REJUVENATION

A Scientific Thriller in the Age of
Biotechnology

W.F. VAN DER HART

ISBN 9789464007329 (paperback)
ISBN 9789464007336 (hardback)
ASIN: B082MR9SV5 (eBook)

To Caroline, Ralph and Norah

Contents

REJUVENATION

1. Stolen dream

The black van was driving away fast in the dark night. Yakov felt he was in a hopeless situation. His right leg was still burning and bleeding, and his right shoulder felt sore. Maybe he should not have fled away like that, but it was in his nature to never give up and always try to find a way out of a difficult situation. Although this time it seemed he had not found a way out and he no longer resisted. He was stuck and had nowhere to go. His head was still bleeding from the blow he had received on his head, and he felt some blood trickling down his neck. His arms were cuffed behind his back and his feet were bound together with a set of chains. They had attached the chains to the metal bench he was sitting on. No way to get loose. To his left sat a heavy, muscular man in black with a mean face. To his right sat another heavy man with a large scar on his cheek. In front of him were two more of these military types, and all four men, heavily armed and carrying assault rifles. Yakov recognized the rifles. They were black AK-12 rifles from the Kalashnikov concern. Sitting on the cold bench, Yakov wondered how he had ended up in this mess.

Three weeks earlier, Yakov had planned to make an announcement to his boss, Andrei Volkov, at Bikov Software, the company for which he had worked for the past five years. Yakov had enjoyed a fast and successful career. As a former national junior weightlifting champion, he knew what hard work was to succeed. After graduating cum laude from Saint-Petersburg State University, Yakov received an offer to come work for Bikov Software. They had made him an offer he could not refuse, and as part of this package, they had sent him to California to get a Master of Science in Computer Science at Stanford University, all expenses paid by Bikov Software. After graduating from Stanford University, he went back to work for Bikov Software in Saint-Petersburg. Over the past five years, he had become the company's star programmer, but Yakov had another dream, and at that point he could not have known that this dream would get him into trouble.

He had reached a major milestone in developing the first version of a "deep-fake" software. He had developed this software using machine learning techniques, and it could basically create indistinguishable videos of someone and have that person say anything you wanted. Yakov had been central to the development of this technology, and they almost had software they could start selling. Yakov had just finished demonstrating the software to his boss. Andrei was impressed with the progress.

"Yakov, you've outdone yourself. This software has become so good now, I think it's ready for the market."

"Thanks Andrei, although I still have to fix some minor bugs."

"Okay, but try to have it ready next week, because we want to present the software at the upcoming Board of Directors meeting."

"I'll do my best."

Yakov hesitated for a moment, but he announced his decision to his boss, anyway.

"Andrei, there's something else I want to discuss with you and it's a bit delicate, but I believe now it's the right time because I've almost finished the software."

Andrei looked puzzled at Yakov.

"Tell me, Yakov!"

"Well, I think I already told you when I started working for you five years ago, but I still have that dream of starting my own company and I feel the time's right to take this big step. I've decided to leave Bikov Software to start my company."

Andrei's face changed and looked grim and startled.

"Yakov, you can't leave us. We need you for the other projects we have in the pipeline. Are you not satisfied with your salary? I'm sure we can arrange something for you."

"No, I'm sorry, Andrei. Since I was young, I've dreamed of starting my own business and I feel this is the right time. It's not about the salary, but about realizing my dream."

"Yakov, you really can't leave us now. We need you. Please consider my offer to improve your package."

"I really prefer to pursue my dream."

"Come on, don't make a hasty decision. Consider my offer to increase your salary, please?"

"Okay… Andrei… I'll think it over, but I'm almost sure it won't change my decision."

Yakov let Andrei hope that he would consider his offer, but he replied only so because he did not want to upset Andrei too much. He was afraid that the discussion might deteriorate further, and he wanted to leave the company on good terms. Over the following days, Andrei tried several times to convince him to reconsider his decision to leave, but Yakov would not budge.

The following week, Yakov presented the finished software to Andrei, and it seemed that the last bugs had been fixed.

"Yakov, you did a superb job. I think it's ready for the market now."

"Thanks, Andrei. When are you going to present the software to the Board of Directors?"

"Well, the meeting is tomorrow afternoon, but I would actually like to ask you to come and demonstrate the software at the meeting. Since it's your baby, it seems only fair that you get all the credit."

Yakov was dumbfounded when he heard this. Yakov had never presented anything to the Board of Directors, nor had he met the members of the Board of Directors, except for the Chairman Adam Bromavich. He was quite impressed with Adam Bromavich, one of Russia's many billionaires. Although he had somehow stayed out of the press, people said he was one of the powerful Russian oligarchs. Yakov had heard that he had amassed most of his wealth in the aftermath of the breakup of the Soviet Union in the nineteen-nineties during Russian privatization. In the past five years of his career at Bikov Software, Yakov had met him only twice, and each time the encounters had been brief.

Yakov was especially surprised to be asked, given the tensed conversation he had had with Andrei the week before. Was Andrei trying to persuade him to stay with the company by offering him this opportunity? He had been clear to Andrei that he had decided to leave, but it was nice of Andrei to let Yakov take credit for the software. In the past, Andrei had always gotten all the credits, so it seemed like he wanted to do him a favor.

"Do I need to prepare anything special, Andrei?"

"No, I think the demonstration you gave me earlier will do just fine. We start at three in the afternoon and I've scheduled your presentation at four-thirty, so be on time!"

Yakov left the meeting with Andrei, still feeling puzzled and he had the feeling there was more behind it.

The next day he felt a little nervous before his first presentation before the Board of Directors. It didn't change his decision to leave the company, but he felt flattered that Andrei had asked him to present before these rich and powerful people. A little after four, Yakov went downstairs to the large room where the meeting was taking place. The wooden door to the conference room was closed, and he waited in front with his laptop under his arm.

About ten minutes later, Andrei opened the wooden door.

"Hi Yakov! You can come in."

Yakov followed him inside and he saw three gentlemen sitting behind the large wooden table. He recognized Adam Bromavich, and he was the first to get up and walk toward him.

"Hi Yakov, it's been a long time since our last encounter. I heard you did excellent work at our company."

"Hello Mr. Bromavich, it has indeed been a long time."

Yakov shook his hand and at the same time he saw the two other men approaching. One had curly dark hair, and the other was bald.

"Hello, I'm Serge Devaux. Nice to meet you." the man with the curly dark hair said with a strong French accent.

"Hi, I'm Yakov Cherepanov. Nice to meet you, Mr. Devaux."

"Hello Yakov, I'm Jeff Broch," the bald man said with a grin on his face.

"Nice to meet you, Mr. Broch."

Yakov shook his hand, which had a firm cold grip that felt unnatural, but he did not dare say anything.

The three men sat down behind the table and Andrei sat next to Yakov on the other side.

"Well, as I said earlier, Yakov will demonstrate our latest version of the software, which I believe is now ready for the market. Yakov, go ahead!"

Yakov felt nervous as he connected his laptop to the projector and dimmed the light in the room. He presented for about an hour. At one point, he gave a demonstration with a video image of himself, and had them type what he had to say. This caused some laughter, and they all got excited about the software.

At the end of the presentation, Adam said, "Thanks, Yakov. My compliments. Very impressive work!"

Yakov closed his laptop and grabbed his notebook and pen. Adam looked at him and then at the others.

"Yakov, before you go, I understood from Andrei that you plan to leave us to start your own company. I just want to clarify that we all believe you're the key to the success of our company, which is why we discussed the matter before you came in. We really want to keep you with our company, so we want to make you an offer you can't refuse. We propose to increase your salary by fifty percent and we're doubling your bonus."

Yakov was surprised to hear the offer, and normally he would have been eager to accept it, but he had been thinking about starting his business for a long time, and he found that money did not change his decision. The three men looked at him seriously, and an awkward silence fell. Andrei broke the silence after a while,

"Well, Yakov, that's the most generous offer this company has ever made to anyone. I hope it can convince you to stay with us."

Yakov felt uncomfortable, because he would obviously disappoint everyone by sticking to his plan to leave. He decided it was probably best not to turn down the offer right away, as that might offend them.

"Thank you for your generous offer. I've been thinking about starting a company for a long time and your offer doesn't make my decision any easier. Let me think about it, and I'll get back to you as soon as possible."

Adam looked a little annoyed now, and the other two men looked grim.

"Okay, Yakov. I would have preferred an answer right away, but I understand you need time to think about it. Let us know your answer by the end of the week."

"Thank you for your understanding, Mr. Bromavich. I'll let Andrei know."

Yakov picked up his laptop and extended his hand to Serge Devaux, who had risen to say goodbye.

"Nice to meet you, Yakov, and my compliments on your presentation!"

"Thank you, Mr. Devaux!"

Adam held out his hand and thanked Yakov as well. Mr. Broch stood up last and shook Yakov's hand, and while holding his hand he said, "Yakov, you've done a great job. I hope you'll accept our offer, because I think it's your only choice. You don't want to disappoint us."

Yakov now felt uncomfortable because Mr. Broch would not let go of his hand and it felt like he had an iron grip. What strength this Mr. Broch had in his hand.

"Do you understand, Yakov?"

"Yes, Mr. Broch, I understand and I will give my answer at the end of the week."

Mr. Broch let go of his hand, and Yakov left the room. Outside, he felt relieved because the tensed situation in the conference room had made him very uncomfortable. The huge increase in his package flattered him, but deep down, he felt that the time had come to start his own business, and money did not change that. It was already getting dark, and he headed home. He got on his heavy motorcycle, on which he rode to work every day, and which allowed him to get to the office on time despite the heavy traffic on the roads of Saint-Petersburg.

Over the next few days Yakov working on, but in his mind, he had decided and felt less motivated. At the end of the week, he knocked on his boss' half-open door after lunch to inform him of his decision.

"Hello Andrei. Do you have a moment to talk?"

"Hi Yakov. Yeah, sure, come in and sit down."

"I came to announce my final decision."

Andrei looked at him curiously.

"What have you decided, Yakov?"

"Well, I appreciate the generous offer you've made me, but I feel the time is right for me to start my company. This isn't about money, but about following my dream. Thanks for all the support, but my decision is final."

Andrei now looked concerned, and his face turned grim. A silence fell after Yakov finished speaking until Andrei finally responded.

"Okay, Yakov, that's clear. I guess there's no other way to convince you to stay?"

"No, Andrei. I'm sorry."

"I hope you realize that the Board of Directors will not be happy about this?"

"Uh… I can imagine, but I hope they'll understand I want to pursue my dream."

Andrei's face now looked sad, and he shook his head.

"I fear that this Board of Directors does not excel in feelings of compassion or understanding."

Yakov started to feel uncomfortable with the whole conversation, but he felt that dealing with the Board of Directors was not his problem.

"Do you want me to finish my one-month notice?"

"Yakov, let me talk to Adam Bromavich first, and then I'll let you know."

"All right. I'll talk to you later, then!?" and Yakov got up to leave the room.

"Yes, and close the door behind you, please!"

Yakov walked back to his desk. The whole situation felt awkward. Later in the afternoon, Andrei came to his desk with a grim face.

"Hello Yakov, I just finished my phone conversation with Adam Bromavich and he wasn't pleased at all. Unfortunately, they want you to stop working immediately and leave your laptop and cell phone here. I'm sorry it has to go this way."

Yakov noticed Andrei was not happy with the situation and was tense.

"No problem, Andrei, I understand."

"I have to go now, Yakov. I wish you good luck."

"Thanks, Andrei," and Yakov shook his hand, and before he could say more, Andrei had already left the room.

Yakov had imagined his farewell to the company to be warmer and nicer, but he also understood that they were not happy with his departure. He handed in his laptop and cell phone to Andrei's secretary, and before leaving, made a small tour of the company to say goodbye to his colleagues. Some were surprised, but some on his team were not, because they already knew of his plan to start his own company. They wished him good luck and agreed to keep in touch. After his farewell tour, Yakov left and pulled the office door shut behind him for the last time.

Outside, he walked to his motorcycle and put on his helmet. With a loud roar, he rode away from Bikov Software. As he pulled onto the main road along the Neva River, he felt relieved. He felt ultimate freedom and excitement now that he was off and about to start his own company. Finally, his dream was about to come true.

After a while, he arrived at his home in the Kolpinksy district. He took the small dirt road behind his house, where he parked his motorcycle. He turned on some music and walked to the room at the back of his house where he had installed his weightlifting equipment and he started working out. As he lay on his weight bench and lifted some weights, Yakov felt like he was starting a new phase in his career and felt excited about it.

The following week, he spent the entire week registering his company and creating a website. He had been working on several software applications in his spare time that he wanted to develop further. He saw the most potential in one of his facial recognition applications. This would allow security companies to grant access to buildings based on facial recognition, but it could also recognize unwanted guests or criminals in stores. He first wanted to find some launching customers to test and further improve the software. He scheduled several meetings to meet some potential customers, and by the end of the week, he felt good about the progress he had made.

On Friday, he stopped working early in the evening and prepared a quick meal because he had a blind date in the evening and had to hurry a bit. He had had little time to date since he had broken up with his girlfriend a year earlier. A few weeks ago, his friends had arranged a blind date for him. He had spoken to her briefly on the phone to arrange a time and place to have a drink together. She had sounded really nice and Yakov was looking forward to it.

After dinner, the doorbell rang. Yakov was startled, because he was not expecting anyone. He looked through the window, but in the dark night, he could not see much. He saw a black van parked in front of his house. He opened the door a few inches but left it on the door chain, because he was not sure what to expect. He saw a muscular man in black standing at the door with a short-shaven head and mean face. Yakov immediately felt an adrenaline rush go through his body, because something told him the man did not have good intentions. Behind the man stood another muscular man, also dressed in black and with a shaven head and a large scar on his cheek.

"Mr. Yakov Cherepanov?"

"Uh… yes, that's me!? Who are you?"

"Please come with us."

"What do you mean? What for and where to?"

"I can't tell you, sir, but it would be better if you just come with us."

"No, sorry, I don't know who you are, so I won't come with you. Good evening, sir."

Yakov wanted to close the door, but it jammed, and when he looked down, he saw the man had stuck his foot in the doorway.

"Please go away. I'm going to call the police!"

Yakov tried to kick the man's foot out of the doorway, but when that failed, he ran to the phone hanging on the wall further down the hall. As soon as he let go, the man kicked the door open, yanking the door chain out of the wall. The two men stormed in and the man in front pushed Yakov away from the phone with such force that Yakov, who was quite strong himself, fell to the floor. The heavy man grabbed him, but in a reflex Yakov pulled the man down to the floor and pushed him into the corner.

Yakov quickly got up and while the man was still on the floor, he pulled one of the large cabinets off the wall and pushed it on top of the man. The other man came after him, crawled over the cabinet and, as Yakov ran to the kitchen, he opened the door to the basement and pushed it with all his strength against the man behind him. The man banged his head against the door and flinched for a moment. Yakov did not hesitate a second and rushed to the kitchen as he saw two other men getting out of the van. It looked like they were carrying some kind of automatic rifles. The adrenaline rushed to his head. He quickly closed the kitchen door behind him and pushed the refrigerator in front of the door. The two men tried to open the door to the kitchen but could not get in.

He searched the kitchen for something he could use as a weapon. Then, in an instant, he got an idea and opened the cabinet under the kitchen sink and pulled out the fire extinguisher. He pulled out the safety pin and pointed the fire extinguisher at the door to the hall, where the two men had already pushed the refrigerator away from the door. The men walked into the kitchen and Yakov pressed the button and pointed it at them. A white cloud of powder sprayed onto the two men and filled the air in the kitchen. They were trying to rub their faces clean when Yakov stormed out through the back door. Outside, he ran to his motorcycle and jumped on it. He put on his helmet and started the engine. With the engine roaring loudly, he rode away as one of the men tried to grab him. When he looked back, he saw them running after him down the small dirt road. Yakov stepped up the speed and left them far behind.

At high speed, he drove off the dirt road, and at the end, he turned onto the paved road. On the paved road, he crossed the road that led to the front of his house. He peered into the road and saw the black van at the end of it. It seemed to be coming toward him. The adrenaline kept coursing through his head and he realized that they saw him pass. He increased the speed further and drove onto one of the main roads next to the Neva River, toward the center. Yakov thought it best to go to the nearest police station. That was a few kilometers away, so as he drove onto the main road, he increased his speed even further.

He no longer saw the black van and thought he might have shaken off his pursuers. He slowed down a bit and tried not to go too fast, because there were speed radars all over this road. At one point, he looked over his shoulder again and, to his surprise, he now saw the black van approaching at high speed. It had almost overtaken him. The van's side door was open, and a man was pointing an automatic rifle at him. Without hesitation, he turned the throttle back and his motorcycle sped up rapidly. He heard the rifle firing behind him. He tried to go as fast as he could, and the distance between him and the van increased again. The Neva River was on one side of him, and on the other were only buildings. This van would never keep up with his heavy motorcycle, he thought to himself as he went faster and faster. He looked behind him and the van was now far behind. He thought he should be able to make it to the police station.

He continued along the river road at high speed until he approached some traffic lights and slowed down a bit. The traffic lights had jumped to red for him, but seeing no cars, he did not stop and just drove on. He looked back over his shoulder and the van was now far away. Looking ahead again, he was startled to see an old man crossing the street and about to hit him with his motorcycle. In a reflex, he swerved, missing the man by inches, but he felt the heavy motorcycle began to slide. He had lost control and was now sliding sideways across the road surface. Bright sparks flew around him from the metal hitting the street. His right shoulder and leg hit the road surface, and he felt a painful burning sensation. Slowly his motorcycle came to a stop, and he felt his leg burning like crazy now. He tried to push the heavy motorcycle away, but his leg was stuck underneath. His pants were torn open and his leg was bleeding. He tried one more time to lift his motorcycle, but it was too heavy.

A moment later, several large headlights approached him, and a car with squealing tires braked behind him. Yakov tried to look, but because he was blocked under the heavy motorcycle, he could not quite turn around. Then he suddenly saw the heavy man, who had rung his doorbell earlier, and another man beside him. He felt the weight of the motorcycle lessen as one of the men lifted it up. The man came closer and grabbed him by his shirt, and Yakov could just see him stretching his fist. A second later Yakov felt a large blow to his head and everything went dark.

After a while, the van seemed to slow down and Yakov looked at the two men in front of him. As soon as the van came to a complete stop, the four muscular men stood up and one of them untied the chain from the metal bench to which they had attached him. They pushed him out of the van and he looked around, but it was dark and he could not see much. They were on an empty big road that looked like a runway, but there were no planes or buildings in sight.

He waited there among the heavily armed men with their AK-12 rifles until he heard a plane. When he looked up, he saw some lights moving in the dark sky, slowly approaching the runway. The sound increased, and he could see the shape of the plane as it approached. He would have loved to run away, but his leg still hurt and with the heavily armed men beside him, that would be madness. The plane stopped in front of them and the door opened. A man in a dark blue uniform stepped out of the plane and looked at the four muscular men in surprise.

"You guys should have put a bag over his head. Now he has seen your faces!"

"Oh shit," muttered one of the four men, and he pulled a dark piece of cloth from his pocket.

"Hold him tight," the man said to the others, and he pulled the bag over Yakov's head.

He could no longer see anything, but felt them pushing him toward the plane. Where would they take him? Who are these people? Then he suddenly felt a sharp pain in his arm, as if someone had stuck a needle in it. A few seconds later, he felt weak and dizzy, and that was the last thing he remembered.

2. The assignment

His board moved swiftly through the raging waves. His long hair was all wet, and he went faster and faster as the wind blew hard into his sail. He closed his sail and his board accelerated even further. He made a strong jump with both legs and with a quick movement, his board was now flowing through the air. What a feeling, like a bird in the sky. He wondered if his girlfriend was watching him from the beach. When he landed back in the wild waves, he looked at the beach, but then suddenly the sun blinded his vision. He fell off his board and landed in the water with a hard smack. He felt something big pass beside his leg, and it scared him. He quickly got back on his board and continued surfing through the waves until he saw a large fin appear behind him. He tried to go faster, but his board did not seem to move. Suddenly, a huge wave swept him off his board and he fell into the water. As he stuck his head back out of the water, he heard the loud roar of the next wave coming at him. The wave slammed into his face and the roaring noise grew louder. His board and the waves disappeared, and everything was now black.

The buzzer roused Dave from his sleep. The awful sound penetrated his ears. He rubbed his eyes and stretched his arms. His bed was nice and warm, so he pressed the snooze button and turned to the other side. He tried to get back into his dream and onto his surfboard, but the feeling was not the same. He felt his stiff limbs and the aching pain in his back. Almost every morning, it was the same painful feeling as if a truck had run over him during the night. He got up slowly and sat on the edge of his bed. In his younger years, he sometimes jumped out of bed, but that was long ago. He lacked the energy, and the fear of hurting his back made him more cautious.

"Is this what aging is all about?" he thought as he slowly tried to get out of his bed. Aging was like a thief in the night. Every morning, it had taken away a piece of energy without you noticing. One day, you realized how much your body had degraded and that you had aged. The problem was that it happened so gradually that Dave could not remember when the pain in his back and limbs had started.

He sauntered toward the bathroom as he carefully stretched. He yawned and looked out the window. Everything was still dark. He turned on the light in the bathroom and stood in front of the large mirror. He stared at his bald head and wrinkled face. The wrinkles did not bother him so much, because they also made him look wiser, except for those bags under his eyes. He hated those bags and dark circles under his eyes, because they made him look older. Over the past twenty years, his hair had gradually thinned until he was bald on top, except for the remaining gray hairs on the back and side of his head. As a child, he used to joke about his father's bald head. Once, his father had become irritated and told him with a cynical smile on his face, "Someday, you'll regret those remarks, boy."

His father had been right, but unfortunately, Dave had never had the chance to tell him. Dave was already glad his son, Andrew, had not made the same comments to him. His son was the greatest gift he had ever received from his ex-wife, Jennifer. He still remembered the day he was born. It was the first and only time in his life that he cried out from sheer happiness. The beauty of newborn life had touched him so deeply. Andrew had grown into a fine man, and Dave was very proud of what his son had accomplished in his life.

Unfortunately, Dave saw him only a few times a year since Andrew had moved from Boston to California six years ago. Before the move, they saw each other several times a month. Andrew would visit his parents in New York, or Dave and Jennifer would go to Boston. In the last few years of Andrew's time at Massachusetts Institute of Technology or MIT, Jennifer did not go with him and Dave went alone. Sometimes he stayed there for a few days and sometimes for a week. After Andrew earned his Ph.D. in Biological Engineering, he accepted a job at a research institute in California. Although Dave often spoke to him by phone, he missed his son very much. They had been very close all these years, and the distance between them made him sad.

In the last few years, Dave felt constantly depressed and lacking energy. Every day was like a struggle, and his body just felt like it was holding him back. The fact that his appearance had changed did not make it any easier. Even the remaining brown hairs on his head were mixed with more and more gray hairs. Henry Hornbauer, his colleague at Science Publications Inc. had suggested shaving off the remaining hair band, believing it would make him look younger. Dave grabbed his razor and thought about Henry's suggestion for a moment. Somehow, he was still attached to the few remaining hairs as a reminder of the past. He put some shaving foam on his cheeks and chin and began to shave. Then he combed the remaining hair band and smeared some anti-wrinkle cream on his face. All those special men's creams promising to reduce wrinkles had had little effect on his face.

The aching feeling in his back was still there as he walked to his dressing room. He slowly put on his suit and shirt, and he sat down to put on his shoes. Every movement hurt him. His mother had insisted he see a doctor.

"All part of getting older. Not much we can do about that. You can take some painkillers," the doctor had told him several years ago.

Apparently, Dave had a form of arthritis and had to live with it. The doctor could not do much about it, and he had left him with this depressing conclusion. He got back up and walked slowly to the kitchen, where he sat down at the table to have some breakfast with his morning espresso. He read the news on his tablet, but his mind wandered again. He thought about what Elizabeth Cooper had told him yesterday. They had discussed his frustration with his life over a glass of wine in one of the local bars downtown. She had asked him why he did not take any action if he wanted to change things and she had said, "You only have one life. Live it!"

She was so right, as Elizabeth often was. His life had dulled by going through the same routine every day, week, and month. Since his wife had left him five years ago, he had focused more on his work to fill the void in his life. But besides his work, he did not have much time or energy left for other things. On weekends, he usually worked or ran errands.

Dave had tried dating a few times, but it had gone nowhere. His back pain often prevented him from going out or when he did go out, it often made him moody and that did not help with a first date. He felt insecure with women with his aged looks. He increasingly felt that he had become a spectator, watching his own life go by without control over its direction. Most people estimated him older than he was, and that morning he felt old and felt that the best part of his life was behind him. Physically, things only went downhill from here, and his love life was non-existent. He continued to read the news as it grew less dark outside.

After a quick glance at the time, he rose from his stool. He put on his long anthracite coat, grabbed his brown leather briefcase and his black hat, and hurried out of the door. He pressed the elevator button, and as he waited, the door of the apartment next door opened.

"Good morning, Mr. Wilson," his neighbor greeted him warmly in her Spanish accent.

"Good morning, Ms. Garcia. How are you today?"

Ms. Garcia, a handsome middle-aged lady, wore a long beige coat and high-heeled shoes. She had a friendly smile and Dave liked her because she was always cheerful and friendly. She looked to be in her forties, but he had heard she was older than him.

"Good, Mr. Wilson. Today is an important day for me," Ms. Garcia replied as they stepped into the elevator. He pressed the button, and the doors closed.

"An important day? You make me curious, Ms. Garcia?"

"We're launching our marketing campaign for our new anti-aging cream today."

She had founded a cosmetics company some twenty years ago and was quite successful. She began to explain that the new skin cream was capable of completely eliminating age spots on older people's skin after a few weeks of use. Unlike most creams that promise to reduce spots, this one worked very well. They had completed all clinical trials last month with great success.

"Wow, that sounds impressive. Maybe I should write an article about that for Science Magazine?"

"That would be great, Mr. Wilson."

He explained he was about to have his weekly Monday morning meeting and would suggest it to his boss. She thanked him and they walked out of the elevator. It was raining outside, and they said goodbye. Ms. Garcia quickly got into the black limousine, which was waiting for her. Her driver, holding an umbrella over her head, closed the door behind her and the car drove away.

"What a fascinating woman," he thought as the car disappeared from view.

Dave continued walking toward the subway station. It was chilly and the gray sky turned darker and the rain was now getting heavier. He pushed up the collar of his coat to cover his neck. He had forgotten to check the weather and had not brought an umbrella. He pushed his black hat lower on his head. Before he had lost part of his hair, he had never worn a hat, but now he took it with him everywhere he went. He had never realized how his hair had kept his head warm until he lost it.

As he got closer to the subway station, it was pouring rain, and he hurried inside. When he walked down the stairs, his shoes and pants were soaking wet. The crowd grew around him. The flow of people always made him giddy. Everyone was rushing to their destination.

Down on the platform, he waited for the C Line toward Euclid Avenue. The platform was full of people, all damp and wet from the rain. The mixture of different people always gave him the impression that all the peoples of the world converged on the subway. Most ignored each other and looked in other directions. When the subway arrived, he shuffled forward into the wet crowd and found a standing place between an old man in a gray suit and a young woman in black. The air was humid and it stank. He hated the feeling of being crammed in like a sardine in a can, but it was the quickest and surest way to get to work.

After seven stops, he wriggled between people toward the exit. When the doors opened, fresh air blew in his face as he walked to the steps to leave the platform. He followed the stream of people to the exit until he found himself back outside on the street among the tall office buildings under the pouring rain and dark sky above. A block away, he hurried inside through the glass doors of the building where Science Publications had four floors.

After working for the same company for nearly twenty-seven years, Dave was no longer impressed with much. He had given up his ambitions to move up the ladder and stuck to writing articles for the magazine. For years, he dreamed of writing a book, but with his lack of energy, he had become a senior procrastinator.

He scanned his badge to pass the entrance gates in the large white reception hall, and he unbuttoned his long and wet coat as he stepped into the glass elevator and pressed the button for the fourteenth floor. He greeted some of his colleagues entering the elevator. In the mirror, from under his hat, he looked at his wrinkled face. The walk had done him good, and his back pain had eased somewhat.

Arriving on the fourteenth floor, he walked out of the elevator. He took off his black hat and long coat and hung them to dry on the coat rack near the entrance to the work floor. As he walked to his desk, he passed Claire's desk.

"Morning, Claire."

Claire Davenport was his department's secretary, and she was always friendly.

"Good morning, Dave," she said with her beautiful smile.

"Did you have a nice weekend?" he asked.

Claire always dressed well. Today she wore a dark knee-high skirt with a blood-red blouse on top. She was more than ten years younger than him. He found her a very attractive woman with her dark brown hair. Four years ago, he had finally dared to ask her out to dinner. They had a nice evening, but at the end of the evening, she gently made it clear he was not her type. Who could blame her, given that he looked aged and almost completely bald except for the horseshoe-shaped fringe of hair on his head?

"I had a great weekend. One of my best friends got married. What a party!"

She smiled and continued talking about her weekend. They talked for a few minutes, then he walked over to his desk. Dave unpacked his briefcase and turned on his laptop. He was just about to sit down when Henry appeared at his desk with a big smile.

"Morning, Dave. Coffee?"

He smiled back.

"That's the best suggestion I heard today. I could use some coffee to warm up after this heavy rain outside," and they both walked to the coffee corner.

He had been working with Henry for almost eighteen years. They were about the same age. Though Henry was a lot grayer than Dave, he still had all his hair. They played tennis together once a week until about five years ago, when Dave's back problems forced them to stop. They still went out for drinks together almost every week. Henry was a lively and charismatic person, always up for a good joke.

With a cup of coffee in his hand, he talked about his date last weekend with a woman about fifteen years younger than him. Henry's wife had died seven years ago, and it had taken him years to get his life back together. A year ago, he had created a profile on several dating platforms, and in recent months, he had a new date almost every weekend. On most dates, not much happened, but this weekend he had apparently hit it off with a sexy blonde woman named Sara. They had met for dinner and liked each other right away. Henry explained they had been talking continuously, and a little after midnight, the waiter came and said they were closing. Only then did he notice that all the other guests had already left and that they were the last guests in the restaurant. Sara convinced Henry to go with her to one of the local clubs and they had danced until five in the morning. Then he took Sara to his apartment, and they spent the night together. Henry tried again to convince Dave to create a profile on the dating site.

"Dave, with a bit a luck you'll live a long life, you can't spend the rest of it alone."

"Listening to your weekend, I should probably do that Henry, but I'm worried about putting my photo online… I mean, who goes out with an old bald guy like me?"

"Ah, come on, Dave. The ladies will line up for you."

Dave laughed, but did not think for a minute that it could happen.

"If your baldness really bothers you that much, why don't you make an appointment with that hair transplant surgeon I recommended to you?"

"Yes, I know. I have yet to call him," Dave answered in a dull voice.

"You're a true master procrastinator. Well, let's plan beers this Friday?"

"All right. Good plan."

Back at his desk, Dave prepared for his department's weekly meeting. His department wrote the content of Science magazine. The magazine was published every month. Each week they discussed the work in progress, new ideas and articles, and the planning of when to publish what. Dave had just completed an article last week on growing livers from stem cells for transplantation. He had been working on it for several weeks and finally finished it last week. He had emailed it to his boss, Craig Pathfinder, who was the Managing Editor, and he had loved the article and had given him many compliments. He had interviewed several researchers from the research team in Cincinnati. He had slept in a hotel there for more than a week to do all the interviews. He had even interviewed the lead researcher, a Japanese researcher, via videoconference. He would have liked to have interviewed the researcher in Japan, but the department had to cut back and they only allowed international visits in exceptional cases.

The research team had grown new livers from human stem cells. This was a breakthrough because there was a shortage of liver donors and transplanted livers were often rejected. This new method made it possible to grow a new liver from the patient's own stem cells, preventing the body from rejecting the new organ and eliminating the ethical concerns of other methods. Previous methods relied on bone marrow and cells from the umbilical cord to grow new liver cells, but these were more difficult and controversial. Other methods used embryonic stem cells in the research, but this was heavily criticized and raised many ethical concerns. The team was very excited because they were about to begin the first human clinical trials to transplant their bio-engineered livers into human patients. He often called his son to discuss the research, since Andrew had a degree in biological engineering and he was working in this field. Because of the additional contact with his son, Dave had enjoyed writing this article.

He had learned a great deal about biotechnology over the past decade, and within the department, they considered him the expert in the field. Since biotech was a topic of growing interest for the magazine, Dave did not have to worry much during the recent layoffs in the company. He had written an article last year that had generated considerable interest and helped his reputation within the company.

It was an article about a Chinese scientist, He Jiankui, who had created the world's first gene-edited babies. The scientist had edited the genes of a human embryo, and through In Vitro Fertilization (IVF) a woman had given birth to the first twins with edited genes on this planet. Dave had a gift for explaining complicated scientific matters in such a clear and understandable way that it became comprehensible to a much wider audience. The Chinese scientist had used a gene-editing technique called CRISPR. Dave had explained that this CRISPR technique allowed a specific part of a gene to be edited. Here, the scientist had eliminated a gene called CCR5 to render the babies resistant to HIV, smallpox, and cholera. The baby's father had HIV and wanted to use this method to prevent his children from inheriting the disease. The birth of the first genetically modified babies had shocked the scientific world and was seen as irresponsible and controversial.

The development had sparked a huge ethical debate and heavy criticism, because changes to an embryo would be inherited by future generations. Eventually, this could affect the entire human gene pool, leading to unwanted mutations. This article had boosted Dave's reputation within the company, and his job was secure. At least this was a bright spot in his life, because if he had lost his job, he probably would have suffered a decisive blow on top of his depression and his struggles in life.

The accelerating biotechnical developments in the world provided the magazine with a large flow of topics and gave Dave relatively good job prospects. He had given up trying to move up in the company, since all his attempts to become an editor had failed. At least he had become a functional expert in biotechnology. He had always had a keen interest in biology in the past, but he had never studied biology or biological engineering at a university. He had started at a newspaper after graduating from The City University of New York with a bachelor's degree in journalism. He had worked his way up to become a journalist with an excellent reputation. About five years later, he left for a job as a writer at Science Publications Inc.

More than ten years ago, he was able to delve into biological engineering, a passion he had shared with Andrew. During Andrew's university time at MIT, Dave visited him often and even attend some lectures. He spent a lot of time in the university library and often had in-depth discussions with his son.

Craig Venter and Daniel Cohen, two of the world's leading genetic scientists, had stated it already in a famous publication:

"If the twentieth century was the century of physics, the twenty-first century will be the century of biology."

Dave truly believed this and had noticed that breakthroughs were happening more frequently, and new developments seemed to happen at an exponentially increasing rate. Science had already eradicated many diseases, and many current research projects focused on tackling the remaining ones. The ultimate topic seemed to be the search for the fountain of youth or man's pursuit of immortality. Either way, there were plenty of topics for him to work on.

To prepare for the meeting, he wrote down all the items he wanted to discuss. On his list, he also put Ms. Garcia's skin cream. Dave was a principled fellow, and if he made a promise, he kept it. Besides, he thought it could make a nice article, but first he had to convince his boss.

After lunch, he hurried back to his desk to grab his notebook, and then he left for the meeting. He felt a bit stressed and felt his back pain returning. The meeting was to take place in the large conference room on the sixteenth floor. As he was waiting in front of the elevator, Henry came rushing toward him.

"Come on Dave, we desk-animals should take every opportunity to move around a little. Let's take the stairs!"

"No, I'm sorry, Henry, my back is killing me… I'm trying to move as little as possible today."

"No problem, old buddy, I'll see you upstairs," and Henry disappeared through the doors into the stairwell. When the elevator doors opened, he saw Sandra Reynolds standing in the elevator.

"Hi Sandra. How are you?"

"I'm fine, Dave. Thanks. And you? Ready for the meeting?"

He nodded. Sandra was a colleague he did not trust or like very much. She was always trying to make herself look better at the expense of others. He always felt she was trying to take over his role as a key senior writer on biotech. She often challenged him in meetings and tried to appear smarter than him. When he entered the elevator, he was much more wary.

"So, any interesting topics for new articles?" she asked.

In the past, he would have been too innocent and answered such a question. But because she had abused that innocence in the past, he had become more cautious. Last year was the last time she had caught him off guard. He had told Sandra about one of his ideas for the weekly meeting. She had immediately raised her hand when Craig had asked who had new suggestions for articles. Without shame, she presented his idea as hers. Dave was so bewildered at the time that he did not know what to say. Anyway, forewarned is forearmed.

"Yeah, I may have a good topic. I'll tell you about it in the meeting."

Clearly frustrated, she shut up and did not speak another word. He looked at her and felt like smiling, but wisely did so only in his mind.

Arriving in the large meeting room with glass windows, about fifteen of his colleagues were already seated at the large, long glass table. Outside, the heavy rain still persisted, and the sky was dark gray. He greeted everyone and sat down on the window side of the table, as far away from Sandra as possible. Craig came in last and closed the door behind him.

He welcomed everyone and sat at the head of the table, flanked by his secretary, Anna Phearson. Anna always took the meeting minutes. Craig had made a flashy career in the company. In less than ten years he had made it to managing editor and, at the age of thirty-six, became the youngest managing editor the company had ever had. Despite the age difference, Dave loved working for Craig. He liked his direct and honest work ethic, and he knew how to motivate people to give their best for the company. Craig started the meeting and looked at Dave.

"Dave, you outdid yourself with that article on growing livers from stem cells. My compliments. That's clever journalism."

Dave saw a jealous look appear on Sandra's face. His article would appear in the upcoming issue of the magazine as the lead article, quite an honor. He relaxed and felt that the extensive hours of work over the past month had been well spent. Craig continued the meeting and asked everyone to give an update on their current work and progress. One by one they gave their update, and all seemed to be going as planned, until we got to James Cullen.

"Okay, James, your turn. Any progress on your interview with that Russian software developer about their 'deep-fake' software?"

"Well, not really, Craig. I got some bad news today. I've been trying to get in touch with this software developer, called Yakov Cherepanov. As you know, he had agreed to a telephone video interview to explain about his software, but on the day of the interview, about two weeks ago, I could not reach him. I tried to reach him almost every day and also called several people at his company, but no one could tell me where he was. Someone told me he thought he had left the company. This morning I tried again and a secretary from the company explained to me that she had heard from the local police that they think Mr. Cherepanov was kidnapped last week."

"Kidnapped!?" Craig asked, and more people in the room looked stunned.

"Yes, amazing, no? I looked for more information about this, but I only found a small article in the Sankt Petersburg Vedomosti newspaper mentioning the abduction. I asked the secretary if there was anyone else who wanted to do the interview with me, and she passed me on to her boss. He was very gruff and rude on the phone and explained that it was their policy not to give interviews. Unfortunately, it seems I have reached a dead end."

"What a story, James. That's too bad. It could have been a marvelous story. Okay, let's continue our meeting."

Craig gave a quick update on Steve Eisman's work. Steve was not at the meeting because he was in Antwerp for interviews with a team of neuroscientists from Belgium and Germany. Steve was working on an article about a study on the effects of space travel on the brain. With all the existing plans for a manned mission to Mars, the topic on space travel was hot at the moment. Steve was the lucky one to be selected for this trip to Europe. Of course, Sandra had tried to get this assignment, but Craig had selected Steve for his background in aerospace engineering.

After discussing all the work in progress, Craig moved on to the next item on the agenda, which was of great interest to all the writers, namely new ideas for articles to write. Craig's practice was that he encouraged everyone to present their own ideas, and if he felt they were potentially interesting enough for publication, he gave the green light. In addition to all these ideas, he himself always compiled a list of potential topics. He then assigned these to the writers he felt most suited to the topic.

Craig began with James Cullen. James shared some slides about a study that showed that drinking coffee reduces the risk of developing Alzheimer's and Parkinson's disease. After James, it was Henry's turn who presented a small piece on a thermal imaging system developed for the U.S. Army. The system would allow soldiers to distinguish details, such as trip wires, booby traps and mortars, even in total darkness. They kept going around the table until it was Dave's turn. He briefly presented Ms. Garcia's new skin cream. Craig looked only mildly interested as he said, "Maybe nice for the section with shorter articles after the main articles. Let's see what you can come up with, Dave."

After approving most of the topics, Craig began the topics he had prepared. Sometimes he would assign a topic to the person he thought was most appropriate, or he would look at who was most interested in the topic and assign it to that person. It always made for an interesting dynamic. The first topic was about a new technological trial called the government's anti-UAV defense system. Apparently, they had developed and tested a new system against UAVs, Unmanned Aerial Vehicles, or drones. It automatically detected and fired a 4-watt beam at drones to block and ground them. Craig looked at Serena Clark, who was sitting to his right.

"I thought of you, Serena, for this article, because you wrote a marvelous piece about drones and the threats they pose to airports."

"Sounds interesting. I'll look into it."

Craig continued.

"The U.S. Army is testing a helmet that uses electrical brain stimulation to improve the performance of the most demanding military roles, like snipers, drone pilots and flight crews. They call it tDCS or transcranial direct current stimulation. It'll probably involve some travel to the Wright-Patterson Air Force base in Ohio. I was hesitating for this one between Henry or Sandra."

Sandra immediately raised her hand.

"I'd love to do this one. While studying psychology, I was already interested in this topic."

Henry looked annoyed by Sandra's quick response. Dave knew Henry did not like to fight over a topic. Still, Henry also responded by saying he would be interest in it, too. Dave decided to help his friend out.

"Craig, perhaps the fact that Henry served in the U.S. Marine Corps and participated in Operation Desert Storm gives him easier access to interview the right people in the military?"

"Ah, of course, Dave. Henry, you're the man for this job!"

If looks could kill, Dave would have been dead at that moment. Sandra stared at him, clearly pissed. Craig continued quickly.

"A topic where I was thinking of you, Sandra, is about a research team developing a painless, microneedle patch that women can easily apply themselves once a month that provides contraception."

Sandra replied, still looking disappointed, "Okay, Craig, I'll get started on that."

Craig continued.

"We heard about an innovative production technique for proteins that have anti-cancer and anti-viral properties. The proteins were very difficult and expensive to produce, but some scientist of the Roslin Institute has added genes to the DNA coding of chickens allowing them to produce the human proteins through their eggs. Apparently, this significantly lowers the cost of productions. James sounds like something for you, doesn't it?"

"Sounds good!" James replied.

Craig moved on to a few more topics, but Dave still had not been assigned a topic.

"The next topic is very interesting, but it requires a lot of research and possibly travel. There are rumors that a research lab in California has tested a new drug on old mice, making them younger. The research lab seems to shy away from publicity, so it won't be easy to arrange interviews."

"That sounds intriguing and I've some family in California, so the travel would be fine," Sandra said before the others could say a word.

Craig looked briefly at her, but then turned his head to Dave.

"Dave, you haven't been assigned a topic yet this meeting, so I thought this could be an appropriate topic for you."

Dave replied enthusiastically, "Sounds very interesting, Craig. I'll get right on it."

Sandra looked at him jealously. Craig ended with a topic on exoskeletons, which allow the elderly to walk and lift things again, and he assigned the last topic to someone else on the team. Then he discussed the planning, and the meeting was over.

Everybody walked out of the meeting room. Dave's back had stiffened during the meeting and he struggled to get out of his chair. He tried to move slowly, so as not to strain his back too much. Craig looked at him, a little worried.

"How's your back, Dave?"

"Thanks for asking, unfortunately not much better."

"Well, if it gets too bad, take a few days off."

"Thanks."

Craig left and Dave noticed Sandra had been waiting to leave until Craig had finished speaking to him, almost as if she was trying to follow their conversation. She now left the conference room and seemed to follow Craig. His friend Henry was waiting at the door with a smile on his face.

"Ha-ha old buddy. I'll never forget Sandra's face when you started talking about operation Desert Storm. I bet she never thought a gray-haired man like me had fought in the war."

"Yeah, it looked like you could use some help to get that fancy project. I've heard about those helmets. Apparently, they're pretty impressive."

"We might be the seniors in the company, but we certainly won't let them push us around."

They both laughed as they entered the elevator to go back to the fourteenth floor. Downstairs, they headed straight to the coffee corner.

"That story of mice getting younger sounds fascinating. If it's true… I guess it will be difficult to arrange an interview. Any idea how you're going to go about that?"

Dave put some sugar in his coffee and replied, "I think I'll check with Andrew, since he works in biotech in California. He might have some useful contacts for me."

"Must be nice to be able to talk to your son about work."

"Yeah, it is. How are your daughters doing? Has the youngest accept her job at that school in Boston?"

"Yes, she did, actually. She's happy with the job so far. Ah, and guess what? My oldest daughter is pregnant, so I'm going to be a granddad. Can you imagine?"

"Congratulations. Well, that means an extra round of beer next Friday."

"We certainly will. Okay, I better get back to work. I have some calls to make before it's too late. See you later."

"Later, Henry."

Back at his desk, Dave first took a painkiller for his back pain and then went over his notes from the meeting. Craig's assignment had been vague, so the first thing he did was search online to see what he could find on the subject. He found many research institutions and companies focused on aging. The more he read, the more fascinated he became with the subject. He read about research on aging, mostly focused on wrinkles, hair loss, dementia or diseases of aging such as Alzheimer's, Parkinson's, arthritis, cardiovascular disease and diabetes. When he searched further, he read about regenerating organs, growing livers and rejuvenating or repairing cells. Experiments by researchers at a life sciences company in San Francisco revealed a chemical switch in genes that apparently triggered cell repair and rejuvenation in roundworms and frogs. The researchers switched the related genes on and off and were able to double the worms' lifespan.

"Because this worm species has many of the same biological mechanisms of cell division and cell death as humans, this species is a powerful model for human health and disease research," one of the researchers stated in some article.

"If this biological mechanism can be found and exploited in humans, this discovery could have important implications in the fight against a wide range of age-related diseases."

All the interesting information he found, he saved on his laptop. This was his usual practice, where he always started by gathering all the information on the subject. He continued his search online. Some scientists in Michigan had blocked a certain molecule in the neurons of a worm, which improved the motor skills of old worms and increased their longevity and overall health. Fascinated, he kept reading and searching, until he suddenly realized it had gotten dark outside. He looked up from his desk and saw that all his colleagues had already left. This had not happened to him in a long time, but he smiled. He already thought it was a great article to work on. Suddenly, he felt the pain in his back again and he stretched and stood up. He turned off his laptop, put it in his briefcase, and hurried to the elevator.

He looked in the elevator mirror at his aging, wrinkled face and bald head. Fascinated by the thought that people might not age so quickly in the future, he wondered if he would live long enough to experience some of these anti-aging developments. He thought of his history lessons and remembered Herodotus' writing, in which he talked about the Fountain of Youth. This fountain contained special water in the land of the Macrobians that gave them exceptional longevity. The research he read gave him the impression that the discovery of this Fountain of Youth was near. He walked out of the elevator and hurried through the crowd on the street. It was still raining, but not as heavily as in the morning. After entering the subway station, he took a seat on the metro and relaxed a bit. As they rushed through the tunnels, he kept thinking about the Fountain of Youth and all the scientific developments he had read about.

This century, humans had unraveled the secrets of nature at an exponential rate. In the year two thousand and three, the Human Genome Project was declared complete. This was an international research project in which researchers had determined the sequence of nucleotide base pairs that make up DNA and had identified and mapped all the genes in the human genome. Since then, developments followed one another at a breathtaking pace. All these new discoveries made it possible for scientists to create genetically modified humans as early as about four years ago. Despite all the ethical constraints scientists had imposed on themselves, it was rather surprising that it was not until last year that the first genetically modified humans arrived. And now we started growing livers and trying to create immortals. The speed of new discoveries and developments was frightening. One began to wonder what would happen to humanity in the coming decades.

A young man with a guitar began to sing on the subway, awakening Dave from his deep haze of thoughts. He checked the name of the subway stop and realized he had to get off at the next stop. He stood up and tossed some coins into the hat on the ground next to the singing man, who blinked at him with one eye as he continued his song. After taking the escalators, he left the subway station and a breath of cold air blew in his face and the light rain poured on his head.

When he got home that evening, it was nice and warm inside and he first prepared some food for himself. He opened a good red wine and poured the red liquid into a large crystal glass. He stuck his nose into the glass to smell the aroma. His sense of smell had diminished over the years, but he still enjoyed a nice wine. Next to his ex-wife Jennifer, though, it became clear that Dave could not smell very well. She smelled the smallest odors in the air. It often made him envious of her. She could smell the mix of aromas in any wine and identify them meticulously. At wine tastings, where they sometimes went together in the past, she could describe the wines, like a professional precisely describing the right taste, smell and texture. Dave, however, could do nothing of the sort. Sometimes he thought back to the old days when, in his twenties, he had a stronger sense of smell and could recognize scents much better. Unfortunately, his smell and taste had become flatter and less profound with age.

The same thing had happened to his hearing, which had also deteriorated. In bars, he often had trouble understanding people, especially if they were in larger groups. Therefore, he preferred to go to quieter places with not too many people. At least then he could follow the conversation. The doctor had tested his hearing and concluded that it had deteriorated, but he had said it was not that bad compared to many of his peers, and he had suggested that if it really bothered him, he should buy a hearing aid. Just the thought of that depressed him.

Over dinner, he watched the stock market news on the flat-screen television in his kitchen. The markets were closed, but he hadn't had time today to look at all the quotes. He had been investing for years, but more than a decade ago, he had changed his tactics and invested his savings only in a few stocks that met his criteria. Dave had attended a conference where a famous stock market guru had said that one should focus his investments only on a few sectors with a clear future and long-term growth prospects to make a nice return. The sectors the stock market guru had pointed out were biotechnology, artificial intelligence and robotics. This guru had impressed him, and Dave followed his advice. He had invested in about thirty companies, all operating in the sectors the guru had mentioned.

The money he had made from these investments had allowed him to buy his current apartment with a bank loan. And a few years ago, he had managed to pay off the entire amount with the proceeds. The fact that he owned his apartment without a mortgage made him feel secure and satisfied. Through his investments, he was already convinced of the growth opportunities in biotech, artificial intelligence and robotics. But all the research he had done recently strengthened his conviction that humanity was facing unprecedented changes.

After dinner, he prepared himself a decaffeinated espresso using the Italian espresso machine he had bought a few years ago after talking to a barista. The smell of roasted coffee rose from his machine and he sat down in his armchair in the corner. He glanced at his watch as he sipped his espresso. Almost ten o'clock, so it was seven in the evening in California. Andrew should be home now, he thought. He turned on his laptop and started up his videoconferencing software. Andrew answered almost immediately.

"Hi Dad! How are you?"

"I'm fine? And you?"

"Pretty good. I just finished a delicious meal that Wendy prepared for me. I love that cooking class she takes. Every week she tries out new recipes. What more could a man wish for?"

Wendy Diaz and Andrew were married last year. They had met three years earlier in Venezuela, when Andrew had taken a diving trip with some friends from his university. He loved diving and had been looking forward to this trip to the Los Roques archipelago. Dave had advised him against going because the country was so unstable at the time. But Andrew always loved adventure. He and his friends had rented a boat in Los Roques, and the archipelago had been breathtakingly beautiful. In the evening, they went to one of the local bars on the beach of Isla Gran Roque, and there he had met Wendy.

She was a beautiful, well-proportioned woman with dark long hair. She was much smaller than Andrew, who was an impressive man with his six feet and seven inches and broad shoulders. She had studied medicine in Caracas, specializing in pediatrics. Her mother ran a hostel in Los Roques, where she was visiting. Andrew and Wendy kept in touch after the vacation and began calling each other regularly. He went back a few times to visit Wendy until the situation in the country became unstable and dangerous. Andrew arranged for Wendy to come to the United States and they began living together in his apartment in San Jose. She found a job in a hospital and got a work permit. A year later, he asked her to marry him while vacationing at the base of a giant sequoia in Yosemite National Park.

Dave had been a proud father on his wedding day. It had been a great day. Only the contact with Jennifer had been awkward. She had brought her new husband, Jack Reeves, to the wedding, a wealthy entrepreneur, just over sixty, about seven years older than Dave. Jack had made his money with a confectionery factory, which he did not hesitate to brag about. Dave was not sure what he disliked most about Jack, his condescending look when he looked at Dave, the fact that he was responsible for his divorce, or the frustrating fact that Jack, unlike Dave, had a thick head of dark hair. Andrew had told him he dyed his hair, which made Dave feel a little better. He had tried to keep his distance as politely as possible that day. Fortunately, he got along well with Wendy's mother. Wendy's father had left them when she was five years old, and they had never heard from him again. Her mother was a very kind and warm person, and Dave had practiced his Spanish with her on the wedding day and on the few occasions he had seen her after that.

"It sounds like I should come over for dinner sometime soon," Dave said jokingly.

"Always welcome Dad!"

"I actually wanted to talk to you about one of my new assignments."

He explained everything about the assignment to Andrew.

"A drug making old mice younger!? That sounds like that myth, the Fountain of Youth, Dad."

"Yeah, sounds too good to be true. Did you hear about any research teams working on that?"

"Well, there's a tremendous amount of research being done on aging and how to prevent or slow it down. And most of the tests are done with mice, so that doesn't help."

"I think Craig had heard it from some professor at MIT at a charity fund-raising event in Boston."

"At MIT? Well, then I guess if I ask around in my network, I could find out more."

"That would be great, Andrew, since I'm kind of stuck here."

"I'd be happy to do this for you, Dad. I'll get back to you as soon as I can."

Dave closed his laptop and looked at the picture of him and his son, which sat on the small table next to the armchair. Andrew kept his arm around him. Their faces looked alike, but his son looked like an athlete with his full brown hair and strong stance. He was about three inches taller than Dave, who was quite tall himself, but because he played sports and had spent his youth swimming, he was much broader. Andrew had won many swimming competitions and even won the MIT championships once. He had never made it at the national level because he had clearly prioritized his studies and not swimming.

Dave had always been there for his son. After Jennifer left him, Andrew became even more important to him. They often called during the week, and that helped him tremendously. Without realizing it, Andrew had pulled him through a difficult period in his life and prevented his depression from worsening. At least once a year they went on trips together, often hiking and fishing.

The silence in his apartment bothered him less than usual that night. Talking with his son always made him feel like life mattered and wasn't so bad after all. He walked to the bathroom to brush his teeth. He looked in the mirror and stared at his bald head. Maybe he should try that hair implant clinic Henry had recommended. Since he read so much about biological advances, he figured that hair clinics had probably gotten better, too. He had always been skeptical about transplants, but maybe it was just a way for him to put off that step. The day had been exhausting, and he now felt his back constantly aching. He took some painkillers and then brushed his teeth. He took one last look in the mirror and wondered how his life had gone by so quickly. Then he walked to his bedroom and went to bed.

A few days later, late in the afternoon, Andrew called him at work. Dave had made little progress with his research. He had spent most of his time in meetings with the editors because his article on growing livers from stem cells was the lead article in the upcoming issue of the journal. They were preparing some additional marketing around the article, and they had involved him to clarify some issues and change some of his article to make it a version for electronic publication. He had found more information about several research teams that seemed to work on ways to slow aging or undo some symptoms of aging. Yet he had found nothing about those researchers who had succeeded in making mice younger.

"Hi Dad. Good news. I think I have a good lead for your story."

"Great, tell me."

"Well, I spoke with one of the current professors at MIT about your assignment and he told me that Dr. Harvey Juncker had left MIT about five years ago to work at a private research institute focused on aging. He had heard a rumor that his team had made old mice younger by giving them the drug they had developed. That sounds like your guy dad! And guess what?!" he said in an even louder voice.

"Well, I don't know," Dave replied.

"I worked several times with Dr. Harvey Juncker on some research projects during my time at MIT. He's a really nice guy, and we always got along well. I called him this morning, and he confirmed he is working on a new drug and that they have managed to make old mice younger. They are preparing a clinical trial for humans. He said they wanted to keep publicity to a minimum, but for me, he might make an exception. He is expecting your call and would be happy to talk to you."

"Wow! That's great, Andrew. Thanks!"

Andrew paused and then continued even more enthusiastically.

"Wait dad, the best news is yet to come. Guess what? Harvey's research institute is in a small town called Novato, north of San Francisco. Just over an hour's drive away from my house, so we can see each other when you come here!"

Dave felt all excited now, too.

"That's great news! It would be great if we could meet up. Thanks again! I'll call Harvey and let you know about my plans when they're clearer."

"You're welcome. I'll mail the contact details right away. Have a nice day, dad!"

"I will and you too. Talk to you soon!"

Dave hung up and stared out the window, a little dazzled by the good news.

As he walked back to his desk after going to the restrooms, he ran into Henry.

"Coffee?"

"Sounds good, Henry."

They walked together to the coffee corner and Henry prepared two coffees from the machine.

"So, and now you have to tell me why you have that satisfied look on your face? Did you finally make that dating profile on that site I recommended to you?"

"No, sorry to disappoint you, but I just got off the phone with Andrew. He has helped me out with that assignment about those rejuvenated mice."

Henry looked interested, but also disappointed that there was no story of a date or anything juicy like that. He thought his friend had been alone a bit too long to be healthy.

"It looks that some research institute near San Francisco has developed a drug that made old mice younger. So, I'll probably have to spend quite some time over there for this assignment, just an hour's drive away from Andrew and his wife."

"Ah, that explains the happy face. Well, then it'll be quiet at the office with you in California and me in Ohio."

They both laughed, finished their coffees, and went back to their desks. He checked his e-mail and was pleased to find Andrew's e-mail already there. He immediately dialed Harvey Juncker's phone number.

"Juvenatrust Research Institute, Mary Lewis speaking."

"Hi, this is Dave Wilson from Science Publications. I'm looking for Dr. Harvey Juncker, please."

"Sorry, Dr. Juncker doesn't speak to the press. Company policy."

"He worked with my son and he's expecting my call."

"Ah, okay. Hold on, sir, let me check with him. Your name was Dave Wilson, you said?"

"That's right."

He was put on hold and heard some music, and he waited a few seconds until a deep voice answered the phone.

"This is Harvey Juncker."

"Hi, I'm Dave Wilson. I'm calling you because…"

Dave got interrupted.

"Hi, yes, Andrew had told me you'd be calling. It was so nice to hear from him. He's such a nice guy. He told me you wanted to write an article about one of our research projects?"

"Yes, that's right. We heard that you have made old mice young again!?"

"We did. Well, I already explained to Andrew that it's our company policy not to talk to the press or any other media. I get requests for interviews all the time and I turn them all down. Because I like Andrew and he has helped me out several times in the past, I'll make an exception to this policy. But we'll have to discuss some clear rules and procedures about your publication, otherwise I could get into serious trouble over here."

"Thanks Dr. Juncker, I appreciate it and I'm fine with following your procedures in this."

"Okay, Mr. Wilson, maybe it would be better if we discussed in person. Will you be in the San Francisco area soon?"

"I can come by next week. What day is convenient for you?"

"Let's meet on Tuesday at two o'clock."

"Perfect. Is the address like the one on your website? 423 Mayhem Drive, Novato?"

"That's right."

"I look forward to our meeting next week. Thank you, Dr. Juncker, and see you on Tuesday!"

"Bye Mr. Wilson, see you next week!"

Dave put the phone down and marked the date on his calendar. He continued to search online for more information about the Juvenatrust Research Institute and about Harvey Juncker. He could only find some general information, but nothing interesting, which was strange since most research companies boast about their research projects to attract more investors. At some point, the office was empty again, so he packed his laptop in his briefcase and left.

The next morning, back at the office, he continued his search online. At ten o'clock, he called Anna Phearson.

"Good morning, Anna. How are you?"

"I'm fine, thanks, and you? Is your back any better?"

"Not really, unfortunately, but I have good painkillers that help me through the day. I was wondering if Craig is available now. I need to have a word with him?"

"Well, he's still in a meeting, but it looks like it could end at any minute. If you come up here in fifteen minutes, I can squeeze you in before his next meeting starts at ten-thirty."

"Perfect. See you in fifteen minutes!"

With all the excitement, he had forgotten the article about Ms. Garcia's skin cream and he knew Craig would ask him about it. He quickly searched his cell phone for his neighbor's number. Fortunately, they had exchanged numbers when he moved into the apartment building. He immediately dialed the number, but it sounded like it was forwarded.

"Ms. Garcia's office, Jane Hudson speaking."

"Hi, this is Dave Wilson. I'm Ms. Garcia's neighbor and I'd like to speak to her. Is she available now?"

He was nervous and feared she might not be available.

"One moment, please."

He waited a bit and then suddenly he was put through.

"Hola, Mr. Wilson. How are you?"

"I'm fine, Ms. Garcia."

"What can I do for you?"

"Remember, I promised to see if we could write an article about your cream against spots. Well, I discussed it with my boss and he thought it was a good idea. I'd like to discuss the planning of the interviews with you."

"Oh great! That's so nice of you, Mr. Wilson. Will you be home tonight?"

"Yes, after eight o'clock, I must be there for sure."

"Good, I'll ask my secretary to prepare an information packet for you and then I'll drop by around eight thirty to discuss this further if that's okay with you?"

"Perfect. See you tonight, Ms. Garcia!"

"See you tonight, Mr. Wilson!"

He hung up and rushed to the elevator. On the sixteenth floor, he walked all the way to the back, where Craig's large corner office was located. Anna was sitting at her desk just in front of the glass doors to Craig's office. She indicated he could go right in.

"Dave, come on in!" Craig shouted enthusiastically from behind his large desk. Dave took a seat in the leather black chair in front of the desk.

"What can I do for you?"

"Well, Craig, I tracked down this rumor about the rejuvenated mice. Apparently, it's true. The Juvenatrust Research Institute in Novato, north of San Francisco, developed the drug. I spoke with the doctor in charge of the research. They have a policy of not talking to the press or other media."

"Mmm, that's not good," Craig muttered.

"The good news is that my son has worked closely with this doctor in the past. The doctor said he's willing to make an exception as long as we work according to their rules and procedures."

"What rules and procedures do they want us to follow?"

"He didn't say, but proposed to meet in his office next Tuesday to discuss it. So, I wanted to check if it would be okay for me to fly over there and stay in a hotel for a few nights to meet with him?"

Since the budget cuts, all expenses had to be discussed in advance, and he did not want to take any chances.

"Yes, of course, Dave. I have high hopes for this story. This could generate quite a bit of publicity, so no problem. Just keep me updated regularly."

"Perfect. I'll ask Claire to make the reservations."

Craig smiled at him.

"And how's that other story going about that skin cream against spots?"

Dave had known Craig long enough to know that he always followed up on everything.

"I spoke with the owner of the company that developed this skin cream and she agreed to meet with me to discuss the planning. With the trip to California next week, it's going to be a bit of a juggling act."

"Okay, Dave, that sounds great. I'm sorry, but I have to leave you now, because I have to rush off to another meeting."

Craig began packing some papers on his desk.

"No problem. I'll see you later."

Dave got up and left Craig's office. Back on the fourteenth floor, he walked straight to Claire's desk.

"Claire, could you…"

He stopped talking when Claire turned her face toward him with red and puffy eyes.

"Claire, what's wrong?"

"I just hung up the phone. It was my mother… my father passed away last night."

"Oh Claire, I'm sorry to hear that. I knew he was sick, but this is unexpected, isn't it?"

"Yes, we were waiting for a new donor liver to become available. He had been stable for a while, but apparently yesterday he had acute liver failure. My mother had called an ambulance, and they had him in intensive care last night. This morning he had a heart attack, and they tried to resuscitate him, but without success."

"I'm sorry for you. I know how close you were to him. Shouldn't you go to the hospital?"

"I still have work."

"Come on, Claire, the work will still be there tomorrow. Follow your heart now."

"I guess you're right. I'll just inform Anna so she can take over for me for today."

She packed her bag. He looked into her eyes and saw her grief. He gave her a quick hug, and she cried again.

"Thanks. You're a kind man. What did you want to ask me, anyway?"

"Nothing, just go now. I'll ask Anna."

"Okay, thanks Dave."

"Take care and let me know if there's anything I can do for you."

Dave continued to his desk. Later in the afternoon, he called Anna to ask her to book a flight to San Francisco and book a hotel room for him for the next week. Anna would check it and email him all the details of the reservation. He hung up and began typing an e-mail, but his thoughts wandered.

He thought about the article he had written on growing livers from stem cells and how a new liver could have saved Claire's father. He had spoken at length with several doctors on the research team. They had explained that the method worked well, and the risks were relatively low. Since they were growing livers from stem cells from the person who needed the liver transplant, they had eliminated the biggest risk, the risk of rejection. They were preparing for the first clinical trials, required by the Food and Drug Administration. It could be years before this new method would be available to all patients. It frustrated him that such a successful method was not available to people like Claire's father. If the scientists had skipped the clinical trials, he might still be alive today. It felt like a sinking boat within sight of the harbor.

That evening he ate quickly because he wanted to clean up his apartment before Ms. Garcia would come over. They had been neighbors for almost eight years now, but their contact had been limited to conversation in the hallway or in the elevator. They had exchanged keys, since they were the only ones on the same floor, and it was convenient to have a spare key with the neighbor. After cleaning up, he quickly brushed his teeth to get rid of the smell of the delicious lasagna he had just finished. Around eight thirty, the doorbell rang. He opened and looked straight into the brown eyes of Ms. Garcia.

She greeted him with a warm smile and kissed him on the cheek. He smelled her subtle perfume. She wore a dark blue skirt with a white blouse. She walked to the large dining table in the middle of the living room and set down a large bag with her company's logo on it. Her high heels made a clicking sound on the wooden floor. He glanced fleetingly at her beautiful figure and the sensual shape of her hips.

"Great, you could come over so quickly, Ms. Garcia."

"Well, I should be the one to thank you, Mr. Wilson. It's so kind of you to write an article about my new skin cream. Also, it's about time we stopped with the Ms. and Mr., isn't? We've been neighbors for so long now, so please call me by my first name."

She smiled at him.

"Perfect, Penelope."

"That sounds much better, Dave. I've brought a bag with me, that my secretary prepared for you. In it are the skin cream, some marketing materials and background information," Penelope said as she unpacked the bag and set some boxes and a stack of documents on the table.

It had been a long time since Dave had had a woman visiting his apartment, especially one a stunning and attractive woman as Penelope.

"Ah, great, that will be a good starting point. Can I offer you something to drink?"

She looked at the bottle of red wine on the bar in the kitchen.

"A glass of red wine would be great."

He walked to the kitchen to get the wine and said, "Okay, let me get the wine and please take a seat."

She sat down on the leather couch in the living room. When he returned from the kitchen with two glasses of red wine, he watched Penelope sitting on his couch with her beautiful legs crossed as she rubbed a hand through her dark hair. She smiled at him as he approached.

"Here you go!" he said as he handed her the glass and sat down in one of the armchairs next to the couch.

She raised the glass to toast.

"So nice, Dave, to be working on an article together. After all these years of living next door to each other."

He smiled and their glasses touched briefly, then they both drank a bit of wine.

"Mmm, delicious wine. What is it?"

"It's a French wine, a Côtes de Bourg from Chateau Bujan, a friend of mine brought it from Europe last year."

The sight of this beautiful woman on his couch made him shy and nervous, and he quickly got up to grab his notebook and a pen. His back hurt him again from sitting too long, and he felt better as he stood up and stretched.

Penelope looked at the picture of him with Andrew on the table.

"Is that your son?"

"Yes, that's Andrew."

"He looks handsome like his father," she said as she held the frame in her hands.

He was speechless when he heard that from her, but thought she was probably just trying to be polite.

"Where does he live?"

"He lives in San Jose in California and works at a research institute. He moved there after graduating at MIT in Boston. We see each other a few times a year."

She put the frame back on the table and said, "He looks like a nice guy. I guess it won't be easy with that distance."

He sat down in his chair with his notebook.

"Yeah, it's hard. But at least we call every week. We get along very well."

He paused and hesitated for a moment, but then asked her,

"Do you have children?"

She looked sad now and replied, "No, I don't. My ex-husband and I tried to have children. For a while, we thought it was because I worked so hard and was too stressed. Later we had some tests done, and it turned out we could never have children together since he was not fertile. I would have liked to have children, but that time has passed."

Dave felt awkward and changed the topic.

"Sorry to hear that. Okay, let's discuss the article. The documents you brought are a good start for me to understand more about the skin cream. Usually, I need several interviews to go deeper into the topic. Maybe we can start with more background on the company and the product and discuss planning for the other interviews later."

She smiled at him.

"Perfect. Where do you want to start?"

"Maybe we can start with the beginning. How did you start your company?"

"Well, when I was young, my mother used to make her own skin cream, which again she had learned from her mother. I remember how she used to sit in the living room with all the ingredients spread out on our dining room table. She mixed them in a certain way. My mother's skin always looked young and well moisturized…"

He looked at Penelope as she continued talking and he realized why he thought she was more than ten years younger than she really was. Her skin looked great and was a nice contrast to her dark hair.

"… when I was at university, I went back to my mother's regularly and she would always give me some of her cream. I've been using it ever since and about twenty years ago, more and more of my friends started asking me about the cream, so I realized there was a great business opportunity there. I founded my company and gave my mother a part of the shares. In the beginning, we outsourced the production, but after a few years sales kept growing and we built our first factory. Meanwhile, we introduced more products…."

He took some notes as he listened to her, regularly asking questions as the hours passed.

"… a few years ago, one of our product developers thought we should do some research on those dark spots people get on their skin as they age. There are a lot of anti-aging creams available, but most do not really work and some are made of questionable chemicals. We created the first effective anti-aging spot cream based only on natural ingredients. For the past few years, we have been doing clinical trials, which showed that the cream is better than any other cream on the market, and last week we launched it..."

She paused, looked at her watch, and was startled.

"Oh my God, look at the time! It's already ten to twelve and I have a very early meeting tomorrow. Maybe we should continue another day, Dave?"

He was also amazed to see how quickly the time had passed.

"Of course. Almost midnight. Time has flown by. What a story Penelope!"

His admiration for her had only grown. What an impressive woman.

"We should probably schedule another meeting together and later I would also like to talk to some of your product development staff. It'll be difficult to schedule anything now, because I'm flying to San Francisco next week for some interviews there. I don't really know how long I'll be staying there, so perhaps it would be best for me to call you next week to plan the follow-up."

"No problem, that sounds fine to me," she said.

He couldn't help but look at her body as she stood up. She really looked beautiful. She had been divorced about four years ago and, as far as he knew, she had hardly dated since then. He could only dream of going out with her, but what was he thinking? An amazing woman like Penelope would never fall for a man like him. Even though she was out of his league, he loved spending this time with her. He had even forgotten about his back until he got out of the armchair and felt the horrible pain in his back.

"You okay, Dave?"

"Yes, thanks, it's my back. It gets stuck when I sit too long and the last few days, it's been extra painful."

"I'm sorry to hear that. Do you see a doctor for that?"

"Yes, I do, but there wasn't much he could do. I guess I'll have to live with it. He gave me some good painkillers, though."

"Okay. Thanks again for writing this article. If it gets published in Science Magazine, it'll be great for our image," she said as they walked to the door. She gave him a kiss on the cheek and left.

"I'll call you next week. Sleep tight."

"Good night," she said as she closed the door and smiled one last time at him.

3. The interview

As the plane approached San Francisco International Airport, it began a slow descent. Dave began to move in his seat and woke up. He looked at his watch and estimated that he had slept maybe an hour. He could not fall asleep for the first four to five hours of the flight because his back hurt too much. After taking some painkillers, the pain had slowly subsided, and he had finally fallen asleep. Dave searched his pockets for gum, as he felt some pressure on his ears. As soon as he started chewing, he felt his ears pop. As the plane approached the runway, he felt anxious. It had always amazed him that such a large object could soar through the air, and he never really felt comfortable flying. The wheels of the plane touched down on the runway and the plane braked, then slowly taxied toward the gate.

Outside the airport, happy to have both feet back on the ground, he walked to the car rental counter, pulling his black suitcase behind him. There were no clouds and you could feel the sun's rays warming the crisp morning air. He felt excited about his assignment and went to pick up his car at the rental agency. It was a nice silver-gray BMW. He put his suitcase in the trunk and typed the address of the hotel into the navigation system, then he started the engine and drove off toward highway I-380W. He turned on the radio and listened to the music.

As he drove across the Golden Gate Bridge, he thought back to his time in college and how he first met Jennifer. He had first noticed her when he was playing basketball with some friends from college. She had beautiful, long, blond hair and a wonderful smile. Dave still had a full head of hair then, and with his tall stature and friendly smile, he attracted quite a bit of female attention. He asked Jennifer out and fell in love with her. After graduation, they married and moved in together. He never forgot the date of his wedding day, as it was the Saturday right after the 1987 stock market crash. He still remembered how the guests at his wedding talked about it. Some had lost a lot of money. Jennifer had given him many wonderful years and, most importantly, she had given him his son, Andrew. The last five years of their marriage had not been as good and had been one of the reasons for the depression he fell into after she left him.

Dave thought of the rejuvenation drug and wondered if it would create the possibility of living forever. He also wondered if people wanted to live forever. Eternal life would only make sense to him if one could live healthily and happily. With his constant back pain, it sounded more like a long punishment to him. The painkillers he had taken on the plane had worn off, and slowly his back began to feel more uncomfortable. After exiting U.S. Highway 101, he arrived at the hotel north of San Rafael. He got out of the car and first stretched his back completely. It was a beautiful day. He got his suitcase out of the trunk and walked to the front desk.

The woman at the reception greeted him kindly.

"Hi, I have a reservation under the name Dave Wilson."

"Let me check, sir," she said, glancing at her screen.

He noticed the basket with chocolate chip cookies on the counter.

"Yep, I found it. A reservation for three nights. I have your key right here. You have a conference suite on the second floor with a view of Lagoon Park. Breakfast is from six to ten in the morning. You can take the elevator over there and I hope you'll have a pleasant stay with us," the woman said, pointing to the elevators.

He pointed to the cookies.

"Could I have one?"

"They're complimentary."

He took a cookie and headed for the elevator down the hall. Arriving in his room, he unpacked his suitcase. His cell phone rang. It was Harvey Juncker.

"Oh hi, Dr. Juncker. I just arrived at my hotel."

"I hope you had a pleasant flight?"

"It was ok. Flying is not my thing, but the weather on arrival compensated for the flight right away."

"I had told you about some rules and procedures and I'd like to ask you when you come here at the reception not to tell them you're from Science Magazine."

"Ah, ok, but what would you rather I tell them?"

"Maybe you can tell them you're from Siemens Laboratory Diagnostics. They're one of our equipment suppliers and they come here regularly with different people, so that'll probably attract the least attention."

Dave was uncomfortable lying, but it had happened before that they had asked him to lie about who he worked for.

"Okay, I'll do that, Dr. Juncker."

"Thanks, see you at two o'clock!"

"Perfect. Bye Dr. Juncker."

After taking a shower to freshen up, he dressed and went downstairs to have lunch in the restaurant next to the reception. The restaurant was quiet and he read the newspaper he had brought from the front desk. He felt his back hurt and took another painkiller so that the pain would not bother him too much during his meeting with Dr. Juncker. He had prepared for the meeting by doing some background research on Dr. Juncker and about aging research. He had found quite a few articles written or co-authored by him, but all from his time at MIT. He had tried to find recent publications, but to his surprise, he had found nothing, nor did he find Dr. Juncker on social media. One of the MIT articles listed his date of birth. He was sixty-eight years old. He finished his cappuccino, grabbed his briefcase, and walked to his car.

After leaving the parking lot, he drove onto U.S. Highway 101 and continued north toward Santa Rosa. About ten minutes later, he took the exit for Novato. He drove through the small town and followed the directions of the navigation system that led him to a large park. Just before the park, he turned onto a small road called Mayhem Drive. Except for a few office buildings at the beginning of the road, it felt more like he was driving through a thick forest with trees to the left and right. There were no signs saying "Juvenatrust," so he was glad the navigation system gave him directions. A few kilometers further on, he saw a gray square building with dark mirrored windows in the middle of the forest. It was a surreal sight. There were many cars in the parking lot, and after finding a spot, he walked to the entrance while hearing birds singing. The sound reminded him of past visits to nature parks.

In front of the building stood a mailbox with only the number 423 on it. There was no sign with the name of the company, nor was it written on the building. It was strange not to see the name anywhere. The sound of birds faded as he entered the building and walked to the reception desk. The entrance hall had a white desk on the left side, with a metal sign on the wall behind it with "Juvenatrust Research Institute" written on it. On the right side were some modern white armchairs with a coffee table with some magazines on it. There was a glass door at the end of the hall with a white corridor behind it. The whole hall felt cold and clinical. A lady with an emotionless and cold face greeted him.

"Hello sir, what I can do for you?"

"I have an appointment with Dr. Harvey Juncker. My name is Dave Wilson."

The woman started checking her computer. Without looking up, she asked him which company he was from.

"I'm from Siemens Laboratory Diagnostics."

Dave felt nervous. The woman grabbed her phone and dialed a number.

"Hi Mary, Dave Wilson is here to see Dr. Juncker. Okay. Bye."

The lady pulled a badge from behind the counter and scanned it.

"All right, Mr. Wilson, Dr. Juncker is expecting you. Here you have your badge, which you must wear at all times during your visit. Go through that glass door. The guard will scan your bag and then you must take the elevator to the second floor. Dr. Junker's secretary will pick you up there to take you to his office."

"Thank you."

As he approached the door, he heard an electronic lock opening, and the door opened automatically. In the hall behind the door, a large security guard sat next to a scanner.

"Please put your bag on the belt, sir."

He put his briefcase on the belt, and it went through the scanner.

"Okay, sir. Have a nice day!"

He got into the elevator and looked at the buttons. Only three buttons marked "G", "1" and "2" and he pressed the button for the second floor. As he looked into the mirror in the elevator, he noticed a black security camera on the ceiling in the corner behind him. He rearranged the collar of his blue shirt and knocked a lint off his dark brown coat. His bald head glowed under the bright elevator spotlights. A friendly looking, older woman was waiting for him as he came out of the elevator. He greeted her. It was Mary Lewis, Dr. Juncker's secretary. He followed Ms. Lewis through the narrow white corridor, passing several doors to the left and right. At the end of the corridor, she stepped into an office. A gray-haired man with glasses eagerly walked up to him and held out his hand to shake his hand.

"Hello, Mr. Wilson, welcome to Juvenatrust Research Institute!"

"Hello, Dr. Juncker, what a magnificent view you have."

"Yes, I guess one of the perks is the forest view. Can we offer you something to drink?"

"Do you have a cappuccino?"

"Yes, and for me, a latte macchiato, please, Mary."

The woman nodded and left the room, closing the door behind her. Harvey looked at Dave and said, "You're almost as tall as Andrew, right?"

"Well, about three inches less. Andrew told me you worked together at MIT, Dr. Juncker?"

"Please call me Harvey. Andrew has worked with me on several projects. He's a very talented boy and a pleasure to work with. I was very pleased to hear from him last week. He seems to be doing well, and the research institute he works for in San Jose has an excellent reputation. Please take a seat."

Dave sat down on the chair in front of Harvey's desk. He watched Harvey as the latter sat down and continued talking. Harvey must have been five foot six and looked quite sturdy. He looked older than Dave, but was very energetic. His office was full of piles of papers. He saw the latest copy of Science Magazine on the corner of his desk. He saw the headline of the editorial, "Growing livers from your own stem cells," the article Dave had written.

"Yeah, Andrew is a bright guy and you can't imagine how happy I was when he specialized in biological engineering, one of the most promising fields to work in."

"Well, Dave, I understood you're becoming an expert in that field yourself. I'm a big fan of Science Magazine. I enjoyed your article on the genetically engineered twins last year. You really know how to explain difficult matters in simple language. I just received the latest edition and saw you wrote the lead article."

They talked for a while about the article until the older woman entered the room with the coffee. While she set the cups on the table, Dave and Harvey stopped talking. Harvey thanked the secretary, and she left, closing the door behind her. Harvey took a sip of his latte macchiato and lowered his voice slightly.

"As I explained to you, it's our company policy not to talk to the press. Juvenatrust is privately owned and the owners prefer to operate below the radar. They've forbidden all staff to talk to the press or release any information about the company or our work on any media. However, we've reached an important milestone this year, with our tests proving that we can make old mice young again with our newly developed drug," Harvey said. He turned his chair and now looked straight at Dave. "I disagree with the owners of the company about keeping such a low profile. I believe the scientific world has a right to know about our amazing discovery and success and since I like Andrew and admire your magazine, I believe the time's right for a publication in Science Magazine. I haven't yet discussed this with the owners. So for now, I prefer to work with you in secret until I've convinced the owners to allow publication."

Harvey shifted slightly forward in his chair and said with a stern look on his face," That's why I think we should first agree on a few things before we proceed with the interview. I asked you to pretend to be someone who works for Siemens Laboratory Diagnostics, because we often have suppliers visiting us. I always handle all these contacts, so to the people who work here it seems normal for me to receive your visit. I also often show our suppliers around our research facility, so under this cover I could give you a tour later on. But under no circumstance should you reveal your true identity and avoid any contact with anyone who works here at Juvenatrust."

"That's no problem for me, although I think I told your secretary that I work for Science Publications when I first called you."

"Don't worry about Mary. I trust her. We worked together already at MIT. She won't tell anyone, but apart from her, you can't reveal your identity. At least not until I get approval from the owners. We have a board meeting at the end of this month where they will all be present and where I'll discuss the publication of the article. Until then, I want you to guarantee that you will not publish or share anything with anyone without my approval."

"No problem, Harvey. It's not the first time I've worked under secrecy."

Harvey looked deeply into his eyes and said in a very serious tone, "Swear on your son's life that you'll keep your promise!"

Dave was surprised that Harvey asked him to do this, but he did not see a problem. He would just have to be clear with Craig, because he normally asked to see some intermediate work when working on longer assignments. He thought Craig would probably accept the terms.

"Okay, I swear on my son's life that I'll publish nothing or share anything with anyone until you give me approval."

Harvey looked more relaxed now and sipped the latte macchiato.

Curious, Dave asked, "Who are the owners of Juvenatrust, actually?"

Harvey looked a little puzzled, and his face turned bleak.

"When I joined Juvenatrust five years ago, they made me sign a confidentiality agreement which stated that I had to keep the identity of the owners of the company secret. So unfortunately, I'm not allowed to answer your question."

It was getting darker outside. Dave looked at his watch and realized the time had passed quickly.

"Okay, I understand. Let's discuss the planning of our interview."

Harvey's face brightened, and he continued enthusiastically, "The timing for an interview could not have been better. Next week, a large group of our staff members will go on an off-site training program, so the facility will be much quieter than usual. This week I suggest coming to your hotel for the first interviews, to avoid people getting suspicious. Next week, when most people are gone for the training, I can show you our research facility in more detail. Does that suit you?"

Dave did not expect to get so much time with Dr. Juncker. All he had to do was to extend his stay at the hotel.

"Sounds perfect to me. We can sit in my hotel room, since they booked me into a huge suite with a separate conference room. That way, we won't be disturbed."

"Great! Tomorrow I can come to your hotel around two, since I have some meetings in the morning. Can you give me the address?"

Dave searched in his coat for one of the business cards from the hotel and handed it to Harvey. He looked at it and said, "Ah, that's only ten minutes from here, perfect. Let me walk you to the elevator."

Dave put his notebook back in his suitcase and stood up. Harvey walked with him to the elevator and Dave saw a man with dark hair and a dark mustache standing in front of the elevator. As soon as they arrived at the elevator, Harvey said, "All right, thanks for visiting and send me your equipment proposal no later than next week. Have a good trip back!"

Surprised, Dave played along.

"I will. Thank you for your time, Dr. Juncker."

In the elevator, he did not speak a word to the man and stared ahead, but the man was checking him out. Downstairs, he had to wait behind the man while the security guard scanned his bag. After the man passed the security check, Dave put his suitcase on the belt. He picked it up on the other side after the guard nodded at him. He handed his badge to the woman at the reception desk and left the building. Outside, it had grown dark, and the sky had turned a dark red. He stretched his back a bit, as all the sitting had not done him much good, and then he got into his car and drove away. He looked back on his day with a positive feeling. The only thing puzzling him was the secrecy surrounding the owners of Juvenatrust. However, this did not stop him from falling fast asleep that night in his comfortable hotel bed.

The next morning, he called Claire to rearrange his schedule.

"Hello Claire, it's Dave. How are you?"

"Hi Dave! I'm fine. How was your flight yesterday?"

Claire knew he did not like flying. She had advised him to take a sleeping pill to relax, but he did not like to take sleeping pills because they could be addictive and had many negative side effects.

"Not so bad. I even slept for an hour without taking sleeping pills. How's your mother doing? The priest who spoke at the funeral last Saturday was very good."

"Yeah, he did well. My mother's still sad, but at least she had some people visiting every day. Tell me, what can I do for you?"

He explained to Claire that he would be staying for at least two weeks longer, maybe even three. He asked her to make the necessary changes to the flight and hotel. Claire told him she would take care of it, and then he asked to be put through to Craig. He got Anna on the line, who explained that Craig was still in a meeting and would call him back in half an hour.

He put a capsule into the espresso machine and made another coffee. He sat down at the large table and stared out at the lagoon park. The birds were flying around from tree to tree. He thought back to the proud on Harvey's face when he confirmed they had succeeded in making mice younger. It would be the first time in the human history that anyone had rejuvenated a mammal. The more he thought about it, the more he realized the importance of this breakthrough. The ringing phone interrupted his thoughts. It was Craig.

"How did your meeting go with Dr. Juncker?"

"Well, pretty good actually, he confirmed they have made mice younger with their drug."

"Wow, I hope you realize this could be the biggest story we've ever covered. Has it become somewhat clear yet what he meant by the special rules and procedures?"

He took a sip of his espresso and replied, "Apparently, it's company policy not to speak to the press, but Dr. Juncker told me he wanted to make an exception for us. He thinks highly of Science Magazine and has worked with my son in the past. He also believes the world should know about the important milestone they've reached. The problem is, he doesn't have any permission from the owners of Juvenatrust. At the end of this month, he has a board meeting and then he wants to convince the owners to allow publication."

"Ah, ok, so we've to wait for the interview until the end of the month?"

"Well, no. Dr. Juncker proposed to go ahead, but I have to work for some equipment supplier. He also made me swear not to publish anything without his approval, nor share my article with anyone. Not even with colleagues."

He paused and waited for a response from Craig.

"Well, Dave, it's awkward, but given the importance of the story, I would accept it all, and it's only a few weeks until his board meeting. Who are the owners of Juvenatrust, actually?"

"I asked him exactly the same question, but Dr. Juncker said he signed a confidentiality agreement that prohibits him from saying anything about the ownership. I searched online yesterday, but found nothing yet."

"I'll ask Anna to look into that. I'm sure we should be able to find something. Okay, so what's the schedule?"

"Well, this afternoon Dr. Juncker is coming to my hotel for the first part of the interview. Next week he's planning to show me the facilities. So, it looks like we can make quite some progress in the next few weeks."

"Great. Well, keep me posted and I'll let you know when we know out more about the owners. I have to go now. Good luck Dave."

"Thanks, Craig."

He took another sip of his espresso. The pain in his back had gotten worse, so he took another painkiller and went downstairs to have lunch. After that, he returned to his room and prepared for Dr. Juncker's visit. The phone rang. It was the woman from reception informing him that Harvey Juncker had arrived. Five minutes later, he opened the door for Dr. Juncker. He made him an espresso and took some water for himself. He grabbed his notebook and pen.

"So, where shall we begin? Perhaps first it would be interesting to know how you ended up at Juvenatrust? Ah, and do you mind if I record our interview?"

"No problem."

Harvey smiled, pushed his glasses back on his nose, and replied, "As you know, I used to be a professor at MIT and had focused my research on the key question of why and how the cells in our body age. After giving a presentation on this topic at a biotech conference, an investor approached me who said he had an interesting job offer for me. They had founded a new research institute, called Juvenatrust, whose main goal was to make people immortal. The funding was basically unlimited as long as we made progress. They asked me if I wanted to head the research department of Juvenatrust, and they made me an offer I couldn't refuse. I had to discuss it with my wife. My daughter had already left the house and had moved to London."

Harvey sighed and swallowed before continuing.

"It was a difficult decision because my wife was being treated for cancer in a nearby hospital. Juvenatrust helped us find one of the best doctors in the country at UCSF Baker Cancer hospital in San Francisco, and that convinced us to accept the job offer. Unfortunately, the treatment didn't help and my wife died two years later."

"I'm sorry to hear that. That must have been a difficult time."

"Yeah, it was. I had a difficult period and started working even harder. Mary was very supportive and helped me through that period. Well, anyway, that's how I ended up at Juvenatrust."

Dave grabbed another water bottle from the fridge and offered Harvey one as well.

"You told me yesterday that you reached an important milestone for the company. Can you explain that?"

Harvey took a sip of his water bottle and said, "To start with the milestone, I can tell you we made old mice young again. We developed a drug that, after injection into the mice, made them younger. This was visible in many aspects. The mice became more energetic and started running on the treadmill instead of sleeping in a quiet corner all day. Their hearts became stronger and organs like the kidneys or liver were healthier and functioned much better after the injections. The fur, which was thin and gone in some areas of the older mice, grew back and became thick and healthy again. Many of the older mice had a hunched posture, but after the treatment, this disappeared and their bodies looked strong and supple again. The most impressive result was actually that the mice lived about thirty percent longer than the control group."

"Wow, that's amazing! How long did this treatment take to show these effects?"

"Well, you're right to call this amazing, because the duration of the treatment makes this rejuvenating process even more amazing. We found the drug worked immediately, and most effects became visible within a few days after injecting the drug. Most of the changes stabilized after three to four weeks."

"That's fast," Dave said. "So, how does this work?"

Harvey looked out the window at the lagoon park for a moment before answering.

"I've been studying the aging process, which is very complex, all my professional life, and even now there're so many things we don't yet understand. It would take a long time to explain everything, but I'll try to explain the most important things to you. Before we talk about treatment, let's talk about aging."

Dave stood up and looked at Harvey.

"Another espresso?"

"Yes, please. Biology has gone a long way over the past few decades. We had so many breakthroughs that we could say that the twenty-first century is the century of the biological revolution. In your article last year on genetically engineered twins, you touched upon some of these developments. Most importantly, this revolution has to do with our increased understanding of the human body and the cells that make it up. We've learned that ninety-nine percent of the human body mass comprises only six elements: oxygen, carbon, hydrogen, nitrogen, calcium and phosphorus. From a molecular perspective we learned that sixty-five percent of the mass of the human body consists of water, twenty percent of proteins, twelve percent of lipids, one and a half percent of inorganic substances, zero comma four percent other organics, one percent of RNA or Ribonucleic acid, and zero comma one percent of DNA or Deoxyribonucleic acid."

He made notes while Harvey continued talking.

"With the sequencing of the human genome, we've gone even further in detail and scale by dissecting the building blocks of the human body. I'll try not to overwhelm you too much, but my key point is that the biological revolution resulted in a technical approach to life, and humans in particular. The human body is made up of building blocks, which we're understanding better and better.

Aging therefore and death in particular have now become a technical problem with technical solutions."

Dave listened spellbound as Harvey spoke so passionately about his research. Harvey spoke at length about all facets of aging. Meanwhile, he continued taking notes during the interview. Harvey continued, after taking a moment to sip his espresso.

"Regarding aging, most research has focused on the aging of the cells out that make up the human body. I built on this existing research and focused on what we call 'senescent cells.' With age, our cells get damaged, or rather, the DNA gets damaged. Our body has some mechanisms to repair the damage, but most of the damage remains. These damaged cells destroy themselves, become cancerous or they become semi-dormant and go into a state called senescence. As we age, our bodies accumulate more and more senescent cells. I believe these senescent cells cause most of the problems associated with aging. For example, certain classes of senescent cells accumulate in the wrong places, such as in the joints. This eventually leads to pain in the joints, malfunctioning joints, or other problems. You can say that these cells, when they accumulate, cause damage and impair functions in the body. These senescent cells contribute to age related decline in tissue function."

Dave nodded and when Harvey paused said, "So, if I understand correctly, it's as if these senescent cells are clogging up our system and body more and more, as we age and causing all sorts of problems or leading to malfunctioning of various body functions?"

Harvey looked enthusiastic, as if pleased that Dave understood the complex matter.

"Exactly! As we age, our body accumulates cells that do nothing, because they are there, they gradually clog up the entire system. These senescent cells affect all the individual functions of the human body and the more of these cells we accumulate, the more problematic these functions become. It's like an accumulation of junk in our body with many negative effects."

Dave asked further, fascinated, "So, for example, these senescent cells could cause us more trouble walking as we age. Or that older people get wrinkles or skin problems, or the diminished taste of older people, or my perpetual back pain... it's all caused by these senescent cells?"

Harvey smiled.

"I believe so, Dave. And that's exactly why I focus most of my research on the key question: How do we get rid of these senescent cells?"

Harvey looked outside. It was already getting dark. He looked startled at his watch.

"Wow, the time has flown by."

Dave checked his watch, too.

"Would you like to have some dinner together?"

"That would be nice, but tonight Mary promised to prepare her special Boeuf Bourguignon for me and, judging by the time, it might already be on the table."

"Shall we continue the interview tomorrow, then?"

Harvey checked his calendar.

"I'm sorry. Tomorrow my schedule is full, but Friday afternoon is possible for me. Let's say at one-thirty in the afternoon?"

"Perfect, and shall we then plan dinner in the evening?"

"Yep, that sounds great. Looking forward to it. I'll come to your room at one-thirty, next Friday then."

Harvey shook his hand and left the hotel room. Dave felt tremendous pain in his back, as the painkiller he had taken had now worn off. He took another painkiller and went for a walk in the lagoon park, since that usually helped against the pain. It was a beautiful evening and still relatively warm. He thought back to his conversation with Harvey. A fascinating story, he thought, and it reinforced his thought that this could be one of the hottest stories for Science Magazine for a long time. Harvey seemed to have developed an intimate relationship with Mary after his wife died. Dave wondered why he had not started any new relationship after Jennifer left him. He presumed his lost hair made his appearance not very appealing to women, and with his constant back problems, he often did not have the energy to go out or go on a date. Back at the hotel, he dined alone at a table in the restaurant, and after dinner, he went back to his room. Feeling down, he called his son, hoping that would cheer him up.

"Hi, Andrew, it's me!"

"Hi, Dad! Nice to get your call in the evening. Usually, you call earlier with the time difference. How is it in Novato?"

Feeling better, he replied, "Not bad. My hotel is in San Rafael, next to a park. Novato is a ten-minute drive from here. Your old professor told me to send you his regards. He speaks highly of you. We started the interview, and he has already given me a lot of time. The good news is that I'm extending my stay here for at least a week."

"Well, in that case, come over and stay with us next weekend. You can sleep in the spare bedroom in our house. Do you have a car?"

"Yes, I have a rental car, so I can easily come to you. Thanks for the invitation. I'd love to stay with you over the weekend. Friday, I have dinner with Harvey Juncker, but Saturday I can come by."

"Perfect. Why don't you come early, so we can have lunch at our house?"

Andrew paused for a moment.

"Perfect timing, Dad! I have a nice surprise for you."

"A surprise? Well, you're making me curious. Saturday lunch sounds good. I'll call you when I get out of here."

On Thursday, he worked all day in his room on his article. He called Anna during the day to check if she had discovered anything about the owners of Juvenatrust. Anna explained to him what sources she had checked, then told him her findings.

"Juvenatrust has six shareholders. All six shareholders are Cayman Islands registered companies. The largest shareholder is a company called Cayman Capital Ltd, which owns twenty-five percent of the outstanding shares. The remaining seventy-five percent is held by BioFace Ltd, ImpactVentures Ltd, FutureSense Ltd, Kavneft Ltd and Track Capital Ltd, which each own fifteen percent of the outstanding shares. Unfortunately, I couldn't yet find out anything about the owners of these companies. I know there's a way to find out, but I need to check with Craig first to see if he agrees to the additional fees. I'll ask him tomorrow when he gets back to the office."

"Okay, thanks, Anna. Keep me posted!"

That evening, he ordered some sushi in his room, as he felt tired and wanted to go to bed early. Friday morning, he got up early to continue working on his article and prepare for his meeting with Harvey. Later in the morning, he received a call from Henry.

"Hi, Henry. How are you, old chap?"

He heard Henry laugh.

"Speak for yourself. I don't feel old. I feel more like reliving my high school days with all this dating. Guess what?"

"I don't know!? Did you find another date in Ohio?"

"Ha, ha, no. Remember that blond woman I told you about, Sara? Well, she's coming over here tonight and staying with me for the weekend. Apparently, she missed me and got on a plane to Columbus. I'll pick her up later today."

"Nice! Not much sleep for you this weekend then… how's your interview going there at Wright-Patterson Air Force base?"

"Very well. Yesterday, I even got to test one of their sniper helmets."

"Wow, that must have been quite an experience?"

"It certainly was. They put some light electric current on your brain and it's a great feeling. First, I had to shoot without a helmet in some virtual building where you're attacked by some criminals and you have to be careful because you are not allowed to shoot any civilians. I only killed six criminals, but also two civilians. Then they made me wear the helmet and do the same shooting exercise. I can tell you it was an amazing experience. It's like your brain goes completely silent and all attention goes to the shooting exercise. Complete focus on the task. I didn't even feel like I had to do anything. It felt like I was on autopilot. When they took off the helmet, I felt so relaxed. They told me the result and I couldn't believe it. I had killed all fifteen criminals and no civilians. The weird thing was that after this experience, I kept feeling like putting that helmet back on. They told me that this feeling is perfectly normal and that it can be addictive."

"Wow, amazing!"

"Yeah, it was fun. Next week they'll show me more applications for the helmets. How's your old mice story going?"

"It's a fascinating story. They managed to make old mice younger with their drug. With the treatment, the mice became more energetic within a few weeks. Their bodies went from a hunched body to a normal healthy position, and their fur grew back and became full and healthy again."

Henry jokingly said, "It sounds like you don't need that hair transplant anymore. You can just take one of their drugs. Maybe you can take a sample with you during your visit, ha, ha."

Dave laughed and continued to explain.

"They're preparing for clinical trials, but it'll take years before it becomes available to humans. But it's fascinating and a pretty big story, I believe."

"Sounds interesting. So, you'll be there for a long time?"

"Probably another week or two, but I don't mind. That way, I can spend more time with Andrew. I'm visiting him this weekend."

"Nice!"

He looked at his watch and it was one o'clock already.

"Sorry Henry, I have to go now. I've my next interview in half an hour and I haven't had lunch yet."

"No problem, buddy, have a nice weekend!"

After his lunch, he rushed back to his room, because Harvey could arrive at any moment. He quickly took another painkiller when he heard knocking on the door. He opened the door for Harvey and gestured him to sit down. He prepared two espressos and sat down on the other side of the table.

"So, Harvey, I believe we stopped yesterday after you explained about aging and senescent cells. You were about to explain that your research focused on how to get rid of these senescent cells."

Harvey nodded.

"Right. Our hypothesis was that if we could get rid of these senescent cells, that the original functions would be restored. Many methods have been tried, like genetically modified mice. These modifications in the genes of mice caused their bodies to kill about fifty to seventy percent of the senescent cells, resulting in the mice becoming younger. The problem with this method is that it's still a huge step to modify humans genetically to kill senescent cells. There's a lot of ethical resistance to genetically modifying humans, and the risks of unwanted side effects are high. So, we looked for a way to kill the senescent cells without genetically modifying the mice. The key question was to find out what was preventing senescent cells from destroying themselves and then to remove this brake, so that the senescent cells could kill themselves. After searching in the molecular traffic inside senescent cells, we discovered that damaged cells usually trigger a protein, let's call it protein A, that initiates the cell's process of self-destruction. We discovered that in senescent cells there's another protein, let's call it protein B, that attaches itself to protein A, somewhat like handcuffs. This protein B prevents protein A doing its job properly and instead of self-destruction, the cells become semi-dormant or senescent. Next week I'll give you more papers describing the whole process in detail, with the actual names of the proteins, but for now I prefer to keep it simple."

Harvey took a sip of his espresso. The sky was clear, and the sun was shining on the lagoon lake, a beautiful sight. Harvey cleared his throat and continued.

"Our research team then designed a special peptide drug. Peptides are compounds composed of two or more amino acids linked in a chain, but I'll spare you the details. This peptide drug pushes itself in between protein A and B, releasing up protein A. Once protein A, the death protein, is released, it performs its function and the cell destroys itself. The healthy cells have no protein B and are not affected by the peptide drug. The main challenge here was that peptide drugs were usually too large to enter cells, so they were not widely used. Recently, however, there's a new technology that can make peptides that can penetrate cells. These special peptides can enter cells and organs after injection. Another advantage is that these peptide drugs, because of their characteristics, can be easily adapted for use in humans."

Harvey's story was quite scientific, but Dave had no trouble understanding it, helped by his years of experience in the field of biotechnology.

"After we had designed this drug, we began testing it on old mice, with all the dramatic effects mentioned earlier, such as regrowth of fur, increased energy levels, improved organ functions, etc. When we saw the effect on the mice, we knew we had reached a very important milestone. We repeated the test several times, but the results were consistent," Harvey stated proudly.

He looked admiringly at Harvey, who was sipping his espresso. Harvey was older than him, but much more energetic and passionate about what he was doing.

"So, what did you do after this successful test?"

Harvey smiled.

"Well, that's the fun thing about working for a private research institute. We presented the results to our board, and they were very excited. They asked us about the next steps and immediately injected more capital into the company. With this funding, we adapted the drug to prepare for a first clinical trial on human patients. Next week I'll show what progress we've already made. We plan to begin the trial with elderly people suffering from certain age-related diseases. Then we can target healthier elderly people in later larger trials. We still have to get approval for the clinical trials from the FDA, the Food and Drug Administration. This may still pose some challenges, because the FDA has become very cautious about anti-aging medical trials. Recently, another research institute tried another drug to eliminate senescent cells in a clinical trial and it caused aggressive cancers in some people who took part in the trial resulting in death."

"Do you have the same risk as this peptide drug?"

Harvey smiled lightly as he shook his head.

"No. We have a different approach than they had, and in the trials on mice, there were no cases of cancer. The fundamental difference is that with the other research institute's approach, the drug also affected the healthy cells, causing some of them to become cancerous. With our drug, all healthy cells are not affected and ignored by the drug, because protein B is not present in them. I believe the clinical trial will be a mere formality, but an important one."

"You sound very convinced that it'll work in humans!?"

"Yes. Given the nature of the drug and the success we saw in the tests with mice, I'm convinced it will work. We also tested the drug on aged human cells full of senescent cells in petri dishes in the laboratory. It completely eliminated the senescent cells from the human cells, and not a single cell became cancerous."

"But if that's true, Harvey, does that mean you're the first in the world to find the secret of immortality? A dream humanity has been seeking for centuries."

"Immortality is a bit far-fetched. If the clinical trials confirm that our drug works on people, we'll make them younger and healthier.

Unfortunately, they can still die. Unnatural death always remains a possibility, but natural death is also still inevitable."

"What do you mean? Doesn't the aging process stop when you remove the senescent cells?"

Harvey looked pleased about the direction of the discussion and shifted forward a bit, gesturing with his hands while explaining.

"Aging is a very complex process, and we are only beginning to understand part of the equation. The removal of senescent cells is a very important factor, but there're more aspects of aging than that. For instance, some tissues lose cells as they age, such as the heart and parts of the brain and some organs. We can probably solve this over time by regenerating or recreating organs from stem cells, as you wrote in your article on growing livers from stem cells. Another problem is that cells can get damaged and become cancerous. The accumulation of senescent cells causes some cancers, and removing senescent cells reduces the risk of getting certain cancers, but for other cancers the risk remains. Despite all this, I firmly believe that in this century, we'll solve most of these other challenges as well."

It was getting dark, and Dave looked at his watch.

"What do you think? Shall we go for dinner?"

"Excellent plan, I'm starving. Do you have a restaurant in mind?"

"I booked an Italian restaurant further down on the edge of the lagoon park, so we can walk over there if you like?"

"Sounds perfect. We'll just have to be a little careful what we discuss, since people might be listening in, but I guess you know how to handle that," Harvey said as he stood up.

They grabbed their coats and left the room. When they got off the elevator, he noticed the lobby was a lot busier than usual. He greeted the woman at the front desk and they walked out into the dark night. They took the route through the lagoon park, and the stars and the moon illuminated the sky.

"What a beautiful night," Harvey said as they walked through the park.

"Yeah, it's nice to have a park next to the hotel. Usually, hotels are depressing places."

"Are you married, Dave?"

"Divorced. My wife left me five years ago."

"Oh, I'm sorry to hear that," Harvey said, and a brief silence followed until Dave broke it.

"Yeah, she left me for another man and had probably been cheating for some time. We were married for twenty-seven years. I guess she'd grown tired of me."

"That must have been hard for you. It's always hard to lose the one you love," Harvey said, and changed the topic. "And how is your son doing?"

Thinking about his divorce made Dave sad, because it had been painful for him. His ex-wife had said many nasty things and after leaving him, she quickly remarried. His son always made him feel proud, and he was glad to talk about him.

"Andrew is doing great. After MIT, he found a great job in San Jose at a research institute and last year, he married a wonderful woman."

Harvey smiled.

"Married? Good for him, although I'm not surprised. I remember at MIT he was often in the company of beautiful women. I guess with his posture and kindness, it's no surprise."

Dave smiled back.

"Yeah, he never lacked attention. But when he met his wife, it was different. He had really fallen for her. And his wife is stunning. I must say, his wife confirms all the stories about the beauty of women from Venezuela. He put a lot of effort into getting her to live in our country, which was not easy to get the right permits and all."

"I'm happy for him. He's a good guy. I always enjoyed working with him. Do you see him often?"

As they arrived at the restaurant and went inside, Dave replied,

"Because of the distance, we only see each other a few times a year, but we call regularly. In fact, I'm going to visit him this weekend in San Jose."

"Ah nice!"

They followed the waitress to their table, sat down on the comfortable leather chairs, and looked at the menu. The restaurant was beautifully decorated with dark wooden panels and pictures in metal frames of famous Italian people. The restaurant was fully booked and the Italian music playing in the background joined the hum of the people. After ordering, Harvey mentioned that he had eaten here once with Mary and that the food was quite good.

"You seem to be often with Mary. How did you meet?"

Harvey's face lit up, and he smiled.

"Mary and I live together. She had worked for me at MIT, and she moved with me to Juvenatrust. We grew much closer after the death of my wife, and last year she moved in with me."

They talked about his relationship with Mary and about Harvey's daughter during the dinner. She had married a British banker and moved to London about five years ago. Harvey had been to London a few times to visit her and had traveled throughout Europe. The evening passed quickly, and they discussed no work in the restaurant. As they left the restaurant and walked back, Dave brought up the rejuvenation drug again.

"When do you think this drug will be available in the market?"

"Well, a lot depends on the clinical trials. If all goes well, it could be on the market within a few years. But it could also take longer, like five to ten years. A lot depends on the FDA and their requirements. Next week I'll show you where we are in the process with the preparation for the clinical trials."

"Speaking of next week, what planning did you have in mind?"

Harvey looked at his phone to check his schedule.

"Monday I'm fully booked, but Tuesday we could meet at two in the afternoon. Most people will be out of the office then because of an off-site training program. Late in the afternoon, I can give you a tour of the laboratory. On Wednesday I'm away, but on Thursday afternoon I also have some time available. Friday will be more difficult. Would that work for you?"

He checked his agenda as they arrived back at the hotel.

"Yep, that works for me."

They shook hands.

"Have a nice weekend, Harvey!"

"You too, thanks for the nice evening and send my regards to Andrew. See you next Tuesday!"

He entered the hotel and went upstairs to his room. He felt tired and his back was hurting him. He took a painkiller and went to bed.

Saturday morning, he woke up to the birds singing outside. He had left the window open during the night and now the birds were giving a nice concert. His body felt stiff and his back ached as usual. He moved his limbs slowly and got out of his bed, careful not to hurt himself. He opened the curtains, and the sun blinded his eyes. The sky was bright blue and today he was going to visit his son and his wife. He looked at the lagoon park and saw birds flying back and forth among the trees.

He thought about the night before and the pleasant conversation he had had with Harvey. Hearing how he started dating Mary after his wife had died made him feel worse about himself. He was still alone, and it had been more than five years since his wife had left him. He walked to the bathroom and started shaving, feeling like an old lonely man. He looked at himself in the mirror, and the sight did not make him happy. What he saw was a shadow of the man he used to be. His hair on his head was gone and only this horseshoe hairband remained. His face wrinkled and dark rings under his eyes on his pale face. The breasts on his chest hung a little, supported by his belly underneath. He was not fat, but his belly had become more droopy and larger in recent years. The muscles he once had were less visible. The worst part, however, was his constant back pain, which made him feel old and depressed all the time, and he stood less erect than when he was young.

He went downstairs for breakfast and greeted the waitress kindly. After finishing his scrambled eggs with smoked salmon, he took a painkiller for the pain in his back. He read the newspaper he had picked up at reception. It had an interesting article about the current heat wave in Europe. Climate change seemed harder to deny. The five hottest years on record were the past five years. Harvey had mentioned yesterday that Americans emit twice as much carbon dioxide per capita as Europeans did. They both agreed that much needed to be done to stop global warming and that the government had to take the lead in doing so. If governments did not act now, it would be a missed opportunity that the next generation would resent us for. As he sipped his coffee, he slowly felt better as the painkiller began to work.

Further into the newspaper, Dave became intrigued by an article about a prominent neuroscientist who had mysteriously disappeared from her sailboat. The woman had just published a paper on a breakthrough in brain stimulation. She had succeeded in getting older people to regain their memory and bring it back to the memory function of a twenty-year-old. She had gone sailing alone on her boat in Cape Cod Bay last weekend off the coast of Plymouth, south of Boston, Massachusetts. She had not returned home and later they had found her boat floating, but with no one on board. The police suspected the woman might have fallen into the water, but had not found a body. A large search team had tried for several days to find her body, to no avail. Family members still believed she could be alive, since the sea was calm that weekend and the scientist was an excellent swimmer.

After breakfast, Dave checked out and drove the silver-gray BMW onto the Interstate highway I-580 heading East. He put on some music as he crossed the San Francisco Bay by driving over the Richmond San Rafael Bridge. The navigation system indicated he had about one hour to go. He called Andrew to let him know he was on his way. After hanging up, he wondered what surprise Andrew had in store for him. It had been over five months since they had last seen each other. Andrew and Wendy had come to New York for Christmas and they had a great time and laughed a lot. Andrew was so cheerful and his wife was adorable. About an hour later, he exited the Interstate highway I-880 in San Jose and drove into the suburb where Andrew and Wendy had their home. He parked in the driveway and before he could even turn off the engine, the big wooden door opened and Andrew came walking up to the car. Dave gave his son a big hug and a kiss on the cheek. Andrew smiled at him and took the overnight bag from his hands.

"Come on in and see the surprise we have for you!"

Dave walked in, and Wendy walked up to him. They kissed each other. Wendy looked radiant and smiled as Andrew entered as well.

"So, Dad, and what do you think of your surprise?"

He had no idea what Andrew was talking about. Andrew put his arm around Wendy and they both smiled at him. Wendy squeezed Andrew's side.

"Stop teasing your father!"

Dave smiled and looked puzzled. His son grinned at him.

"Apparently, it's not visible yet, but you're going to be a grandpa!"

A powerful feeling of joy overwhelmed Dave, and his eyes became wet with tears.

"Wow!" he said, and kissed Wendy and Andrew. "Congratulations, what wonderful news!"

He looked at Wendy now, trying to detect some belly, but he saw nothing.

"When are you due?"

Wendy smiled as she touched her belly.

"I'm almost four months pregnant. We've only told my mom so far. You're the second to know."

"Well, you look great! How are you feeling?"

"Pretty good now. In the beginning, I was often nauseous, but now I'm doing much better."

They walked to the dining room. Dave gestured for Wendy to go before him.

"After the two of you, then."

She laughed. They had prepared a sumptuous lunch in the dining room. Dave gave them the gifts he had brought.

In the afternoon, they went for a walk together in a park not far from the house. The weather was still very nice, and they were having a great time. At some point, his back hurt again and they returned to Andrew's house. He immediately took another painkiller and Andrew walked him to the guest room so he could lie down a bit. In the guest room, he patted Andrew on the shoulder.

"Hey, I'm thrilled for the two of you. So nice, the family is expanding with a child."

"Thanks Dad, we're going to prepare dinner. Try to rest!"

He lay down on the bed, and the thought of becoming a grandfather made him very happy. The prospect of helping and spoiling his future grandchild excited him. It added an extra dimension to his life. He had always been there for Andrew when he needed him. He thought back to when his son was still at university. After a night out with his friends, Andrew had walked the last part to his home alone. A mugger ambushed him on the way, stabbed him in the stomach and took his wallet. Andrew had called 911, and an ambulance took to the hospital. He had lost a lot of blood and urgently needed a blood transfusion, but he had a rare blood type. Dave, who had the same blood type, rushed to the hospital as fast as he could and donated his blood. He stayed all night in the hospital with his son. Andrew meant the world to him, and now there would be a grandchild. After half an hour, the pain in his back had subsided, and he went downstairs to help Andrew and Wendy prepare dinner.

On Sunday evening, he said goodbye and drove back to San Rafael. The whole weekend had passed in the blink of an eye, but he had enjoyed every moment. They talked about so many things, about work, their lives and the expected baby. He had the impression that Andrew was happy and enjoying his work and life together with Wendy. That was all he could wish for. On the way back, he thought about his own life. He felt like the best part was over. He felt physically old, and the divorce had made him insecure about himself. In recent years, when he was still with Jennifer, they had argued so much. She often complained that all he did was work. When they were together, and she suggested going out together, he often declined because of the pain in his back. At some point, she started going out with her friends on weekends, or at least that was what she had told him. They grew apart and did not have sex together for years.

It did not really surprise him when Jennifer announced she was leaving him. However, he felt hurt by the last conversation they had when she made her announcement. She had mentioned that she did not feel attracted to him anymore. Dave had long suspected that she was cheating on him and when he asked her, she simply admitted and all her frustration came out. She had insulted him and had said she was tired of living with a man who acts like an old man. She felt Dave was letting life pass by without living it. After she left him, she quickly remarried. He later learned that Jennifer had cheated on him with Jack for years. Dave had been alone for almost five years and his work, friends, and Andrew kept him going. His son had been a great support to him, probably the only good thing from his failed marriage, and he was very proud of him. Seeing Andrew so happy with Wendy filled him with satisfaction and happiness. With the San Francisco Bay to his left, he thought with a big smile on his face about the baby his son was expecting. He was going to be a grandfather.

Looking at the lights of San Francisco across the bay, he told himself to change his life and try to make the best out of it. He did not know how many more years life would give him, but he felt he had already wasted too many years and it was time to live a fuller life and change things up. Arriving in his hotel room, he had a good feeling about his weekend and that night he fell asleep almost immediately.

4. Tour of the lab

O n Monday, Dave remained at the hotel and after breakfast continued working on his article. Once he had made himself an espresso, he sat down at his laptop and began writing down everything he had learned from Dr. Juncker over the past week. The more he wrote, the more he realized that Harvey and his team had made an amazing discovery. It had the potential to change the world. If this drug would get available to everyone, people would all live much longer and healthier. The population would then grow much faster because the mortality rate would drop. He started contemplating what that might mean for society, for pensions, for health care, for pollution, and so on. Could our planet support that many people? How much would the drug cost, and would it be affordable for everyone? And what if not everyone could afford the medicine? Would we get a split in society between people who would live longer and healthier lives and people who could not enjoy these benefits? His head began to spin with thoughts. He tried to jot down as many questions as he could, which helped him prepare for the upcoming meetings with Harvey this week.

A reminder popped up on his screen that took him out of his concentration. Last week he had forgotten to call Penelope Garcia, so last weekend he had set an automatic reminder for today. He looked at his watch. It was now two in the afternoon, in New York. He dialed Penelope's number on his cell phone.

"Ms. Garcia's office, Jane Hudson speaking."

"Hello, this is Dave Wilson. I'd like to speak to Ms. Garcia, please."

"Hello Mr. Wilson, please hold on. I'll see if she's available."

There was a silence on the line for a moment and he looked at the strange modern painting on the wall. Some art can be really ugly, he thought to himself.

"Hola, Dave! I would almost think you forgot me?"

"Hi, Penelope. How could I forget you? Last week has been very busy and went by in a blink of an eye. I'm sorry I didn't call you sooner."

"It's doesn't matter. I'm just teasing you. I missed running into you in the hall last week. How are things in San Francisco?"

He was amazed at how hearing her voice made him feel better.

"San Francisco is nice. I'm actually north of San Francisco. Lovely weather."

"That's not too far from your son, is it? Have you met him?"

"Yes, I visited him and his wife last weekend and stayed with them all weekend. It was great and guess what great news I got?"

She was silent for a moment.

"I don't know Dave, tell me!"

He could not hide his enthusiasm and said in a louder voice, "I'm going to be a grandfather! Andrew's wife's pregnant."

"Congratulations. How nice."

He realized again how kind she was and how close he felt to her, as if they had known each other for a long time. He had brought along all the documentation he had received from her to work on the article. He could have interviewed her over the phone, but he preferred not to in order to keep a good excuse to meet her again.

"Thanks! I'd like to briefly discuss the planning for the article with you. I'd like to schedule a visit to your company and research facilities, and next to that I'd like to meet with you once or twice to continue the interview if possible? This week I'm still here in San Francisco, but perhaps we can plan something for the following week? There's a small chance I might have to stay here longer, but maybe it's good to plan a meeting now. Only if you promise not to get upset with me if I have to stay here longer and we'd have to reschedule our appointment after all."

"Sounds perfect and don't worry, I won't be upset. Let me see. How about next Wednesday at four o'clock for the visit to my company? That day I should be available most of the afternoon to give you a tour."

Dave checked his agenda.

"Perfect. And shall we also schedule some time for interviews?"

"Well, I thought it might be a good idea to have the interview over dinner? I know a very nice restaurant not too far from my office. I can make a reservation for Wednesday night if that suits you?"

He was amazed, but already felt excited about dinner with his beautiful neighbor.

"That sounds great!"

"And if you have to reschedule because of your work in San Francisco, of course, that's no problem. You'll just have to buy me dinner the next time."

He laughed.

"No problem, with pleasure."

"Ok, then I'll see you next week. I have to go now. It was nice to hear your voice again, Dave."

"The pleasure was all mine. See you next week!"

He hung up and got up from his chair to stretch his back. As he stared outside at the lagoon park, he felt better. He was already looking forward to seeing her again. She had proposed dinner. Was it just her kindness, or was there more? He didn't know, but he kept telling himself not to imagine he had any chance with a beautiful woman like Penelope. Still, he had enjoyed the conversation with her, and that was good enough for him.

He made another espresso and took a painkiller, for the pain in his back was getting worse. He continued working, but after about half an hour he got hungry. He looked at his watch. One o'clock already. He went down to the hotel restaurant. He greeted the woman at the front desk. He checked the newsstand, but his favorite newspaper was out. A little disappointed, he took another magazine. When he turned around, the woman from reception walked toward him with a newspaper in her hand and a big smile on her face.

"Hello Mr. Wilson, I had kept a copy of this morning's newspaper for you behind the counter."

"Thank you, that's very kind of you. I was just looking for it."

He walked to the restaurant. The waitress also recognized him and took his order after he sat down next to the window on the lagoon park side. He enjoyed his salmon steak while reading the newspaper. The lead article was about the drought and wildfires in California. There was a map in the newspaper with all the different fires marked on it, some quite close. He could not figure out the scale of the map, and asked the waitress, "Excuse me, Miss. I read this article about the forest fires and wondered how close this one is."

He pointed his finger at the map in the newspaper. The waitress stood beside him and looked at it, then she replied, "Oh, don't worry, that's still about twenty miles away from here. Horrible for all those people who lost their homes."

"Thank you!"

The woman continued clearing the tables in the restaurant, while Dave continued reading. In the article, a scientist explained that climate change was to blame. He looked out the window. He had noticed the increase in extreme weather events in recent years. He had read some of his colleague's articles on climate change in Science Magazine, and all the warning signs were there. His concerns about global warming had only grown over time, but now he wondered if his grandson would still have a future. After lunch, he took a walk in the lagoon park and then worked the rest of the day in his hotel room.

On Tuesday, he worked at his hotel in the morning. After lunch, he drove to Juvenatrust in Novato. The parking lot was empty compared to the week before. He walked to the front desk and told the woman he had an appointment with Dr. Juncker. She got on the phone and a moment later, handed him a badge.

He took the badge and walked through the door. The large security guard was sitting next to the scanner reading some comic book. Dave put his briefcase on the belt. The security guard scanned his bag and handed it back to him. He pressed the button for the elevator. Nothing happened. Then he remembered his badge. He scanned the badge and pressed the button again. Now it lit up. The painkiller he had taken at lunch had worked. He still felt stiff, but no more pain. Upstairs, Mary was waiting for him and she smiled at him. He found her friendlier than before. They chatted a bit about the weather as they walked to Dr. Juncker's office. As he entered, Harvey looked up from his desk and stood up to shake his hand.

"Hello Dave, how was your weekend with Andrew?"

"Great!"

Mary was still standing at the door and looked a bit in a rush.

"Sorry to interrupt, but can I bring you something to drink?"

"For me, a cappuccino please," Dave said.

"And for me, the usual, thanks Mary," Harvey said, smiling at her, then he stood up to open the window to let in some fresh air. Mary left and closed the door behind her.

"The weekend was really nice and Andrew had a big surprise for me. I'm going to be a grandfather. His wife is almost four months pregnant."

"Congratulations! What a wonderful news!" and Harvey shook his hand again to congratulate him. They sat down and continued talking about Dave's weekend until Mary returned with their coffee. After she left, Harvey started discussing the planning for that day.

"Okay, I suggest we start with your questions first and then around five, I'll give you a tour of the building. I think it's better later in the afternoon, because most people will have left by then. This way we attract the least attention."

"Sounds good to me," he replied, pulling out his notebook and voice recorder and placing them on the desk.

"So, let's start where we left off last Friday. I believe we discussed that this drug, assuming it will work on humans, will make people younger and healthier, but they'll still die. You explained that aging does not stop but merely slows down. I wondered how this works. Does taking away the senescent cells not make the cells younger?"

Harvey shifted in his chair and now looked serious.

"Our drug removes the senescent cells and as a result, the other cells function better. Not that the cells become younger. They stay in their full-grown status. It's not like you sometimes see in cartoons were someone takes a magic potion and becomes younger, like an adult becoming a child or baby. The cells remain as they were when they were fully grown. The crucial difference is that the cells function again as they did when you were around twenty-five to thirty years old. You can compare it to a car with an engine that is cluttered and therefore cannot drive. Our drug removes all the debris and cleans the engine, so the car work as well again as it did when it was new. And in this example, if the tires are worn out, our drug doesn't change that. So, if an organ has lost too much cells, it would eventually have to be replaced by a new or regenerated organ to make it work again as it worked in perfect condition. The liver is the only exception here, as it's the only organ that can regenerate itself. Or, for example, if you would have a hole in your heart valve, removing senescent cells would not repair the hole."

He took notes, and when Harvey finished talking, he asked,

"So, what might happen to an elderly person if they took your drug?"

"This person would feel the effect of the drug treatment after a few days. The person would feel more energetic. The skin would look younger and dark spots would disappear, as would their wrinkles. Lost or thin hair would grow back and would become thick and healthy again. Probably the senses would improve, such as more feeling in the hands, better smell, taste, hearing and vision. Usually, elderly people shrink somewhat and stand in a bent posture. The main reason for this is that over time, the cartilage between their joints wears down and osteoporosis causes the spine to shorten. The removal of senescent cells in the bones and the rest of the body will drastically improve the tissues and cells. The bones will become strong and flexible again, and the cartilage between the joints will recover and become healthy again. The pain elderly people have in their joints would disappear. The result would be that the elderly person would regain their uprightness and the height they had when they were about thirty years old."

"Impressive! That would drastically change humanity. You mentioned people would still die, for example, from worn-out organs or cancer. What do you think your drug could do for human longevity?"

Harvey put his coffee cup back on the table and he thought for a moment before answering, "Well, the average life expectancy of a human of sixty years old is now about eighty years. Judging from the increased longevity we observed in the trials with our mice, I think people with our drug treatment could probably reach a life expectancy between one hundred and five and one hundred and ten years. That's an average life expectancy, of course, because some people will die earlier and some will live much older, just as they do now."

Harvey paused for a moment as he stared out the window at the forest.

"But I think with all the other developments in science, humans can probably get much older. Assuming we'll be able to regenerate organs and find new treatments for cancer and other diseases, human beings can get much older, maybe a hundred and fifty years or more. I don't believe there's a real limit to longevity and I believe that, as a result of scientific progress, it'll continue to rise in the future. As our understanding of human genes and how they work increases, so will our ability to further extend lifespan. Genetic selection and genetic manipulation will be two key drivers of further advances in longevity."

"Can you explain exactly what you mean by genetic selection and by genetic manipulation and how that affects longevity?"

Harvey pushed his glasses back on his nose and continued explaining, "Genetic selection is basically checking the genes before a child is born and deciding to abort pregnancies if one finds genetic diseases or malformations. We have been doing this for a long time. For example, we test for Down syndrome or neural tube defects like spina bifida or a 'split spine.' Every year we discover more diseases related to genetics, and over time we'll include more and more checks in these pregnancy tests. We call this genetic selection. Genetic manipulation goes a step further, and you described it very well in your article about the gene-edited twins in China. It's also called genetic engineering or genetic modification. It can be done by genetically modifying embryonic cells or even by genetically modifying cells of already grown humans. We'll be able to change our genes and prevent cancers or diseases like Alzheimer's from developing. I believe that developments with both methods will accelerate this century and increase lifespan even further. Of course, these genetically modified people will no longer be the same as the humans we know today. Genetics will make it possible to create superhumans with enhanced abilities."

Dave sipped his cappuccino, and a silence fell for a moment. He enjoyed Harvey's views on the future of biotech and humanity, but also felt they were straying too far from the subject.

"Very interesting, Harvey. Clearly, this century is the century of biology. I had another question about your drug. I was wondering what would happen if people would stop taking the drugs at some point?"

"Good question. The answer may surprise you, maybe. Since the drug only removes senescent cells, stopping to take the drug will stop this removal process. After stopping the drug treatment, the body and all cells would just resume the normal aging process and new senescent cells would form. You could even say that the effectiveness of the drug diminishes over time, because after a few weeks of use, most senescent cells are gone. Taking the drug longer does not do much more. Only if new senescent cells arose would the drug remove them again. In the mouse trial, most effects were visible in the first week, and after a few weeks, we no longer observed any changes. Normal aging continued when we stopped treatment, but they still lived about thirty percent longer. I expect similar results in humans."

Harvey looked at his watch and then at the stack of documents on the corner of his desk.

"Dave, I've gathered more background information for you about our drug treatment and the test results from the mouse experiments. You can take those with you."

Harvey handed the stack to Dave, who shoved it into his briefcase. It barely fit, and his briefcase had doubled in size. Harvey's phone rang, and he answered.

"Hello, Mary. Thanks for letting me know."

He hung up and looked at Dave.

"Most of the people have left and now is a good time to give you a tour of the company."

Harvey stood up and walked to the coat rack in the corner of his office and put on a long white coat. Then he handed one to Dave.

"Please put this coat on during the tour."

Dave also stood up and put on the white coat.

"Ok, let's go!" Harvey said.

They walked down the long corridor. Most of the offices were empty, except for one. Dave saw a dark-haired man with a mustache sitting behind a desk. As they passed, the man stared at them. He vaguely remembered seeing the man at the elevator the week before. He looked back into the hallway as they turned the corner to walk to the elevator, and he saw that the man was still watching them. The man quickly disappeared when he saw Dave looking. They entered the elevator. Harvey scanned his badge and pressed the button to the first floor. Dave looked in the mirror and found he now looked like a real scientist in the white coat.

"Our building has three floors. On the second floor, we only have offices and two large meeting rooms. The best views of the forest are on this floor."

He smiled at Dave. When they got out on the second floor, Harvey scanned the sensor next to the door with his badge and they walked through a glass door.

"On the first floor, we have our animal testing area, a laboratory, and more offices. On the ground floor, we have our storage space, another laboratory, and an area where we prepare the clinical trials."

They walked down another white corridor with offices on either side. Most of the offices were empty except for two. Harvey greeted his colleagues and continued the tour. He explained many aspects of the building. Such as the ventilation in the building and all the safety measures they had to take to get official federal certification. At the end of the corridor, there was a glass door with a large open workspace full of laboratory equipment. Harvey scanned his badge again and opened the glass door.

In the large workspace, a man and a woman were still working, both dressed in white coats. Harvey greeted them and continued to explain all the safety procedures they had to follow. The two people stared at them. Harvey explained about all the equipment they had in the lab and told Dave which ones they might need to replace. He also explained what new equipment they were looking for. Dave thought it was a little too detailed for him, but he suspected Harvey was trying to make it seem realistic that he was from an equipment supplier. At one point, Harvey even blinked at Dave, so he decided to just play along. He asked some questions about what functionalities they were looking for. At the end of the lab, there was another glass door, and they walked to the next room.

As soon as they entered the room, Dave smelled something you would expect in a zoo. The smell of animals. The large room was full of large racks with cages in them. There was no one in this room, and Harvey looked more relaxed.

"Here we can speak more freely," Harvey continued as he opened one of the windows to let in some fresh air.

"This is the testing area, as you might have smelled, where we do the tests on mice. On the left side, we have older mice that have taken no drugs, our control group."

Dave looked into the cages and saw in the corner several mice sleeping on top of each other. The mice had thin fur, and some even had bald spots. In one of the cages, a mouse walked to drink something from the bottle hanging in the cage. The mouse was sauntering and had a hunched posture.

"They look old. I never really noticed. I guess I've only seen younger mice."

"Most people don't notice, because the older mice usually sleep in the corner, while the younger ones run and attract all the attention."

They walked between all the racks to the other side of the room. Here there was more noise. Unlike the area with the old mice, where hardly any sound came from the cages, here the place vibrated with life and Harvey continued explaining passionately.

"In this area, we have the mice that have received our drug treatment. As you may have noticed, there's a lot more activity here."

Dave looked in the cages and saw mice running around. They were running on treadmills at high speeds. He saw two mice fighting or playing. He wasn't sure. The mice looked very active, and they had beautiful dark fur full of hair. When Dave stood in front of one of the cages, the mice immediately noticed him before continuing what they were doing.

"The mice on this side are about the same age as the mice on the other side. They're healthier and more active. We've examined the mice extensively and almost all the functions significantly improved. They eat better and more, since they burn more calories every day. All body systems improved, such as the digestive system, respiratory system, muscular system, nervous system and cardiovascular system. The old mice would easily break a bone, but these treated mice have much stronger bones. We had first started our experiments on old mice with age-related diseases like cardiovascular diseases and osteoarthritis, a common form of arthritis, a degenerative joint disease. Later, we tested the drug on old mice with no obvious disease. We observed the same results in all groups."

"Impressive! It really looks like this could be one of the biggest scientific milestones in a long time. Maybe you could even win a Nobel Prize with it?"

"I'm glad to impress someone like you who has already seen so many impressive developments in his life. Our board responded with similar enthusiasm and wanted me to move forward as quickly as possible to prepare the clinical trials on humans. That's also why I believe I can convince them to publish an article on it."

"How quickly did this drug treatment work and how long did you give the mice this treatment?"

Harvey looked at the mice in the cages.

"The mice you see here all stopped the treatment. We injected a small dose of our drug into their shoulder every day, and from there the blood flow spread the drug throughout the body. After the first week, we reduced the injections to every other day, and the week after that only twice a week, and the weeks after that only once a week. In the first two weeks, we saw the most dramatic changes, and after four weeks, the change process had stabilized and we observed no further changes. We have a group of mice where we stopped treatment and another group where we continued with one injection per week. So far, we have seen little difference between the two groups, except that the first group began to age normally again and senescent cells slowly returned, as you would except with normal aging. The second group remained young and no senescent cells returned."

Harvey saw fascination on Dave's face as he stared at the mice.

"Thursday, I'll show you some videos we took during all these experiments. That'll give you a good idea of what we observed."

"That would be great," Dave said.

Harvey closed the open window and suggested going back. He used his badge to open the door, and they walked back to the laboratory where now only one man was peering through a microscope. When the man looked up, Harvey greeted him.

"Good night, Rob!"

"You too, Harvey!" the man replied, and nodded at Dave.

They walked through the laboratory and Harvey opened the next glass door and they continued down the white corridor. Now all the offices were empty, and Dave looked at his watch. It was already ten past six. Time had passed again in a blink. It had grown darker outside. In the elevator, Harvey pressed the button to go to the ground floor.

"Fascinating stuff. You must get great satisfaction from your work?"

Harvey smiled as they walked out of the elevator.

"Absolutely. That's why I left MIT at the time to come work here. I could have retired already, but when they offered me this job, I didn't hesitate for long."

On the ground floor, the security guard watched them as they walked away from the reception area to the glass door in the back. Harvey greeted the guard, who stared curiously at Dave.

Harvey opened the glass door with his badge. The white corridor on this floor was much smaller, and there were only a few offices and a few closed doors with no windows. All offices were empty. After opening another glass door, they entered what looked like an even larger laboratory. There was only an Asian-looking woman sitting behind a few machines, but she was packing her bag. Harvey smiled at her.

"Have a nice evening, Suzy!"

"You too, Harvey! Don't work too late," the woman said without any facial expression. The woman nodded to Dave and then left.

"What a luxury to have the whole laboratory for ourselves. During a normal week, it would still be full, even at this hour," Harvey said as he smiled at him. Dave looked around the laboratory curiously.

"This lab looks even larger than the one on the first floor. What do you do in this lab?"

"The two laboratories function almost as one. Roughly speaking, you could say the one upstairs focuses primarily on the mouse experiments, and this one primarily on the human clinical trials. We developed and adapted the drug in here and tested it on human cells. All the results so far confirm that it's very likely to work on humans, but to get FDA approval to use it on humans, we need to do clinical trials. We're preparing a first clinical trial to start within a few months. Initially, we faced a challenge. If we claim to have a drug that makes people live longer, how do you know it works? Another issue is that aging is not officially a disease which complicates the process with the FDA. A clinical trial usually lasts a year or two, but to verify that the drug added ten years or more to someone's life is difficult to prove."

Dave nodded as he understood the issue. It would take too long to prove you had extra longevity, because the proof would only be there after such a long time. It would involve a trial of decades. Dave glanced at the large microscope next to Harvey.

"So, how did you solve this problem?"

"We didn't. We found a clever way around it. We simply focused the first trial on treating age-related diseases. Curing the patients' disease would prove that the drug works. This way we could market it as a treatment for those specific diseases, and over time it would also prove that it extends lifespan. As with the mice, we're starting with a few groups at the same time. One group of elderly people over seventy years with osteoarthritis, this degenerative joint disease. Another group of elderly people with cardiovascular disease. We expect the same results as in the mice. When all the observed changes from the mouse experiments will occur in the humans in our clinical trial, we believe we can claim the rejuvenating effects of the drug. If we successfully pass these initial clinical trials, it should be easier to get FDA approval for a more general clinical trial on elderly people without specific age-related diseases and prove the rejuvenating effect of the drug."

"Smart. More of a two-step approach. First, get approval to use the drug to treat specific age-related diseases and then use the results to get approval for a more general use of the drug to rejuvenate people. So how long would it take to get the rejuvenation drug on the market?"

Harvey thought for a moment.

"Hard to say. Approval of the drug for these specific diseases could take three to five years, if all goes well and smoothly, but it could take even much longer. For the rejuvenation drug, it could take an additional five to ten years."

Harvey looked at his watch and continued walking toward the end of the laboratory to another glass door. He opened it and Dave followed him among all the machines in this room. In the back were several rows of fridges with glass doors that emitted a blue light. It was relatively warm and smelly in this room.

"This is where we make the drugs in preparation for clinical trials. All the ingredients are in the storage room next door."

Harvey pointed to the closed door in the back, behind the rows of refrigerators. Dave could see the darkness outside through the windows next to the door. Harvey walked to one of the windows in the back and opened one. Dave looked puzzled at the windows.

"We produce our drug on these machines. These machines have enough capacity to produce the quantity we need for the clinical trials. When we get the FDA approval, our owners will probably invest in the construction of a larger plant to make the drug. Currently, we can only use injections to get the drug into the body. Normally, we'd develop some kind of pill. Unfortunately, there's still a problem with using a pill, because the acid in the stomach destroys most of the drug before it can begin to work. So, for now, injections are the only way. We're exploring alternatives such as patches with microneedles and I'm sure by the time we finish the clinical trials we will have found a more comfortable way to administer the drug."

"Harvey, how come you can just open a window on the ground floor in such a top-security building?"

"Yeah, I know, it's not usually like that, but we're having some problems with the air conditioning on this floor and those fridges in the back produce quite a bit of heat, so we temporarily unlocked the windows. Someone will come on Friday to fix it and then all the windows will go back to being locked. The guard now locks all windows every night, but normally everything stays locked during the day."

Dave looked curiously at the huge number of very large and tall refrigerators in the back. The strange blue light coming from them reminded him of a scene from a science fiction movie.

"What are all those refrigerators for?"

"Our owners want to proceed with the clinical trials as soon as possible, so they've asked us to produce a huge amount of stock. The drugs can stay well for a few days outside of the refrigerator. But cooled at fifty-four degrees Fahrenheit, like the temperature in a wine cellar, we can keep them good for a very long time. What you see here is a stockpile large enough for all the clinical trials we envision, and we're still producing more."

Dave looked into a refrigerator, which was filled with metal boxes. Harvey proudly opened one of the refrigerator doors and took out a box, placing it on the table. The box contained one layer of tubes. He opened the box and took out a small glass tube.

"This is one dose of the drug. Our test persons will start with one injection of this dose every day during the first week. Then during the second week we decrease to one dose every other day, the third week one dose twice a week, and from the fourth week on only one dose a week. Each metal box contains one hundred doses."

Dave looked at the fridges. Each refrigerator seemed to hold a hundred boxes, and there were so many fridges.

"How many doses do you have in stock here?"

"Phoe, I don't know exactly, but it could be hundreds of thousands."

"What's the blue light for?"

"Uh… nothing actually, but one of the owners wanted blue light. He thought it made everything look more impressive," Harvey replied with a grin on his face.

Suddenly, Harvey's phone rang.

"Hello Mary. Yeah, I'm sorry. I'm still at work. I'm leaving right now."

Harvey looked stressed now.

"Sorry, Dave, but I guess I lost track of time. It was Mary. She's waiting for me, apparently with dinner ready, so we'll have to finish this Thursday."

He walked over to the open window and closed it, then they walked through the glass door together.

"No problem. I'm already grateful you're spending so much time with me. All this is really helping my article tremendously."

They hurried back through the laboratory and down the corridor.

"I hope Mary isn't too mad at you?" he asked as they got into the elevator to return to the second floor.

"No, of course not. She's an angel. It's more. I feel guilty for making her wait with dinner ready."

When they returned to Harvey's office, they took off the white coats. Dave took his briefcase, which was now much heavier with all the documents Harvey had given him. They walked back to the elevator and went downstairs. There, the security guard stood up as they arrived. They put their bags on the scanner and the guard looked at Harvey.

"I take it you were the last ones in the building?"

"I think so, James, but you better double-check during your round. You never know in this company. Have a good evening, James!"

"Same to you."

The air was crisp outside. The night was clear and there were bright stars in the sky. There were only three cars left in the parking lot. Just before getting into his car, Dave called out to Harvey.

"What time shall I come to your office on Thursday, Harvey?"

Harvey quickly checked his agenda on his phone.

"Let's meet at two thirty in the afternoon."

"Perfect! Have a nice evening!"

"You too!"

On his way back to the hotel, he could think of nothing but this huge supply of drug doses for the human clinical trial. Harvey seemed so convinced that the drug will work in humans. As he felt the pain in his back, he thought about how that drug could probably solve his back problems. How wonderful that would be: a life without back pain. Then he could finally find the energy to do all those things he had put off for so long. He had several things he still wanted to do in his life, and the older he got, the more he felt time was running out. One of his wishes was to take a trip around the world and travel for a few months to visit all those wonderful countries and places the world offered. Now, even a shorter journey would be too much, since his back would trouble him throughout the trip.

He wondered if he should ask Harvey if he could join the first clinical trial. Since he had arthritis, it would make pretty good sense. Just the thought of no longer having back pain made him more optimistic about his life. He already imagined lifting his grandchild without difficulty. Then he began to have doubts again. Harvey had clearly said elderly people over seventy, so he would not fit the criteria. Maybe he could make an exception for him, because they got along so well? No, the FDA would never allow that, and Harvey did not look like someone who would break the rules.

He parked his car in front of the hotel and got out slowly. His back ached with every movement. He tried not to move too abruptly as he walked to the trunk of his car. He took out the heavy briefcase, filled with documents. The pain only got worse. He tried to ignore it as he walked inside. He greeted the woman at the front desk and entered the elevator. The first thing he did when he entered his room was to drop the heavy briefcase on the floor. In the bathroom, he immediately took a painkiller and then he sauntered to his bed to lie down.

On the comfortable king-size bed, he thought back to his day as the effects of the painkiller slowly kicked in. It amazed him how close they were to the start of the clinical trials. Soon those test people would rejuvenate and become world news. Again, he wondered if he should ask Harvey if he could take part in the clinical trial? Thinking it over again, he concluded there was no point in asking, because he would surely refuse. No, he had no choice than to wait at least another five years until the drug was available to the public. At that moment, he realized he had forgotten to ask Harvey how much the drug would cost. He got up and took a pen and notebook from the full briefcase, and went downstairs to eat at the restaurant.

Over dinner, he wrote down a list of questions he wanted to ask Harvey on Thursday. Later, he returned to his hotel room. When he got off the elevator and walked down the corridor to his room, he could not believe his eyes. His heart began to beat faster when he saw that the door to his room was slightly open. He peered through the opening. When he saw no one inside, he pushed the door open further. He was sure he had closed the door before going to the restaurant. Someone had entered his room.

He looked around to see if anything was missing. He first looked at his suitcase, but nothing seemed to be missing. When he looked at the desk, he noticed his briefcase was now on it, even though he was sure he had left it on the floor next to it. Next to his briefcase he saw the stack of documents, which someone had taken out. His laptop was still in his briefcase. He had no idea if anything was missing from the stack of documents, because he had not looked at it yet. Did they take any documents from the pile, or did they just look at them? Who had entered his room? He called reception and explained what had happened. Five minutes later, the manager of the hotel appeared at the door, clearly startled. Dave let him in and explained what had happened.

"I'm really sorry, Mr. Wilson. I checked with the staff, but no one was on this floor tonight. All the cleaners had already stopped working in the afternoon, so it must have been someone external who opened your door. Are you missing something?"

"Well, that's the problem. I'm not missing anything from my belongings, but I had just received a stack of confidential documents today and I don't know if anything is missing, since I haven't had a chance to look at them yet."

"I'm so sorry. I can call the police and you can file a report with them?"

Dave hesitated because he did not feel like all the hassle, and he was not even sure anything had been stolen. He felt tired and his back hurt. No, he preferred to go to bed early tonight.

"Maybe it would be better I go through the documents first to see if I'm missing anything before we contact the police."

"All right, well, let me know if you change your mind. Again, I'm really sorry, Mr. Wilson. I'll check with the front desk to see if they've noticed anything suspicious, although I doubt that they'll be much help since it's been so incredibly busy since we're fully booked."

"No problem. I'll contact you if I miss anything. Good evening."

"Good night, Mr. Wilson."

Immediately afterwards, Dave double checked all his belongings. But again, he missed nothing. The only thing he could not check was whether they had taken anything from the pile of documents. He quickly scanned through the pile, but he saw nothing strange or missing. He wondered if he should tell Harvey what had happened and check with him to see what could be missing. He hesitated, however, because he had promised Harvey not to share anything with anyone without his permission, and this would not look good. He postponed his decision until he had spent more time going through the documents. But not tonight, because it was already late, and he was exhausted. He still felt a bit overwhelmed by all he had learned and seen that day and what had happened in the evening. He was so tired that he fell asleep quickly that night.

The next morning, he woke up, and it was another beautiful day. He could get used to this Californian weather. Looking out the window at the lagoon park, he saw all the birds flying back and forth again. He saw some kids running in the park and he imagined how nice it would be to run like a child again with endless energy and no muscle pain anywhere. Suddenly, he remembered he had promised to call Andrew. Andrew and Wendy had invited him last weekend to visit the next weekend as well. He had said he would call them on Monday or Tuesday to let them know, but he had completely forgotten. He immediately dialed his number.

"Hi, Dad! I thought you forgot about us."

"Yeah, sorry, my work has absorbed me a little too much lately, but I just wanted to let you know I'd love to visit next weekend if it still suits you?"

"Of course. Can you come over as early as Friday? I thought it would be nice if we could go fishing together in Yosemite National Park this weekend. There's a nice lake called Lake Tenaya, where we can rent a cabin and fish on the lake on Saturday and Sunday, if you like?"

"That sounds like a great idea. I still have some work on Friday, but I could try to leave here in the afternoon and then we can have dinner together on Friday and prepare for the trip."

"Great, Dad! I'm looking forward to it. See you this Friday then!"

"All right, see you on Friday!"

The last time they had gone hiking and fishing together was more than a year ago, and Dave had been hoping to go fishing with his son again for some time. It sounded like a perfect way to spend his last weekend here in California with his son.

He spent the rest of the morning going through the stack of documents Harvey had given him. He did not seem to miss anything, and it occurred to him it might be best not to tell Harvey anything about what had happened in his room yesterday. He was more careful and put all the documents and his laptop in the safe in his room as he went for lunch. After lunch, his phone rang. It was Henry.

"Hi Dave, how was the weekend with your son?"

"Hi old buddy, good to hear from you. Yeah, the weekend was great, and Andrew had a big surprise for me."

"Oh yeah? What kind of surprise?"

"Well, I'm going to be a granddad," Dave said proudly.

"That's great news! Congratulations!" Henry said cheerfully and added laughing, "Now we can exchange granddad-experiences soon."

"Yeah exactly, I couldn't let you go through the granddad experience alone, no?"

Dave continued, but now in a more serious voice, "Andrew and Wendy look so happy. I'm going to see them again next weekend. Andrew suggested we go fishing together all weekend, which I'm looking forward to."

"Nice! Lucky bastard! It almost sounds like you're on a vacation instead of working? How is your interview going?"

"Very well. Dr. Juncker is a nice guy, and he's already spent a lot of time with me. Yesterday he showed me the facilities, all very impressive. They're about to start the first clinical trials. So maybe in five years we'll all be taking his drugs and getting younger, like those mice."

"Wow, Dave, this could be a huge story! With all the buzz around immortality and the quest for eternal youth, people will really be interested in a development like this."

"And how was the visit from that blond woman you're dating? What was her name again?"

"Sara. It was great, although I hardly slept the weekend. What an energy that woman has. I wonder how long I can keep up with her."

Dave laughed.

"And how's your helmet story coming along?"

"Good, I'll probably stay here this week and should be back in New York next week. They showed me all kinds of videos with experiments they did and the results are impressive, I must say. Those helmets work really well. A sergeant here told me off the record that apparently several helmets were stolen a few months ago and they haven't recovered them yet. There's still an extensive investigation into the theft. You would think theft wouldn't happen so easily at a heavily guarded Air Force base. Unfortunately, I'm not allowed to write about it, maybe when they finish the investigation. So, when do you plan to return to New York?"

"Well, it looks like I'm done here this week, but since I'm spending the weekend with Andrew, I'm thinking of going back on Monday."

"Okay buddy, sounds good. We can catch up over a cup of coffee next week then. I'll see you next week."

"See you next week, Henry. Good luck with your story!"

Dave hung up and walked over to the espresso machine to prepare another cup. He emailed Claire to reserve a flight for Monday. He told her he would stay with his son over the weekend, so he only needed to stay in the hotel until Friday and then one hotel night on Sunday. As usual, she would take care of it.

He had trouble falling asleep that night. His mind was too active. He thought about the theft at the heavily guarded Air Force base. About what happened in his room and how someone had gone through his belongings. He thought about the wonderful plans he had made with Andrew. The rejuvenation drug was also on his mind. He even considered convincing Harvey to give him some samples. The more he thought about it, however, the more he concluded Harvey would never do that. Nor would allow him into the clinical trial. He would probably tell him to wait until it was on the market. Dave did not want to wait. He felt miserable so often, and this drug could change his life. Then he started thinking about the fishing trip and his future grandchild. At two in the morning, he felt exhausted and moved his alarm clock from eight to eleven in the morning. After hours of tossing and turning in his bed, he finally fell asleep.

The next morning, he awoke at eleven o'clock to the sound of his alarm clock. As he moved in his bed, he felt his back pain again. He got out of bed, drank a glass of water, and then took a painkiller. He was glad he had set his alarm clock later. At least he had gotten a few hours of sleep. He dressed and looked again at his list of questions for today's meeting. He added a few more, put the documents and laptop back in the safe, and went downstairs for lunch.

He was starving since he had skipped his breakfast. He said hello to the woman at the front desk and saw a man in jogging clothes enter the hotel. The man looked about his age, which painfully reminded him he had stopped exercising years ago. He always lacked the energy to do anything, even though he knew it would be good for him. When he sat down, he ordered without seeing the menu. By now, he knew it by heart. He took his time for lunch and read a newspaper. His eye fell on a picture of a French man of a hundred and two who had set a new speed record on a bicycle in the over-a-hundred category. He thought how ironic this was, because in five years, many elder people would be much fitter thanks to Harvey's drug. He realized what a tremendous change awaited humanity.

After lunch, he packed his briefcase, but left the documents in the safe. A little later, he drove up the highway toward Novato under a bright blue sky. He thought of the huge refrigerators at Juvenatrust with that mysterious blue light. Given the huge stock they had produced, he wondered how they kept track of the inventory. Did they count their stock regularly? Did they keep a thorough inventory? Then he thought about the questions he wanted to ask Harvey. As he drove up Mayhem Drive, he realized it was probably the last time he would drive here. The parking lot was relatively empty. He picked up a badge at the front desk, greeted the security guard, and ran his briefcase through the scanner. On the second floor, Mary was waiting for him. As they walked to Harvey's office, they chatted a bit. Mary had become friendlier to him since he had developed a closer relationship with Harvey. Most of the offices were empty. In one office, he saw the dark-haired man with the mustache again. As he passed his door, he saw him looking up from his desk.

He entered Harvey's office, and Harvey greeted him enthusiastically. He had installed a beamer on his desk and had just finished adjusting it. It projected a white image on the whiteboard on the wall.

"Can I offer you something to drink?" Mary asked.

"A cappuccino please," Dave replied.

Mary looked at Harvey and he said, "The usual for me, please."

She left the office and closed the door behind her.

"Our last day together already. I hope you have enough material for your article?"

Dave sat down and put his notebook and recorder on the desk. He hesitated whether to tell him about the mysterious burglary in his hotel room.

"I think I have almost everything I need. I've gone through all the documents you gave me and am quite advanced with my article. I just have a few more questions and would like to ask if I can take some pictures today?"

Harvey looked at him, a bit puzzled.

"What pictures would you like to take?"

"Well, several pictures of you and maybe a few of the lab, the mice and of the refrigerators downstairs."

"No problem."

He took his camera out of his briefcase and put it on the desk. Mary came back in with the coffee and set the cups on the desk.

"Mary, can you take a picture of us?" Harvey asked her.

"Sure."

They stood up and went behind the desk. Dave handed the camera to Mary. They posed for the camera while she took a few pictures.

"Maybe it would be nice if you both posed with the white coats on?" Mary said.

"Excellent idea."

They put on the white coats and posed shaking hands, then she handed the camera back to Dave. He now handed his smartphone to her.

"Could you take some extra with this camera?"

"Yeah, sure."

She took more pictures and handed the smartphone back to him.

"Thanks, Mary!"

She left and closed the door behind her. Dave took a few pictures of Harvey sitting behind his desk, then put the camera down. Harvey looked in one of his drawers and pulled out an envelope of photos handed it to Dave.

"Here, we took some comparison photos of the mice before and after the treatment."

Dave looked at them.

"Remarkable. What a difference!"

The mouse in the pre-treatment photo looked bald, hunched, and a little wrinkled. The mouse in the photo after treatment looked very healthy with nice, thick, dark fur and no wrinkles.

"This is perfect, Harvey. Can I get some copies?"

Harvey looked at him and smiled.

"You can keep the whole envelope. I have more sets in stock."

"Thanks. Those are great," he said as he looked at the pictures and took a sip of his cappuccino.

"What is the planning from here, Harvey? I can send you a draft of my article next week. When do you have your board meeting?"

Harvey looked at his phone to check his agenda.

"Next week would be perfect for the article. The board meeting is Monday over a week, so not next Monday but the one after. Right after the board meeting, I should be able to give you the green light for publication."

"Perfect," Dave replied, and looked at his list of questions. "We talked about clinical trials last time. When do those start?"

Harvey took a sip of his coffee.

"That's a topic for the upcoming board meeting, but I expect we'll begin the trial in two weeks. It also depends on the meeting that I have the next week with the FDA."

Dave took notes and reflected on his thoughts of the past few days.

"In two weeks? I assume you've already selected patients to participate in the clinical trials?"

"Yes, we already have a list of patients and have them all registered as part of the FDA approval process."

Dave looked out disappointed as he realized that his chances of participating in the trials had already evaporated. He looked back at his list of questions.

"Any idea about the chances of success of the clinical trials?"

"Oh, I believe it will work. The trials are merely a formality we have to go through."

"When the drug gets to market, what will a treatment cost?"

Harvey suddenly sat up straight and looked puzzled.

"The price hasn't been set yet."

Harvey grabbed the voice recorder from the desk and turned it off. He looked very serious.

"I'm sorry, but I have to answer that question off the record, because it's a very sensitive issue. Right now, I'm still in discussions with the board about pricing. The production cost of the drug is low, and I'd like to see the drug reasonably priced, so it's affordable for most people. But the board disagrees wants a higher price. They think the drug will make them more money that way. We also have a more ethical discussion about how widely spread the drug should be. The board believes that the world cannot handle eight billion people with a prolonged longevity. They want to sell it only to the richest people on earth at an outrageous price."

"What is outrageous?"

Harvey looked down, as if embarrassed.

"The exact price point hasn't been determined yet, but in the discussion, they were talking about amounts in the hundreds of millions for treatment."

Dave looked stunned when he heard this.

"Wow! That's outrageous! That would make it available only to the super-rich in the world."

"Exactly! You can't tell anyone about this pricing to anyone and you can't put it in your article, or I could be in deep trouble. I only tell you this because I trust and respect you and I still hope to convince the board to change their opinion on this subject."

"Don't worry! Your secret is safe with me. Let's move on to my other questions."

Dave turned the recorder back on and asked his questions. Then Harvey closed the blinds and turned on the beamer. They watched the videos from the mouse experiments, and Harvey commented on them. The footage confirmed the stunning results of the drug treatment. During the presentation, Dave's thoughts wandered. He thought about that outrageous price, making the drugs unavailable to ordinary people like him. This drug could fix his back problems, improve his looks, and allow him to enjoy his life like as he used to. Taking part in the clinical trial did not seem possible. He felt there was really only one option left, but that was not one to be proud of. He felt bad having these thoughts and focused again on what Harvey was telling about the movie. The corner of the moved showed the timing. The speed of the changes amazed Dave. Within a week, the mice transformed from old to young. People with no knowledge of the drug would probably think those images were hoaxes or fakes. He knew better by now. Harvey had developed a miracle drug. A drug people had dreamed of since the beginnings of their existence.

"That was all of it," Harvey said at the end, turning off the beamer and opening the blinds. Harvey looked at his watch. It was already ten past five.

"Shall we go downstairs so you can take the pictures?"

"Yes, great!"

Dave stood up, grabbed his camera from his briefcase, and put on the white coat.

"Could you please hide the camera in your pocket?"

He put the camera away and followed Harvey into the hallway. Dave saw the dark-haired man with the mustache still sitting in his office. The man looked up as they passed. In the elevator, Harvey looked at him seriously.

"If we run into people, please don't take any pictures in their presence. I'd rather not make people too suspicious."

"No problem."

When they got out on the first floor, they walked down the hallway. There were only two people talking in an office. The rest looked empty. There was no one in the lab, so Harvey signaled to him that it was okay to pull out his camera. He took some pictures and asked Harvey to pose in front of a microscope. They walked on to the room with the mice. No one was there either. He took quite a few pictures and even filmed some of the mice. It was getting dark outside. They walked back to the elevator and when they passed the office in the corridor, there was only one man left.

"Have a nice evening, Peter!"

"You too, Harvey!"

In the elevator, Harvey pressed the button to the ground floor after scanning his badge. On the ground floor, they greeted the guard, who was reading another comic book. Harvey opened the glass door and walked down the corridor. The offices were all empty, but when they entered the laboratory, there were three people inside. Two men were discussing something behind a microscope, and a woman behind a desk was packing her bag.

"Hello!" Harvey said.

The two men and the woman looked up.

"Hi, Harvey!"

Dave had not seen these people before. He greeted them, and they nodded back. Harvey walked straight to the room in the back and said to Dave,

"I'll show you the mixing machine. It's in the back room."

As Harvey closed the glass door behind him, he looked at him.

"Sorry about that, but I prefer you to have as little contact with other staff members as possible."

"No problem, I understand."

He pulled out his camera and took a few pictures of the machines.

"Maybe one of you in front of this machine?"

Harvey moved in front of the machine and posed. They continued walking to the back, toward the blue-lit refrigerators.

"I'd really love a picture of you holding one of those tubes in front of these blue refrigerators. Would that be possible?"

Dave looked excited, and Harvey grinned.

"Yeah, that makes a nice picture."

He opened one of the refrigerator doors, took out one of the boxes, and placed it on the table. He took out a tube and held it in front of his face as if studying it. Dave took a picture with his camera. Suddenly, they heard the electronic lock of the glass door open. Harvey looked startled and immediately put the tube back in the box.

"Harvey, are you there?" a male voice asked.

They could not see the man since they were standing behind a row of refrigerators. Harvey rushed to the door and looked at the man.

"Oh, hello Michael! What can I do for you?"

"Well, I was just discussing a sample we examined under the microscope with Adish, and we'd like your opinion. Do you have a moment?"

Harvey looked at the row of refrigerators where Dave was still standing behind.

"No problem. Mr. Wilson, excuse me for a moment."

Harvey left with Michael and walked back into the laboratory. He heard the door lock. His heart beat faster as he looked through the glass door. Harvey stood next to the two men and peered into a microscope. He suddenly thought of his idea from that afternoon. A storm of thoughts raced through his mind. He could even hear Henry laughing in his head as he said, "Maybe you can bring a sample with you during your visit."

He looked at the door again and saw Harvey still talking to the two men. Dave looked back at the refrigerators and at the huge number of boxes. His brain suddenly sensed all this stress. He thought about the ridiculous prices of the drug. He looked at the ceiling and the walls, but he did not see any surveillance cameras. Realizing he was all alone now with the drugs that could make him feel young again, he figured it was now or never.

He tried the handle on one of the windows and it opened as he had hoped. He hurried to a refrigerator in the back and took a box from the bottom shelf. He set it on the floor next to the refrigerator. Then he began moving all the other boxes in the row forward, in a way that left a space at the very back. He closed the door again and looked at the refrigerator. It was not visible that a box was missing in the back. Satisfied, he took the box and rushed to the window.

Cautiously, he peered around the corner of the row of refrigerators toward the laboratory. He saw Harvey still talking to the two men, but judging by the body language that he was finishing the conversation. He began to move slowly toward the glass door. He felt the adrenaline rushing to his head and did not hesitate another second. He walked to the window with the box in his hands and looked outside. It was completely dark. He slipped the box through the open window, bent down, and set it close to the wall on the ground between some bushes. Then he closed the window and rushed back to the table where he stood with Harvey earlier. He heard the electronic lock of the door and Harvey entered the room. Dave's heart pounded like crazy in his chest and he tried to calm his breathing. As Harvey turned the corner of the row of refrigerators, he looked at him.

"Sorry about that."

Harvey looked concerned now.

"Are you ok, Dave? You look very pale."

Dave felt his heart pounding rapidly and tried to calm down.

"I feel a bit dizzy. I just realized I forgot to have lunch today."

Harvey walked back to the other side of the room.

"Let me get you a glass of water."

He filled a glass with water and handed it to Dave.

"Thanks," and he began to drink as he slowly calmed down.

"I guess we're done here, right?"

Dave put the glass on the table and grabbed his camera.

"One more picture of you with the refrigerators and then I'll have enough."

He took the picture and Harvey put the box with tubes back in the refrigerator. They both walked to the laboratory. The woman had left and only the two men stood behind the microscope. As they passed, the two men looked at Harvey.

"Thanks for your help, Harvey. Have a nice evening!"

Harvey tapped one of the men on his shoulder.

"Keep up the good work and don't make it too late!"

They smiled at him and continued their conversation. When they got in the elevator to return to the second floor, Harvey explained the men were testing new ways to administer the drug. On the second floor, they walked to Harvey's office. Only one office still had someone in it, and as they passed, the dark-haired man with the mustache stared at them strangely. Dave found it suspicious and felt nervous about what he had done downstairs. In Harvey's office, they took off the white coats. Dave put the camera in his briefcase.

"Well, Harvey, I'd like to thank you for all your time. It has been a real pleasure, and you really went to great lengths to help me with my article. Thank you for that!"

He pulled a wrapped package from his briefcase and smiled at Harvey.

"As a token of my appreciation, I brought you a small present to thank you for all the time you took to explain everything to me."

Dave handed it to Harvey.

"You shouldn't have," Harvey said as he opened the package.

"Oh nice, a book about the history of Science Publications. Well, thanks, that is very kind of you. Let me walk you to the elevator."

They walked down the hallway, and Dave saw the man looking again. At the elevator, he shook Harvey's hand.

"Thanks for everything, Harvey, and good luck with the board meeting next week. I might call you next week if I need to verify some things, and I'll send you my draft next week."

Harvey smiled.

"Thanks Dave, it was a pleasure working with you and you can call me anytime. Give my regards to Andrew."

Dave entered the elevator, and the doors closed. As he looked at himself in the mirror, he thought, "You thief!"

He had never stolen anything in his life and was perplexed about what he had done.

Downstairs, he passed his briefcase through the scanner and wished the guard a pleasant evening. When he arrived in the parking lot, there were still five cars parked. The air was fresh, and it was dark. As he walked to his car, he looked around the side of the building at the bushes next to the windows. He decided it was too risky to pick up the box now. Imagine someone coming out of the building as he walked to his car with the box. He looked up at the building, and suddenly saw a man watching him from a second-floor window. He quickly got into his car and looked again through his windshield at the second floor. The man was still staring at him. It looked like the dark-haired man with the mustache he had seen earlier on the second floor, but against the light it was hard to tell. He turned on the engine and slowly drove away.

At the end of Mayhem Drive, at the point where he would usually turn right to go back to his hotel, he stopped for a moment. He saw a gas station further along on the left and drove there. He parked his car in the parking lot and looked toward Mayhem Drive. After five minutes, he saw a car coming out of the street and it turned away from the gas station. Only three cars left, he thought. He looked at his watch. It was almost seven o'clock. Then he saw a second car leaving. This one turned left, and he feared it might stop at the gas station. He felt relieved when the car drove on without stopping. Two more remained. When he turned his head back to look at the Mayhem Drive exit, he saw another car turn right. One more left. He waited another twenty minutes and then the last car appeared. It turned left and braked in front of the gas station. His heart began to pound rapidly, but then it continued slowly on without stopping.

He waited another five minutes to make sure none of the cars returned. Then he started the engine and drove back to Mayhem Drive. At the building, everything was now dark. He parked his car with the trunk facing the building. The building was in a dark shadow among the trees, and it looked eerie. He walked to the left side of the building, and as he tried to find the right window, he saw the blue light shining vaguely from some of the windows. He started looking behind the bushes in front of the windows, and it did not take him long to find the box.

Suddenly, he heard a branch cracking among the trees behind him. He immediately turned and looked at the forest, but saw nothing. He quickly picked up the metal box and walked carefully back to his car through the darkness. He opened the trunk and put the metal box inside. He got into the car while nervously looking around to see if anyone was there, but it was completely dark around him. He heard an owl further ahead. Then he started the car and drove off. He was still afraid of running into someone on Mayhem Drive. It would be hard to explain why he was there. As he turned right onto Main Street, Dave relaxed, and his heartbeat slowed.

As he pulled onto the highway, he turned on the radio. Some wild rock song was on the radio and he laughed when he heard the song. He tapped the steering wheel and felt great as he sang along to the song. When he had heard the price of drug treatment, it had somehow pissed him off. Then, when he got this exceptional opportunity at the refrigerators, he could not resist the temptation. Strangely, he felt good now, even though it was the first time in his life he had stolen anything. He felt this drug could change his life in ways he never thought possible. Still, he felt guilty. Harvey had been so nice to him, and now he had betrayed his trust.

Later, he thought about what Harvey had said about the proper temperature to keep the drugs. He feared the drugs would get too hot. As he made the turn toward his hotel, he saw a "Megamall" sign on the left. Instead of turning right toward the hotel, he turned left. Arriving at the mall, he got out of the car and asked an older man if there was an outdoor or hiking store in the mall. The man explained that there was one further down the mall. Inside the store, he walked straight to the cooler section. As he looked at the wide assortment of coolers, a store clerk walked up to him.

"Can I help you, sir?"

"Well, I'm looking for a medium-sized cool box that can keep white wine at the right temperature for a long time."

The store clerk walked over to the cool boxes and took out a white one.

"Sir, you can plug this cooler into your car power or a regular outlet and you can regulate the temperature. After disconnecting the power, it has a battery pack that provides cooling."

Dave looked at the box and examined the inside. The box looked big enough to hold the metal box with the drug doses, and there would even be some room left over.

"Perfect. After cooling it to fifty-four degrees Fahrenheit, how long after disconnecting would it stay at that temperature?"

The man thought for a moment and then picked up a blue ice pack.

"On the battery alone, and if you keep it closed, it could stay cold for about two days, but if you place this ice pack next to the bottles, it could probably stay cold a day longer."

"Okay, I'll take both then."

He paid at the counter and walked back to his car. He looked around to make sure no one was looking and opened the trunk. He put the metal box in the cool box. Then he put the cool box on the floor next to the driver's seat, plugged it into the car's power supply, and drove to the hotel.

At the hotel, he parked his car in the parking lot. He grabbed the cool box and his briefcase and locked the car. It was a clear night, and the stars shone brightly, competing with the moon. He looked up and felt a mix of excitement, guilt, hope, and shame. He greeted the woman at the front desk. She handed him the evening newspaper, and he took the elevator. In his room, he immediately plugged the cool box into the power socket. He was so excited he could not wait any longer, and looked in the cool box, and opened the metal box. Inside the box were a hundred tubes, and he stared at them for a moment as if looking at some kind of treasure. Then he closed the box and ordered room service. His back hurt a lot now, and he took another painkiller. That night, he put a chair behind the door to prevent anyone from entering the room without hearing, and then he went to bed.

5. Family time

Friday morning, he woke up at nine thirty. The night before, he had felt tired and had not set the alarm clock. He had not closed the curtain properly and a ray of sunlight shone on his bed. For a moment, he thought he had dreamed all the events at Juvenatrust the day before, but then he saw the cool box standing next to his briefcase. It was not a dream. He had actually stolen a large quantity of the rejuvenation drug. It could be worth hundreds of millions if Juvenatrust indeed priced it so high. For Dave, it was a ticket to a possibly younger and healthier life. On the one hand, he felt content to have the drug in his possession. On the other hand, he was scared and worried about the theft. The risk of getting caught, but also the risk of the drug itself. If he used it, he might die in a terrible way instead of becoming young. For now, he decided not to worry too much, as he could always decide not to take the drug and return it to Juvenatrust. Getting out of bed, he felt the pain in his back and took a painkiller. He got dressed and wanted to have breakfast, but he did not dare to leave the cool box alone in the room, so he ordered room service.

After breakfast, he sat down at the desk and began working on his article. About an hour later, his thoughts wandered again. He felt guilty. Harvey had been so kind to him, and now he had breached his trust. If he ever found out that he had stolen the box of tubes, he could not look him straight in the eye. For now, he did not have to worry too much. He could always deny it was him. Anyone could have stolen from the huge stockpile of drugs. He stood up and prepared an espresso. He looked inside the cool box again and stared at the glass tubes, then he continued working on his article. Around one o'clock, he got hungry and ordered lunch in the room.

He had just finished his lunch when suddenly the phone rang. His heart started pounding hard, and he felt adrenaline rush to his head. Had they already found out about the theft? He picked up the phone nervously.

"Oh, hi, Claire. How are you?"

"I'm fine. Ready for your weekend of fishing with your son?"

She sounded cheerful.

"Yes, I'm looking forward to it. It has been a long time since our last trip."

She changed to a more serious tone.

"Nice. I just have a little problem with the flight back. I couldn't find a flight on Monday at a reasonable time, only at eleven in the evening. I know you hate flying at night. I can book you on the ten-thirty flight on Tuesday morning if you like?"

"Tuesday morning sounds much better."

"Okay, then I'll book that and also an extra night for you in the hotel."

"Perfect. Thanks, Claire."

He spent the rest of the afternoon working hard on his article. He wanted to leave the hotel before five, hoping to stay ahead of the heavy traffic on the highway. At four-thirty, he started packing his things. His back hurt again, and he took another painkiller. Ten minutes later, he put his suitcase, briefcase and cooler in front of the door and checked the room one last time. He checked out, loaded his luggage into the car and drove away.

As he drove across the Richmond San Rafael Bridge, he finally relaxed a bit. He had been tensed all day. He turned off the radio to call Andrew. The line was busy, so he left a voicemail that he would arrive in an hour. He hung up and began thinking back to the rejuvenation drug. He was still unsure whether to take the drug. The risks could be tremendous, despite what Harvey had told him. They had not injected the drugs into any human yet, so how could Harvey be so sure it would work? Maybe there would be terrible side effects. But Dave felt unhappy with his life as it was now, and this drug might change all that. Sometimes he felt so indifferent that he cared little whether he die or not. The more he thought about it, the more convinced he became he wanted to try the drug. It even seemed better to him to take the first injection before he got to Andrew. At least then, if something happened to him, Andrew would notice right away and could take him to the hospital. He had decided. Today would be the day.

During the drive, he thought about all the supplies he still needed to inject the drug. He had almost arrived and exited the Interstate highway I-880 in San Jose. Instead of driving straight to Andrew's neighborhood, he turned the other way to the mall. He parked in front of a large pharmacy and went inside. Inside he looked for syringes, but could not find them. A store clerk came his way,

"Can I help you, sir?"

Dave felt like a kid doing something sneaky and made up a story.

"My wife has diabetes and couldn't find her syringe. She sent me to buy another one, but I can't find them in the store. Do you sell syringes?"

The store clerk nodded.

"Yes, we do. You'll find them in aisle six. Over there."

The store clerk pointed to the other side of the pharmacy. Dave walked to aisle six, grabbed a pack of five syringes, and put them in his basket. He added some disinfectant. He also put a small insulating cooler bag in his basket, where he planned to keep some tubes. That way, he would not have to carry the cool box around all weekend. He walked to the cash register and paid as the adrenaline coursed through his head again. He felt nervous and his hands were clammy.

Back in the parking lot, he looked around nervously to check if anyone was watching him. There was no one around, so he opened the trunk and opened the cool box. He filled the small insulation bag with three tubes and put in one syringe and the disinfectant. He put the other syringes in the cool box and closed it. He put the insulation bag in his suitcase and then closed the trunk. He got into the car and drove off.

Five minutes later, he arrived at their house. He parked his car in the driveway in the carport's shade and took out his suitcase and his briefcase. As he closed the car, the door to the house opened, and Wendy appeared in the doorway.

"Hola Dave! Come on in!" she said with her Spanish accent.

"Hi Wendy! Good to see you again. You look good."

He kissed Wendy on the check and followed her inside.

"Andrew called that he's going to be a little late, but he should be here any minute. You might want to put your suitcase in the guest room already."

"Thanks, Wendy! I'll do that and freshen up a bit."

He walked upstairs and felt nervous as he entered the guest room. Was it wise to inject the drug? Technically, it was the best moment. If something would happen to him, Andrew and Wendy would be there for him. What if the drug did not work or worse, if it made him very sick? He felt stressed and weak, and his forehead grew warmer and sweaty. He felt his back ache again. The adrenaline rush returned, and suddenly he had made up his mind.

He opened his suitcase and took out the insulation bag. He unbuttoned his shirt and took it off. He took out a syringe and a tube. He unpacked the syringe and stuck the needle into the rubber top of the tube while holding the tube upside down. He had seen it many times in those hospital series on television. He filled the syringe with all the liquid from the tube. Then he held the syringe upright and tapped it twice and pressed it slightly to let all the air bubbles out. He rolled up the short sleeve of his T-shirt so that his shoulder was exposed. He looked at himself as he stood in front of the mirror. He thought of a quote from Mark Twain: "Twenty years from now you'll be more disappointed by the things you didn't do than by the ones you did do."

He waited no longer and stuck the injection syringe into his shoulder. The needle stung, and it felt weird to stick it in his own skin. He slowly emptied it completely and removed the needle from his arm. He waited for a moment and looked in the mirror. He felt nothing. Nothing different. He saw nothing different. He still had rings under his eyes and looked tired. He disinfected the syringe and put it back in the isolation bag. He hid it under some clothes in his suitcase. He looked in the mirror again. Nothing. He had been thinking about this moment for a long time, imagining all kinds of scenarios. Not this one. Nothing. No difference at all. The door slammed downstairs, and he heard his son call out.

"Dad?"

He walked downstairs. Andrew stood at the bottom of the stair.

"Hi Andrew! Good to see you."

He walked up to him and gave his son a big hug.

"How was your drive? Not too tiring?" Andrew asked as he looked at his father.

"It was okay. I took another painkiller before I left, so my back didn't bother me too much in the car."

They walked together to the living room.

"What do you want to drink?"

Dave thought about the injection and alcohol probably was not a good idea now with this drug in his body. You never know if there would be any chemical reaction, and the mice certainly had not mixed it with alcohol.

"Just some water, please."

Andrew went to the kitchen and got the drinks. Wendy was in the kitchen preparing dinner and could smell the food when Andrew returned from the kitchen.

"Here you go!"

He handed the glass of water to Dave.

"Through a friend of mine, I've booked a cabin for tomorrow night at Lake Tenaya. It's a great package and includes a boat and a fully equipped cabin."

He smiled at Andrew but was still distracted by his concerns about the injection.

"That sounds great. I'm looking forward to it. The weather forecast is good, so we should probably pack some sunscreen."

"I already packed a bottle. I still remember how you burned last time. You were as red as a lobster," Andrew said with a smile on his face.

They both laughed and talked further about the fishing trip. After dinner, he helped them to clear the table and clean up the kitchen. Wendy had announced at her work that she was pregnant and her female boss had not reacted well.

"I believe it's because my boss is trying to get pregnant herself and apparently it's not working out."

"Well, if there's one thing I've learned about bosses, it's that you shouldn't listen to them when they try to tell you what to do with your private life. If you're sick, it won't be your boss standing by your bedside," Dave said.

"You're absolutely right," Wendy said with a smile.

Andrew poured more wine into his glass and asked,

"Dad, are you sure you don't want any wine? This is a great red wine from Chili. I'm sure you'll love it."

He felt uncomfortable because he always loved to drink wine and his son knew that very well. He came up with a lie.

"No thanks, it's very tempting, but I'm trying to stop drinking for a while. A friend of mine quit drinking and lost quite a bit of weight, and I want to try that too."

He had chosen the wrong lie, and Andrew teased him.

"Come on, Dad, compared to the average American, you're not overweight at all. At your age, you're not becoming one of those diet freaks."

Dave was not fat, that was true. He had a small belly, but nothing too extreme.

"Well, I think it's good if I try, anyway. Maybe I'll feel better."

"Come on, encourage your father. It's very good he's trying to cut down on alcohol," Wendy said.

Andrew backed off, sipped his wine and said,

"I've already packed all the fishing gear in my car. So tomorrow we just need to add the bags and the food I've prepared in the fridge, and then we'll be ready to go. I wanted to leave early, so we can have lunch there. It's about a four-hour drive to the lake, so I was thinking of leaving at seven thirty, if that's okay with you?"

Dave felt a bit tired and looked at his watch.

"That's fine with me, but I'd better get to bed. My week has been rather tiring, and it's already eleven o'clock."

He got up, thanked Wendy for the dinner, and gave her a kiss. He patted his son on the shoulder.

"Good night, and I suppose you'll wake me up tomorrow?"

He gave his father a hug.

"Sure Dad, sleep well."

Upstairs, he brushed his teeth and looked in the mirror. Still nothing to see. He did not feel any better and looked tired. He had been looking tired all week. The dark circles under his eyes looked worse than usual. He looked at his shoulder, at the hole left by the syringe. At least he had not died instantly or suffered an epileptic seizure or something. He did not feel completely relieved, however, because it might take more time for the effects of the drug to kick in. He lay down on the large bed in the guest room and turned off the light. Maybe he would not wake up anymore and his son would find his cold, stiff body in the morning. Trying to feel better, he thought about how Harvey had said the drug would work on humans. Harvey was the expert, so he just had to trust that. He tried to relax by thinking about the fishing trip he was going to take with his son, and after a while, he finally fell deeply asleep.

The next morning, Andrew stood beside his bed and called out,

"Dad, Dad, wake up!"

Andrew pushed Dave a bit, and he lifted his head from under the blanket. He looked at his son, who jumped away and looked frightened.

"Dad?"

Andrew took a few steps away from him and looked shocked.

"Jesus, is that you, Dad?"

His reaction startled Dave, and he touched his face. His face felt strange and wet. He felt large pustules on his face, and his skin felt rough and slimy. Frightened, he thought of the drugs he had injected the night before. He looked at his hands and they were dark red and bloody, with pustules all over his hands.

"What the fuck? No… no…"

Dave got very nervous and looked at his nails. They were all yellow. Andrew took a few more steps away from him, as if he was afraid of him.

"Dad, is that you? What happened to you?"

Dave put his feet on the floor and looked at them. They were all red and bloody, like his hands. Pus was dripping out of the large pustules on his feet. He started babbling and said,

"No… no… no… this can't be…"

Wendy entered the room and looked at Andrew at first.

"What's going on, Andrew?"

She now looked at Dave and began to scream out loud as she clasped her hands in front of her mouth.

"What… what… what's that?"

Dave stood up and shivered with fear. He did not dare look at himself. When he turned on the light, he looked in the mirror and saw his face was all bloody and pus was coming out of the huge pustules on his face. He began to scream. He heard Andrew's voice again.

"Dad! Dad! Wake up!"

Dave was back in his bed, and his son stood beside his bed.

"I tried to wake you up, Dad, but it was like you were having a nightmare or something."

Dave immediately looked at his hands, but they looked normal. He touched his face, and it felt normal.

"Yeah, I guess I had a nightmare."

He slowly got up and looked in the mirror. His face looked normal. He felt relieved.

"I'll make breakfast," Andrew said as he left the room.

"Ok, I'll be right down."

He looked in the mirror again at his bald head and wrinkled face. He noticed nothing different. He moved a little closer to the mirror, thinking for a moment that the rings under his eyes were less dark and less thick. He looked again and concluded there was probably no difference. He shaved and got dressed. Then he packed his suitcase and took it downstairs.

He put his suitcase next to Andrew's backpack, which was standing in front of the door. Andrew was busy in the kitchen.

"Do you like an omelet, Dad?"

"Yep, sounds good."

Andrew cut the omelet in half and put half on his and half on Dave's plate.

"You look less tired than yesterday. Did you sleep well?"

"Thanks! Yes, I slept deeply," Dave replied.

They ate their breakfast, and Dave took a painkiller. His back did not hurt yet, but felt stiff, and with the long drive ahead, he thought he'd better take one. They talked about the fishing trip and checked that they had packed everything. After breakfast, they filled Andrew's cool box with all the food and drink he had prepared. Wendy appeared in her pajamas in the opening of the kitchen door, still looking sleepy.

"So, you have everything you need?"

"Morning, Wendy."

"Morning, Dave. You look less tired than yesterday."

"Yeah, I slept like a rose. I was really tired from last week."

"Okay, let's go, Dad!" Andrew said as he kissed Wendy goodbye.

He carried the cool box, grabbed the backpack and Dave's suitcase, and carried them all at once to his car. Dave gave Wendy a kiss.

"I'll bring him back to you on Sunday."

She smiled.

"Enjoy your trip! Andrew has been really looking forward to it."

"Thanks! See you on Sunday!"

Andrew started the engine as Dave took the seat next to him. They both waved at Wendy and drove off toward Yosemite Park. It was a sunny day, and the sky was clear. They talked about their previous fishing and hiking trips. They both started laughing when they talked about that time they went fishing in Canada. They had gone fly-fishing for salmon for the first time in a river north of Quebec, called Sainte-Marguerite. They had rented gear in a nearby town called Sacré-Coeur and they both wore those wading suits, long waterproof fishing pants. They had been in the river for at least two hours and had caught nothing. The place was infested with mosquitos and, despite all the anti-mosquito spray, they had been bitten several times. At one point, they were moving around a bit and laving through the deep water, when Dave suddenly stepped into some deep hole. He sank into the water up to his neck and all the water poured into his pants. He was soaking wet. With Andrew's help, he could swim back toward the bank. His wading suit was now much wider and larger now and full of water. Halfway, he started yelling at his son.

"I think something is moving in my pants."

Andrew roared with laughter as he helped his father climb back onto the bank. When he was finally safely out of the water again, Dave pulled off his pants. He warned Andrew to have his fishing net ready. He slowly stepped out of the wading suit and they both looked at the fish, laughing. Andrew pulled out the small salmon with his fishing net.

"Well, that's the first time in my life I've seen someone catch a fish with his pants, Dad."

Just talking about that trip made Dave laugh so much that he had tears in his eyes.

As they were chatting pleasantly, it felt like the drive to Yosemite went by quickly and they soon arrived at the Big Oak Flat

Entrance. They registered at the entrance station and Andrew picked up the key to the cabin he had booked. After three hours of driving without stopping, Dave did desperately need to go to the restroom. Inside, he looked in the mirrors above the sinks. Wendy and Andrew had been right. He looked less tired. His rings seemed less thick and the dark spots under his eyes were less visible. Other than that, he noticed little of the drug he had injected the night before. He entered the bathroom stall and suddenly realized that his back did not hurt as much as before, but he felt a little stiff. It had been over three hours since he had taken his painkiller and usually the pain would come back slowly, especially after a long drive in the car. Outside, the sun was shining on his face and Andrew was waiting for him beside the car.

"Ready to go to Lake Tenaya?"

"Yep, let's go!"

They got in the car and continued on State Route 120 into the park, heading east. They had to drive much slower there, and the last forty miles took them an hour, compared to three hours for the first one hundred and sixty miles. After an hour, they saw the lake appear before them. Mountains surrounded the lake, and the water looked clear and teal. They took the turnoff on the dirt road next to the lake, and after five minutes of driving through the forest, they arrived at their cabin.

It was a small wooden cabin with a covered terrace among some large pine trees. The terrace faced the lake and had a beautiful view of the lake with the mountains beyond. Andrew opened the cabin, and inside there was a small kitchen with a small living area next to it. Behind the living area was a small bedroom with a bunk bed. His son looked a little worried at the bunk bed and then at Dave.

"Do you think it's okay for your back?"

"Well, it's only one night, so I'm sure I'll survive."

Next to the bedroom was a small bathroom with a shower and a toilet. They carried all the luggage into the cabin, and they filled the refrigerator with the food and drinks. Andrew grabbed the fishing gear and put it on the patio.

"Dad, can you prepare the sandwiches and drinks? I'll get the boat ready in the meantime."

"Okay."

Andrew walked away, and Dave disappeared into the kitchen. Further along on the right was a jetty with all the fishing boats. Andrew looked into one of the storage boxes next to the dock and took out their boat's outboard motor. He mounted it on the boat and then he brought all the fishing gear aboard. Dave had prepared the table on the patio for lunch and filled a large thermos with coffee.

After lunch, they cleared the table and closed the cabin. Dave smeared some sunblock on his face and arms and handed the bottle to his son as he put on his hat.

"Here, with this sun, you better put on some sunblock, since we'll be outside for the rest of the afternoon."

Andrew took the bottle and smeared some on his face and arms, then they walked to the boat and climbed on. Andrew started the engine and untied the rope from the dock.

"Here we go!"

He steered the boat to the middle of the lake. At one point, he turned off the motor and, since there was no wind, they let the boat drift. They both grabbed their fishing rods and put the bait on them. Andrew threw out his rod first. Dave quickly followed him, then they both waited in the sun. After forty minutes, it was Dave's fishing line that pulled first. He waited a moment and then gave a quick tug on his rod to make sure the fish was hooked. Then he enthusiastically began pulling in his fishing line.

"I think I'm the first one this time."

A few minutes later, he held his rod in the air and a beautiful gray spotted trout was twitching around on the line.

"Nice one, Dad! At least we'll have something for the barbecue tonight."

Dave smiled and grabbed the fish, untied it, and tossed it into the bucket in the middle of the boat. He put some fresh bait on his hook and threw out his fishing line.

At the end of the day, they went back to the dock. They loaded the gear and the bucket out of the boat. Andrew stowed the outboard motor back in the storage box and they walked back to the cabin.

"That was a beautiful day," Dave said. His face felt all warm, and he was afraid the sun burned him after all.

"A great day indeed. Let's see how these babies will taste after we grill them on the barbecue!"

When they arrived at the cabin, Dave remembered that he had injected the medicine around this time the day before. He figured it was probably best to take the drug at the same time every day. Just the thought of injecting the drug made him nervous again. Andrew lit the barbecue and looked at him.

"Maybe you can prepare the table, Dad?"

"Okay, but first I really need to go to the toilet."

Inside, he looked in his suitcase for the small insulation bag under his clothes. Then he looked out the window to see where his son was. Andrew was standing next to the barbecue. He took the insulation bag into the bathroom and closed the door behind him. First, he looked in the mirror. Still nothing special to see, although his face looked red from the full day in the sun. He wondered if the medicine was really working. He felt no change, except perhaps that he felt no pain in his back. Normally, his back would hurt a lot after a day in a car and on a boat. Today, however, he felt no pain, nor had he taken any painkillers since that morning. It was probably too early to think much of it, but no pain for a change was already a relief for him.

He rolled up the sleeve of his T-shirt to expose his arm. He took the syringe and a tube from the insulation bag. He filled the syringe with the liquid from the tube and tapped the syringe to get the air out. He took a deep breath and inserted the needle into his shoulder. As he slowly emptied the syringe, he looked at himself in the mirror. He felt like a junkie. Hiding in this small, shabby bathroom to take the drug secretly while his son was waiting outside. He slowly removed the needle from his arm and disinfected it. He put the syringe and empty tube back in the insulation bag, and as he closed it, he was suddenly startled when Andrew knocked on the door.

"Are you all right, dad?"

He had been in the toilet for almost twenty minutes now. His heart pounded when he heard his son's voice.

"I'm fine, just a little constipated, I think."

He flushed the toilet and washed his hands. He tucked the insulation bag in his pants under his shirt and stepped out of the toilet. Andrew was in the kitchen cleaning the fish. He quickly slipped into the bedroom and hid the insulation bag under some clothes in his suitcase.

Dave walked to the kitchen and prepared the table on the patio. The barbecue was on and a plume of smoke came from it. He went back inside, cooked some potatoes for five minutes, wrapped them in aluminum foil and put them on the grill. Andrew finished cleaning the fish and put them on the grill.

"Not bad for a first afternoon."

"Should be enough for us, but nothing compared to that trip to Lake Champlain two years ago," Andrew said with a smile.

"Yeah, I remember that trip. We had caught so many fish we had to hand them out to all our neighbors at the lake. I'll never forget their faces when they saw the quantity of fish we had caught."

Andrew laughed and grabbed a beer from the fridge.

"You want one, too?"

"No, thanks. Maybe some iced tea for me."

Dave still thought it best not to drink while taking the drug. Andrew handed him a can of iced tea.

"With you doing all healthy here, I start to feel guilty," Andrew said and handed Dave a can of iced tea.

"Just wait until you're my age," Dave said, laughing.

The fish on the barbecue smelled delicious.

"I think this fish is done. Hand me a plate, Dad."

Dave gave it to him and checked the potatoes, which looked good. Enjoying the sunset on the lake, they savored their catch.

"Nothing tastes better than freshly caught trout," Andrew said.

"Absolutely, our reward for our hard work today. Speaking of work. How are things at?"

"Good. They're pleased with my performance and I can expect a promotion at the end of the year."

"Sounds good. What's the promotion about?"

"Well, as you know, I used to work on only one research project at a time. My boss told me they might promote me to the position of senior research manager by the end of the year. The main difference would be that I would then be responsible for multiple research projects instead of just one, and I expect a salary increase. To test me and prepare me for the change, they have already made me responsible for two projects and by the end of the year, they may add more."

"Nice challenge. What projects are you working on?"

"Let me grab another beer first. Would you like another iced tea?" Andrew asked as he stood up.

"Yes, please."

They had their love of biological engineering in common, and they could talk about it for hours. When Andrew returned with the drinks, he said, "We're working on a new type of eye scan that tracks the thinning of the retina. With this scan, we want to detect Alzheimer's disease at an early stage, often long before the obvious symptoms of the disease appear. We've found that patients with Alzheimer's have a reduced density of blood vessels in the retina compared to healthy people. We can probably also use the same eye scan to detect patients with Parkinson's disease early on, before major symptoms appear."

"Wow, that sounds like quite a breakthrough, because both Alzheimer's as Parkinson's disease are often discovered late when the disease is already well advanced. Very interesting."

Andrew nodded and continued, "The other project focuses on regeneration. We're studying the regenerative capacity of different species of marine worms. All the worms can regrow the tail part of the body. Only a few worm species were also found to be able to regrow their head and brain. We're trying to identify the genes responsible for this regenerative ability. In doing so, we hope to discover how this process works. Perhaps in a follow-up project, we can then try to discover how to enlarge the regenerative capacity of humans. Humans have some regenerative abilities, for example, to grow skin over a cut, or regenerate whole parts of organs, but these abilities are very limited compared to those of these worm species."

"So maybe in the future we can regrow a lost arm or leg?"

"Yes, exactly. That would be something, wouldn't it?"

They cleared the table, and Dave boiled some water for tea.

"Would like some tea, too?"

"No thanks, I'll stick with my beer."

They sat back down at the table. It was completely dark now. The wind was blowing through the forest and then they heard an owl.

"Last weekend you told me about your article on senescent cells. How did it go last week?"

Dave shared what he had learned and seen over the past week. Andrew was fascinated and amazed that Juvenatrust was so close to the first clinical trials on humans.

"What do you think about Dr. Juncker being so convinced that the clinical trials will confirm that the drug also works on humans?"

Andrew thought for a moment.

"Well, given that the mouse trials worked without complications and the fact that the laboratory trials on human cells also confirmed it worked, I would think Dr. Juncker was probably right."

Andrew took a sip of his beer and continued, "I mean, they could still be wrong about the right dosage of the drug, but it sounds like the risk of complications in this case is low. There's always a chance it could turn out differently and there could be complications. That's why the FDA always obliges clinical trials before a drug is allowed on the market. Some people may develop cancer or something, you never know for sure."

The latter did not please Dave. Perhaps he had made a huge mistake by injecting the rejuvenator. He felt like telling his son everything. About the theft and about the injections he had taken, but he hesitated and felt afraid to tell him everything. Andrew might get very worried or worse, he might be disappointed in his own father, especially since Andrew had made the introduction to Harvey Juncker.

"The first clinical trial will be on a group of patients with osteoarthritis. Can you imagine the irony? My doctor in New York told me I have that. So, this drug might solve my back problems. I considered asking Dr. Juncker to let me participate in this first clinical trial."

Andrew looked a bit surprised.

"Why didn't you ask him?"

"Well, Dr. Juncker explained the FDA had already registered and approved all patients. So, I didn't think it would be possible anymore."

"Ah, yes, once the approval process has begun, it's difficult to make changes. Probably Dr. Juncker would have refused. But hey, the good news is that if the first clinical trial deals with osteoarthritis, it could mean that in two or three years you can buy the drug. And at least you don't have to take the risks of a clinical trial."

"Well… the problem is that the drug may not be available to everyone."

"What do you mean?"

He saw Andrew's bewildered face and hesitated, then continued, "Well, you're not supposed to know this, so please keep it a secret. I had asked Dr. Juncker what he thought the drug would cost if it came to market. When I asked him that, Dr. Juncker turned off my voice recorder and told me he only wanted to tell me off-the-record and that I should put nothing about it in my article or tell anyone. He told me the drug is not that expensive to produce, but that he's having a huge discussion with the owners of Juvenatrust about the price. The owners want to make the drug extremely expensive, making it available only to the super-rich of the world."

"But that's outrageous! The entire world should have access to this drug."

"So agrees Dr. Juncker, but the discussion is ongoing."

"Can you imagine the global outrage if it comes out that only the rich may rejuvenate and live longer? That would cause a division in society and much opposition to it," Andrew said, astonished.

"The owners apparently believe the world can't handle eight billion people with an increased longevity. It could pose huge issues, for instance, with the environment and with pensions."

Andrew thought for a moment.

"When I look at the environmental problems we already have, I imagine that if all these people live longer, global pollution will also increase dramatically. Even without this rejuvenation, I sometimes worry that my future son or daughter may not have much world left to live in. Apparently, scientists are warning that the problem of global warming is getting out of control and we could be facing an ecological collapse. Many countries are taking measures to curb carbon dioxide emissions. It makes me ashamed and sad to see our government still denying the climate problems."

"Yes, that's an immense problem. At least here in California they are taking some measures, but I wonder if it will all be enough. I've also read somewhere that we're fast approaching some tipping points, that could further increase global warming and make it difficult to reverse the trend even if we were to reduce the carbon dioxide emissions drastically. I remember two examples of that," Dave said, and took a sip from his tea before continuing. "One is the fact that all the polar ice is melting, so less sunlight is reflected, so the earth absorbs more heat and the temperatures rises even more. Another is that the permafrost in the Arctic is thawing. The permafrost is soil that stays frozen year-round. The Arctic landscape stores in its frozen soil one of the world's largest natural reservoirs of organic carbon. But once thawed, soil microbes in the permafrost convert that carbon into the greenhouse gasses carbon dioxide and methane, which then enter the atmosphere and contribute to global warming. This creates a feedback loop in which rising temperatures lead to increasing release of carbon dioxide and methane, which in turn leads to rising temperatures. Although these conclusions come from our own NASA, our government prefers to stick its head in the sand like an ostrich."

"I heard about that, but I didn't know it was our own NASA that had come out with this report. That makes it even more shocking our government is not taking enough measures. I suspect there must be an ecological catastrophe in our country before people take the required drastic measures."

Dave nodded. Besides biological engineering, the problem of climate change was one of their favorite discussion topics. They continued their discussion until midnight, after which they went to bed.

The next day was another beautiful day, and the sky was bright blue. Dave had slept on the bottom bunk bed. Normally by now his back would be broken and he would have woken up from the pain. This morning, to his surprise, he woke up with no pain in his back. It took him some time to realize it as he got up and walked to the bathroom. He felt stiff, but no pain. Andrew was already in the preparing breakfast.

It was a strange feeling. He actually felt no pain and felt good. In the bathroom, he looked in the mirror and saw that his face was less pale. He could not tell if he was more tanned from a day in the sun or if his skin was healthier. The rings under his eyes were much smaller and barely visible anymore. It could be a coincidence, and maybe he had just slept well after a healthy day outside. Or was the drug working? He couldn't really tell. He shaved and washed his face. Normally bending to wash his face would be difficult with the stiffness and pain in his back, but today he felt nothing. The stress he had felt over the past few days about the drug slowly gave way to a feeling of contentment. Perhaps he had made the right choice in taking the risk. He got dressed, walked to the kitchen, and gave his son a friendly tap on the shoulder.

"Did you sleep well?"

Andrew was frying an omelet and did not look at Dave but at the pan.

"I slept like an ox. And you? Was the bed okay for your back?"

Dave prepared the table for breakfast.

"I haven't slept this well in a long time."

Andrew looked at him in surprise as he sat down at the table in front of him.

"Wow, your face! You look so rested and tanned. Is that because you got sunburned yesterday? The outdoors is doing you good."

He continued to stare at him as if he could not believe what he saw. Dave felt uncomfortable and felt he had to justify.

"When I arrived at your place, I felt so tired and overworked. I had spent little time outside in the last few months. I think the outdoors and the good night's sleep did me good."

Andrew smiled and sliced his omelet.

"Well, then I'm glad I proposed this fishing trip. If I had known it would have this effect, I would have suggested it much sooner. You look younger like that."

"Thanks!"

Dave did not know where to look and felt a bit embarrassed. He took a big bite of the omelet.

"I suggest we fish until noon and then have lunch here. If we leave around one thirty from here, we'll be home around five thirty. At least then we can eat with Wendy before you drive back to your hotel. Would that suit you?"

"Perfect. Let's hope we catch a lot of fish then so we can eat them for dinner tonight."

"Great! Let's clean up and then we'll go back on the lake," Andrew said as he stood up.

They fished all morning and caught more fish than the day before. At eleven thirty they had caught already twelve brown trout. The daily limit was five brown trout per day per person, so they threw back two fish and returned to the cabin.

"What a catch today!"

Dave nodded and said, "Let's eat four fish for lunch and then keep the other six fish for dinner."

Andrew walked over to the barbecue and turned it on. After a delicious lunch, they cleaned up everything. They packed their luggage and took one last look at the beautiful lake before driving back. After an hour's drive, they were back at the Big Oak Flat Entrance. Andrew returned the keys to the cabin while Dave went to the restrooms. He washed his hands after coming out of the restroom and looked in the mirror. He looked much more rested and had much more color on his face. His face had always looked pale and gray. He still hesitated to tell his son everything. He found it difficult and decided to wait with it. He was still ashamed of his theft.

He walked back to the car, and they continued west on the State Road 120, leaving Yosemite National Park. What a wonderful trip it had been! They were constantly so busy talking in the car that Dave was surprised to see their home suddenly looming before them. The long drive had passed in a blink. Andrew drove up the driveway, and they got all the luggage and gear out of the car. Dave put his luggage in his car and helped carry the rest inside. As soon as Andrew opened the door, Wendy came walking out of the kitchen. She kissed Andrew and stared at Dave.

"What happened to you?"

Dave did not know where to look and gave her a kiss.

"Wow, you look so rested and tanned! Your rings are almost gone. Amazing, I guess I should go fishing too."

They laughed.

"I've been so tired and haven't slept much lately. In the woods, though, I slept like a baby, and I guess the sunshine did me good. It was a great weekend with great company."

Andrew confirmed and showed her the fish.

"Today we caught so much. Enough for lunch and for dinner."

"Wow, what a catch. Well, then we better start preparing dinner."

Wendy had a big smile as she looked at the fish. She walked with them to the kitchen and they cleaned all the fish. After preparing the food, they sat at the table together and enjoyed their home-caught meal. Andrew poured some wine into his glass and asked Dave if he wanted some, but he refused again.

"Mmm… this fish tastes delicious. What a difference from the fish from the supermarket. You can go fishing like this more often."

Andrew smiled back at her.

"Nothing better than a freshly caught fish, my dear."

Wendy stared at Dave's face again.

"The tan makes you look younger. I guess you don't get outside much in New York?"

"Yeah, I've been working so hard the last few months and have barely been outside. This trip was great and I have to say Yosemite Park is amazing. It's very colorful. We even spotted some deer drinking water on the side of the lake."

He took a bite of the fish and continued, "How's the pregnancy going? Still tired?"

"Well, it's a little better. My appetite has increased a lot."

Andrew said with a smile, "Yes, you could say she's eating for two. Last week, she finished an entire sausage in one hour, whereas it normally takes us a couple of days together."

Dave smiled at them.

"I remember when Jennifer was pregnant with Andrew that she ate for two. She usually went back to the kitchen after dinner and ate so much, like she was having a second dinner. One time, she woke up at night and asked if I would order pizza for her. No, you better get used to it, Andrew."

They laughed and continued their dinner. Around ten o'clock, Dave looked at his watch.

"I better get going, because I still have to drive all the way back to my hotel."

He thanked them for dinner and the great weekend. They walked with him to the door and kissed him goodbye. Andrew and Wendy stood in the doorway waving to him as he drove his car out of the carport. He waved one last time at the happy couple and drove off.

As he pulled onto the highway, he felt great. He had had a superb weekend with his son. It was dark outside, and the highway was calm. Suddenly, he felt his heart pounding as he realized he had forgotten to take his injection. He had tried to stick to a set time, but now the cozy dinner had made him forget completely. He looked at the signs on the highway and, five minutes later, he saw a sign that said there was a gas station in about five miles.

A while later, he took the exit and drove toward the gas station. There was a large parking lot in the back. He drove there and parked the car. When he got out of the car, he looked around to check if anyone was watching him. The parking lot was almost empty, only next to the gas station were some cars parked and a large truck. He opened the trunk and removed the insulation bag from his suitcase. He closed the trunk and looked around one more time before getting back into the car. He took off his jacket and rolled up the sleeve of his T-shirt to expose his shoulder. He opened the insulation bag and took out the syringe and the last full tube. He sucked the drug into the syringe and removed the bubbles. He looked around the car one more time and then stuck the syringe into his shoulder. Slowly, he squirted all the liquid into his arm. As he removed the syringe from his arm, he was suddenly startled by a pickup truck parking one spot away from his spot. He looked at it and saw a bearded man looking at him. He did not wait a second and put the syringe back in the insulation bag and started the engine. When he looked back up, he saw the bearded man was still watching him. His heart was pounding hard again. He immediately drove off. That was close, he thought to himself, and turned on the radio.

While he was driving, he decided to program his phone to give him an alarm every day at seven o'clock to remind him to take his shot. In the car, he had finally some time to think about the week ahead. He would stay at the hotel for two more nights before flying back to New York on Tuesday. On Wednesday night, he had scheduled his interview and dinner with Penelope Garcia. This gave him a few days to work on his article, because he knew Craig would ask him about it as soon as he got back. When he arrived at the hotel, he parked in the parking lot and took out his luggage and the cool box. Inside, he greeted the woman sitting at the front desk.

"Good evening, Mr. Wilson. Welcome back," she said with a sweet smile, but then she stared at his face.

"You look tanned, Mr. Wilson. Did you spend the weekend outside?"

He grew nervous at the attention, but tried to act normal.

"Yes, I fished all weekend in Yosemite and we had great weather."

She smiled back, but kept staring at his face.

"Well, it did wonders for your looks. I gave you the same room and kept a newspaper for you."

The woman handed him his key and the newspaper.

"Thank you. Have a nice evening."

He walked with his luggage to his room. There, he realized that his back did not hurt at all. Even with today's long drive, he felt nothing, nothing at all in his back. He turned his attention back to the cool box, which had been unplugged in the back of his car all weekend. He wondered if it was still cold inside. He opened it and stuck his hand in to touch the metal box. It felt cold. The guy in the store hadn't lied. The cool box was working fine. He closed it again and plugged the cable of the cool box into the power socket in his room. He felt satisfied that everything was going as planned so far.

He looked at his watch, and it was now close to midnight. He walked to the bathroom, brushed his teeth, and he looked at himself in the mirror. His rings were almost gone and there were no longer any dark shades under his eyes. His skin looked tanned and pinker than before. The pale and gray tint on his face was gone. The drug seemed to be working. He still felt guilty that he had violated Harvey's trust by stealing from his laboratory, although deep down, he felt he made the right decision. He had been miserable for so long, and this drug could change his life. In bed, he felt his head itch slightly. He turned onto his other side and almost immediately fell asleep.

6. A trip back in time

Dave walked through the main hall of the airport with his luggage. Arriving at the security checkpoint, he placed his luggage on the security belt. He took off his belt and emptied his pockets, placing all his belongings on the security belt. He stepped into the body scanner and raised his arms. The security guard nodded that he could continue walking. He waited for his luggage to pass through the scanner. A security guard behind a screen called his colleague in, then the man pointed at Dave. Suddenly the security guards moved in, an alarm sounded and a red light began flashing on the security tape. Two security guards approached him.

"Sir, is this your luggage?"

They showed him his bag with the metal cool box with the tubes in it. Dave turned all red and stuttered.

"Well... uh... I guess..."

He started sweating and felt like running away. The guard grabbed his arm and pulled him toward a nearby office.

"Please come with us, sir!"

Dave started struggling, trying to get out of the security guard's grip. He was sweating even more, and he began to twist and turn, trying to get away. He turned again and then he fell and suddenly he was back in his hotel room. He felt hot and sweaty and pulled the blanket off him. It was still dark, and he looked at the alarm clock. It was ten past five in the morning.

He thought back to his dream and realized he could not take the plane on Tuesday with all those tubes. He had a worrisome problem. Maybe he had to send the tubes by mail. Although that would probably cause similar problems. Ever since those threatening anthrax letters had appeared in the country after the nine eleven attacks on the twin towers, the postal services thoroughly scanned all packages and mail. He tried to think of other solutions, but he saw no alternative but to drive the car back to New York with the tubes in the trunk. He turned on his side and fell back asleep.

About two hours later, he woke up again and felt rested. As he sat on the edge of his bed, he did not feel his back as he normally would in the morning. However, his head did itch slightly. He rubbed his bald head with his hand and to his surprise, his head was not smooth as before. His head felt rough, like sandpaper. He hurried to the bathroom and looked with his head bowed in the mirror. His head had a gray tint on the place where it used to be shiny and bald. His head felt rough, just like his cheeks and chin before shaving. He moved his head close to the shaving mirror, which had a curved side to magnify the image. To his surprise, he saw tiny little hairs were growing back on his previously bald head.

He got all excited when he realized that the medicine worked the same way it did for mice. No hair had grown on top of his head for the past ten years, and now suddenly small hairs were growing. However, the remaining band of hair on the sides of his head was unchanged. He took another look in the mirror and his face looked rested and without rings under his eyes. He even had the impression that his wrinkles were smaller.

Suddenly, he realized that he should have taken pictures of himself before taking the drug for comparison. A moment later, he remembered that Mary had taken pictures of him with Harvey. He hurried out of the bathroom and walked to his briefcase. He took the camera out of his bag, turned it on, and scrolled through the pictures. Then he found the pictures of him and Harvey together. He zoomed in on his face and was amazed. He looked back in the mirror to compare his face to the photo. The biggest difference was the color of his face and the rings under his eyes. But his wrinkles had gotten smaller and his head in the photo was shiny bald, but now looked grayish. Now, with the photo next to it, he already looked noticeably younger. The medicine seemed to work exactly as Harvey had predicted.

After shaving and washing, he went downstairs to have breakfast. The woman at the reception greeted him and handed him his newspaper. She kept staring at his face the whole time, and he felt uncomfortable. He walked quickly through to the restaurant and sat down in his usual spot next to the window. Five minutes later, the waitress came walking his way. She had the same puzzled look on her face as the woman at the front desk.

"Hello, Mr. Wilson. Did you have a nice weekend?"

"Yeah, I had a great weekend, thanks."

The waitress kept looking at him and then she said, "You look different, Mr. Wilson."

He felt uncomfortable with the whole conversation.

"Yeah, I got pretty burned last weekend. I'd like the omelet with smoked salmon and some fresh-squeezed orange juice, please."

The waitress noted down the order but did not seem convinced with his explanation. He felt his heart pounding again and felt like a child caught doing something naughty. He looked away, avoiding the waitress' eyes, as if she could see in his eyes what he was hiding from her.

"Coming right up," she said and as she walked toward the kitchen, she turned her head to look at him again.

He read his newspaper until the waitress returned with his breakfast. He tried to avoid eye contact and pushed his newspaper aside to make room for the plate. He thanked her politely and immediately continued reading as she stared at his head again. She walked back to the kitchen, and he saw from the corner of his eye that she was looking at him again.

After his breakfast, he walked back upstairs. As he walked past the front desk, the woman greeted him, but kept staring at his face again. Feeling increasingly uncomfortable, he felt he should try to leave the hotel as soon as possible. As he exited the elevator, he walked to his room, but then he saw a heavy, black-clad man standing in front of his room. He felt adrenaline rise to his head as he realized the man was trying to open his room.

"Hey, that's my room, sir!?"

The man looked startled and let go of the door handle. The man was muscular and had a broad face with a thick neck.

"Oh, I'm sorry. I must have confused it with my room. I'm sorry, sir," the man said as he hurriedly walked away.

He did not like the look on the man's face, the look of a ruthless, mean person. He stared at the man until he disappeared around the corner into the hallway, then he quickly entered his room to see if anything was missing. He rushed to the cool box, but it looked untouched and all the drug doses were still inside. He checked all his belongings, but nothing seemed to be missing. Was it just a coincidence, or had the man tried to break into his room? The second time now, he found it all too suspicious and wanted to leave the hotel as soon as possible.

He prepared himself an espresso and then unpacked his briefcase and opened his laptop. He typed in the route from his hotel back to his apartment in New York, and it showed that it was a drive of about forty-four hours. If he didn't want to drive more than eight hours a day, it would take him a week. On the map, he saw that Yellowstone National Park was not far off the route, and that had been on his bucket list for a long time. If he drove back all the way to New York, a quick stop in Yellowstone National Park would not make much of a difference, he thought. He realized Craig would not be pleased with his changed plans, especially since he expected him to deliver the article on rejuvenation. Harvey had told him his board meeting would be next Monday, so they could publish nothing before Monday anyway, and Craig knew that. Dave had worked hard all his life, so he felt he deserved this detour to Yellowstone National Park. He thought for a moment about how to get the story to Claire and to Craig. The newspaper he had read at breakfast gave him a great idea.

He took a sip of his espresso and dialed Claire's number. They chatted, and Dave asked how things were at the office.

"It has been quiet. Henry just got back from his trip today."

"Claire, I need to discuss a delicate situation with you. I don't know what I have, but ever since I read this article in the paper this morning about that crashed Boeing in Ethiopia last weekend, I haven't been feeling very well."

"Ah, I read it too. Horrible, all those deaths. Everybody is comparing it to this crash in Indonesia last year. It seems to be a similar problem with a sensor."

He was glad she had read the article because it supported his story.

"Well, you know I'm already not a big fan of flying, but now I'm all stressed out. I don't think I'll be able to fly back tomorrow."

"When I read that article, I was already worried about you. My sister also has a fear of flying, and she now only takes the car or train to get around. If you want, I can cancel your flight and you can drive back here. My sister drove back that last year from Seattle, and it took her less than a week. I think it's about the same distance from San Francisco."

He could not believe his ears, which is why he liked Claire so much.

"Ah, Claire, you're an angel. What a great idea! Although I'm not sure how to bring this to Craig."

"Ah, don't worry. Craig is currently still in the Monday morning meeting, but I'll talk to him about it right after. I'll call you back after I talk to him."

Feeling relieved, he looked out the window. The lagoon park looked colorful in the morning light. He realized that his life was becoming more complicated and that he would probably have to lie more, now that the drug seemed to work. He was not happy about that, but he felt he had little choice. He sat back at the desk and worked on his article to forget his worries for a while. About an hour later, his phone rang. It was Claire.

"Hi, Dave. I just talked to Craig and explained everything to him. He wasn't too keen on it, but I convinced him. He started complaining about going over the budget with your expenses. As a compromise, he agreed to the extra car rental, but you have to pay for the hotels along the way. I assumed you wouldn't mind this, so I canceled the flight. I extended the car rental and arranged for you to drop it off in New York instead of at San Francisco International Airport."

"Great! Thanks for all your help. What would I do without you?"

"You're welcome. Craig asked me to put you through to him. If I don't speak to you again, good trip back. Hold on, I'll put you through now."

He was put on hold and waited a moment.

"Hi, Dave. How's the interview going?"

"Hi, Craig. Very good. I met with Dr. Juncker for a few days last week, and he showed me around the premises. He was very open with me, and I believe I have more than enough information to finish my article. Next Monday, Dr. Juncker has the board meeting and expects to get approval for the article."

"That sounds good. We checked the shareholders of Juvenatrust and it was not easy. These shareholders seem to have gone far in hiding their identities through this complicated shareholder structure. It's not often to see such a rich and powerful group of investors together. We discovered that the largest shareholder, Cayman Capital, is owned by another company from Switzerland called Grossfinanz GmbH. The owner of this company is a wealthy billionaire named Jeff Broch, who has both U.S. and Swiss citizenship. He isn't on the Fortune five hundred list, but according to one of my sources, he should be on it. Jeff Broch seems to avoid all media, and we couldn't find much about him. He seems to own many companies in the IT, technology and pharmaceutical sectors. BioFace Ltd is owned by a Chinese investor called Liu Zhidong, who seems to have made his fortune with various internet media companies and biotech companies. FutureSense Ltd is indirectly owned by an Indian billionaire called Rahul Dasani, who owns several companies in the pharmaceutical industry. Kavneft Ltd is a company indirectly owned by a Russian billionaire called Adam Bromavich, a Russian oligarch who owns many companies. Track Capital Ltd, is indirectly owned by a French billionaire named Serge Devaux, who owns several companies in the telecommunication and arms industry. We're still working on ImpactVentures Ltd, which is owned by a company called Tratro Ltd registered in the Republic of Vanuatu. Unfortunately, we couldn't find more information about this company, but our research department is working on it."

"The Republic of Vanuatu? I thought I knew every country in the world by now, but I've never heard of this one?"

"Yeah, I had to look it up, too. It's a group of islands in the South Pacific, formerly known as the New Hebrides. They've been hiding for a long time, but with all the new laws since the financial credit crisis, it's a lot easier for us to track down the ultimate owners. So, Dave, I heard you'd rather drive back here?"

Dave felt awkward, but had expected the question.

"Yeah, I feel more comfortable this way, but I'll use the time in the evenings to finish the article."

"Okay, no problem. I understand. Keep me posted on the progress next week. We've to wait for approval next Monday, anyway. How's that article on the anti-age spot cream coming along?"

Here he was caught a little off guard, having forgotten about his scheduled meeting with Penelope Garcia on Wednesday night.

"Well, I haven't spoken to Ms. Garcia yet. Originally, I was supposed to meet her on Wednesday, but now with my changed schedule I'll have to reschedule that. I'll let you know as soon as I can."

"All right, Dave. I have to go now. Have a good trip home and keep me posted. Bye."

He looked back at the map on his laptop. Over three thousand miles he was going to drive, but at least he could bring the precious tubes with the rejuvenation drug back to New York without risking too much. With the stop at Yellowstone National Park, the drive would be nearly three thousand two hundred miles and take about forty-nine hours. Traveling a long distance in a car would normally be torture for him, given his back problems. But now he felt optimistic, having had no pain in his back since last weekend.

He had read and seen a lot about the geysers in Yellowstone National Park, and he was happy to get to see them with his own eyes at last. He was glad for the change of plans and tried to worry less. He had already taken the huge risk of injecting this experimental drug into his body, and now he would just have to enjoy the ride. He had no way of predicting what would happen to him, anyway. Now that his back was no long hurting him, he felt a new energy bubble up within him and felt he should try to enjoy his life. He had wasted so much time already. He might end up in jail for the theft, but he didn't care. He was going to enjoy this long drive to New York and after that… well, that he would see after.

Suddenly, he heard knocking on the door. His heart skipped a beat. He was not expecting anyone, so who could it be? He got up to walk to the door when he heard a voice.

"Housekeeping!"

He looked through the peephole in the door and saw a woman in a hotel uniform standing at the door. He opened the door a little and stuck his head out.

"Hello, you can skip my room today."

"No problem, sir! Have a good day!"

"You too," and he closed the door.

He worked on his article for a few hours until he got hungry. After all the strange looks at breakfast and the strange man at his door, he thought it best to order lunch in his room. About thirty minutes later, a waiter knocked on the door. Dave let him in and the waiter put the lunch on the table. The waiter glanced at the cooler. Dave tipped him, then the waiter left the room. After lunch, he looked at his watch. It was two-thirty. He still had to call Penelope Garcia to cancel his Wednesday night dinner. It was now five-thirty in New York.

First, he tried to think for a moment about what to tell her. Driving back by car also meant missing dinner with her, and he had been looking forward to it. It had been a very long time since he had gone out with a beautiful woman. He hoped she would not be too disappointed. He dialed her phone number and got her secretary, who put him through.

"Dave! So nice to hear from you. How are you doing? Are you back from San Francisco yet?"

"Hi! I'm doing fine, but I'm still in San Francisco, though. I feel a little bad, but there is a change in my plans. I can't have dinner with you Wednesday night, because I'm driving back from San Francisco to New York."

"Drive back!? That's far, isn't it?"

"Yes, it's far. I know this might sound strange, but I'll try to explain it to you later. I really need to take some time for myself next week. We'll have to postpone our dinner for at least another week, but I'd rather not set a date yet, because my schedule is still unclear."

"No problem. It's very good to take some time for yourself. Life goes by so fast that most people just continue on the treadmill without taking time for themselves. I did look forward to our dinner, though, but we can plan that when you get back. The good thing is that you have to buy me dinner now. I'm already curious to see what nice restaurant you're going to surprise me with," she said jokingly.

"You're funny. I promise to come up with a big surprise next time we meet. Why don't we try to call at the beginning of the next week to plan something?"

"Perfect, let's do that! Take care of yourself next week and you can call me anytime."

"Thanks for your understanding. Let's call next week. Have a nice day!"

For a while he stared out the window toward the lagoon park, thinking about Penelope. He was looking forward to seeing her again. From the beginning, he had been attracted to her. In the apartment building, he was always shy in his encounters with her. But since the interview, they had gotten to know each other better, and he felt more at ease. The image of Penelope sitting on the leather couch in his apartment with her beautiful legs crossed was etched in his memory. When they talked together, he felt good and had the impression that she liked him. She had told him he could call her anytime. That was more than just friendly and he resolved to call her later in the week, just to chat.

He spent the rest of the afternoon working hard on his article. He worked so intently that he did not even notice that the sun was setting outside. At some point, it had gotten dark, but he was still typing. Suddenly, the alarm from his cell phone took him out of his concentration. He looked at his phone, and he saw the reminder that he needed to take his injection. He got up, turned on the light in the room, and closed the curtains. To avoid contact, he ate in his room again. The hotel's room service menu was still on the table, but by now he knew it by heart and had tried everything. Another reason to leave this hotel. He ordered dinner and then went to the bathroom to take his injection. He took off his shirt and looked at himself in the mirror. He had the impression that not only the skin of his face had changed. But the color of the skin of his entire upper body looked less white and more pink and healthier. He emptied the syringe into his arm and put the syringe back into the insulation bag. He kept the empty glass tubes in a plastic bag.

Ten minutes later, someone knocked on the door of his hotel room. He looked through the peephole and opened the door for the waiter. He put his food on the table and Dave tipped him. He closed the door again and sat down at the table. The food tasted better than last week and he felt like having wine with dinner, but he thought it was too risky to drink alcohol. He would have loved to call Harvey now to ask if he could consume alcohol besides the drug, but alas.

As he enjoyed his food, he wondered if anyone had already discovered his theft at Juvenatrust. Since he had left a space at the very back of the huge refrigerator, this was unlikely. They would have to count their inventory to find out about the theft. He hoped they did not do that too often. Most companies only counted their inventory once a year. Even if they found out about the missing box, they would still have to link the theft to him. He worried again that one day he would get into trouble. However, something deep inside told him not to worry too much. He thought of a saying he had once heard: "Worry is like a rocking chair: it gives you something to do but never gets you anywhere." He got up, made tea, and turned on the television to relax a bit.

The next morning, he woke up before his alarm clock went off. It was ten to seven and felt wide awake. He jumped out of bed and stood a little bedraggled beside his bed as he realized what he had just done. He had not jumped out of bed like that in a long time. He thought of his childhood and university time when he occasionally jumped out of bed. His body filled with energy and he felt no pain or stiffness in his back. For more than a decade, his back had been in constant pain. Not feeling that pain anymore was everything he had hoped for when he stole the drug. He felt happy and jumped into the air. He threw his fist up and shouted, "Yes!"

He opened the curtains and looked at the clear blue sky. It was another beautiful day. He was going to miss the nice Californian climate. Today, he was going to start his long drive east and wanted to leave early. He ordered breakfast from his room and went to the bathroom. He washed himself and noticed that the gray area on top of his head had darkened. He could now see little brown hairs where he used to be bald. Most of his thick wrinkles had disappeared, and his face looked younger and healthier.

After breakfast, he packed up and went downstairs. At the reception, the same woman greeted him. He told her he would like to check out. When he handed her the key, her eyes almost seemed to fall out. She stared at his head.

"You look different this morning, Mr. Wilson?"

He felt uncomfortable and did not feel like talking to the woman, so he completely ignored her question.

"I'm in a bit of a hurry. May I see the bill, please?"

"Oh, I'm sorry. I'll print it right away," she said and blushed.

He looked at the bill and checked all the items.

"Okay, it looks correct."

"I'll charge it to the company account. I hope you had a pleasant stay with us, and I wish you a pleasant journey home, sir."

Outside, the sun shone on his face and he felt relieved. He put his luggage in the trunk and plugged the cool box into the power outlet. He started the engine and drove toward the highway. His long drive back home had begun.

On the highway, he headed north toward Novato, which gave him mixed feelings of guilt and fear. Those feelings faded as he left Novato behind and headed east on the Interstate I-80 toward Sacramento. He was still worried about how to explain his changed looks, but deep down, he felt that this long journey would give him time to find all the answers. He felt his life was changing, and it felt good. The burden of his back pain had subsided, and it looked like his bald head would soon be a thing of the past. These were things he had hoped for when he stole the drug, even though he realized he might end up in jail or die from it. The thought of feeling young and fit again had driven him to something he had never thought himself capable of. Now he felt it had been worth the risk, and he planned to enjoy the ride as long as he could. He turned on the radio and relaxed, listening to the music.

About two hours later, he drove among the beautiful forests and mountains of Tahoe National Forest. At a gas station, he refilled his car while looking at the mountains. He still felt no pain in his back. When he went inside to pay, the store clerk did not pay much attention to him. It was good to be on the road. No one would wonder about his changing looks. He did not know how much further his body would continue to change, but he would certainly have something to explain to his son, colleagues, and friends. In Yosemite, he had felt it was not the right time to tell Andrew, but he felt bad about it. They had always been very open and honest with each other, and he felt bad keeping such a big secret from him. He looked at his face in the restroom, and as he got closer to the mirror, he saw the tiny hairs on his head. His face looked much healthier, and his wrinkles had diminished. As he walked out, he felt great and felt like changing some things in his life. It was time to enjoy himself and make the most of his life.

Around noon, he arrived in Reno, Nevada's second-largest gambling city, after Las Vegas. He cared little about gambling. He had never really understood why some people got hooked on it. It seemed a rather silly activity to him, since the odds were always against the players and in favor of the casino owners. He decided not to drive too deep into town, but stopped at the first decent-looking restaurant after leaving the highway. He ordered a salad and a large pasta dish to satisfy his hunger.

After finishing his lunch, he ordered a large cappuccino for the road. Before getting into his car, he looked at the beautiful mountains behind Reno. He had always loved nature. Pleased, he thought about his trip with Andrew last weekend. He drove the rest of the day, making short stops every two to three hours to stretch his legs and refill his coffee. He had originally planned to drive about eight hours or stop earlier if his back hurt him. Surprisingly, his back did not hurt at all that day. It was about five thirty in the evening when he left the Interstate I-80 near the town of Wells and turned onto U.S. route 93 northbound. He still did not feel tired, so he drove on.

An hour later, he got hungry and stopped in a small town called Jackpot, on the far edge of the state of Nevada, about a mile from the border with the state of Idaho. He had never heard of this town before, but he smiled when he saw the name pop up and realized the irony of its location next to the state border. It was a small town, and the presence of casinos surprised him. He did not feel like searching long for a restaurant, so he parked in front of "Cactus Pete's." Before going inside, he watched the beautiful sunset. Inside, he remembered why he did not like casinos, and the noise immediately got on his nerves. The noise felt even louder than he remembered. As he gazed at the huge room full of slot machines and blackjack tables, a waitress approached him.

"Welcome to Cactus Pete's! What can I do for you?"

Dave put his hands on his ears as he answered, "What a noise! I'm looking for the restaurant."

"Please follow me, sir."

He walked through the doors of the restaurant and the noise of the slot machines faded as the waitress pointed him to a table in the back. He ordered and read the small brochure about Jackpot. Apparently, the town was founded in nineteen hundred and fifty-four after Idaho banned all forms of casino gaming. Two casino owners named "Cactus Pete" Piersanti and Don French moved their slot machine operations from Idaho to Jackpot, creating Cactus Pete's and the Horseshu Club, respectively. Initially, the land commissioners named the town "Horse Shu", despite protests from Cactus Pete. Because the club owners could not agree on a name, the land commissioners renamed it "Unincorporated Town No. 1" a month later. The clubs reached a compromise a year later with the name "Jackpot." About five years later, Cactus Pete's management took over the Horseshu.

Funny story, he thought, and after he finished his food, he started looking on his smartphone to see how far away he was from Yellowstone National Park. It would be too far to get there tonight and realizing hotels would fill up later in the evening, he thought it would be better to look for a hotel now. He paid for dinner and checked out the hotel next to the casino.

The alarm on his phone rang. It was time for his daily drug injection. He walked to the car and looked around, but there were too many people in the parking lot. He opened his trunk, removed the insulation bag from his trunk, and took a tube from the cooler. He put the insulation bag away in the inside pocket of his coat and walked to the hotel. The terrible noise of slot machines echoed in the hall, and he hurried to the restrooms. He hung his jacket on the hook in the toilet cubicle, unbuttoned his shirt and hung it on the hook as well, and rolled up the sleeve of his T-shirt. He prepared the syringe and filled it with the liquid from the tube. It was already becoming routine, and a few minutes later, he injected the drug into his shoulder. But just as he was about to remove the needle from his arm, the door opened. A man stared at the needle, shocked.

"What are you doing with that needle? Drugs are illegal and we don't want junkies here. I'm calling the police!"

The man rushed out of the restrooms before Dave could say anything, but he did not hesitate for a moment. This was not good. How could he have forgotten to lock the door? And how was he supposed to explain this to the police? No, he had to get the hell out of there. He put the syringe in the insulation bag in his coat and put back his shirt and coat, then he rushed out of the restroom. He saw the man talking to a woman at the front desk who was talking on the phone. The man saw him,

"That's him! That's the junkie! He's got drugs in that bag!"

Dave got scared, and the woman called a man at the back, who came storming toward him.

"Can you come with us, sir?"

He did not wait a second and rushed to the revolving door. The man came after him, and he realized he would never make it to his car. So as soon as he passed through the revolving door, he looked at the man, waited for him to enter the revolving door, and then pushed against it with all his weight. The man received the door with a big smack in his face and fell to the ground. He ran to his car in the dark and started the engine. With squealing tires, he drove off as he saw in his rearview mirror the man along with another man running after him. They quickly disappeared from sight and a few minutes later, he left Jackpot's bright, flashing neon lights behind him. That was close, he thought to himself. He looked several times in his rearview mirror to see if anyone was following him, but the road was empty and he tried to relax. He hoped they had not noted his license plate number, but for now, he had gotten away.

He turned on the radio and continued north on U.S. route 93. About forty-five minutes later, he arrived in Twin Falls. He stopped at the first decent-looking hotel. The parking lot was full, and he was afraid the hotel would be full. But he was in luck. In his room, he plugged in the cooler and took his laptop out of his briefcase. Yellowstone National Park had been on his bucket list for a long time, and since he realized he would arrive in the park as early as tomorrow, it seemed wiser to book an overnight stay in the park in advance. After an Internet search, he found a cabin not too far from the Old Faithful geyser, which he booked for two nights. It looked like he would have to drive six to seven hours tomorrow, compared to the ten hours he had driven today, although with all the stops, it had taken him thirteen hours. Yet he felt no pain in his back, nor did he feel tired. He could never have made today's trip a week ago. What a difference this medicine had made. He read more about

Yellowstone National Park and then continued working on his article until he went to bed at midnight.

He woke up around seven the next morning and he had slept wonderfully. He walked to the bathroom and washed his face. The little hairs on his head were longer, and his bald head now looked more like the short-cropped head of a Marine. He touched his head and loved the feeling of having hair on his head. But the contrast of the short hair on top of his head with the band of longer hair on the side was a weird sight. He thought it might be better to wear a hat until his hair had grown longer. After shaving and dressing, he hung the "Do not disturb" sign on his door and hurried downstairs to the front desk.

"Good morning, sir. Could you tell me if there's a mall anywhere nearby?"

The man at reception stared at his weird hair and then pointed to the door.

"Yes, there is. You turn right and then one block further you should see the mall on your left. Although I believe they're still closed. They should open in an hour."

Dave felt uncomfortable with the staring and did not feel like waiting for an hour.

"Do you know where I can buy a hat somewhere at this hour?"

The man nodded and pointed to the right.

"Our hotel shop is open. It's on the right at the end of the corridor. I believe they sell some hats."

"Thank you."

"You're welcome."

He walked down the hallway to the small hotel store. It sold some souvenirs and snacks. The woman in the store greeted him and also stared at his hair. In the corner, he saw some baseball caps. He chose a dark blue cap with "Twin Falls" written on it. After paying, he immediately put it on and looked in the mirror. He noticed that the woman at the cash register looked at him from the corner of her eye and smiled. At least now he looked normal and not like some lunatic with a messed-up haircut.

At the front desk, he took a newspaper from the counter and headed to the restaurant to get some breakfast. Inside, he noticed the smell of fresh bread and fried bacon and eggs. At the buffet, he ordered an omelet and took a bowl of fruit salad. He had the impression that his sense of smell had improved, or maybe he had just slept better. He could recognize the smell of the different fruits in the fruit salad and even could smell the sesame seeds on the bread.

While enjoying his breakfast, he read an article about the suspension of a nuclear treaty between the United States and Russia. The writer implied that with the suspension, a new nuclear arms race had begun. The suspension of the treaty, combined with the development of new hypersonic missiles and new drone armies, was the start of an entirely new arms race. Hypersonic missiles could change the entire balance of power in the world. Current missiles were either subsonic, traveling slower than the speed of sound or supersonic, traveling faster than the speed of sound, called Mach-1, but slower than Mach-3, which was three times the speed of sound. Our famous Tomahawk cruise missile was an example of a subsonic missile. Although easier to intercept, it still had some advantages, such as its fuel efficiency, low production cost, its accuracy and its ability to abort an attack even after launch. The Indian and Russian Brahmos missiles were examples of supersonic missiles, which were much faster and therefore harder to intercept, but also had less time to abort an attack after launch. Now many world powers like the US, Russia, India and China were developing hypersonic missiles, traveling at over five times the speed of sound, for which there were no operational or reliable defense systems that could intercept these strategic weapons. The writer explained world powers were also developing large drone armies that could attack many targets at once, like a huge swarm. Having read this, he only hoped that our leaders would have the wisdom never to use these weapons and use them only as a political deterrent. All this just confirmed to him we were amid a great biological and technological revolution that would change the world in ways we had never seen before.

After breakfast, he felt energized, and strangely, he felt like running. It had been over ten years since his last run. He had not run for at least a good ten years. At the nearby mall, he bought running shoes and sports clothes. Then he changed and looked at the tourist map on the desk. About five miles from his hotel, there was a park called Shoshone Falls Park. He did not want to leave the cool box in the room, so he took it in the trunk of his car. When he arrived at the edge of Shoshone Falls Park, the sky was clear and the sun was shining brightly.

As he came out of the car, he could hear the rumbling noise of the waterfall. He approached the viewpoint for the Shoshone Falls and the sign read, "Welcome to Shoshone Falls, the Niagara of the West". At the edge, he could see the wide waterfall thundering down the rocks with a deafening noise. The white and clear water flowed down, forming a cloud of mist at the bottom in which he could see a rainbow. To the left he saw a sign that said "canyon rim trail" and he started running in that direction. The air was still fresh, and he felt the warm rays of the sun on his body. It had been so long since he had last run, and now it felt great. Back then, he had stopped running because he had too many injuries and his back always hurt afterwards. The sound of the waterfall slowly muffled the farther he ran from it. The river's water was dark green-grayish now and still flowing fast. As the sound of the waterfall became more distant, he heard birds and even bees and other insects. He slowly increased his pace and enjoyed his run. After about forty-five minutes, he returned to the parking lot. He was sweating and breathing faster, but felt good. His head felt clear, and he felt he could go on even longer. He stretched his muscles as his breathing and heartbeat slowed. He took one more look at the beautiful falls before returning to the hotel.

Back at the hotel, he took a quick shower before getting dressed and packing his luggage. As he put the baseball cap back on his head, he looked in the mirror and his face had more color than before. He smiled and felt good. He checked out and a few minutes later drove onto Highway I-84 heading East. He drove northeast toward Yellowstone National Park all morning. After a quick stop in Idaho Falls for lunch, he continued on Route 26. About half an hour later, his phone rang. It was Henry. He was happy to hear his friend's voice.

"Hi, Henry! How are you, old chap?"

"Good, although it was lonely at the coffee machine today."

He started laughing as Henry continued.

"I heard you decided to take a horse and carriage home, because a plane dropped out of the sky on the outskirts of Africa."

Dave burst out laughing, and Henry now laughed too and asked, "Where are you now? Gambling away your paycheck in Nevada?"

Dave had to recover from laughing for a moment before he could answer.

"No, I've already left Nevada. I'm in Idaho now."

"Idaho? You've driven quite a lot then. How's your back holding up?"

"Not bad actually, I take regular breaks and that helps a lot."

"How was the fishing trip with your son?"

They continued talking for a while about the great weekend with his son. Later, Henry started talking about his girlfriend, who wanted to move in with him, but he thought it was too early for that. Dave thought he should start preparing his friend for his changed looks, so as not to give too much of a shock when he returned to the office.

"Guess what, Henry? I finally did something with your advice."

"What advice? I guess I'm forgetting my own recommendations."

"Last week I did a hair transplant."

"Really? I thought you'd never do it. How was it? Was it painful?"

Dave paused for a moment.

"Actually, I didn't feel much, because they sedated me and afterwards, I took some painkillers."

"Wow, I'm sure you won't regret that. How does it look?"

Dave felt he was merely twisting the truth and thought it was better than telling the whole truth, which could get him in trouble.

"Little hairs are growing on my head and it's strange to see hair growing there after such a long period of baldness."

"Well, I'm happy for you. Soon, the ladies will be lining up for you."

Dave laughed.

"I have to go, my friend. When will you be back in New York?"

"Well, I'm not exactly sure how long this trip will take, but I hope sometime next week."

"Ok, buddy. Hope to see you next week, then with your new hair. Take it easy. Bye."

"Will do, Henry. Have a good evening. Bye."

He felt relieved that he had told Henry about his hair, and that way, slowly prepared his return to the office. He still was not sure if they would believe his story, but he saw no other option for now. Meanwhile, he had already crossed the Wyoming state line and passed Jackson, the last town before the southern entrance of Yellowstone National Park. The mountains were getting higher and more. Driving north on Route 191 was getting increasingly more scenic. On his left, he passed Jackson Lake, and he parked at the next stop to take some pictures of the beautiful scenery. The Grand Tetons, huge mountains, were behind the beautiful lake, which also reflected a mirror image of these mountains in the water. The highest one they called the Grand Teton at thirteen thousand seven hundred seventy-seven feet, and it was the second highest peak in the state of Wyoming. He stared at the breathtaking scenery for a while and felt better than he had felt in a very long time. The fresh air, the bees and other insects circling around, and the scent of the flowers and plants around him filled the air. He could not remember ever smelling flowers so strongly before. Images from his childhood came to him. He remembered standing in a lavender field as a child with the aromatic scent in the air. Gradually his smell had diminished, but he had the impression that he had his sense of smell back.

He drove on, and about half an hour later, he arrived at the South Entrance of Yellowstone National Park. From there, it was less than an hour's drive to the cabin he had booked. The surrounding forest grew thicker as he drove further into the park. He relaxed as he listened to a song on the radio. His thoughts wandered to Penelope, and he realized he missed the contact with her. Suddenly, out of nowhere, a huge elk appeared in front of his car. He hit the brakes and heard the tires squeal. In the back, the luggage moved, and he heard the tubes tinkling. His heart pounded, and he felt adrenaline rush to his head. The huge elk passed a few inches away from his car and walked on as if nothing had happened. The big brown elk, which was about five feet tall, had huge antlers and stared at him before disappearing among the trees. He hurried out of the car, fearing the tubes had broken from the shock. His precious rejuvenation drug might be gone. He saw the black skid marks on the road behind the car. He opened the trunk. The cool box had fallen on his side, and he set it back upright and opened it. He looked inside the metal box and inspected the tubes. To his relief, the tubes were all still intact. He closed the trunk and drove on, but now much slower.

The route swirled along the high pine trees until a large wooden lodge loomed in front of him. He parked his car and walked to the lodge. Bird chatter was all around, and the scent of pine trees and forest filled the air. Inside the lodge, there were many visitors in the large reception area and he walked up to the front desk. A young woman greeted him with a friendly smile.

"Welcome to the Old Faithful Lodge, sir."

Dave smiled back.

"Hello, I made a reservation for a Frontier Cabin in the name of Wilson."

The woman stared at the computer screen on her desk.

"Yes, I have a reservation for two nights."

She handed him the keys and a map of the premises. She explained about all the facilities and where the cabin was. He thanked her, entered the small shop next to the reception, and bought some water bottles and snacks. As he walked out, he noticed the restaurant with its huge windows. There were many people standing in front of them, so he got curious and went to take a look. At the window, he smelled the mix of odors from sweat to perfumes of the people standing around him. Just as he peered outside, he saw a huge fountainlike stream of water and steam bursting high up into the air. The erupting Old Faithful geyser was a magnificent sight, and he felt he had made the right decision to add Yellowstone to his itinerary. After the eruption, he walked back to his car and drove down the small dirt road to his cabin.

The wooden cabin consisted of a small bedroom with a desk and a small bathroom, nothing compared to the huge suite he had in San Rafael, but for him, it was perfect. He connected the cool box to the power socket and unpacked his luggage. Despite the long drive, he felt energetic and took a walk to see the nearby geysers. The fresh forest air blew in his face, mixed with a noxious smell he could not place. As he passed the Old Faithful Geyser, which showed no activity, the noxious smell became much stronger and he smelled the hydrogen sulfuric gas from the geyser that resembled the smell of rotten eggs. He followed the Upper Geyser Basin trail and passed several smaller geysers, all marked by a plume of steam coming out of the geyser hole. Further on, a group of people were waiting next to a geyser called the Grand Geyser, and he stopped next to a couple to look. The man of the couple, who looked about his age and had thick gray hair, pointed to Dave's baseball cap.

"Have you been to the Shoshone falls?"

"Yes, I went running this morning in the park next to the falls. They are magnificent."

The blond, younger woman next to the man smiled with her twinkling blue eyes at him and said, "This morning, nice. We visited them yesterday. What a gorgeous place! Must be nice to run down there?"

"Yes, it was great."

An increasing noise and activity in the geyser interrupted the conversation.

The woman called out, "Look, it's going to erupt!"

Moments later, the geyser spewed out a wide column of water and steam with a thunderous noise. The geyser continued to erupt and spew water and steam for nearly ten minutes.

As the sun was setting, he walked back with most people to the Old Faithful lodge. His phone started ringing. It was the alarm showing it was time for his injection. He walked back to his cabin, took a tube out of the cool box, took the syringe, and injected the drug into his arm. The empty tube he put in the plastic bag with the other ones. He locked the cabin and went for dinner in the restaurant.

Later, when he walked back to his cabin, it was almost eight thirty, but he still felt full of energy. At the cabin, he saw in a brochure, there was a fitness center, open till ten o'clock. He quickly changed into his sport clothes and walked to the fitness center. There were only two other people inside. A young man was pressing weights and a young woman was running on a treadmill. He started running on the treadmill next to the pretty woman with the slim figure. It had been a long time since Dave had gone to a fitness center. At university, he went to the gym several times a week, but later he went less and less. The running had warmed him up and he began pressing weights on the various fitness machines. He switched from machine to machine, following a similar sequence of exercises as he had seen the young man do. He was not sure how to do the exercise on one machine. The young man noticed and explained it to him. Dave noticed the young woman, who was cycling on a bike now, smiled at him. He chatted with the man and explained he had not done much exercise for a long time.

"Well, you still look pretty fit," the young man said.

"Thanks."

They continued talking while doing their exercises and just after ten, an older man with a uniform appeared and announced they were closing.

"Ah, what a pity I felt like going on longer."

Then the young man, called Mike, said, "Tomorrow we are going whitewater rafting, and we still have a spot available. Maybe you'd like to join us?" Mike pointed to the slender woman who had been training next to them.

"Rafting, I've never done that before, but it sounds exciting."

"Ah, don't worry. You look fit, so you'll be fine and we'll explain everything."

The woman approached, and Dave held out it his hand.

"Hi, I'm Dave."

"Hi, I'm Taylor. Nice of you to join us tomorrow."

They walked out while Mike explained the details of the trip and where to meet the next day. Dave said goodbye to them and walked back to his cabin. The exercise had done him good, and he felt his muscles were harder than before the workout. In the cabin, he took off the baseball cap he had worn all day and looked in the mirror. His face looked younger, and he had the impression that the longer hair on the side of his head looked less gray. As he approached the mirror, he noticed that each gray hair was now only half gray, only at the edges. Close to his head, the hairs were brown, like his gray hair was disappearing. He took a shower and went to bed. That night, he slept like a log.

The next day, he woke up feeling great. He put on his running clothes, put on the baseball cap, and locked the cabin. After a light breakfast, he ran into the woods. The fresh forest air blew in his face as he began to run. He followed the designated trails and passed the Old Faithful Geyser and later the Grand Geyser. After an hour of running along the Firehole River, he arrived at a strange-looking, colorful lake. The sign next to it said it was the Grand Prismatic Spring, the largest hot spring in the United States, three hundred and seventy feet in diameter. He had seen nothing like it before. They named the lake after its striking colors, corresponding to the rainbow dispersion of white light through an optical prism: red, orange, yellow, green, and blue. In the center, the lake was blue and outward it colored green and then around the edges the color changed from yellow to orange and then the brown ground all around. Steam plumes came out of the lake, making the whole scene even more mystical.

He was walking back when the blond woman, from the couple he had spoken to the night before at the Grand Geyser, came running and approached him. She was wearing a tight sports outfit that exposed her sexy, slender figure. She smiled and looked a bit tired.

"Hi, I saw you running by. You're in pretty good shape."

He vaguely remembered passing over several people during the six-mile run, but apparently had not noticed her.

"Thanks. You seem pretty fit yourself. It's quite a distance from the lodge. Your husband didn't come along?"

She smiled, still catching her breath.

"No, he stopped running a few years ago. His knees were hurting him too much. He's a lot older than me. I think we younger people should enjoy running before we get too old for it, right?"

He could not believe what he was hearing. Did this young woman really think he was her age? He got curious and couldn't resist.

"Ah, so what age would you give me?"

The woman smiled and stared at his face, trying to estimate his age correctly.

"Always hard to estimate, but more around mid-thirties like me."

He was amazed to hear that, and squinted when he said, "Well, I'm more in my early forties."

She looked stupefied.

"You look younger."

"I would have thought you were younger too," Dave flirted.

"Thank you," the woman smiled, with a naughty look in her eyes.

"Well, I'm running back to the lodge."

"I'm going to check out the hot spring first. Maybe I'll see you later," the blond woman answered.

"See you later," he said.

Back in the cabin, he took a cold shower. He had not felt this good for a long time, and it reminded him of his university days when he was physically very fit and got a lot of attention from women.

Later, he walked in his sports clothes to the meeting point, where a yellow minibus was waiting. Mike and Taylor were waiting for him. He greeted them and the other people in the minibus. After an hour and a halve drive, they arrived at Grand Teton National Park at a cabin by the river. Everybody got out of the bus and more people arrived on another bus. The instructor explained they would raft on the mighty Snake River and that only fit people could go. Dave looked at the flowing water behind him and thought it did not look too wild, but then the instructor explained this was a calmer part and it would get much wilder later.

After the safety instructions, the fifteen people donned their life jackets and helmets. He got into a boat with Mike and Taylor, another couple and a guide. The latter told everybody to grab their paddle as he pushed the boat away from the shore. Some boats had already left, and their boat was also picking up speed. The river went through the forest and the scenery was magnificent. They all paddled to steer the boat away from the rocks in the water. The water became wilder and whiter and the current increased. From time to time, the boat sped up and dropped into the cascading river, splashing water all over them. He got soaking wet, and the faster they went, the more he felt his adrenaline rush. It was a sensational bonding experience. The whole rafting trip lasted over two hours. At the end, the boat slowed down in a wide bend in the river where the water was calm and they got out.

"How did you like it?" Mike asked him as they dried themselves on the shore.

"Thrilling! It was great, Mike!" he said, noticing Taylor watching him with a flirty smile. She looked sexy with her well-shaped figure as she dried off. They all got on the bus and talked nonstop during the trip back.

Mike suggested they all go to dinner at the restaurant. They arrived at seven thirty at the lodge and Dave told Mike that he would change first and join them in fifteen minutes. The real reason he went back to the cabin was that it was time for his injection. At the cabin, he quickly undressed and changed into clean pants. With his upper body still naked, he took a tube from the cool box, filled the syringe, and injected the drug. After cleaning the syringe, he stored everything away. He put on a clean dress shirt and hurried to the restaurant. Taylor waved at him as he entered. They had arranged two long tables for all the people who had gone rafting, and he was the last to arrive. Mike had saved a spot for Dave next to him.

"A beer, Dave?" Mike asked him as the waitress approached them.

"No, an iced tea, please."

They were talking about the grizzly bear they had seen on the side of the river.

"Taylor and I have been trying to spot a grizzly bear the past five days, with no luck. Finally, today we saw one and, of course, I had left my camera on the bus."

Later, Mike asked him again, "Beer?"

"No, thanks. I'll have another iced tea. I can't drink alcohol since I'm on medication."

"Nothing serious, I hope?" Taylor asked.

"No, it's for my allergies, but I get sick when I combine it with alcohol."

Mike ordered beer for everybody and an iced tea for him. After dinner, they all went to the bar. He talked with Taylor for a long time, while Mike danced with Steve, Mandy, and another girl. Mike looked drunk, and he started loudly telling Taylor and Dave to dance. Taylor took Dave's hand and pulled him along to the dance floor. They danced and had a great time. He had not danced since Andrew's wedding, and was having a great time. They danced until midnight, when most people left. Mike was completely drunk.

"Fn... fnext... year... I... am... tu... turning... thirsty... I... mean... thirty. Depwessing," Mike murmured to Dave.

Taylor looked at Dave.

"How old are you, Dave?"

"How old do you think I am?" he replied in a teasing voice.

She smiled and thought for a moment as she looked at him with a sultry glance.

"Difficult, from the looks I'd think early thirties, but from your behavior I would rather think mid to late thirties."

"Ah, not bad," he replied with a grin on his face.

Suddenly, Mike fell from the bar stool to the floor. Dave and Taylor helped him back to his feet.

"Could you help me carry him back to our cabin?"

"Sure, Taylor."

They carried Mike together, and he stumbled between them to their cabin. When they arrived at the cabin, Taylor opened the door and Dave helped Mike inside. They laid him on the bed, and he immediately fell asleep and began snoring. Taylor smiled at Dave, who made his way back to the door.

"He should have quite a hangover tomorrow. Sleep well!"

Taylor hurried after him and blocked the way.

"Wait, let me thank you for your help."

She looked at him with a naughty look in her eyes and suddenly kissed him on the mouth. He smelled her sweet perfume, felt her soft lips, and she wrapped her arms around him. He touched her neck with his arm and her skin felt soft and smooth. He felt her soft, warm body against his and felt her breasts against his chest. They kissed for a moment, but then Taylor began to touch his ass and opened his pants. He was a little overwhelmed while she was already sliding her hand down his pants. It did not feel right to him. In his mind, he pictured Penelope's face with her kind smile.

"Your boyfriend! Taylor," he said and flinched.

"He's asleep," she said in a soft voice as she smiled and put her arms back around his shoulders.

"No, you'll regret this tomorrow," he said and walked away.

Back at his cabin, he wondered what had happened. He should have jumped at this chance to have sex with Taylor, since he had not had sex since his divorce. Besides, she was a beautiful and sexy woman. He realized maybe he had more feelings for Penelope than he thought. All his life he had been quite serious about love, and he had only slept with women for whom he had strong feelings for. Still, he wondered if he was foolish to pass up the opportunity with such a beautiful woman. He went to bed and immediately fell asleep.

The next day, when he went for breakfast, he saw Steve, Mandy, and Taylor sitting at a table. They gestured him to join them. Mike was still in a coma, Taylor explained. They laughed and talked about their great rafting trip. After breakfast, Steve and Mandy left for a mountain biking trip and Taylor smiled at him.

"Thanks for yesterday! I believe I had a little too much to drink. Thank you for not taking advantage of it. Mike doesn't know his limit when he drinks, but I love him. We're getting married at the end of the year."

Dave smiled at her.

"Congratulations! You're a cute couple."

He looked at his watch. It was eleven thirty.

"I'm sorry, Taylor. I have to go."

She stood up and kissed him with her soft lips on his cheek.

"Have a nice trip home, Dave. You're a good guy, you know."

"I wish you well, Taylor. Say goodbye to Mike for me!"

He packed and put his luggage in the car. On the way to the reception, he threw the plastic bag with the seven empty tubes into a trash can. He checked out and drove to the South Entrance to leave Yellowstone National Park. He looked back on a few wonderful days and felt in a way he had not felt in a long time. He felt young again.

7. A different turn

After passing Jackson Lake, he stopped in a town called Moran for a quick lunch. So close to Grand Teton National Park, he could not help thinking back to that thrilling ride on the Snake River the previous day. Never too old to try something new, he thought. He had not felt the excitement he had felt during the raft ride in a long time. After lunch, it became cloudier, and he drove farther east on Route 26. The ringing of his phone interrupted the song on the radio. It was Craig.

"How's your long drive back?"

"I'm in Wyoming now and on my way to Nebraska."

"And how's the article going?"

"Well, I have a good draft ready, but still need to revise it a bit."

"When can you send me a first draft to read?"

"We should probably wait for that until Dr. Juncker gives his approval."

"I prefer to see it as soon as possible so we can publish it quickly when Dr. Juncker gives his approval."

"I understand Craig, but Dr. Juncker made me swear on my son's life not to share it or publish it without his approval. We discussed this at the beginning and you said you agreed to his terms. Besides, he should get back to us on Monday."

"Okay, but make sure it's ready then, and let's call Monday as soon as Harvey finishes his meeting."

He felt relieved that Craig backed off, as he could be persistent.

"Don't worry, I'll review it tonight and over the weekend. Monday, I'll have my final version ready."

"Okay, drive carefully and let's call on Monday."

Around five o'clock, he already started looking for a hotel, because he wanted to work on his article that evening. He was driving south on route U.S.-287 and had just entered a small town called Rawlins. It did not take him long to find a good hotel next to a small park. In his room, he plugged in the cool box and unpacked. He had been taking the drug for a week now, and he was following the exact schedule Harvey had mentioned. He adapted his alarm to alert him every other day at seven in the evening. Tonight, it would be the first night in a week he would not take the drug.

Despite the long drive, he felt full of energy and went for a run in the park. He put on his sport clothes and hung the "do not disturb" sign on his door. An hour later, he returned to the hotel, but still felt like exercising more and went for a workout in the gym for another hour. Satisfied, he then headed back to his room.

In the shower, he had the impression that his belly had gotten a little smaller and his muscles tighter. He felt great, and when he stepped out of the shower, he looked at himself in the mirror. His whole body looked healthier, and his muscles were more visible. He looked at his hair and on top his hair was more than half an inch long now and he could no longer see his bald head through the brown hair. On the side, his hair was a lot longer, which gave him an odd look, and it was time to go to the barber to cut just the sides shorter. After dinner, he worked on his article till midnight.

The next day, he woke up early before his alarm clock. He felt fit and had slept amazingly well. The urge to run again came soon after waking up, but it was pouring outside. He went to the gym, ran on the treadmill, worked out on the various fitness machines, and then he went back to his room. He ordered some breakfast in his room. Today he planned to drive to Omaha about nine hours away. After checking out, he drove onto Interstate Highway I-80 heading East.

Around lunchtime, he stopped in Sidney, Nebraska, and found a hair salon next to the entrance of the local supermarket. He went in and the hairdresser, who had a funny accent, looked at his hair, a bit confused. She mostly cut off the band of hair on the side of his head with the gray ends and cut it back into shape. The woman called it a buzz cut and had done a good job. He was happy with it and decided not to wear the baseball cap anymore. In the car, he looked in the mirror a few times. He liked his new look, very short dark brown hair and not a single gray hair left. It felt great to have his hair back. He bought a sandwich at a gas station and then continued on Interstate Highway I-80.

The landscape was dull compared to Yellowstone National Park, and he passed town after town through the treeless prairie landscape while listening to the radio. His phone rang, and he was surprised but delighted to hear Penelope's soft voice.

"Hi, Penelope! How are you?"

"I'm fine, and you? How far along are you with your long drive?"

"I just passed Paxton, Nebraska, an hour ago, and am now on my wat to Omaha."

"Omaha, well, you certainly get to see a lot of our countryside. Dave, my schedule for the next week has changed and I'll be in Chicago on Monday. I'm flying over there tomorrow for a presentation on Monday and will be there until Tuesday. So, if you like and can get to Chicago by then, we can try to meet up?"

He loved the idea. It was about a seven-hour drive from Omaha to Chicago, so he should be able to arrive on time tomorrow.

"What a great idea. I can arrive in Chicago tomorrow later afternoon."

"Great, then why don't we meet at seven in my hotel?"

"That sounds perfect. I'll book the restaurant, since I canceled our last appointment. Any preference for food?"

"No. Surprise me. I'll email you the address of my hotel and I'll see you tomorrow."

"Perfect! Looking forward to it. See you tomorrow!"

He hung up and stared at the horizon. He felt excited about meeting Penelope in Chicago. He wondered if she also had feelings for him or if it was just work for her and he misinterpreted her kindness. Promptly, he realized he had forgotten to tell her the story about the hair transplants to prepare her for his changed looks. Should he just show up in front of her or call her back now? He put it off till tomorrow.

A bit before sunset, he arrived in Omaha and checked into a modern hotel next to the Missouri River, which was right on the border between the state of Nebraska and the state of Iowa. While checking in, his phone's alarm went off. It was time for his injection. He asked the man at reception, "I noticed you have a fitness center. What are the opening hours?"

"It's open twenty-four seven. May I have your passport, please?"

He handed him his passport. The man looked at his picture and looked back at him, a little puzzled.

"Quite a difference in hairstyle from your passport photo. You don't see that often."

Dave felt uncomfortable and realized that this was the first time he checked in without wearing his baseball cap.

"Yeah, the picture's outdated since I did hair transplants."

He looked at the man, who had a bald head with a band of hair on the sides like Dave had before taking the drug. Suddenly, he understood the man's curiosity.

"Wow, impressive. They did a good job. Sorry to be so nosy, but I've been thinking about getting hair transplants myself. It's impressive to see how they succeeded with you, sir. Do you have any tips for me?"

Dave felt more at his ease now and blustered.

"Well, I'd take the time to compare different doctors and ask for references to see their work. A good doctor is key. More than the price, I'd say. There're quite a few sharks waiting to get their hands on your money by offering false hope of a cure for baldness."

The man handed him the keycard for the room and said, "Thanks for the advice. I hope you enjoy your stay with us, sir."

Upstairs in his room, he plugged in the cool box and took a tube out. A bit later, he injected the drug slowly into his arm. After putting back the syringe in his suitcase, he looked in the mirror and rubbed his short hair. All the gray edges of the hair on the side of his head were gone, and he looked so much younger now. He moved closer to the mirror to look at his wrinkles, but he could no longer see any wrinkles. They had completely disappeared. This drug was amazing. He felt satisfied he had stolen it from the laboratory. He put his sport clothes on and went to the fitness center. After working out, he ate in his room while he worked on his article. Around eleven thirty, he finished it, and satisfied with the result, went to bed.

The next morning, he jumped out of bed and felt like running again. He put on his sports clothes and ran to the Missouri river. He ran along a beautiful path along the riverbank. The sky was clear today, and he could feel the warmth of the sun as he ran through the crisp morning air. He arrived back at the hotel about an hour later and checked out after breakfast. Around nine o'clock, he drove up Interstate Highway I-80 eastbound. The route was monotonous and went mostly through farmland. He thought about how to explain his changed looks to Penelope. The hair transplant story seemed right to him, and he wondered particularly how to explain his healthy, younger skin. He could say he had stayed a lot outside, but feared that she would look through his story. She was a sharp, perceptive woman. The ringing of his phone broke his thoughts. It was Andrew.

"I'm glad to hear your voice. A welcome change from driving through the boring farm country here in Iowa."

"Iowa? What are you doing in Iowa? I thought you would be back in New York by now!?"

He realized his stupidity and felt embarrassed.

"Oh, I'm sorry. I meant to call you earlier, but things were pretty hectic. That plane crash in Ethiopia last week freaked me out, and my secretary suggested I drive back by car, so I canceled my flight."

"I thought you were over your fear of flying. I can imagine that the plane crash did not help. What a horrible crash. Driving to New York must be about three thousand miles, right? How do you cope with your back?"

He felt bad about it, but he had to lie again.

"Yes, it's a long drive, but with the painkillers I'm holding on. I should arrive in Chicago tonight."

"Ah, but then you didn't drive so much per day. A friend of mine drove from San Jose to Chicago in three days."

This triggered Dave to tell his son the same story he'd told Henry. They often video called, and he would see his hair soon enough.

"That's right, I took some time for myself. Remember, we talked about hair transplants in the past, well I had the procedure done last week."

"You did? Wow! I thought you would never do it. Well, I'm happy for you. Did it go well?"

He hated lying to his son, but saw no other choice, because he knew he would resent his theft and the injection of an untested drug, and he would probably become very worried.

"Very good. They sedated me and I didn't feel much. I'm still amazed at what the doctors can do these days. I'll show you when I get back to New York, but I have hair growing on top of my head. It's still short, but it's there. I'm glad I did it."

"I'm happy for you, Dad. I can imagine it was a big step. I look forward to seeing your hair. I have to go now. Wendy's calling me. She has prepared lunch, and I'd better not keep her waiting."

"You're absolutely right. Never keep a woman waiting. Give her my regards and I'll call you when I get to New York."

Around one o'clock, he got hungry and left the highway in Davenport, Iowa. During his lunch at a restaurant near the highway, he searched online for a restaurant in Chicago. He wanted to make a good impression on Penelope, so it had to be one with top food. He checked the restaurants with a Michelin star rating in Chicago. There was only one with three Michelin stars, three with two stars, and eighteen with one star. Although he had little chance of getting into any of them on such short notice, he tried anyway. He started calling the restaurants and after being turned down several times, he finally got lucky. One of the one-star restaurants had some late cancelation, and it was only two blocks away from Penelope's hotel.

After lunch, he continued east on Interstate Highway I-80. He still had about three hours to drive, and it looked like he might arrive well before six in the evening. That would give him ample time to find a hotel, freshen up, and change for the dinner. His navigation changed his route to Interstate Highway I-88 due to traffic further down I-80.

After passing Aurora, a suburb of Chicago, he suddenly felt a thump and the steering wheel pulled to the right. He heard a flapping noise and slowed down. He parked the car on the hard shoulder and got out. His right front tire was flat. He looked in the trunk, but there was no spare tire. Just my luck, he thought, and called the road assistance number.

"Hello, this is road assistance. How can I help you?"

"Hi, this is Dave Wilson. I have a flat tire and there's no spare tire in the trunk. I'm on I-88 past Aurora heading toward Chicago."

"Okay, sir. Could you give me the license plate number?"

He read the number to the man on the phone.

"I'll send someone over to you as soon as possible, but the wait may be a little longer than usual because it is Sunday."

"How long do you think it'll take? I'm in a hurry, so the sooner the better."

"I understand, sir. Let me check."

"They should be with you within an hour, sir."

After hanging up, he looked at his watch. It was a quarter to five. He checked his navigation. Still about an hour left to drive. If all went well, he could still be on time for his appointment. He called Penelope.

"Hi Dave, you're not going to cancel again, are you?" she said jokingly.

"I wouldn't dare. No, I'm just calling to let you know I might be half an hour late. I'm about one hour's drive away from you, but I have a flat tire and I have to wait an hour for roadside assistance."

"Oh, annoying. No problem. I'm in my hotel room. Room nine hundred and six."

"Okay. I also have two surprises for you."

"That sounds good. I love surprises."

"Well, I have a reservation at an excellent restaurant not far from your hotel."

"Sounds good!"

"The other surprise I'd prefer to tell you about now, so as not to shock you too much when you see me. I had a hair transplant last week, so you might not recognize me with my brown hair."

"Wow! That's quite something. Did it hurt?"

"No, they put me under anesthesia."

"Well, don't worry. I think I would have recognized you anyway, but thanks for letting me know. I'm curious."

He felt relieved now he had told her about his hair. He waited beside his car until the roadside assistance truck arrived. It took the man about twenty minutes to change the tire. He thanked him for his help and got back on the highway toward Chicago a little after six. He tried to pick up speed, but the road was crowded and he barely got near the speed limit.

Despite the heavy traffic in Chicago, he still arrived at Penelope's hotel at ten past seven. Fortunately, there was a large parking garage in front of the hotel. There, he changed his clothes.

He saw no one and quickly changed his pants. A car passed just as he had put on his pants. Then he quickly put on a nice dress shirt and a dark blue jacket. At twenty past seven, he entered the hotel.

He waited for her in the impressive hotel lobby with its high ceilings. He looked into one of the large mirrors and rearranged his shirt a bit. He stared at his brown hair, still not used to the idea that his hair had grown back. The elevator doors opened, and he saw her walk out. She looked beautiful in her red dress and high heels as she walked elegantly into the lobby with her long, shiny, dark hair. He waved at her. She looked in his direction and her smile turned into a look of surprise

"You look amazing, Penelope."

She stared at his face.

"Thanks, but I ought to say the same about you. Your hair, but also your face. You look so much younger! What happened to you? Can I touch it?"

She looked fascinated and reached out to touch his hair.

"Of course, go ahead."

She stroked his short hair with her hand.

"Wow! They did a good job. So well-spread out and thick."

She was now looking at his face with amazement in her eyes. "Your skin looks different, much healthier, and your rings are gone. What did you do?"

He was beginning to feel uncomfortable now.

"Well, uh, the same clinic as my hair clinic also gave me a skin treatment, and I spent a lot of time outdoors. That has done me good."

She stopped asking questions, but still looked puzzled. He could see in her eyes she was not buying his story. What was he thinking, trying to fool a woman whose business is to make skin look younger? Uncomfortable as he felt, he changed the topic.

"I'm so glad to see you. Great to meet in Chicago now."

She smiled at him and said, "Yeah, that's funny, isn't? When my secretary mentioned this meeting, I immediately thought of you. So great that you could make it."

"After all my cancelations I didn't dare say no," he said with a smile, and they both laughed.

"I made a reservation at a very nice restaurant about two blocks away. Would you rather go by car or walk?"

"Let's walk since I haven't been out much, and the weather looks good."

The night was clear, but it was still relatively warm. Penelope held his arm as they walked to the restaurant. He felt good walking next to this beautiful lady and asked her about the presentation she had to give tomorrow. At the restaurant, the doorman opened the door for them and inside, a host welcomed them and escorted them to their table in the back. He ordered champagne because he wanted this evening to be perfect and had no desire to spoil the evening by not drinking. He felt he could risk it now, since he had taken the injection yesterday and would not be taking it tonight. She asked him how his trip to San Francisco had been and if he had met his son a second time. He started talking about his fishing trip with Andrew in Yosemite. Not for a moment did they stop talking, and the evening passed quickly. The five-course dinner was excellent, and they laughed a lot. He had not had such an enjoyable evening in a long time, and they kept talking until at one point they noticed that almost all the guests had already gone home. They laughed and left the restaurant.

It was cold now, and Dave noticed she was shivering. He wrapped his jacket around her shoulders, and she held his arm. He felt great. They continued talking until they arrived in the hotel lobby.

"Well, I really had a great evening. It feels like it passed in a blink of an eye. We should definitely do this more often."

She looked at him and smiled.

"I had a great night too. I even feel there's still so much more to talk about."

She paused for a moment.

"Perhaps you'd like to come upstairs for a cup of tea and we'll continue our conversation longer?"

"I'd love to."

They walked to the elevator and inside he looked her into her eyes and kissed her. Her lips were soft and her skin smelled wonderful. She wrapped her arms around him as they continued to kiss until the elevator arrived at her floor. They walked down the hallway, holding hands like two young lovers. She smiled at him, took her key, and opened the door. She had a huge suite with a living area. He walked up to the large windows and looked out.

"Wow, you have an amazing view of Chicago!"

He could see some skyscrapers on the left and Lake Michigan on the right, with the moon and stars above in the clear sky. As he looked out, he felt her soft hand touching his hand. He put his arm around her and looked at her.

"Beautiful."

He kissed her soft lips again. She had taken off his jacket, and he felt her soft skin through the thin fabric of her dress as they embraced. He caressed her back as they kissed. He felt her unbutton his shirt, stroking his chest.

"Maybe we should move to the bedroom," she whispered.

He kept one hand on her back, and with the other one, he lifted her off the floor. As they continued to kiss, he gently carried her into the bedroom and laid her down on the king-size bed. He caressed her arms and her body. She had soft and warm legs. She opened his shirt further, and he pulled it off. She looked at him.

"You look more athletic than I imagined."

She pushed him onto his back on the bed and kissed him on his mouth and then on his neck. She kissed him as she moved down. She opened his pants, pulled them down, and then she stood next to the bed, turned and asked him to unzip her dress. She turned around again and dropped the dress to the floor. He looked at her well-figured body. She was even more beautiful than he had imagined. He took off his trousers completely, and she climbed back on top of him and they kissed. The kissing slowly turned into making love as they moved closer and closer, and a night of passion followed.

The next morning, he woke up and realized it had not been a dream. Beside him, Penelope was still sleeping like an angel. She began to move and slowly opened her eyes. She smiled when she noticed he was looking at her.

"Morning, Mr. Love," she said with a dreamy look.

"Morning, and what a pleasant morning it is, waking up next to such a beautiful angel."

"Mmm... I don't know what you did to me yesterday, but it was amazing."

She began caressing his chest.

"That's what you get with an amazing woman," and he kissed her and thought back to last night. He had surprised himself. Never had he made love like this. It lasted longer than he had ever lasted. Before, he would get tired or get aches or cramps somewhere, but not yesterday. He enjoyed it and when he saw she liked it too, he got even more excited. While kissing, they slid closer and began making love again. A while later, they were lying next to each other on their backs.

"Wow, you know how to please a woman," she said and turned on her side to look at him and she gently stroked his hair. He noticed she looked for a moment at the alarm clock.

"What time do you have to go to your meeting?"

She looked back at the clock, which showed almost eight thirty.

"Well, I have a short meeting with my team at eleven and my presentation is at two thirty. If you like, we can try to have lunch together between the two meetings?"

"That sounds like a great plan."

"Super! But first I'll order breakfast for both of us," and she called room service.

They stayed in bed, and she looked closer at his face as she caressed him.

"Your skin is amazing. I've never seen a treatment so effective in my life. And it's not just your face, but the skin on the rest of your body looks young too."

He felt bad about his lie, and it was obvious she knew he had lied. She had been in the beauty industry all her life, and there was no way of fooling her. He really liked her and felt something beautiful had started between them. With some hesitation, he corrected his mistake.

"Penelope, I believe in honesty and don't want to start off on the wrong foot with you. But what I'm about to tell you could get me into big trouble, so please don't tell anyone."

She looked at him a little worried, and then they heard knocking on the door. He put on the white hotel bathrobe to open the door and a waiter brought a trolley with their breakfast. He wheeled it into the bedroom, and she looked at him from the bed with a worried look.

"You can trust me, Dave. Are you in trouble?"

He paused for a moment, as he found it difficult to begin.

"Not yet, but I might get into trouble someday. Do you remember I told you about my interviews in San Francisco?"

"Yes. They were at some research institute that had developed a new drug."

"They've developed a drug that successfully rejuvenated mice. The drug has been tested on human cells in the laboratory and proved successful. The company is about to start a clinical trial on humans in the coming weeks and they have everything prepared."

She looked puzzled.

"What does that have to do with your hair and skin treatment?"

"The old mice that took the drug started running actively all day. Their fur grew back and became thicker and healthier. All wrinkles they had before disappeared and their skin looked young again. Their senses and body functions improved on all fronts."

Her mouth fell open in amazement as she began to grasp it.

"No... did... did you take this drug?"

He looked away, ashamed.

"Yes, actually I did."

She was shocked and looked concerned.

"But that's an untested drug. That's very dangerous. How could you do something like that?"

He sighed and recounted how he had felt bad about himself and his appearance for years.

"Dave, I liked you before you took this drug, just the way you were."

He was glad to hear that, but felt he had to explain the complete picture.

"It wasn't just my looks, but especially my chronic back pain, limited my life tremendously and caused a huge amount of my unhappiness."

He went on to explain how he had come to his decision to steal the drug. He told her about the interviews and the company visits and about how he stole the drug and began injecting it during his weekend with his son. He also told her what happened to him after that. How his body changed, about his long drive and his trip to

Yellowstone National Park. After listening attentively to his entire story, she looked at him in amazement.

"Wow! Rafting, running, working out. That's some rejuvenating drug. You have quite some guts to just inject this experimental drug, even though you were afraid it might kill you. It must have been a weird experience to go through all those changes."

"Yes, it was and still is strange, but since my back pain is gone, I feel happier and more alive."

She kissed him and looked at him with an infatuated look.

"Thanks for sharing. I guess you worry they catch you for stealing?"

"Yeah, sometimes I worry about that, but I'm glad I told you. I don't want to lie to you."

She hugged him and smiled.

"I'm happy you did, and I understand now why you did it."

He looked at her as he felt close to her.

"Did I tell you already that I think you're an amazing woman?"

She kissed him.

"I better go shower and change, or I'll be late for my meeting."

He stayed on the bed while she showered. He stared at the ceiling and thought back to the wonderful night. A feeling of complete happiness filled him, and for a moment, he forgot his worries. It felt good to tell her everything, as if a burden had fallen off his shoulders. She came walking out of the bathroom in a white bathrobe with a towel wrapped around her hair.

"You can stay in the room if you want. I'll call you when I finish my meeting. I'll leave the key on the desk. They gave me two anyway."

He got out of bed, kissed her, walked to the shower and said,

"I'm already looking forward to it."

After showering, he walked back to the bedroom in the white robe and she was now dressed in a blue suit.

"You look beautiful."

"Thanks! You look handsome in that bathrobe, too. I have to go now."

She gave him a hug and a kiss.

"See you at lunch," he said as she walked out of the door.

He smelled the scent of her perfume long after she had left. What an amazing woman, he thought. He got dressed and ate one of the leftover croissants. He went to get his luggage from his car and then walked back to the hotel. In the elevator, he could not help to think back to last night when he kissed her there.

Back in the room, he made an espresso and checked his e-mail. He reread his article and made some minor changes. Overall, he was quite satisfied with the article. He looked at his watch and grew curious about Harvey's board meeting. He sent him a text message:

"Hello, Harvey. How are you doing? I was curious about your board meeting. Any news yet? Kind regards, Dave Wilson."

About half an hour later, he received a message back:

"Hi Dave. Good to hear from you. The board meeting has been postponed until two o'clock this afternoon. I will call you or send you a message as soon as I have news. Kind regards, Harvey Juncker."

He looked at his watch and realized it would mean that around four o'clock in the afternoon Chicago time, the board meeting would start. He emailed Craig to inform about the delay.

He worked the rest of the morning on the article about the anti-spot cream and prepared a list of remaining questions. Around twelve thirty, Penelope called him and he went downstairs. She was waiting for him in the lobby. She looked beautiful and confident in her business suit. She smiled at him and they went to the hotel restaurant.

"How did your meeting go?"

"Very well, although it was mostly a preparation for the presentation later today at one of our biggest clients. And you? Did you have a nice morning?"

"I worked on the article about your cream."

They talked a bit about the article and then about all kinds of other things. They laughed a lot and time passed quickly. At two o'clock her phone rang and after hanging up she said,

"They're waiting for me in front of the hotel. Unfortunately, I have to go now. After my meeting, I'll come to the room and then we can see where to have dinner tonight."

"Sounds good! I'll be waiting for you. Good luck with your presentation."

They walked back to the lobby. She gave him a kiss on his lips and disappeared into the car that was waiting in front of the hotel.

He went back to the room, where he still smelled her scent. He felt like exercising and went to the fitness center in the hotel. He ran on the treadmill for an hour, then did a workout on the fitness machines. He slowly increased the weights and pushed his body further and further. He spent an hour working out before returning to the room. He took a quick shower, dried off, and looked in the mirror. His body looked more athletic, and his muscles were more pronounced. After dressing, he prepared an espresso and continued working on his article.

After six, the door opened. He looked up from the desk and looked into Penelope's brown eyes. She looked a little tired, and he got up to give her a big hug.

"How did it go?"

"Pretty good! They're going to distribute more of our products. It was quite an intense afternoon and I think I'm going to lie down for a while."

He walked her to the bedroom, and they lay down together.

"Maybe you'd like a massage?"

She looked surprised at him and smiled.

"That would be wonderful!"

He went to get some oil while she undressed. When he came back, she was lying on the bed in her underwear. He began massaging her back.

"You should come on all my business trips," she said with a smile on her face.

He looked at her body as he massaged her. Her body was well shaped and her skin was soft.

"I wouldn't mind spending my time with such a beautiful lady. Shall I fill the bathtub for you?"

"Oh, yes, please."

When it was full, she got up and walked to the bathroom and a moment later she called from the bathroom, "Aren't you joining me?"

"I thought you wanted the bath to yourself, but I love to join."

He took off his clothes, and she looked at him.

"You look even more athletic now."

"I worked out in the fitness center in the afternoon," he said with a smile as he carefully stepped into the bathtub. They sat close together and talked for a while.

After dressing, they were ready to go for dinner when the alarm on his phone rang. It was time for his injection. He felt awkward.

"Ah, I completely forgot, but it's time for my drug injection. I'm taking it every other day this week. It won't take long."

He took the insulation bag from his suitcase and prepared the syringe. He took off his shirt and inserted the needle into his shoulder. She watched him as he injected the drug, and he noticed her gaze.

"Maybe you want to try it, too. I have more than enough in stock?"

"I'm not sure I want to. I feel good in my body the way it is now, and how can you be sure there won't be any side-effects?"

"You're absolutely right. I don't know all the risks, and it's been too short to be sure there won't be any negative effects. But if you ever want to take it, let me know."

"Thanks. Who knows, I may one day change my mind"

He put his shirt back on, and they left for the restaurant. Dinner passed in an instant, as they had a great time. On their walk back to the hotel, they held hands. He felt in a way he had not felt for a very long time. He felt in love. He stopped walking and stood in front of her and put his arms around her.

"You make me happy," he said and kissed her.

She looked at him sweetly and lovingly. At ten o'clock, they were back in the hotel, and when he noticed the time on the large clock in the lobby, he suddenly realized he had not heard from Harvey. He checked his pockets, but he did not find his phone.

"Is something wrong, Dave?"

"Well, I was expecting an important call about this article I'm writing, but I guess I must have forgotten my phone in the room."

They went back upstairs, and he found his phone back on the desk. He had one missed call from Harvey's cell phone and a voicemail.

"I'm sorry, but I really need to make a call now."

"No problem, I'll change into something more comfortable."

He listened to his voicemail:

"You have one new message. Press one to listen to your message."

He pressed the one on his phone.

"Hello Dave, it's Harvey. The meeting didn't go well at all. The board members got very upset when I explained I had talked to you and wanted to publish an article about our milestone. They forbade me to publish the article, but I strongly disagree with them. I want to make everything public, so please go ahead and publish it. You can publish it in my personal title, as I legally don't need official permission from Juvenatrust. The sooner the better. You have my permission…"

He suddenly heard a bang and then heard Harvey say in a startled voice,

"… What the f…." and then the line dropped.

The message baffled him. Harvey sounded very agitated and stressed. He dialed Harvey's cell phone number and waited, but he was put through to his voicemail. He left a message.

"Hello, Harvey, it's Dave. Please call me back when you get this."

After hanging up, he immediately called Craig on his cell phone.

"Sorry to disturb you so late, Craig, but I just got a weird message from Harvey."

"No problem, Dave."

"Apparently, the board won't allow him to publish the article, but Harvey wants us to publish it anyway and as soon as possible."

Craig chuckled.

"Funny situation. Well, since he gives his permission, we can proceed. Can you forward me the voicemail message? I'll double check with our lawyers tomorrow, but I think we should just publish it."

"Okay, I'll forward the message. The article's ready, so I'll also email it to you now. Call me if you want to discuss it."

"Thanks, Dave! I will! When will you be back in the office?"

"Well, I'm in Chicago now. I should be back on Wednesday."

"All right, sounds good. Drive carefully and take your time with your back problems. We can probably discuss most things over the phone, anyway. Thanks for calling and have a nice evening."

"You too. Bye."

After hanging up, he forwarded the voicemail message to him.

"Everything all right, Dave?"

He opened his laptop as he answered, "Well, quite a surprise with my work. I need to send a few e-mails urgently. Just give me a few minutes."

"I'll be waiting for you," she said in a sensual voice from the bedroom.

He checked the article one last time, then emailed it to Craig, and closed his laptop. He walked to the bedroom and, as he walked through the door, his heart skipped a beat. She lay naked on the bed in a sensual pose and smiled at him with a naughty look. What an amazing woman, he thought to himself and he began to kiss her from head to toe and they hugged and kissed. He undressed and slowly, the kissing and caressing turned into lovemaking. He could not get enough of her, and they lost track of time in another night full of passion.

The next morning, they sat in bed having breakfast. He explained what had happened with his work the night before and told her about the surprising message. She told him not to worry too much about it, since it would not change much, anyway.

"Maybe you can try calling him later in the morning?"

"I will. At what time are you flying to New York today?"

She checked her ticket.

"At twenty-five past one."

He looked at his watch.

"I'll take you to the airport. What time do you want to leave from here?"

She looked at her watch.

"At eleven should be good, I think. That leaves us two hours before we have to leave."

She smiled naughtily at him and moved the breakfast tray away from the bed. They began kissing as she slowly climbed on top of him.

At eleven thirty, he parked the car in front of the departure hall at O'Hare International Airport. He got out and carried her luggage out of the car.

"Thanks, Dave. I had a great time and I hope this is the beginning of much more."

"I hope so too. I miss you already. I'll call you tonight when I get to my next hotel."

They kissed and hugged, and then he walked back to his car. He got in and drove toward the highway. As he drove onto Highway I-90 eastbound, he thought about the strange message from Harvey. He had never heard Harvey's voice so agitated. He called him. The call again went straight to his voicemail, and this time, he left no message. Normally, the call would be transferred to his secretary and he would get Mary on the line, but that did not happen, either. He had a bad feeling about all this and was worried. He decided that at his next break he would look up the general number of Juvenatrust in his notes and try calling again.

About an hour later, he left the highway to put gas in his car. After refueling, he looked up the number and dialed it right away. To his surprise, he got a general voicemail and hung up without leaving a message. This had never happened before, and he found it strange. Maybe they had a problem with the internet connection, he wondered. He started his car and drove onto the highway I-90 toward Cleveland in the state of Ohio.

8. Suspicious events

The sky was dark and cloudy and looked threatening. He had just passed Southbound, a town along the Interstate I-90 highway in the state of Indiana, when his phone rang. It was his boss.

"I've read your article and I love it. I think this might be one of the most groundbreaking articles for Science Magazine of all time, and we should publish it as an editorial in the next issue."

"Great, I couldn't agree more."

"Since we have permission from Harvey Juncker and not from Juvenatrust, I made a few minor changes and added a disclaimer to the article. I'm still expecting comments from our legal department, but I'll mail you a copy now. Could you have a look and send me your comments? Preferably as soon as possible?"

"Okay, I'll stop at the next exit and review the changes over lunch."

"Perfect. Any news from Harvey?"

"No, nothing. I got his voicemail again and also tried the Juvenatrust's general number, but no one answered. I hope nothing bad has happened to him."

"Strange. Well, check my comments and then call me."

"I will. Bye, Craig."

He took the next exit and stopped at a restaurant near the highway. He ordered some food, opened his laptop, and checked Craig's comments and changes. Meanwhile, he ate his lunch, which smelled delicious. Since he had injected the drug, he had noticed a huge improvement in his sense of smell. Even Penelope's natural scent had not escaped him, and he loved that smell. It even wound him up.

He had once written an article on pheromones, the natural smell of people. Scientists in osphresiology, or the science of the sense of smell and the production and composition of odors, had found that both sexes were attracted to each other by chemical messengers called pheromones. These pheromones stimulated sexual arousal, desire, hormone levels, and even fertility when released. Because pheromones increased attractiveness and led to a better sex life, fragrance and cosmetics companies had made efforts to bottle the scent of certain pheromones in perfumes. At first, he thought it was her perfume that attracted him to Penelope. But after spending some time with her, he noticed it was her natural scent. He had also noticed that with some people, their pheromones had the opposite effect on him, and he felt repulsed by it. Since he smelled better, he also felt his taste had gotten much better. He noticed that because of the drug, he now tasted much more different flavors in his food. Like now with his sandwich it, each ingredient left him with a distinct taste.

He sent his comments to Craig and called him on the phone. They briefly discussed the article, and then he continued his drive east. He turned on the radio and it was raining now. He wondered why Harvey had not responded. About two hours later, his phone rang. It was Craig again.

"Hi Dave! You won't believe what just happened here. I'm absolutely flabbergasted. Four sharp dressed lawyers showed up at my office about half an hour ago. They told me they're representing Juvenatrust and accusing you of theft."

Dave's heart began to pound, and the adrenaline rushed to his head. Had they already found out about his theft? They must have checked their stock of tubes. He never thought they would find out so soon. He did not know what to say.

"They did what?"

Craig continued, all excited now.

"They're calling your interview with Dr. Juncker a theft of intellectual property and confidential information. Can you imagine?"

As soon as he heard this, he relaxed a little and his heart rate slowed. Thank God, he thought. They had not found out about his theft yet.

"They talked nonstop for about an hour and fired all kinds of arguments and accusations at me. Basically, they forbid us to publish any information about Juvenatrust's activities or any other information we've received from or obtained through Dr. Juncker. They want us to turn over all information in our possession and destroy all copies of it or they'll sue us."

Dave worried about all this and wondered if all his work might have been for nothing.

"What a mess! What do you want to do with all this, Craig?"

Craig chuckled.

"Ha! You think a few suits impress me! I've handed over the case to our legal department, but I'm not impressed and we'll just go ahead with publication. We have the personal approval of Dr. Juncker, and I believe that should be enough. I was planning to send everything to the printer at the end of this week and just publish it next week. Legal is reviewing it right now, and they'll let me know tomorrow if they foresee any problems."

"Sounds good. Totally agree, it would be a shame not to publish this article. Well, let me know if you have any news."

"I will, Dave. If those lawyers call you, just transfer them to me, okay? I'll take care of them."

He was glad to hear this. In all the years he had worked with Craig, he had appreciated that he always shielded journalists from lawyers and other aggressive people. If someone tried to sue us over a publication, he always took the heat as the Managing Editor.

"Okay, thanks! I will."

It was a bit after five when he arrived in the city of Toledo, in the state of Ohio. He made a quick stop to stretch his legs and buy a cappuccino. He felt good and his back was holding up fine, despite the long drive. He drove on down I-90 toward Cleveland. After a while, the phone rung and now it was Claire.

"How's the long drive going?"

"Not bad. I'm about an hour away from Cleveland. I should be back in New York tomorrow."

"Craig just told me. That's why I'm calling. He asked me to book some time in your calendar to go over the final details for the publication with you and some people from the legal department. What time would suit you?"

"Mmm… I don't know exactly what time I'll arrive. It depends how far I get today. Maybe later in the afternoon is better?"

"Let me open his calendar one moment."

"He still has some time at five thirty. Shall I book that for you?"

"Perfect!"

"How is your back with all that driving?"

"Not bad. It's a comfortable car."

"Henry told me you've had hair transplants. Is that true?"

Dave laughed. He had hoped Henry would tell people in the office. This way, his return became easier.

"Yes, that's true. After much hesitation, I finally decided to have it done and I must say, I'm glad I did. They did an excellent job."

"Nice! I'm happy for you and I'm looking forward to seeing your hair tomorrow. I'll see you tomorrow afternoon then. Drive carefully."

He drove on, and around seven, he passed Cleveland. He wanted to cover more distance that day, so he ate a quick dinner and continued on I-80 east. His goal was to arrive in Youngstown, Ohio, around eight o'clock in the evening. That would leave less than four hundred miles to New York or about a six-hour drive for tomorrow. In his rearview mirror, he saw the sun setting. The clouds had thinned, and the sun had found an opening to shine through. His phone rang again. Now it was Penelope.

"Dave, I have some terrible news!"

"What's wrong?"

"I just came home and found the door of your apartment ajar. Someone broke in. I've immediately called the police and then looked inside. There was no one there, but it was a complete mess. They emptied all your closets onto the floor. I don't know if they stole anything."

He was shocked and also worried about Penelope. She took a risk going inside and could have gotten into trouble.

"Are you okay?"

"Just a little freaked out, but I'm fine now. The burglars drilled the lock to get in. The police just left and asked me if you can come to the police station to file a report."

"Thanks for your help. Can you do me a favor and call a locksmith to fix the lock?"

"I've already called them. They should be here any moment," she said, sounding more relaxed now.

"Thanks! What would I do without you? This is all a little too coincidental, though. First, the strange message from Harvey and not being able to join him. Then a bunch of lawyers showed up at the office today, threatening to sue if we publish the article about Juvenatrust's drug. And now someone broke into my apartment."

"You had lawyers showing up at your office?"

"Yes, my boss just called to tell me about it. They threatened us and urged us not to publish."

"Aggressive. And now?"

"My boss was not impressed and wants to proceed with the publication. Tomorrow we'll discuss the next steps with our lawyers."

"Oh, the locksmith is here. I have to go now. I'll talk to you later, okay?"

"Okay, and thanks again for your help, Penelope. I miss you."

"Me too. Bye."

Around eight, he entered Youngstown, and checked into a hotel not too far from the highway. He had made sure they had a fitness center, since the running and fitness had become like an addiction to him. After a long day in the car, he really felt like it. In his room, he quickly changed his clothes. He ran on the treadmill for about an hour, and then he worked out on the fitness equipment for another hour. Feeling satisfied, he returned to his room after ten. He took a quick shower, dried off his body and looked at himself. It still felt strange to see himself so fit and young. He worried about tomorrow.

The prospect of seeing his colleagues scared him a little. He now had a good explanation for the hair, but lacked a good story for the other changes to his face. He hoped most people would focus on his hair and not bother to ask more. But people like Henry would notice and ask more, and the idea frightened him. He had considered not going to the office and avoiding his colleagues. But he could not do that forever. He had even thought about starting a new life all over and move to a place far away, but he loved his job and did not want to cut off contacts with his friends, colleagues and family. While on the road, he had avoided this problem, because nobody knew him. But now his journey came to an end. He had been open and honest with Penelope, but with his colleagues and friends, that would be more difficult. He could end up in jail if he told too many people the truth.

He turned on the television to distract himself. There was a disturbing documentary about the Great Barrier Reef, the world's largest reef, in Australia. Global warming had caused extensive damage to the reef, and scientists declared that the coral might never recover. Baby coral in Australia's Great Barrier Reef had declined by ninety percent last year due to massive bleaching in the two previous years. A professor in a white coat explained how the reef suffered from the recent extreme heat.

Suddenly, he thought of Harvey and tried his cell phone again. Again, he got the voicemail, and he began searching for Mary's phone number, since she was the most likely person to know Harvey's whereabouts. He tried to remember her last name, but it did not come to him. Then he remembered she had mentioned her name, when he had called Juvenatrust for the first time. He began searching his notes and a few seconds later found it. Her name was Mary Lewis. He sent an e-mail to Claire asking her to find Mary's private number for him.

He worried again about going to the office tomorrow and called Penelope. He was so glad he had told her the truth. At least now he had someone he could talk to openly with and who understood his problem.

"Hi, Dave. The locksmith put in a new lock. It's still a huge mess inside. I didn't touch anything, so you can check yourself on what's missing."

"Thanks. I'll check tomorrow what they stole. I'm in Youngstown, Ohio, and tomorrow I still have to drive about six hours. I should arrive early in the afternoon."

"I have your new keys with me. Why don't you call me tomorrow when you know what time you'll arrive? Depending on the time and my schedule, you can pick them up at my office or at home if I go home earlier to work from home. I'm hoping for the latter, but I'm not sure about my schedule tomorrow."

"Perfect. Let's do that! I wanted to discuss something else with you. I don't know what to do tomorrow, and maybe you have some good ideas."

"Tell me!?"

"Well, tomorrow I'm meeting my colleagues and I'm wondering what to tell them. I can't tell them the truth. I told a colleague that I had a hair transplant, so that covers part of the change. The problem is more how to explain the change in my face and skin, and you're the only one I can discuss this with."

"I understand. I guess people who don't know you well will focus more on your hair and might not ask about your face. They might think you've been out in the sun. The people who know you well will notice. I noticed it right away too. From a distance, it's the healthier look, but if they look closer, they'll see that your rings and wrinkles are completely gone."

"Exactly! Some people may not dare to ask anything, but I have a few colleagues who are like friends and they'll ask. Originally, I thought to tell them I had some skin treatment done and try not to give too many details. Unfortunately, that didn't work with you either, so now I thought to tell them I had a facelift. What do you think?"

"You might get away with that. It's not so common in men, so most people don't know what it looks like."

"The problem is more that given the article I'm writing, some people might suspect that I've taken the rejuvenation treatment."

"That's far-fetched. The drug is not yet in a clinical trial, and no one will think you're taking an untested drug. I had trouble believing you did that, even though you told me you did. No, I don't think you should worry too much about that. I just thought of something else that you could do. You could make your face look older again. A colleague of mine sold some products for the film industry. They use special makeup to make people look older. We could bring back your wrinkles and rings that way, and if people don't get too close to your face, they won't notice anything."

"That's a great idea. Maybe I should do that."

"The only problem is that you'd have to reapply make-up every day."

He thought for a moment about the prospect of pretending and hiding behind a layer of make-up for a long time.

"Yes, I don't think that would not make my life much easier and I could still be exposed if I get caught in the rain or something. No,

I think the best option is to tell the story about a facelift and maybe pretend to be a little embarrassed about it."

"It sounds like the easiest option and remember that most people won't dare to ask anything about such a delicate and personal topic."

"Thanks, Penelope. It's nice to talk to you about this. If you were next to me now, I would give you a big kiss."

"It was great waking up next to you this morning. You made my trip to Chicago unforgettable and I miss you here beside me tonight."

"Me too."

"You should come sleep with me tomorrow night with all this mess in your apartment."

"I'd love to. I don't think I'll have much time to clean up my apartment tomorrow."

"What a day! After that tiring flight home and now this burglary, I think I can sleep. I look forward to being in your arms again. Goodnight and call me tomorrow as soon as you know what time you'll arrive in New York, okay?"

"I will! And thanks again for all your help. Sleep tight."

He went to the bathroom to brush his teeth and took another look in the mirror. His face looked like it did when he was under thirty. What an amazing transformation! He put on some music. He felt energetic and danced along to the rhythm. He felt great jumping and dancing. He felt young again. What a feeling! He thought of Penelope, and he had not felt what he felt for her in a long time.

The next morning, he woke up around seven and jumped out of bed. He did some push-ups and then dressed. After breakfast, he checked out around eight and drove up Interstate Highway I-80 toward New York. It was gray and cloudy outside, but at least it was not raining. The road was busy, but it was driving fairly well as he passed the Pennsylvania state border. After about an hour of driving, his phone rang.

"Hello, is this Dave Wilson?" a male voice said on the other end of the line.

"Speaking, but who's this?"

"This is Marc Fender. I'm working for Benderson and Figwitz and we represent the company Juvenatrust."

He felt his heart skip a beat. He wondered how they had gotten his cell phone number.

"Sorry to interrupt, Mr. Fender, but I have explicit instructions from my boss, Craig Pathfinder, not to talk to you. You can contact him if you have anything you want to say or ask."

"I understand, but I just have a few questions for you, Mr. Wilson."

He was getting irritated now.

"I'm sorry, Mr. Fender, but you'll have to go through my boss. Have a nice day," and he hung up the phone.

The call from the lawyer stressed him out, and he kept wondering how they had gotten his cell phone number. Neither Craig nor Claire would ever release his number. He turned on the radio, but almost immediately, the phone rang again. This time, he looked at the screen to see who it was. It was Claire.

"Hi, Dave. I found Mary Lewis' phone number. I'll send it to you right away. Any idea when you'll be in the office today?"

"Well, I should arrive in New York around two thirty, but I have to go home first. Apparently, they broke into my apartment yesterday."

"What, that's terrible! Do you need help to change the locks or something?"

"No, thanks. My neighbor took care of that yesterday. I'll probably have to check what they stole and clean up the mess a bit before I come to the office."

"Do you want me to reschedule the appointment with Craig?"

"No, that meeting is urgent and I should be able to make it. Could you tell Craig, though, that some attorney named Marc Fender from Benderson and Figwitz called me and that I referred him to Craig?"

"Of course. I'll tell him. Amazing, he called you on your cell phone. They had already called in the office and I referred them to Craig. I wonder how they got your number?"

"Yeah, me too. Ah. And Claire, tomorrow morning I'll probably go to the police station first to report the burglary."

"Okay. Well, let me know if there's anything I can do for you."

"Thanks. And thanks for the phone number."

"Drive carefully!"

He looked at his watch. With the time difference, he would have to wait another three hours before he could call Mary. The sun appeared between the clouds and the road became less crowded. He listened to some music and enjoyed the cappuccino he had bought on the way. All the events still puzzled him. He had a bad feeling about Harvey's message and hoped Mary could tell him how to reach him.

While bored in the car, he called Elizabeth Cooper. He had not spoken to her in weeks. Elizabeth and Dave had become friends about eight years ago. He had written an article about the new medication for Parkinson's she had developed with her team at the biochemical research institute where she worked. He always called her the exception to the rule that friendships between man and woman rarely last. She was married to a nice guy with whom he got along well. She had always tried to convince Dave to make some changes in his life, as he often complained to her about his health and relationship problems. With all the changes in his life, he felt it was time he gave his friend an update.

"Hi, Dave! It's been a long time. How are you doing?"

"Hi, I'm doing great. I finally took your advice to heart and made some changes."

"I'm happy to hear that, and you're making me curious now."

"Well, I guess it's too much to tell you everything over the phone, but the most important thing is that there's a very nice woman in my life now. I think I'm in love."

"Wow, Dave, that's great news. Tell me more! How did you meet her?"

He began to explain how they had met and after that he also told her about his hair transplants and the facelift. She was stunned by all the news, and they agreed to call the weekend to plan something. After he hung up, he felt good. He could share the changes in his life with Elizabeth, although he remained uncomfortable about the lies as well. He had always had a great difficulty lying, but in this case, he had no choice and would have to get used to it.

After a quick lunch on the way, he called Mary.

"Hi, Mary, it's Dave Wilson from Science Magazine. I'm calling you because I have been trying to call Harvey for a while, but I can't seem to reach him. Every time I get his voicemail and the general number at Juvenatrust doesn't seem to work either. I was wondering if you know where I can reach him?"

There was a silence on the other end, and then he heard her voice trembling.

"That'll be difficult, Dave, because the police think Harvey may be dead."

The line was silent again, and he heard crying. He could not believe his ears.

"What? That's horrible news. What happened?"

Half crying, she answered, "He hadn't come home after work on Monday and I couldn't reach him. I had left the office at six and he was still in his board meeting then. Later that evening, I got a call from a colleague that the Juvenatrust building was on fire. I rushed to the office to have a look, and because I was worried about him. The police wouldn't let us near the building, because it was too dangerous with the flames and heat. I told them that Harvey had not come home. Flames were coming out of the windows on all floors, and the firefighters were trying to put out the fire. It was horrible. I finally went back home but couldn't sleep because I was so worried about Harvey. Yesterday, the police told me they had found four burned bodies in the building. They think Harvey could be one of them, because they found his badge on one of the bodies. This afternoon I have to go to the coroner to identify him."

She stopped talking and began to cry harder.

"Jesus, Mary. I'm so sorry. What a nightmare," Dave said.

"Let me know if there's anything I can do for you."

After some silence, she stopped crying and regained her breath.

"Thanks. I have to go now."

"Well, Mary, I'm deeply sorry for you. I wish you lots of strength for the identification later today. Is it okay if I call you tonight to hear how it went?"

"That's fine Dave, I'll talk to you later."

"Bye, Mary, take care!"

In shock, he drove on, unable to believe what he had just heard. Harvey might be dead. A profound sadness filled his mind. So many questions haunted him. He wondered if the fire had anything to do with those forest fires caused by the drought. The weird message he had received from Harvey also puzzled him. He should tell Mary about it in the evening. He also wondered what had happened to that huge stock of drugs for the clinical trials. Had they noticed his theft before the fire, or had the fire now erased all traces? How did Harvey end up in this fire? He turned on the radio to distract his mind a bit. At less than a half-hour drive from New York, he called Penelope to check where to pick up the keys to his apartment.

"Hi, Dave, how's your drive?"

"Good, I arrive in New York around three. Do I pick up the keys at your office?"

"No, I just arrived home. I felt like seeing you. It wasn't too busy today, so I work from home in the afternoon. You can just come straight to my apartment, so I can give you a big kiss and your new keys."

"Perfect, I'll drop the car off and be there around three."

"Are you all right? You sound different?"

He was amazed how she could immediately sense his mood.

"Well, I guess I'm still in shock. I just got some terrible news. I spoke to Mary Lewis, the girlfriend of Harvey Juncker, the doctor I interviewed in San Francisco. He probably died in a fire at the company last Monday."

"That's horrible! Poor woman, she must be devastated."

"Yes, she cried a lot and today she has to identify him at the coroner's office. Apparently, they've found four burned bodies in the building and the police suspect one of them is Harvey."

"Do they know what caused the fire and how those people got caught in the fire?"

"No, I couldn't ask her much because she had to leave and was crying a lot, but I'll call her back tonight to find out how the identification went. After Harvey's voicemail on Monday, I already had a bad feeling that something might have happened to him and now he might have died in a fire."

"Do you think someone may have killed him?"

"Well, I don't know. It's all a bit too coincidental for me. I'll investigate over the next days."

He arrived in New York and the road was getting busier.

"I'm about to drive into the Lincoln Tunnel. I'd better hang up now and concentrate on the road. Let's talk later."

After dropping off the car at the rental office, he carried his suitcases and the cool box to his apartment building. Claire had made sure the car rental office was close to his apartment, and he only had to walk three blocks to arrive home. When he stepped out of the elevator, he looked at the door of his apartment and noticed the new lock. He rang Penelope's doorbell, and a moment later, when she opened the door, a sweet smile appeared on her face. They kissed, and he entered her apartment and put down his luggage in the living. She looked at the cool box.

"Do you keep the drug doses in there?"

He smiled and asked, "Do you want to have a look?"

He opened the cool box and showed her the metal box with the tubes.

"Wow, how many doses do you have in there?"

"It fits a hundred doses, but I've used nine already. More than enough for me and also for you, if you ever want to try. I understood that if I stop the treatment, my body will continue to age at its normal rate. So, I can stop occasionally and then start back when I need it again. I should probably store them in a safe place, especially given the recent burglary."

"Yeah, you better do that."

He had already thought of a place, as he had thought about it in the car. He looked at his watch.

"Probably I should check out my apartment first."

"Yes, it's a huge mess. I left it the way I found it."

She opened a drawer in the hall closet and handed him the set of keys for the new lock.

"I kept one of the spare keys as part of our neighbor deal, but I'd like you to check if they didn't take my keys from your apartment. Yesterday that kept me awake."

He took the keys and put his arms around her, and kissed her.

"What would I do without you?"

They kissed for a while and then he said, "Well, I better check my apartment."

"Okay, I'll let you do that alone. Otherwise, I'll just get in the way. Let me know if you need any help at some point."

He walked to his apartment and opened the new heavy lock with his key. He pushed the door open and looked inside. The hall looked normal, but in his living room, the floor was littered with papers. All the drawers of the cupboards were half open or had been pulled out completely and thrown on the floor. He took pictures with his phone of his entire apartment. First the living room, then the kitchen. Then he walked over to his bedroom, where all his closets had also been emptied. The dressing was the biggest mess since all his clothes were in a big pile in the middle, even the bathroom was a dump. He looked at the mess and did not know where to start. He looked first for the key to Penelope's apartment. He had hidden it in the small storage room near the entrance, where he had his washing machine. They had thrown some stuff on the floor. He looked in the door of the fuse box, where on the inside was a small space to hang keys. The key to her apartment was still hanging there, and all his other keys were there, too.

As he walked back to the living room, he picked up the frame with the picture of him and his son. He looked at it and was shocked to see himself and how much his appearance had changed. He started cleaning up the bathroom first, because that was the smallest. Then he cleaned up the bedroom and, surprisingly, they had not taken any of his jewelry or expensive watches, which he kept in a drawer in his bedroom. He found everything back on the floor and missed nothing. He continued into the living room. While he cleaned up and put all his things back in place, he checked to see if he was missing anything. About an hour later, the living room was also back in its original state. He looked at his watch and stopped for now because it was four-thirty already and he returned to her apartment.

She was on the phone when he came in, and he took his luggage to his apartment. There, he opened the cool box and took out ten doses, putting them in a large cup in his refrigerator. That should be enough for the next two months, he calculated. He took the cool box with the remaining doses into the elevator. To get to the basement, he had to use a special key in the elevator. He stuck his key in the elevator lock, turned it, and pressed the down button. Now the elevator continued down along the ground floor until it reached the basement. He looked down the narrow, dark corridor in front of the elevator. He stepped out and waved with his hand to trigger the motion sensor. The light came on and he walked all the way to the back, past the doors of the other residents' storage rooms. He walked left into the second corridor he crossed and there, at the end on the right, he put the cool box on the floor as he unlocked his storage room. He turned on the light. On the right side was a mountain bike, his tools, and several boxes. On the left side was a large rack with his wine collection. He had always loved wine, and over the years, he had amassed a sizable collection of over four hundred bottles. The temperature in the storage room was ideal for wine and thus for his drug doses.

He emptied one of the wine racks and pushed it aside. He took out one of the floorboards under the wine rack. He had a safe deposit box installed under the floor in his storage room when he bought the apartment. He opened the safe and took out a stack of papers and the kilo gold bar he had kept in it. During the financial crisis after the collapse of Lehman Brothers, he had lost faith in the banks and had bought the kilo gold bar. Initially, he had kept it in a safe deposit box at a bank, but when he bought this apartment, he kept it in here. He took the metal box out of the cool box and put it inside. Then he placed the gold bar next to it and the papers on top. He felt relieved that it all fit in his safe. He locked it and put the floorboard back over it. He put the wine rack back on top and filled it with the wine again. The cool box he put in the corner next to his bike. He locked his storage room and took the elevator back upstairs.

Penelope walked up to him as he entered her apartment.

"And? Anything missing?"

"Well, the good news is that your keys are still there. I haven't checked everything yet, but so far, I'm missing an old spare laptop I kept in a desk and the USB sticks next to it are all gone. Strangely, they didn't take any jewelry or money from my apartment. I still need to clean up the kitchen and my dressing room and check some of my papers, but so far it looks like they came for my laptop. That will disappoint them because I had my laptop with me and they took my old one. I wonder if the burglary has something to do with those lawyers trying to stop the publication of my article."

She looked concerned and said, "If that's the case, they might come back and try to steal the other laptop."

"Yep, tomorrow I'll report it to the police."

He looked at his watch.

"I have to go to the office for my meeting. I'm still worried about what people will say when they see my changed face."

She suddenly looked up and pulled him by his hand toward the bathroom.

"I thought of something yesterday after we hung up. I have another solution. Come with me!"

They walked to her bathroom, and she pulled some make-up from a cabinet.

"I was thinking instead of using full make-up to make your skin look exactly as before, maybe it would be better to use a little make-up to create some dark circles under your eyes. That way the difference from before is less, but we don't have to apply a thick layer of make-up."

"Sounds like a great idea."

"Okay, don't move."

She carefully put some make-up on his face and then he looked in the mirror. His face looked paler, less healthy, and he looked tired. It was closer to how he used to look. His hair now drew the most attention. Instead of bald at the top, he now had short, thick brown hair.

"Perfect. You're an angel."

"You're welcome."

He took his briefcase and headed for the door when she asked,

"Do you want to have dinner together tonight?"

"I would love to! Although I'm not sure what time I finish my meeting. I should probably be back at seven, but it could be later."

"No problem. Why don't you call me when you leave the office?"

"Perfect," he said, and gave her a kiss.

He left the apartment building and walked toward the subway station. He did not notice the large black SUV with tinted windows parked in front of the building across the street. On the subway, he felt comfortable in anonymity, where everyone ignored each other. In the window, he saw his reflection and felt nervous about returning to the office with his changed looks. He rehearsed the story he would give people if they would ask anything. The less he told people, the better it was. At the seventh station, he got off the metro and took the escalators. He entered the glass doors of the office building at twenty minutes past five. He scanned his badge to pass through the gates and took the stairs to go to the Science Publications office. On the fourteenth floor, he hung his coat on the rack near the entrance to the work floor. Normally, he would be completely out of breath after fourteen floors of stairs, but he did not feel tired. He walked over to Claire's desk to see which room the meeting would be in. She was looking at her screen, but when she looked up and saw him, she stared at him with in amazement and her mouth dropped open.

"Hi, Claire! Do you know in which conference room I have to be in for the meeting with Craig?"

She still stared at his face and was silent for a moment before she answered.

"Hi, Dave. Wow! You look so different. You look great!"

"Thanks!"

She kept looking at his face with her mouth open.

"How was your trip back? Everything went well with the rental company?"

"Everything went fine, and thanks for all your help."

He looked at his watch as he was now a few minutes late for the meeting. She noticed and looked a little embarrassed at her screen to check the location.

"I'm sorry, you're in a hurry. The meeting is on the sixteenth floor in the Evolution conference room."

"Thanks, Claire. I'll see you tomorrow after my visit to the police and then we can catch up. All right?" he said apologetically.

"No problem. See you tomorrow! And I love your hair," she said with a friendly smile.

He rushed up the stairs to climb the two floors. On the sixteenth floor, he ran into Steve Eisman.

"Hi, Steve! How was Antwerp?"

Steve looked puzzled and stared at him.

"Oh, hi, Dave! Sorry I didn't recognize you. You look changed. Your… your… your hair has grown back? How can that be?"

Dave smiled at him. Apparently, the hair transplant story had not reached everyone in the office.

"Yeah, weird, huh? I got hair transplants. Impressive what they can do these days."

Steve stared bewildered at his face and hair.

"You can say that. They did an impressive job. Nice! Where did you have it done?"

Steve's hair had grown thinner over the years and he was going bald on top of his head.

"In California. I'm sorry, Steve, but I'm already late for my meeting with Craig."

Dave hurried on toward the conference room.

"No problem, you better not keep the boss waiting," Steve said with a grin on his face.

Dave opened the door to the conference room. Craig was inside talking to another man in a dark suit. He had seen the man's face before in the company, but had never actually met him. They both stood up as he entered the room.

"Sorry I'm late, but they broke into my apartment."

Craig stared at his face with an inquiring look.

"Hi, Dave, a break-in? Wow! This is Wayne Davidson, the head of our legal department."

He shook his hand and took a seat at the conference table.

"Anything stolen from your apartment?" Craig asked while he continued to stare at his face and hair.

"I haven't had time to check everything yet, but I did notice they stole an old spare laptop of mine and all my USB sticks. Oddly enough, they didn't take my jewelry or money."

"That's strange," Craig said while still looking at Dave's face, trying to figure out what was different.

"Exactly. It looks like they were looking for documents and data, which makes it suspicious and startling considering it coincides with those lawyers trying to stop the publication of the article."

Wayne nodded. Craig nodded, too, without taking his eyes off Dave's face.

"Yeah, a little too coincidental. By the way, Dave, they did a great job with those hair transplants."

"Thanks," he said as he unpacked his notebook and took a pen in his hands. Wayne now stared at his hair.

"The purpose of today's meeting is to discuss the legal issues of publishing the article on the rejuvenation drug developed by

Juvenatrust. I've prepared a small agenda and listed the main points to discuss."

He handed out a paper, and both looked at the list.

"Is there anything missing from the list that we should also discuss?"

"There's an important development I just heard about. I spoke with Mary Lewis today. She's the Dr. Juncker's secretary, but also lives with him. She told me that Dr. Juncker had not come home Monday night after attending the board meeting at the office. That same evening, a fire broke out in the Juvenatrust building and after the fire was extinguished, they found four burned bodies in the rubble. Police believe one of the bodies may be Dr. Juncker. Ms. Lewis is going to the coroner today for identification, and I'll call her later tonight to find out if it was Dr. Juncker."

They both stared at Dave with wide-open eyes and astonished looks. A silence fell, then Craig spoke.

"Jesus! That's shocking news, and this could complicate matters."

Wayne nodded and said, "The lawyers of Juvenatrust could use this to their advantage, since Dr. Juncker is no longer there to support us and back up our story. What proof do we have that he authorized the publication?"

Dave put his phone on the table.

"Well, I have his voicemail. I'll make you listen to it."

He put his phone on speaker and played the voicemail message. They listened intently and after the message end Wayne said, "The message is clear and proves that he fully approves of the publication. At the end of the message, it sounds like something happened to him. I think we should report this to the police in Novato and give them a copy of the message. It may shed a new light on what happened to Dr. Juncker and how he got caught in the fire. I'll ask our IT department to make a copy of the message and the call-log on your phone."

Dave nodded and Wayne called someone from the IT department. They talked further about the legal issues, while someone came to pick up his phone to make a copy. Half an hour later, he got his phone back. Then the alarm on his phone went off. It was the reminder to take his injection. At the end of the meeting, they made some changes to the article to better position it and make it harder for Juvenatrust's lawyers to stop the publication. They decided to go ahead with the publication and include it as an editorial in the next issue of Science Magazine, which would be on newsstands next Friday. Around seven thirty, the meeting was over. Craig and Wayne returned to their office, and Dave called Penelope as he walked downstairs.

"Hi, I just finished my meeting, so I should be with you around eight."

"Perfect," she said. "I don't really feel like cooking. Shall I order some Thai food?"

"Sounds good. I'm leaving right now. See you in half an hour."

After picking up his coat, he took the stairs down the remaining fourteen floors. Outside, it was getting dark and chilly. He closed his coat and walked to the subway station. The metro was not too crowded, and he got off seven stops later. The street in front of his apartment was full of parked cars and he did not notice the large black SUV with tinted windows parked among the other cars.

Five minutes later, he opened the door of his apartment and rushed to the fridge. He pulled out a dose and took the syringe from his suitcase. He filled it with the drug, then he took off his jacket and shirt and emptied the syringe into his arm. He disinfected the syringe and put it in his bathroom. He put back his shirt and hurried out to cross the hall to his neighbor. Penelope opened the door for him and gave him a sweet kiss.

"Would you like something to drink?"

"Just some water, please."

She filled a glass with water and handed it to him.

"How was it at work? Did people say anything about your face or hair?"

He took a sip from the glass.

"It went pretty well, to my surprise. The people who know me a bit better all stared at me in amazement. Some complimented me on my hair transplants, but no one asked about my skin. You were right that most people don't dare to ask. Although I only saw a few people and I didn't see my best friend Henry yet. I'll probably see him tomorrow afternoon, so I'd like to put the make-up back on again since it seemed to have worked today."

"Of course, I would do it at least this week and then maybe we can slowly phase it out. Let me get the make-up off your face."

She took a bottle of make-up remover from her bathroom and some cotton pads. He sat on one of the bar stools in the kitchen, and she stood very close to him. He loved her smell and could not resist kissing her on her neck. She smiled, but told him to sit still. With a cotton pad, she cleaned his face until all the make-up was gone. She inspected his skin up close.

"Your skin is amazing. Perfectly smooth and very healthy."

They ate at the kitchen table while talking about all sorts of things. He realized he felt very comfortable around her and, besides getting along, he was also physically attracted to her. Just smelling her scent of her body made him want to kiss and hug her. They had barely finished eating and were joking and laughing when he suddenly felt a strong urge to make love to her. He started kissing her, and she wrapped her arms around him. He lifted her in his arms and carried her to the bedroom. Gently, he laid her on the large bed and started kissing her all over her body. Not much later, they made love passionately. He felt so good and energetic that he just couldn't stop.

Around eleven, they lay side by side, and she gently stroked his chest. He felt happy and enjoyed the moment. A little later, she asked him if there was any news from Dr. Juncker, and then he realized he had forgotten to call Mary Lewis. He looked at his watch and it was a little after eight in the evening in Novato. He put on his boxer short and a T-shirt, walked to the living room and grabbed his phone.

"Hi, Mary. It's Dave. How did it go today?"

"Hello, Dave. It was horrible. I tried to identify him, but his body was so burned and black that I couldn't recognize him. I could only recognize the glasses on his burned face and the watch, which I had given him as a gift. I guess it was him, but the body was so badly burned. The smell was horrendous, and I fainted. Fortunately, my brother had come along and was able to catch and break my fall. I woke up in the coroner's office. The police asked me if the burned man was Harvey and I said I didn't recognize him, but that the watch and glasses were definitely his. I gave them permission to access his dental records and perform an autopsy to verify his identity. It may sound strange, because it was probably Harvey, but I'd like to make sure."

"You're absolutely right to request an autopsy, and I believe it's quite common in these cases. Any idea how long that'll take?"

"They told me they'll have the results next week."

A silence fell, and he hesitated to tell her about the voicemail.

"Mary, there's something else I wanted to tell you. I'm not sure if it is the right time, but I had received a voicemail message from Harvey on Monday night after his board meeting and I thought it was suspicious."

"What was suspicious about it?"

He opened his laptop and looked for the e-mail he had received from the IT guy in his office containing the voicemail recording.

"Well, maybe it would be better if I let you listen to it yourself. I can play it for you if you want?"

"Please do, Dave!"

"Okay, here it comes."

He held his phone close to his laptop and played the message for her. After the message, he heard her crying. He waited for a moment for the crying to subside.

"Are you ok? I know this must be hard for you, but I thought you needed to hear this."

She still sounded very sad, but was no longer crying.

"I'm glad you made me listen. He sounded so stressed, that's not like him. It was like he was afraid of something. And the ending is strange, like something happened to him. He rarely uses language like that."

"Yes, it puzzled me too, and now that he seems to have died in the fire, it sheds a different light on the message. Moreover, on Tuesday, the lawyers of Juvenatrust threatened us with a lawsuit and ordered us to stop the publication of the article."

Her voice changed tone, and she sounded angry now.

"They had the nerve to do that!? They've no right to do that! The development of this rejuvenation drug has been his life's work, and if anyone has the right to make it known to the world, it's Harvey. I hope you won't stop the publication?"

"No, we intend to go through with it. This voicemail message will serve as proof that we have Harvey's consent."

"Well, if you need more proof, I'm happy to testify. Harvey felt it was time to let the world know of his discovery, and he was so proud to get an article in your magazine. He worked hard all his life for this recognition. His old colleagues did not believe he would succeed and even ridiculed him. So please, publish the article. The sooner the better. This article is the crowning glory of his work. Those board members are only interested in making money, and Harvey's drug is about so much more than that."

He was pleased with her response and admired her fighting spirit.

"Mary, I had my boss and our company lawyer listen to this voicemail today. The lawyer will forward it to the police in Novato, because he thought it was all a little too suspicious."

"He's absolutely right! Thank you for doing that. I hope they investigate. Next Friday there's a meeting in Novato in the morning where the police and fire department will give more details about the fire. I'll ask them if they're going to open an investigation. I really need to know what happened to Harvey."

He became more curious about the whole thing the more they talked about it.

"Could you call me after that meeting, because I'd like to know more about all this? I also wonder how this fire will affect the research and all the work Harvey did."

"Sure. I'll call right after, Dave. Thanks for calling. Bye."

"Take care, Mary!"

9. Hunted down

The next morning he woke up next to Penelope. He stared at her, still a bit in disbelief. She looked beautiful in the morning light with her dark brown hair. Her alarm clock started buzzing at fifteen to seven, and she opened her eyes and noticed he was looking at her. She smiled at him.

"Good morning, handsome."

They kissed, and he began caressing her. They stayed like that for a few minutes, and when he aroused her a little too much, she stood up and looked at him with a flirtatious smile.

"Tempting, but I really need to hurry today. I have some clients coming by in the morning and my driver is waiting at the door at seven thirty. So, hold that thought till tonight, please?"

He smiled and got out of bed as well. After breakfast, she put the same make-up on his face as the day before to make him look older. They left her apartment together and kissed goodbye in front of the elevator. He entered his apartment to clean up the remaining mess.

First, he made an espresso and then began cleaning up the kitchen. They had thrown many cups and bowls on the floor, and many were broken. About an hour later, the kitchen was back in its original state and he had grown thirsty. He took some cold water from the bottle in the fridge. When he put back the bottle, he saw the cup with the nine doses of Juvenatrust's drug. He knew that, with the fire at Juvenatrust, the drug doses he had stolen were probably worth even more. He had better hide them better. He kept only three doses in the cup, one he would take this Friday and then two doses for the next week on Tuesday and Friday. Next week, he would switch from one dose every other day to two doses for the whole week and the week after to one dose per week. He put a milk carton in front of the cup with the three doses to keep them out of sight. He stuck the other six doses with duct tape under the lid of the bottom drawer, at the very back, completely out of sight. Then he closed the refrigerator and began cleaning up his dressing room. He had to refold all his clothes, and it took him more than an hour for everything to be back in place. His entire apartment was now tidy, and he concluded that only his old laptop and the USB-sticks were missing.

At ten thirty, he went to the nearby police station to report the burglary. He packed his briefcase, because straight after filing the police report he would proceed to the office. He had to go to the Midtown Precinct North of the New York Police Department, and that was about six blocks away from his apartment building. He walked in the southern direction. This time he noticed the large black SUV with tinted windows on the other side of the street, but paid little attention to it. After walking for about ten minutes, he arrived at the Midtown Precinct North. Inside, it was very crowded, and he had to wait for his turn.

After more than an hour, he could finally file a report. He was skeptical that they would ever catch the burglars, but to his surprise, the police officer who filed the report told him they had just received the video surveillance files from the cameras in his apartment building. The officer gave him a phone number to call after four o'clock for the results of the analysis of the video surveillance files. Around noon, he left the police precinct building, satisfied that they were taking this burglary seriously.

Outside, he walked onto Eighth Avenue and continued to the 50th Street subway station. He bought a sandwich in front of the station and walked down the stairs of the subway entrance. It was calm in the metro, one of the advantages of going later to the office. He looked at himself in the window's reflection, liking his appearance with his dark hair. Six stops later, he got out and left the Spring Street subway station. One block further, he arrived at the office. He noticed a similar large black SUV with tinted windows, as he had seen in front of his apartment building earlier that morning. He vaguely saw the shape of two men inside. He entered the building and walked straight to the stairwell. Full of energy, he walked up the fourteen flights of stairs.

On the fourteenth floor, he walked to his desk and passed Claire's desk, who was probably away for lunch like most people in the office. On the entire floor, only two people were sitting at their computers. He passed Barbara Saunders, whom he did not know well. She looked up from her desk, stared at his head and when then smiled at him.

"Hi, Dave. I like what they did to your hair. Looks good."

"Thanks, Barbara," he said as he continued on to his desk.

She stared at his face for a long time before looking at her screen. At least it seemed to help that Henry had told some people about his hair transplants. Further on, James Cullen sat at his desk, and he looked up from his screen when Dave arrived at his desk. He stared at Dave's face and hair and after a moment of silence, he said, "Wow, Henry had told me about your hair transplants, but your hair looks better than I expected. I've seen some hair transplants in the past, but with you, they did an excellent job."

"Thanks, James. It's a wonderful feeling to have my hair back," he replied, smiling.

James continued to stare at his face.

"Well, California seems to have done you good. Nice tan. How did the interview go?"

He told him about it, but also about the recent developments. He was amazed to hear about the fire and the death of Dr. Juncker. After that, James continued working and Dave could finally get to work. He made the changes to the article he had discussed with Craig and Wayne the day before. An hour later, he was about to send the revised article to his boss when he felt a firm hand pressing on his shoulder.

"Who's this hairy fellow sitting at my best friend's desk?" Henry said jokingly in his deep voice.

Dave laughed and said without looking up at him, "Hold on, buddy. I have to send this e-mail first."

After clicking the send button, he looked up at Henry, who was looking at his hair. His smile disappeared and his mouth fell open the moment he saw Dave's face.

"What's that? What happened to your face?"

Dave had been afraid of this. Henry was his best friend and they were always very honest and direct with each other about everything. Now he wished the ground would open up and swallow him. He looked slightly concerned at James Cullen, but he did not seem to have heard anything. Dave stood up and tapped Henry on the shoulder.

"We have a lot of catching up to do, buddy. Let's get some coffee?"

Henry still looked a little puzzled as he walked with Dave to the coffee corner.

"Good plan. It has indeed been too long."

On the way, another colleague looked at him.

"Hi, Dave. Nice hair!"

"Thanks!"

Henry smiled and looked at Dave's hair again.

"They did an amazing job. It makes you look a lot younger."

Dave pressed the button of the coffee machine as they arrived in the coffee corner.

"Thanks, Henry, and you know what? It's thanks to you. You had suggested it to me so many times already and now that I've finally done it, I wonder why it took me so long."

Henry smiled, and Dave handed him a coffee cup.

"You're welcome, Dave. Better late than never, no? But it looks like your gray hairs are also gone!?"

"Yes, I figured I'd better dye my hair after the hair transplants to make it look nicer," he lied.

Henry nodded, but stared at his face as he tried to understand what had happened to it. Dave noticed and wondered how to divert the subject and not tell him too much.

"You look different, younger," Henry said.

"Thanks. Californian sun, I guess. I must say I feel a lot better, too. But I guess I've other reasons for that."

Henry noticed the mysterious smug smile on Dave's face.

"Well, you're making me curious. Tell me, did you win the lottery? Got an inheritance? No? Did you meet someone?"

Dave shook no and smiled when Henry suggested he had met someone. Henry looked stunned with eyes wide open.

"No!? You've met someone? Tell me! Tell me!"

"Well, as you know, I'm working on an article about an anti-aging cream!? The CEO of the company, Penelope Garcia, is also my neighbor. I have always found her a very attractive woman, but thanks to this article, we have now become much closer. We had scheduled a meeting for an interview, but because of my visit to San Francisco, I had to postpone it. During my long drive back to New York, she called me to say that she would be in Chicago for a few days and we agreed to meet. We went out to dinner together and we had a great night. We kissed and have been seeing each other ever since."

"Wow, I'm happy for you! That sounds like a great time in Chicago."

"Yes, it was."

Dave looked at his watch and hoped to get away without talking about his face.

"We should probably plan some drinks soon to catch up. So much has happened lately. It feels like a rollercoaster ride," Dave said.

"Why don't we have drinks after work today?"

Henry stared at his face again as he moved closer to put away his empty coffee cup.

"All right, let's do that!"

"Perfect," Henry said, suddenly pointing at Dave's face.

"Your face looks changed. You look less tired and your skin looks so young. Did you have something done to it?"

Dave swallowed deeply and knew he could not avoid the subject much longer. He looked around to check that no one else could hear them.

"Okay, I'll tell you, but please don't tell anyone, because I'm kind of embarrassed about it. I had a facelift done. I figured I'd better do all the repairs in one go."

"I knew it was something like that! Your face looks so much younger and less wrinkled! Hey, but don't worry, your secret's safe with me. You'll definitely have to tell me more about it tonight."

Dave felt a little relieved after his reaction.

"Yeah. Well, there's so much more to talk about. I haven't even talked about the burglary, the fire, and Dr. Juncker's death."

His mouth dropped open.

"What!?"

Dave smiled and patted him on the shoulder as they walked back to their desks.

"Tonight, my friend. Too much to tell and you even haven't even given me an update from your side yet."

Henry smiled and as he walked away said, "Okay, I'll pick you up around six."

Back at his desk, he checked his e-mail. Craig had already responded. He gave some compliments on the updated article and asked when he could expect the article on the anti-aging cream. Dave had already written most of it, but had yet to visit the company and interview some of the company's researchers. He dialed Penelope's number and got her secretary on the line.

"Hello, Mr. Wilson, just a second. I'll check. She had told me to block all her calls during her meeting."

The line was silent for a moment and then Ms. Hudson said, "Mr. Wilson, she's still in her meeting, but it looks like it's almost done. Do you want to hold the line?"

"Yes, please."

He waited and meanwhile checked his mail until, at some point, he heard her voice.

"Hi. How was it this morning at the police station?"

"Well, I had to wait a very long time, but I was positively surprised. They're seriously investigating the burglary, and they're checking the video surveillance files of our apartment building today. I didn't even know we had video surveillance in so many places. I mean, I saw the camera in the elevator, but apparently there're also cameras in the reception area and in the hallways on every floor."

"Well, then they must have some nice footage of us kissing in the hallway."

He chuckled.

"Penelope, I'm calling about the article on your anti-aging cream. When can I visit your company and interview the researchers who worked on this cream? My boss is after me to get the article."

"Let me check," she said, and there was a silence for a few minutes.

"How about ten o'clock tomorrow morning? After the visit and interviews, we could have lunch together?"

He checked his calendar.

"Perfect! Ah, before I forget, I'm seeing Henry tonight for drinks and bites, so I'll be home late tonight. If you like, we can meet up afterwards. I was also wondering if you like to go out to dinner with me tomorrow night!? I know a really nice restaurant in the neighborhood."

"That sounds like a great plan and good to know for tonight. I've a lot of work today, so I'll probably be home late anyway, but just stop by after your evening with Henry. How was it? Did he ask a lot of questions about your looks?"

Dave lowered his voice slightly to keep those around him from hearing.

"Yeah, way too much as expected. I told him what we discussed together, but let's talk tonight."

"No problem. Have fun tonight and I'll see you after then."

He hung up the phone and e-mailed Craig that he was going to visit the company tomorrow and expected to send him a draft by Monday. Then he searched for information about the fire at Juvenatrust. He could find surprisingly little about it. In one article, a Juvenatrust spokesperson said that some explosion in the lab on the ground floor might have caused the fire, and that if it had happened during the day, the number of casualties would have been much higher. Other than that, he did not find much, and continued to work on the article about the anti-aging cream.

After four, he called the police officer of the Midtown Precinct North. They had looked at the video surveillance files and seen two burglars break into his apartment at one thirty Tuesday afternoon and left with a laptop. He asked if they had seen their faces, but apparently, they had black motorcycle helmets on. The police had even checked the video surveillance files from the cameras on the street in front of the apartment building. On one of the cameras, they had seen the two men with the black helmets leave the building and get into a black SUV. Unfortunately, they could not see the license plate number. He thanked the police officer and asked for a copy of the report for his insurance. He had an uneasy feeling about the whole break-in, thinking they would probably never catch the perpetrators. After the phone call, he continued working until Anna Phearson called him to say that Craig would like to see him in his office. He went straight to his office.

"Hi Craig, you wanted to see me?"

He looked up and stared at Dave's face.

"Hi, yes, I did. More to inform you, I just received a subpoena for the lawsuit filed by Juvenatrust. They've started a summary judgment to stop the publication of the article. I'll attend the first hearing with Wayne next Monday."

"That's quite serious. Do they have a chance to win?"

Craig chuckled.

"Wayne told me they don't stand much of a chance given Harvey Juncker's approval. We'll just proceed with the preparation and I don't expect they'll get the judge to stop publication, but you never know for sure."

"Is there anything I can do?"

Craig looked at him as if trying to figure out what was different about his face.

"Not for now. I believe a journalist should not be directly involved in lawsuits, so I'll take care of it on Monday. I just wanted to warn you, because Wayne told me there's a chance that they might approach you to get a statement from you to use in the lawsuit."

"Okay, I understand, so I should be wary if anyone asks anything."

"Yep, that's all. Other than that, I want you to work on the article about the anti-age cream. Impressive that you could get an appointment on such short notice."

Dave smiled mysteriously.

"Yes, I get along well with the CEO. I think I should be able to finish the article on Monday."

Craig looked back at his desk, signaling the meeting was over.

"Great, Dave. If you get it done earlier, you can always email it to me."

"I'll do that, Craig. See you later!"

Dave worked on until Henry appeared at his desk with a big smile and with his hand in the air, making a drinking gesture. He smiled back, closed his laptop, and packed his briefcase.

"Let's take the staircase down," Dave said.

Henry looked at him a little perplexed and jokingly said, "You look younger with that hair, but now you're starting to act younger, too."

"Going down is a lot easier than going up. No, seriously, I'm trying to move more. We old guys have to move every chance we get."

"How's your back pain?" Henry asked as they walked downstairs.

"A lot better. The doctor told me to move as much as I can. I need to train my back muscles more, that helps to reduce the pain. So, I'm trying to move more."

"Good to hear it's going better. Since I've been Sara, I've also been exercising more and trying to watch my weight a bit."

"Sounds like things are getting more serious with Sara?"

On their way downstairs, Henry explained how it was going and how she was eager to move in with him, but he was putting it off because he liked his freedom. They left the building and walked down the bustling street, headed to a bar two blocks away where they went often. As usual, they had a great time, and Dave was happy to catch up with his best friend. He told him about his interviews, about the trip back, and about Penelope. He diverted a few times the conversation when Henry asked about the hair transplants or the face lift. He did not feel good about hiding the truth from his friend, but he had no choice. He changed the topic back to his interviews at Juvenatrust and the strange things that had happened after, like the fire, Harvey Juncker's death, the burglary in his apartment, the lawsuit. Henry was fascinated. They talked about his article on the electrical brain stimulation helmets, which was also planned for the next issue of the magazine.

Around nine thirty, they left the bar and said goodbye. Dave took the subway back to his apartment. When he arrived in front of his apartment building, he noticed the dark SUV further down the street and thought about his conversation with the police officer in which he mentioned a dark SUV. As he entered the hall of his apartment building, he looked up at the ceiling and noticed for the first time the security camera hidden in the corner. He went upstairs. First to his apartment to put his briefcase away and freshen up a bit.

He felt energetic and was not at all tired when he rang the bell of her apartment. She opened, and they kissed. She asked how the evening had been with Henry, and he explained that he seemed to believe the story about the face lift. Then he talked about what the police officer had told him that day, but he did not tell her about the black SUV in the street. He did not want to scare her and was not even sure it was the same car as the burglars. She talked about her busy day and that she wanted to sleep early. He smiled and said he thought that would be an excellent idea, and began kissing her on the couch. He carried her into the bedroom, and they made love for a very long time. They could not get enough of each other. Around midnight he fell asleep feeling happier than ever before.

The next morning, he woke up a little after and looked at Penelope sleeping beside him. She looked beautiful and peaceful in the morning light. He felt lucky to wake up next to her. He was very careful not to wake her when he got up. He got dressed, left her a note, and went back to his apartment, where he changed into his sport clothes. He had been meaning to go run for a few days. The air was fresh outside, and he ran to Central Park, which was just a few blocks away. It was a beautiful morning. When he entered Central Park, he noticed how calm it was. Only a few people were walking their dog or running. He ran north and turned the music on his phone to something more energetic. He ran faster than usual and felt in better shape than ever before. He began to push his body to its limits more. His condition had improved over the past weeks, and he ran for about an hour before returning to his apartment. He arrived in the hall of the apartment building all sweaty and greeted an old lady called Mrs. Robinson, who lived two floors below him.

"Hello Mrs. Robinson, it's a wonderful day today."

"Oh, hello, sir! Yes, it's sunny."

In the elevator, he realized that poor Mrs. Robinson probably had not recognized him, partly because of his changed looks and partly because of his sweaty sportswear. He took a quick shower before returning to Penelope. When he entered her apartment, she was getting dressed. He started preparing her a nice breakfast and boiled some eggs. A bit after, she came to the kitchen and looked at him.

"Morning. You were up early..."

"Yes, I went running in the park. It's a beautiful day, and I was bursting with energy."

She kissed him as she stroked his chest.

"I noticed yesterday," she said with a flirtatious smile.

They had breakfast together at the kitchen table. At one point, she looked at him and said with a smile on her face, "You look even younger today, with your pink cheeks. Soon people will think I have a toy boy. We'd better put the make-up back on."

He laughed and then she put the make-up around his eyes to make him look older. They had another coffee together until her driver arrived, then they kissed goodbye.

"See you at ten o'clock!"

"All right! Bye, my love."

He retrieved his briefcase and coat from his apartment and took the elevator down. Outside, he looked down the street and noticed the large black SUV further down on the other side of the street. This time he pulled out his phone and took a few pictures using the zoom on his camera, making sure the license plate number was visible on the photo. On his way to the subway station, he called the police officer and explained what he had observed the past few days. The police officer was very interested, and Dave sent him the photos.

About twenty minutes later, he walked out of the Spring Street subway station toward the office. When he arrived in front of the office, he saw another large black SUV parked across the street. He took some pictures of this car as well and made sure the license plate number was visible. He had the impression he saw someone sitting in the car, but with the tinted windows, it was hard to be sure. When he arrived at his desk, he also sent these photos to the police officer with a message that he had taken them in front of his office. He found it suspicious and hoped that the police officer could figure something out. He checked his mail and then began looking for topics for new articles in preparation for the team meeting next Monday.

At one point, he went to the restroom, and when he arrived back at his desk, the phone rang. It was Claire.

"They called from reception to say that there are two visitors waiting for you there."

"Do you know who they are?"

"Oh, I'm sorry, they didn't say, and I completely forgot to ask. Do you want me to ask them?" she said in a bit stressed.

"No, it's all right. I'll go check at the reception."

He took the stairs up to the fifteenth floor where the company reception desk was. As he came out of the stairwell, he saw two men standing in the waiting area with their backs to him. He looked at Stacey Brooks, the receptionist, and she gestured to the two men. They noticed her gesture and turned around. One of them was a blond man in a dark suit with a white shirt and striped red tie, and the other man was wearing a gray suit with a light-blue shirt with no tie.

Dave froze when he saw the face of the man in the gray suit, who had dark hair and a dark mustache. His heart began to beat faster as he recognized the man whom he had seen several times at Juvenatrust. The blond man had a slick face and held out his hand to him.

"Mr. Wilson, I presume? I'm Marc Fender from Benderson and Figwitz. We spoke briefly on the phone last week."

He wanted to leave immediately, as he felt extremely uncomfortable. The man with the dark hair and the mustache looked at his face in amazement and said in disbelief, "Are you Dave Wilson? You... you... you look different from the last time I saw you?"

He felt his heart pounding in his chest and broke out in a cold sweat. The man with the mustache had recognized him, and that worried him. He wanted to leave, but he was also curious who the man with the mustache was.

"Excuse me, but who are you?"

The man with the mustache continued staring at his face and held out his hand with a strange grin on his face.

"I'm Yuri Petrovski and I work for Juvenatrust. I believe we ran into each other a few times in the corridor, although you look very different now. You had no hair on top of your head the last time I saw you and you look much younger than I remember?"

Dave noticed Yuri Petrovski pulling out his phone and looked at pictures on his phone. He was feeling worse by the minute and had to get out of there.

"I'm sorry, Mr. Fender and Mr. Petrovski, but I'm not allowed to talk to you. You'll have to talk to my boss, Craig Pathfinder."

Marc Fender looked concerned when he saw Dave moving back toward the stairs.

"Mr. Wilson, we just have a few questions for you."

He made a turn and walked away, but Yuri Petrovski grabbed him by the arm.

"Mr. Wilson, is that you?"

He showed Dave the screen of his phone. There it was, the picture of himself in a white coat next to Harvey Juncker in his office. The picture Mary Lewis had taken during his interview with Harvey. Dave felt worse by the minute and wondered how this Yuri had gotten hold this picture. He was getting scared now, and without reacting, he hurried away. He walked to the stairwell and opened the door with his badge. He was about to close the door when he heard Yuri call out to him.

"Mr. Wilson! Look at me!"

Without thinking, he turned his head and looked back. Right at that moment, Yuri took a picture of Dave's face. Dave stressed out and immediately closed the door and ran downstairs. He heard them trying to open the door to the stairwell, but it remained locked. Back on the fourteenth floor, he passed Claire's desk, visibly agitated.

"Everything all right, Dave?"

"I'm okay. I was just caught off guard by those visitors. They were from Juvenatrust and that law firm representing them and started asking me all kinds of questions. I referred them to Craig."

"I'm sorry. Next time, I'll ask who's visiting and check better."

"No problem, Claire."

He walked to his desk and looked at his watch. It was already a quarter to ten. He started to pack his briefcase since he now had to rush to his appointment at Penelope's company. He rushed down the stairs, hoping not to run into this Yuri fellow and the lawyer. As he walked down, he called Craig and his secretary answered. She connected him through immediately this time.

"What can I do for you, Dave?"

"Well, I'm on my way to this company from the anti-age cream, but just about ten minutes ago a lawyer named Marc Fender and a man from Juvenatrust, called Yuri Petrovski, showed up at the reception to ask me some questions. I refused to say anything and referred them to you."

"Okay, thanks for telling me, but I haven't seen them yet. This Fender guy was there last Tuesday too, but that Yuri Petrovski is new to me. You have done well. Just send them to me."

"Thanks Craig!"

"No problem, and good luck with your meeting!"

He continued walking downstairs, wondering where the two men would be now. Did they leave already, or were they going to Craig's office? On the ground floor, he peeked around the corner of the stairwell door and scanned the entrance hall. He saw no sign of them and walked toward the exit. Suddenly, he stopped and looked outside as he noticed the two men walking away to the right and crossing the street in front of the building. He hurried through the glass entrance doors and turned left immediately. He was about to disappear around the corner, but cast one last glance at the two men. His heart skipped a beat when he saw them get into the back of a large black SUV with tinted windows, the same type he had seen earlier. One of them looked his way, and he rushed around the corner and walked at a brisk pace toward the subway station. As he went down the escalator, he looked around one more time. He saw no black SUVs, nor any sign of the two men.

Her office was only two stops away from the subway. He was still nervous about what happened at his office. He entered the building and reported to the reception desk. He had to wait a few minutes in the large reception hall. On the wall hung huge pictures of healthy-looking young people in front of beautiful landscapes. Jane Hudson came to pick him up. She was a young, pretty woman dressed in a perfectly fitting business suit. He followed her to the elevator, and Ms. Hudson pressed the button to the fifth floor. There, they walked to Penelope's office all the way in the back. She was sitting behind her modern desk in her spacious office and looked stunning. When Jane closed the door behind her, they kissed passionately.

"How was your morning?" she asked, and his face turned grim.

"Well, not so good, actually. I'm in trouble."

She looked concerned now, and he explained what had just happened. He even showed her the photo Yuri Petrovski had on his phone.

"I don't get how he got this picture. I only sent it to Harvey, and I don't believe he would have given it to anyone else. And with Harvey dead, I find it strange. How did he get this picture?"

She stared at the photo.

"Wow, compared to this picture, you look a lot younger now!"

"I know! And at the reception, he took another picture of me with his phone! I'm afraid he might have made the link and suspects me of stealing the rejuvenation drug."

"Well, I wouldn't worry too much about it. A few pictures aren't enough to prove that. Okay, maybe I should start giving you a tour around the company?"

He looked at his watch and smiled nervously and still agitated.

"Sounds like a good idea."

He spent the rest of the morning touring the company and interviewing two researchers who had worked on the anti-aging cream. Around noon, he finished, and they took him back to her office. They went for lunch together at a restaurant down the street. They had a great time together until Jane called to remind Penelope of her next appointment. They kissed each other goodbye, and he took the subway back to Science Publications. As soon as he got there, his worries returned. He looked down the street in front of the office, but did not see the black SUV anywhere. He took the stairs and walked up the steps fourteen floors up and felt fit. Even if they put him in jail, he thought it had all been worth it, considering how much better he felt.

He walked back to his desk and, with the extensive company visit and interviews, he now had more than enough material to finish his article. He wanted to finish it today so he would have the weekend off to relax and do other things. After he had progressed quite a bit with the article, he felt like a break. He walked over to Henry and when he looked up at him, Dave made a drinking gesture with his arm, to which Henry smiled and got up. After a short break, he continued working on the article and about an hour later, his phone rang. It was Mary.

"Hi Mary, how are you?"

"A bit better, given the circumstances, thanks. I just came back from the meeting that the local police and the fire department had organized for all the Juvenatrust employees and the victims' families. They told us they believe the fire was caused by an explosion in the laboratory on the ground floor early in the evening. The fire department is still investigating what caused the explosion and why the fire could spread so quickly throughout the building. They said it may have been an accident, but they're not ruling out arson either, as they found traces of gasoline in the building. They found two bodies in the laboratory on the ground floor and two bodies in a room on the second floor. The room upstairs was locked and the police are keeping all options open. They will perform autopsies on all the bodies to establish the exact cause of death and to make sure they have correctly identified them. Until then, they cannot release the bodies. The locked room was enough reason for the police to launch a criminal investigation. The video recordings of the security system were lost in the fire, but the police are still checking whether a backup is available. I had asked them if all the research work was lost in the fire and they replied that the company had made backups of all digital work, but that all equipment, the stock of drugs and the cages with mice had been destroyed by the fire. They had found the fridges still full of tubes on the ground floor, but they were all burned. At least with the backups, most of Harvey's research has not been lost."

He listened intently and her update reinforced his suspicion that the whole fire was deliberately set and that Harvey Juncker might have been murdered.

"That's quite some news. Good to hear that Harvey's work isn't completely lost."

"That's not all Dave. Before the meeting, some security guy from Juvenatrust had called me and told me to bring the company laptop Harvey had at home to the meeting."

"That's odd and quick, considering Harvey's recent death. Did you give them the laptop?"

She chuckled.

"Well, I did, but I made a backup on my own PC first. I thought it was suspicious, but I don't want any trouble with them."

"Did they say when they expect to have more news about the investigation?"

"Well, they said they would inform us of any new developments as soon as possible."

"Okay, well, thanks for the update and keep me posted if you hear anything. Juvenatrust is trying to obtain an injunction against the publication, and there's an initial court hearing next Monday, but basically, we're planning to publish the article next week."

"Good luck with that, Dave! I really want that article published. Harvey's research findings should be public. That's what he wanted. Let me know if I there's anything I can do for you."

"Thanks, Mary. I will. Let's keep in touch!"

He continued working. Around five thirty, he had finished a first draft. He was going to go for dinner at seven with Penelope and wanted to call Andrew before that, so he packed his briefcase and hurried down the stairs. Outside, he noticed the large black SUV parked in front of the building. The subway was packed, and he stood the entire seven stops back home. He enjoyed the walk from the subway back to his apartment through the fresh air. His worries returned, however, when he saw another large black SUV across the street in front of his apartment building. He checked the license plate number, but it was a different one than the one from this morning. He took another picture and entered the apartment building while he sent it to the police officer. Back in his apartment, he put his laptop on the living room table and closed the blinds to make it darker. He had promised to call Andrew, and they always used a videoconferencing application. He went to the bathroom to check that his make-up was still okay, and then he called his son. Andrew answered and his mouth fell open when he saw his father.

"Wow, Dad! Nice hair! What a difference! You look much younger."

"Thanks! I guess I should have done it a lot sooner."

"You had told me about hair transplants, but this looks much better than I imagined. I have to show this to Wendy. I'll take a screen shot and maybe you can send me a picture of you?"

Dave grinned a bit after his son's reaction.

"No problem. How's Wendy doing?"

He explained how her pregnancy was going, and then he asked how Dave was doing. He explained that he had fallen in love with Penelope and how their first date went. Andrew was delighted to hear that his father had finally found a new love and was looking forward to meeting her. Then, they talked about all the developments around his article, the fire, Harvey Juncker's death, the lawsuit, and the burglary. Andrew was deeply shocked to hear about Harvey and amazed by all these developments. After a while, his son had to go back to work and, as Dave had hoped, he had said nothing about his younger face. He still felt guilty for not telling him, but he felt with time he would find a way to tell him.

A bit before seven, Penelope called to say she was running late. After hanging up, Dave checked the article one more time and then sent it to Craig and closed his laptop. Enough work for today, he thought. His phone's alarm went off to notify him it was time for his shot. He walked to the bathroom and grabbed the syringe. Back in the kitchen, he took one of the three doses from the cup and filled the syringe. He took off his shirt and injected the dose into his shoulder. Next week, he would switch to two doses a week. He realized he had just finished two weeks of drug treatment and his body had gone through an amazing change. He had noticed no negative effects so far and had not regretted his decision for a moment. He was still walking around in his bare chest, feeling energized. When he was at university, he had been able to do about a hundred push-ups, but he had never managed it since. He tried, and to his surprise, he succeeded. He went to the bathroom to freshen up a bit and still felt his arms from the exertion. He put on a nice dark blue dress shirt and a navy jacket and combed through his short hair. While looking in the mirror, he felt good about himself and his appearance. He walked to her apartment and rang the doorbell. She answered and was wearing a red dress.

"You look stunning," he said as he kissed her on her lips.

"Thank you! Shall we go straight to the restaurant?"

"Yep, let's go."

He noticed the big black SUV still parked in the street, but he decided not to say anything to Penelope and they walked to the restaurant a few blocks away.

After a romantic dinner, they walked back to the apartment building. She held him by the arm. When they arrived at the building, he peered down the street, but he did not see the black SUV anywhere. Maybe he had worried for nothing. They entered the elevator, and she looked at him with dreamy eyes. He kissed her until they arrived at their floor. She walked down the corridor.

"Shall we get some tea in my apartment? Or…"

Her mouth fell open as she looked at Dave's apartment. His heart began to pound when he saw they had forced his door open. He listened at the door, but heard nothing, and pushed it open. They had thrown nothing on the floor this time. He walked slowly inside, and Penelope followed him. He quickly checked all the rooms.

"No one inside. Let's see if I'm missing anything."

This time, no open drawers, no things thrown on the floor, and he saw the empty spot on the table in the living room.

"They took my laptop! It was on the table and now it's gone!"

She stared at the table, still in shock. Stressed, he rushed to the kitchen and opened the fridge. He looked inside and the cup lay on its side. The two doses were gone.

"Oh no! They took the drug doses. I wonder if…"

His heart began to beat faster now, and he dropped to his knees in front of the fridge to check the bottom drawer. The six doses were still taped under the lid of the bottom drawer.

"They didn't find these, but they took the two doses I still had in the cup. Shit, they know!"

She looked at him, puzzled.

"Who knows what?"

He looked at her a little desperately.

"Remember that guy I met at work today who took my picture? I feared he was on to me, but I wasn't sure. I saw them leave in a large black SUV and before dinner I saw a similar SUV across the street in front of our apartment building. I thought I was just being paranoid, but it seems they came looking for the drug and now they've found it."

He rubbed his hands over the side of his face and ran them through his hair.

"Now they could accuse me of theft and sue me. I might end up in jail!"

She tried to calm him down and touched his shoulder.

"Don't worry too much. It's not so easy for them to sue you. Since they stole the doses from your apartment, they can never use that as evidence in court."

He nodded and realized she had a point. Although his worries did not go away.

"Well, I guess I'll just call the locksmith and the police. I'll report the stolen laptop, but I won't say anything about the stolen drugs."

She nodded.

"Meanwhile, I'll prepare some tea."

She walked back to her apartment while he went to make the calls. About two hours later, the locksmith had put a new lock on his door. He had now become paranoid and went to check the storage room in the basement, but no one had broken into it. Back on the fourth floor, he went to see Penelope.

"I have a new set of keys for you. You must have a nice collection of keys by now," he said and showed her the keys with a smile. "I also spoke to the police. I'll have to stop by the station tomorrow morning to file another report. They are going to ask for the video surveillance files from the building again. I wonder if they'll find something this time. I also notified Craig. Fortunately, I had sent him the article about your cream just before dinner."

Penelope poured him a cup of tea.

"Well, time to relax, then. I'm curious what your boss thinks of the article."

He sat down next to her on the couch and took a sip of his tea.

"Yes, me too. It won't be in the coming issue, but probably appear in the next one. I think he'll like it."

He stared wearily ahead, thinking again about the break-in and the stolen doses.

"I've told the police that I suspect Juvenatrust is behind the burglary, because they're trying to stop the publication of the article. They said they would investigate."

She pressed a finger to his lips and turned on some music.

"Stop worrying! It's time to relax now."

As the music played, she began to kiss him. Slowly, he relaxed and enjoyed her soft touch and wonderful scent. They continued kissing, and they started touching each other, and after a while, they undressed. They made love and moved from the living to the bedroom, where they continued to make love until they fell asleep.

The next morning, he woke up next to her. She was still deep in sleep. He slipped out of bed and walked to the kitchen. It was a beautiful sunny day and his eyes had to get used to the bright light in the living room. He prepared breakfast for the two of them. The moment he had just finished preparing the kitchen table for breakfast, he noticed her in her bathrobe, standing in the doorway of the bedroom. She still looked sleepy.

"Morning. I made breakfast."

She kissed him, gave him a hug, and looked at the table.

"Mmm... looks good!"

They sat down at the table and had breakfast while discussing their plans for the weekend. She knew a nice restaurant near Battery Park, so they decided to have lunch there today. On Sunday, her brother, Andy, and his wife had invited them to go sailing with them for the day on their sailing boat. She thought it would be a good moment to introduce Dave to her brother. He liked the idea, and she called her brother to confirm. He cleared the table while she phoned Andy. He wanted to go running in the morning before going to the station to file a police report. Penelope had a yoga class in the morning. After the call, they kissed goodbye, and he went back to his apartment.

He changed into his sports clothes and put on his running shoes. In the elevator, he attached his cell phone to his arm, put on some music, and walked outside. The air was still fresh, and he felt sun's rays on his face. It was a beautiful day. He peered out into the street and noticed the black SUV was back. It was parked further down the street in the opposite direction of where he was going. He ran toward Central Park, away from the apartment building and the black SUV. It was ideal weather for running, not too hot and a nice clear sky with a fresh breeze.

He looked back one more time and, to his surprise, he saw the black SUV was making a U-turn. He turned the corner and continued toward Central Park. He arrived at Broadway. The pedestrian light was green, and he ran across the street without stopping. After crossing, he looked back into the street and saw the large SUV stopped in front of the traffic lights on Broadway. It could still be a coincidence, but he had the impression that the car was following him. He increased his pace a bit. Just before he reached Central Park West Avenue, he saw the approaching black SUV from the corner of his eyes. It halted a few feet in front of him and two men, wearing black motor helmets with dark-tinted visors, jumped out. Dave startled and jumped away from them, feeling a hand on his arm from one of the two men. He made a quick sideways motion and jerked his arm loose, then he accelerated and sprinted away. He ran as fast as he could.

Just before crossing Central Park West Avenue, he glanced left and right. Several cars approached, but he ran right in between them. Some cars honked and one car stopped with screeching tires. He noticed the driver raise his fist at him. He ran on as fast as he could and jumped onto the sidewalk on the other side. He continued to run at high speed along the sidewalk northward. He quickly looked behind him and saw the SUV had now also crossed Central Park West Avenue and was coming his way at high speed. He continued as fast as he could, but as he approached the park entrance, the black SUV passed him and stopped with screeching tires in front of the park entrance. As he almost reached the entrance, two men jumped out of the SUV, blocking the park entrance. They both extended their arms and were about to grab him. He reacted in an instant. Instead of running through the park entrance, he turned and without hesitation jumped over the three-foot high stone wall that marked the boundary of Central Park. After landing on the grass on the other side, he ran as fast as he could into the park. A little further into the park, he looked over his shoulder. He no longer saw the two men and slowed down. He turned and looked back at the entrance. The black SUV and the two men were gone.

As he slowed down, the adrenaline rush he had felt earlier slowly dissipated. He looked back again to check that nobody was following him and called Penelope.

"This is the voicemail of Penelope Garcia. You can leave a message after the beep."

He remembered she had a yoga class and left a message.

"Hi Penelope, it's Dave. I went running in Central Park and that large black SUV I told you about was following me. Two men with black helmets jumped out. I think they wanted to kidnap me. I slipped away, but they might try again. I'll try to run to the precinct now. Try to call me. I love you with all my heart."

He hung up and still felt stressed. Fearing the men in the SUV would wait on the edge of the park for him, he kept running through the park until he would figure out a way to avoid his assailants. He felt relatively safe in the park, because the black SUV could not get there. While he was running, he thought about what to do next. They probably expected him to return to his apartment. It seemed best to go straight to the precinct. With a bit of luck, he could talk to the same police officer and explain everything. Feeling fit and energetic, he ran all the way to the north side of the park, and as he approached the edge of the park, he peered into the street, but there was no trace of the black SUV. He felt relieved when he realized he had shaken them off. He ran on and felt better. On his way back south, he ran through the middle of the park, avoiding the major streets on the side of the park. He passed the Turtle Pond and approached Belvedere Castle. There were fewer people in this part of the park, which made him feel less at ease.

Suddenly, he saw the two men with the black helmets coming out of a path, and they walked onto the road on which he was running. He got startled by the sudden appearance so close to him, and before he could turn around, he was staring into the barrel of a black gun that one of the men pointed at him.

"Mr. Wilson, come with us now or I'll have to shoot you!" the man with the gun said in a low voice.

Dave stopped and stood in front of them. The other man grabbed his arm. The man with the gun pointed at the small path going down.

"That way, Mr. Wilson."

He looked at the path and realized it led down to the 79th Street Transverse. They probably had their car parked down there, and he was afraid they would kidnap him. Suddenly, he saw a mountain biker coming up behind the two men at high speed. Dave saw his chance and in one swift move, he pushed the man, holding his arm against the man with the gun. The man on the mountain bike got startled and could no longer avoid the men, and crashed into them.

They fell to the ground, groaning in pain. He did not hesitate a second and ran as fast as he could toward Belvedere Castle. He ran as if his life depended on it and kept sprinting southward through the park. At some point, he glanced quickly over his shoulder, but there was no more sign of the two men. He continued running until he crossed the bow bridge over the lake. He slowed down and looked behind and around him, but the two men had disappeared.

He called the police officer he had spoken to earlier about the burglary. He looked for the number on his phone and then dialed it.

"This is the voicemail of Donald Russel at the NYPD Midtown North Precinct. I can't answer your call right now, but if you leave a message with your phone number, I'll call you back as soon as possible."

He felt unlucky and left a message.

"Hi Mr. Russel, this is Dave Wilson. I spoke to you last week about the burglary in my apartment and the suspicious SUVs in front of my building. You showed me men with black helmets on the video footage. I ran into these same men with these black helmets and their black SUV today. They tried to kidnap me and pointed a gun at me. I escaped and I'm now trying to get to the Midtown North Precinct. I'm in great danger and need protection. I think Juvenatrust has something to do with it. Someone broke into my apartment a second time yesterday and they stole my laptop. Please try to call me back as soon as possible."

He kept running southward, constantly looking around him to see if those men were anywhere near. It seemed better to him not to leave the park at Columbus Circle, because it was on the way to his apartment building and they might be waiting for him there. He left the park near Seventh Avenue. When he got to the edge of the park, he saw the traffic lights at Fifty-Ninth Street and waited to leave the park until the pedestrian lights turned green. The moment they did, he ran out of the park as fast as he could and crossed Fifty-Ninth Street. To his surprise, he saw to his right the black SUV waiting behind another car at the stoplight. He wondered how they knew he was going to leave the park here. Were they tracing his phone? The fact that they were waiting for him at the Belvedere Castle had been a little too coincidental.

He knew this neighborhood well and ran as fast as he could to the next street. He heard a car approaching fast. When he looked to his left, he saw the black SUV passing him over. When he got to Fifty-Eighth Street, he turned right onto it and was lucky it was congested with cars and because it was a one-way street, they could not follow him there. He ran as fast as he could to Broadway, then he turned southwards on Broadway. Several people on the street stared at him, because he was running very fast. He was approaching Fifty-Seventh Street, and he knew that if they were tracking his phone, they might be waiting there for him. As he peered into Fifty-Seventh street, he saw the black SUV parked on the side and the two men with black helmets were waiting for him. He felt pursued, and they came closer and closer.

He needed to get to the Precinct as fast as possible. He ran to the left and crossed Broadway, running. He barely managed to dodge an oncoming car, and cars were honking all around him. People were now staring at him as if he was a madman, trying to commit suicide. When he got across the street, he immediately ran on and crossed Fifty-Seventh Street to continue southbound on Broadway. He noticed the black SUV was driving along with him on the other side of the road. Because it was stuck on the one-way street on Broadway between Fifty-Seventh and Fifty-Sixth Street, he turned around and ran back onto Fifty-Seventh street eastbound. He looked around to see if he saw any police officers anywhere, but he had no luck today. He thought of one of Henry's comments: that the police were always there to give you a fine, but when you needed them, they were nowhere to be found. Today was just one of those days.

As he ran back toward Seventh Avenue, he knew they would probably take Fifty-Sixth Street and then Seventh Avenue to come his way. He thought he better go to the Fifty-Seventh Street subway station, at the corner of Fifty-Seventh Street and Seventh Avenue, because that seemed to be the only way to get rid of the black SUV. As he approached the entrance to the subway station, he saw the black SUV arrive on Seventh Avenue, which was behind the station entrance. He ran as fast as he could toward the subway entrance, feeling he had a good chance of making it and if he could take the subway, he would be able to shake off his pursuers. When he was almost at the entrance, he looked at the SUV on the street behind the entrance, but then suddenly another black SUV stopped next to him with tires screeching. Two men wearing black helmets jumped in front of him. One of the men pushed an elderly lady. She fell to the ground with a big smack and started screaming loudly, "Ah… ah… help! They broke my arm! Those bastards pushed me!"

More people stopped and stared at the scene. Meanwhile, one of the men with the black helmets fired a taser at Dave. Suddenly, all his muscles contracted, and he felt paralyzed as his body ached everywhere. He fell onto the sidewalk and the two men pulled him upright. A man in a suit, watching the men drag Dave to the SUV, shouted, "Call the police! Call the police!"

Dave saw a young man who seemed to be filming everything with his smartphone. It shocked him no one came to help him as the men pushed him into the back of the black SUV. A man inside the SUV leaned toward him with a black bag and pulled it over his head. He could no longer see anything. He felt another man next to him and they pushed him. He heard the door close and the man next to him yelled, "Go! Go!"
He heard the car's engine whine as the car pulled up fast.
Everything was dark and as he felt the car move, the man next to him pushed him forward and then he felt a blow to his head.

10. Lost freedom

The first thing he felt when he regained consciousness was the excruciating pain in his head. It was pitch dark around him and he could see nothing at all, but it felt like everything was moving. Slowly, he became more aware of his surroundings and heard a whooshing sound. He had the impression he was sitting. It felt like he was tied to a chair, and both his ankles and wrists were attached. He could barely move. The whooshing sound reminded him of the sound you had in airplanes. Then he felt the vibration and felt his seat moving slightly. He was almost certain that he was on a plane. The way it moved gave him the impression it was not a very large plane, either. Other than the loud whooshing of the plane, he heard nothing else. No voices, as if he was all alone onboard.

His head ached horribly, and he felt like touching it, but he could not move his hands. His mouth felt dry, and he was thirsty. He tried to lick his lips to moisten them, and his tongue touched the cloth of the bag that was over his head. He thought of those prisoners in a war he had seen on the news with black bags over their heads, and now he felt like them. Helpless and unaware of what was going on around them, except for the noise and smells. The air smelled stuffy.

He heard two loud thumps in the plane, and then only the whooshing sound continued. Then he heard a rumbling sound, as if there was a change in the engines' gyration and the engine was revving up. He felt a change in pressure in his ears and tried to equalize by swallowing, although it was more difficult with his dry mouth and he kept more pressure on his ears than usual. It felt like the plane was descending. He heard someone pass beside him. Dave was worried and wondered why he had been kidnapped and by whom. Was it really Juvenatrust or someone else? And what were they going to do with him? He did not understand and thought of Penelope. He hoped he had not put her in any danger and that she was all right. Maybe they did not know about their relationship, and that would probably be safer for her. He also wondered if people had started looking for him.

The plane kept descending. At some point, he heard a high-pitched whirring sound. It sounded familiar to him, for he had often flown and had always been afraid. Every sound used to scare him, but this time he did not think about that. He was worried about what would happen to him. Now he heard what could be the sound of a hydraulic pump and then a thud. He recognized it as the sound of the landing gear coming out. He kept swallowing to relieve the pressure in his ears, and the plane seemed to descend faster. Then suddenly he felt the plane hit the ground and from the way it bounced, he realized it was a small plane. He was pushed forward in his chair as the plane braked on the runway.

Normally, a flight attendant would have announced something, but so far, he had heard no one speak. It all felt eerie. The plane came slowly to a stop, and he heard the engine stop. He heard people moving around him and heard a door open, and then a man said, "Bring him outside!"

He heard someone approach, and then he felt an arm close to his hands. He heard some chains rattle and someone touched his ankles, and then opened his seat belt. His hands, still tied together, were pulled up by someone, and he heard a deep male voice.

"Mr. Wilson, stand up and follow me carefully."

He pushed himself upright and slowly walked sideways in the direction where he felt the strap around his hands pulling him. His head still hurt, and he felt like touching it, but his hands were pulled forward. There was now someone behind and someone in front of him now, and suddenly he felt a breeze of fresh air on his face. A voice said, "We're going down the stairs now. Be careful and move slowly."

He felt a little afraid to go down a flight of stairs seeing nothing, and he moved more slowly now. He slid his feet forward until at one point he felt the edge of the stairs, and then slowly moved one foot down until he hit the first step. Thus, he slowly moved down the stairs until, at some point, there were no more steps and he touched the ground. The fresh air did him good, and despite the bag over his head, he was breathing better. It was hot outside, and sweat was dripping off his head. He slowly shuffled forward until he felt a hand on his head pushing him down.

"Get in the car, Mr. Wilson, and sit down!"

He felt a hand on his leg, helping him get into the car, and he slowly slid in. A hand pushed him further, and he slid onto a seat until he felt a large and heavy man next to him. On his other side, another man sat down and he was sitting in between the two now. He could smell their sweat, especially one of them smelling bad. He stayed like that while the car started moving. He had the impression the ride was long, and at some point, he even dozed off. After waking up again as the car moved over rougher terrain, he gathered enough courage to ask, "Where're you taking me?"

The complete silence after he had asked this terrified him. He thought there were at least three other people in the car with him, but none of them answered, not a word. The entire ride, none of them spoke. He could hear the breathing of the man next to him. It sounded like he had the lungs of a heavy smoker. No one said a word. He asked nothing more and just waited as they took him to an unknown destination. Wherever he was going, it was not cold, because he was still sitting in his running shorts and felt warm. With his bare knees, he touched the seat in front of him. The upholstery felt like leather.

After what felt like hours to him, the car stopped and he heard the man next to him open the door. A hand touched him on his shoulder and he heard a man's voice.

"Follow me!"

He slid across the seat to the side of the car and put his feet out of the car on the ground. He felt a hand on his head as he stepped out of the car. He could see nothing and it was still pitch black, but he felt warmth on his face and body. He moved slowly and the hand on his shoulder guided him a little. There was only the sound of the wind and the sound of his own footsteps and those of the surrounding men. The ground felt loose, as if he was walking on a dirt road.

After five minutes of slow shuffling, he came to a harder surface and heard a door open, and the hand guided him inside. The heat he had felt on his body disappeared and he now felt cool air on his legs and face. He had entered some air-conditioned room, and it felt a lot cooler than outside. The floor felt different, much smoother and harder. They led him through a long hallway until he felt like he was crossing some kind of threshold. He heard doors closing and suddenly he felt the ground move like an elevator, as if they were going down. At some point, the moving stopped, and they led him down another corridor. Occasionally, he heard people walking and passing by, but no one spoke. It all felt surreal to him. He walked over another threshold, but this time, the floor did not move. A door closed behind him and he heard what sounded like some electronic lock. Complete silence followed, and he now heard only his own breathing.

He shuffled across the room until he hit the wall. As he moved in another direction, he bumped his leg against an edge that felt like a bed. He turned and sat down on the bed. He was cold in his sports clothes, in this air-conditioned room. He tried to pull the cloth bag off his head, but it seemed to be stuck around his neck. The more he pulled, the more his neck hurt. Then he heard the door open, and he immediately sat up straight when he heard a man's voice, "Mr. Wilson, I'll untie you. Please remain calm and don't try to escape or the guard next to me will have to taser you."

"Okay," Dave replied and did not move an inch, terrified of being tasered again.

He felt someone pulling on the straps around his wrists until suddenly his wrists were loose. He rubbed them and moved his hands to ease the stiffness. Now he felt someone touch the cloth bag around his head until it came loose around his neck. A second later, the bright light hurt his eyes as they pulled the bag off his head. He immediately covered his eyes, as the light was too bright. He heard the man say, "I'll get you some clothes. Try to relax, Mr. Wilson."

He looked up at the man and saw a dark man in a dark blue uniform. He had a friendly face. Behind the man he saw a tall heavy man standing in a black uniform and he had a taser in his hands. The guard looked menacing and had a scar above his eye.

"Where am I?"

The man smiled at him and as he walked away, he said, "We'll be back in about half an hour, Mr. Wilson."

The guard also left, and he heard the door lock behind them. He looked around the room. The walls and ceiling were light gray. On one side, there was a bed, and on the other, a small desk with a chair in front of it. He saw a toilet and a sink next to the desk. In the middle, opposite to the door, was a window. Or at least it looked like a window, but there were no bars or anything. He got up and walked toward the window and he looked out at a green forest. As he wondered where he was, he touched the window and felt the glass surface. It was only the image of a forest on a television screen and not a real window. Maybe there was no forest outside. He saw it was recessed into the wall, making it look more like a window. There was a vent in the ceiling next to the lamp. The door looked like heavy metal and there was a small hatch inside it.

He wondered where he was and wanted to look at his watch to see what time it was, but his watch was no longer on his wrist. His phone was also gone. His head still felt sore, and he groped it with his hands. He felt a huge bump on the back of his head and noticed a little blood on his hands after touching it. He stretched his legs and walked to the sink to wash his hands and face. Then he dried himself with the towel hanging next to the sink. There was no mirror. It was chilly, and he took the blanket from the bed and wrapped it around him and lay down a bit to rest.

After a while, he heard the lock on the door move, then the door opened. He got up and sat on the edge of the bed. The friendly dark man was back, followed by the guard with the scar. He was carrying a pile of perfectly folded light blue clothes. As he put the pile on the desk, Dave saw some metal wristband lying on top of the pile. The man took it and looked at him.

"During your stay here, you'll wear this wristband. It'll show you the time, and occasionally, it'll show messages. Please hold your hand forward."

Dave looked at the metal wristband, which looked like a large electronic watch. On the inside of the band, it looked strange though, as he saw some wires and pins inside. He looked at the dark man and tried to assess him.

"And what if I don't want to wear your wristband?"

The armed guard with the scar stepped forward, and in a deep voice, he said, "Then I'll make you wear it, but I advise you to listen to my colleague."

Dave looked at the armed guard, who was looking menacingly at him with the taser in his hand. He extended his arm to the dark man, who put the metal band on his wrist and closed it. It made a heavy clicking noise. He looked at it and could see the time on it. It was five o'clock in the afternoon, but he did not know if he was still in the same time zone as New York since they had flown him somewhere.

"Where am I?" he asked the friendly dark man.

"Please take off all your clothes, Mr. Wilson, and put on these clothes. I'll be back in ten minutes, and then we'll take you upstairs."

"What's upstairs?"

But the two men walked away without answering and closed the door behind them. He looked at the metal band on his wrist to see how he could take it off, but there was no opening mechanism on the back. He tried pulling on it and bending it to open the back, but nothing worked. The metal watch remained closed on his wrist. He looked at the pile of light blue clothes. He got up and checked the pile. It was a complete set, and it even included light blue underwear and light blue socks. He was still cold, so he started taking off his clothes to put on the light blue ones. He undressed completely and then put on the light blue underwear, which felt comfortable and soft. Then he put the light blue trousers and the light blue shirt on. They seemed to have picked out exactly his size because it fit him perfectly. He put his running shoes back on and put all his clothes in a pile on the desk.

He was hungry, and even though he had no clue how long he had not eaten, it felt like a very long time. He began to worry about what would happen to him now. If they were willing to kidnap him, they might also be willing to kill him. But then he realized they could have easily killed him already if they had wanted to. It probably would have been easier to kill him than to kidnap him. Whoever had kidnapped him wanted something from him. But what?

The mechanical sound of the door unlocking startled him out of his thoughts. The friendly dark man entered the room, followed by the mean-looking guard.

"Hello Mr. Wilson. Perfect. I see you're ready. Please, follow me!"

He followed the man and passed the guard, who seemed to watch his every move. They walked out of the room into a long corridor painted in the same light gray color, which had as many as twenty doors. They walked on and he saw an elevator at the end of the corridor. There were no windows anywhere. The dark man passed his wrist along the sensor next to the elevator door and it opened. Dave noticed the man was wearing a similar metal wristband to the one he was wearing. There was a double door next to the elevator with another sensor next to it. Dave looked at the electronic panel in the elevator and saw they were on the floor, marked minus nine. The buttons went from minus ten to plus five and he deducted he suspected he was deep underground. The dark man looked at him now.

"Mr. Wilson, please scan your wristband here on the sensor every time you enter the elevator."

Dave moved his wristband close to the sensor. The dark man pushed the button to the fourth floor, and the doors closed. The elevator moved at high speed and Dave suddenly felt heavier and felt some pressure in his ears. He noticed a camera in the elevator's corner and then he looked in the mirror. He looked healthy and young again without the make-up he had been wearing that week. His dark hair was shiny and thick. He noticed the guard was watching him. Dave looked at the taser the guard had in his hand, and then he saw the guard was also wearing a metal wristband. When they reached the fourth floor, the elevator braked, and he felt his stomach rise. He looked toward the door now, wondering where he had arrived.

The door opened, and they walked into a bright white corridor. To the left and right, he saw a long corridor with a window at each end and many doors in between. Right in front of him, there was another corridor, and he followed the dark man into this one over the black marble floor. Everything looked much more luxurious, nothing like the bare gray floor he had just come from. Still, the place felt cold and creepy. At the end of this corridor, they walked through a large double door from thick, black wood and entered a reception area. A blond woman in a navy-blue business suit sat behind the reception counter. Next to it was another double door in the same black wood with a large man in a black uniform next to it.

The man, armed with a gun and what looked like a taser, stared at him but did not move an inch. The dark man spoke to the blond woman.

"I have Mr. Wilson here for Mr. Broch."

The woman looked at the screen of her computer and replied, "He's still on the phone. Please take a seat in the waiting area."

The blond woman pointed to the chairs next to the counter. There were no windows, but on the walls hung several large Cubist-style paintings. On the paintings, he saw what looked like humans with cyborg extensions. He had heard that name before, Mr. Broch, but could not remember where. After a while, the woman from the reception walked up to them and he noticed her beautiful long legs under the short dark blue skirt.

"Mr. Broch will receive you now."

She opened the left door of the heavy double door and the dark man walked in and gestured Dave to follow him. As he walked through the door, he noticed it was probably thicker than his leg. He entered what looked like a huge office. On the left and right were doors and in front of him was a seating area and next to it was a large desk with floor-to-ceiling windows behind it. He immediately looked outside, curious as he was for clues as to where he was. He saw a vast dry desert-like landscape with a mountain range in the distance. It reminded him of landscapes he had seen in Arizona or Texas, but it could also be in Mexico. In front of the windows sat a bald man at the large desk. The man stood up and walked toward him. He was almost as tall as him and wore a dark blue suit with a light blue dress shirt.

"Welcome, Mr. Wilson!" the man said as he held out his hand.

Dave shook his hand, which felt strange, hard, and different from a normal hand. The man continued to hold his hand as he continued talking.

"I'm Jeff Broch…"

Suddenly he remembered. Jeff Broch was Juvenatrust's largest shareholder and one of the more mysterious billionaires in the world.

"… and I'm sorry for the inconvenient trip you had to make up here…"

He felt very nervous, and the fact that Jeff Broch kept holding his hand did not help. Jeff stared at his face as he continued talking and moved closer to his face, making him feel even more uncomfortable.

"... but I didn't have much choice when I heard you stole something from me. I can feel your fear. Don't worry, Mr. Wilson, if I wanted to kill you, you would have been dead already. I wanted to see you with my own eyes. I couldn't believe my ears when one of my men told me he suspected you had stolen our rejuvenation drug and probably used it on yourself."

He looked at his left wrist, on which he wore a metal wristband wider than Dave's, with a large screen on it. When Jeff looked at the screen, it came on and showed the picture of Dave and Harvey together in their white coats. Jeff looked at it and then stared back at Dave's face. He examined Dave's face and hair up closely.

"Amazing! How long have you been taking the drugs?"

Dave was not sure if he should be open and honest with this man and admit his theft. He hesitated. Perhaps it was better to deny in order to prevent them from suing and convicting him.

"I... I... I don't know what you're talking about."

Jeff squeezed his hand harder now. It was not a normal hand, because the power in the grip was amazing. It was as if Dave's hand got stuck in a heavy metal molding press and the pain in his increased. Jeff looked him in the eye and said with a complacent smile, "It's no use lying to me, Mr. Wilson. I have a lie detector sensor in my hand, a convenient extension of my body. Answer my question!"

Dave squirmed in pain and said, "It... it's now been two weeks since the first dose."

Jeff's firm hand squeeze loosened, and Dave felt the blood circulating in his hand with a tingling sensation in his fingers. Jeff touched Dave's hair.

"Two weeks, impressive! I've always been skeptical of Dr. Juncker's claims, but you're living proof."

Jeff let go of his hand and walked back to his desk. Dave looked at the hand that had held his hand so strongly, but he did not notice anything odd. It looked like a normal hand, perhaps a little too perfect. As Jeff Broch walked back to his desk, Dave noticed a small metal cap on the back of his head with a thin wire going down in his shirt. Jeff Broch sat back at his desk as the meeting was over. He still had many questions, though, so he asked, "Mr. Broch, why did you bring me here?"

Jeff looked up from his desk and replied with an emotionless face, "You're the first human in the world to have taken our rejuvenation drug. We're keeping you here to examine you. You've taken a drug that has not even been tested in a clinical trial yet. Our scientists will be thrilled."

He kept looking at Jeff and asked, "How long are you going to keep me here?"

"As long as it takes, Mr. Wilson," Jeff replied, and then added, "Just to be clear. You're here because you stole something from me and you'll remain here as long as we deem useful. You'll be assigned a room downstairs with the others."

"What do you mean by the others?"

"You'll see that soon enough, Mr. Wilson."

He did not like the prospect of going back to this gray prison cell, and he was starving.

"Can I get something to eat?"

Jeff was smiling now.

"At seven, dinner will be served for all of you. Just to make a few things clear about your stay here. As my guest, you're free to roam around in the areas where you're allowed. Don't try to escape or resist any of us, or we'll have to take measures. If you attempt to enter any area where you're not authorized, you'll receive a warning via the wristband on your arm. If you persist in trespassing, you'll be punished. That's all for now. James and Henry will escort you to your quarters. Goodbye, Mr. Wilson!"

Jeff looked away and stared at the computer screen on his desk. He felt a hand on his shoulder. When he turned his head, he looked into the friendly eyes of the dark man.

"I'm James, Mr. Wilson. Please follow me."

Dave quickly turned his head to take another look out the windows and stared at the landscape, desperately searching other buildings, but he saw only a dirt road and, for the rest, a dry arid landscape. He walked with James and the guard back to the elevator. When they passed the reception, he looked at the guard.

"So, you're Henry?"

The guard did not smile, he just grunted a little. In the corridor, they walked toward the elevator and he started talking to James.

"James, where're we going? Do I have to stay in this gray prison cell?"

James shook his head.

"No, Mr. Wilson. You'll get a room with the other people."

"You can call me Dave. What do you mean by the other people?"

James smiled at him as they approached the elevator.

"Dave, you'll see that downstairs. You're not the only one staying here. You get your own room, and you're allowed to move freely on the floor. You'll get permission to go to some of the other floors, for example, to eat in the restaurant at seven o'clock."

He opened the elevator with his wristband. James pressed the button to go to floor minus three. When the doors closed, James continued talking as the elevator quickly descended.

"I'm part of the support staff, just like everyone else, in a dark blue uniform. If you need anything, you can always ask us or you can use your wristband. If you hold your other hand on it and ask something, you'll get an answer on the screen."

James took his hand and showed him how to do this.

"Go ahead, ask, for example, which room you'll be staying in."

He looked at the wristband, held his other hand on it and asked, "Which room will I stay in?"

The dark screen showed a message in yellow letters and it said: *"Dave Wilson's room is -3.12."*

Meanwhile, the elevator slowed down, and the doors opened. James walked out and continued explaining.

"The three is for the third floor below ground level and the twelve is your room number on this floor."

As they walked down the hallway, he noticed the walls were painted in the same white color as on the fourth floor and there were twenty doors. To his surprise, he saw some people walking down the corridor. Many doors were closed, but some were open. In the room with the first open door he passed, he saw an older-looking man with glasses in a light blue uniform, just like the one he was wearing. The man looked at him and then anxiously at the guard in a black uniform. Dave looked at him and waved his hand.

"Hello."

Immediately, the guard pushed against his arm to indicate he should move on. The man in the door greeted him back.

"You'll have plenty of time to get acquainted with the other people down here. First, I'll show you your room," James said.

He noticed the numbers next to the doors, and they stopped halfway down the corridor at the door with number twelve on it.

"Please hold your wristband next to this sensor!" James said as he pointed to the sensor on the door.

He held his wrist next to the sensor and heard the electronic lock open. He entered the room, and with its white walls, it seemed larger than the prison cell downstairs. There was a bed on the left and a desk with a chair on the right, but no toilet and no sink. Next to the desk, there was a large closet. Under the desk he saw several drawers and on the desk a paper and a pen. Next to the desk was a small refrigerator with a kettle on it, and some cups and instant coffee, tea, sugar, and milk. The window looked exactly like the one in the prison cell, and he recognized the forest outside. There was also a remote control on the desk. James saw him looking at it, picked it up and pointed at the window.

"This is the remote control for the television. That's not a window, it's a screen and you can watch television on it. If you need anything, you just ask your wristband or the support staff. You can freshen up in the washing room down the hall. That's also where the toilets and showers are and there's a locker with your room number on it with toiletries, which you can open with your wristband. The wristband is waterproof, so you can wear it all the time, even in the shower. It is now fifteen minutes past six and dinner is at seven on the second floor, but they will notify you before. I'll leave you alone now. Have a nice evening, Dave."

Dave wanted to ask so many more questions, but James and the guard were already walking away.

"Thank you, James!"

He touched the back of his head and the bump was still painful, but he felt the headache was easing. He looked around the room and opened the closet. Inside, it was full of light blue clothes neatly folded on several shelves. He inspected them and there was even light blue sportswear and a pair of light blue swim shorts.

He went to the restroom. He looked left and right but the hallway was empty he walked to the end. He passed some doors that were half open, but there was no one there either. There were two doors at the end, one on the left with a sign for men and one on the right with a sign for women. He entered the men's washroom and saw the older-looking man with the glasses he had seen earlier combing his gray hair in front of a mirror. He walked up to the man and held out his hand.

"Hi, I'm Dave Wilson."

The man shook his hand with a friendly smile on his face.

"Hello, I'm Dr. William Ashton. I'm sorry I was gruff before, but I'm always careful around those guards."

Dave noticed he was also wearing a wristband.

"How long have you been here?"

"Over a year now, since they locked me in here. I assume you just arrived since I haven't seen you here before?"

Dave nodded.

"I was kidnapped this morning, I think. Although, I don't know how long I was unconscious, but I suppose today is still Saturday. Is that right?"

"Yes, it's Saturday. Where are you from and what's your specialization, Dave?"

"I'm from New York and am a journalist for Science Magazine, and you?"

William looked puzzled.

"A journalist? That makes you the first one in here. Everyone else here is a scientist. I'm from Boston and previously worked in at a research center. I'm a neuroscientist with a specialization in brain stimulation and brain implants. They force me here to work on several projects in that field. This is the first time I've seen a journalist in here. Any idea why they brought you here?"

Dave looked down, as he felt ashamed. Since Jeff Broch knew what he had done, he no longer saw the need to lie about it.

"Well, I don't know exactly what they plan to do with me, but I stole experimental drugs from one of Jeff Broch's companies and took them myself. They hadn't even started clinical trials yet."

William looked astonished.

"Taking drugs before they've gone through clinical trials can be very dangerous. What's this drug supposed to do?"

Dave grinned and looked at William, who looked at least something like sixty years old.

"Well, let me ask you first, what age do you think I am?"

William looked a little puzzled and was now looking at Dave's face.

"That's difficult since I would guess from your behavior that you're older than you look, but I would say somewhere between twenty-five and thirty years old."

He was pleased with the answer, as it proved his point.

"I'm fifty-four and the drug I took makes my body young again, like a rejuvenation drug."

William looked flabbergasted and stared at his face.

"Fifty-four and not a wrinkle in your face, nor gray hair or bald spots. Remarkable."

Dave checked the time, and it was already a quarter to seven.

"I'm sorry William, I'd love to talk longer with you, but they told me we're having dinner at seven and I still want to freshen up before. They told me there would be some toiletries down here. Do you know where I can find them?"

"No problem, Dave! Let me show you around."

William showed him his locker and demonstrated how to open it with his wristband. In the locker, he found everything he needed, from towels to shaving gear, toothpaste, toothbrushes, even shampoo and all kinds of creams.

William returned to his room while Dave washed himself. He went to the toilet and after that washed his hands. Suddenly, he felt the wristband vibrate. The screen flashed and displayed a message:

"Proceed to the restaurant on floor 2."

He left the washing area toward the elevator. He now saw several people walking in the same direction. A man with long gray hair and a gray beard emerged from a room. He looked like an old hippy. Noticing Dave, he said with a friendly smile, "Hello there! A new face!? I'm Larry Miner."

Larry held out his hand, and Dave shook it.

"Hi, I'm Dave Wilson. They kidnapped me and brought me here today."

As they walked together toward the elevator, Larry continued, "That's how we were all brought here, unfortunately. I've been here for four months now. I'm a specialist in artificial intelligence and machine learning. What's your specialty?"

The question no longer surprised Dave, as he was under the impression that everyone here had some sort of specialty as a scientist.

"Well, I'm a journalist for Science Magazine."

A woman dressed in a similar light blue uniform came out of another room and when she heard what he said, her mouth dropped open.

"A journalist? That's the first one here. Let me introduce myself. I'm Margaret Jones and I've a background in biological engineering. I work in 3D bio-printing. I was kidnapped about five months ago."

He shook her hand and explained to Margaret and Larry how he had ended up with them. They saw William waiting for the elevator next to an older-looking bald man with thick rings under his eyes and round glasses on his nose. Dave said, "Hi William."

William smiled back and at the others.

"Hi, Dave. I see you've met Margaret and Larry. I think this first day can be overwhelming with all these new faces. Let me introduce you to Pierre Lavoisier."

He shook the hand of the bald man to whom William pointed.

"Hi, I'm Dave Wilson. I'm a journalist for Science Magazine."

The bald man looked surprised and in a strong French accent said, "Ah bon, a reporter!? I'm a specialist in medical engineering. How did you end up here?"

He explained the whole story to Pierre Lavoisier, who responded, "Ah, the first day. That's always an overwhelming experience. On top of it, it's quiet on this floor today. Most of the people were still working in one of the laboratories downstairs. You'll meet them in the restaurant."

Dave smiled back at the group.

"Yes, I still feel like this's a bad dream and I'm hoping to wake up. I've been so…"

He stopped talking, his mouth fell open and he could not believe his eyes. The elevator door had opened and there were about five people inside, all dressed in light blue uniforms. One of them was Dr. Harvey Juncker. He was wearing a different model of glasses, but he recognized him immediately. Harvey looked puzzled at him. After staring at Harvey for a few seconds, Dave said, "I can't believe my eyes. Harvey? I thought you were dead!?"

Harvey stared at him and stuttered, "D... D... Dave? What happened to your face? All this hair on your head?"

"You're alive!" Dave said and was so happy to see Harvey that he gave him a hug. After that, he still kept his hands on Harvey's shoulders and looked at him, still in disbelief. He looked older and more tired than the last time he had met him in Novato. The elevator doors closed behind them and it moved upward as he continued talking to Harvey.

"Mary told me you died in the fire at the Novato office and now you're here in front of me. Unbelievable!"

"Poor Mary! She must be devastated."

Dave nodded.

"Yeah, poor Mary. She had to go to the coroner last week for identification. She had told me the body they had shown her was badly burned and unrecognizable. She had only recognized your glasses and your watch."

Harvey listened to him, but continued to stare at Dave's face.

"Yes, they took my glasses, but they realized I'm like a mole without them and they had to get me a new pair quickly last week, as I couldn't see a thing. But Dave, tell me what happened to your face and hair, and what the hell are you doing here? You look so much younger than the last time I saw you? How can this be? I would almost think you took our rejuvenation drug, but no one is that crazy."

He was embarrassed looked down at his feet. Harvey looked at him in bewilderment.

"No!? No, you didn't?"

The elevator arrived on the second floor, and the doors opened. Everybody headed to the restaurant area, but they remained talking in front of the elevator. Harvey looked pissed and raised his voice.

"How could you? I trusted you! You thief!"

People turned their heads and stared at them. Dave stared at the floor and said, "I'm sorry, and I feel terrible about what I did. I know I betrayed your trust. I'm deeply ashamed."

Harvey calmed down a little, but still looked upset and said, "And then to think of all the time I spent with you, helping you with your article. The same article that got me into this mess. A thief!? You, of all people!?"

Dave tried to calm him down as a guard came their way and raised his taser threateningly. Harvey looked frightened. The guard gestured for them to walk on, then they quickly continued to the restaurant. They joined the line and Dave tried to explain to him why he had stolen the drug. He talked about his ongoing back problems and aging issues and how this had made him unhappy, depressed and insecure. They both took a platter of food from the self-service counter and walked to an empty table in the back in front of the large windows overlooking the same mountain range he had seen in Jeff Broch's office. The light outside was beautiful, as the sun was already hiding behind the mountain range and was about to set. Dark shadows already shrouded part of the desert. Dave explained how he could hardly enjoy his life because of the constant pain. Harvey still seemed very upset, but he nodded and said, at some point, "I don't know if I ever can forgive you, but at least now I understand better why you did it."

Dave still felt bad about betraying Harvey's trust and looked down at the tabletop. Harvey stared at Dave's face, his professional curiosity distracting him from his anger and disappointment. He stared at his hair, examining it more closely now.

"Amazing! Just like the mice. How long have you been taking it?"

Harvey baffled him, but he was happy to change the subject.

"It's been two weeks now, but most of the changes occured in the first week."

Harvey touched his hair and then moved very close to his face as he looked at his skin.

"Remarkable! Your skin looks like that of a twenty-year-old man. The hair on your bald head has completely regrown and looks healthier, plus all the gray hairs are gone. How do you feel?"

"Like a young, healthy man. I've started running again and I try to work out whenever I can. I feel very energetic all the time and have a daily desire to go running or exercise and, more importantly, my back pain has completely disappeared."

Then Harvey asked him about his experiences in the first few weeks after beginning the treatment. He explained in great detail the transformation he was going through, and Harvey listened with fascination.

At eight o'clock, both their wristbands vibrated, startling them from their deep conversation. He looked at the little screen on the wristband and it read:

"Please proceed to floor -3."

As they stood up, Dave took one last look at the dark desert outside.

"Eight already. Let's go back downstairs, Dave. I'm also on the third floor under the ground, so we can continue our conversation on the way back."

The restaurant was almost empty now, and they continued talking while they waited for the elevator with some other people. When they got off the elevator and stepped into the corridor of minus three, they walked to his room.

"Wow, it's much busier now," Dave said.

Harvey nodded.

"Yes, we're not the only ones deprived of our freedom. All these scientists are from different places around the world. There're three others from Juvenatrust here. Let me introduce you."

They walked to the third room on the left. The door was ajar and Harvey knocked on it.

"Adish, I want to introduce you to someone. May we come in?"

The door opened, and he saw an Indian-looking man, whose face looked familiar to him.

"This is Dave Wilson, a journalist from Science Magazine. This is Adish Bharara, one of the top scientists of Juvenatrust."

He shook Adish's hand as Harvey continued.

"Dave stole our rejuvenation drug two weeks ago and took it himself. They brought him in today."

Adish first looked at Harvey in disbelief and then he stared at Dave's face in amazement, and after some silence, said, "Amazing!

I think I remember seeing you in the laboratory, but I hardly recognized you. What a difference! You used to be bald on top of your head before, if I remember correctly?"

Dave smiled and nodded.

"Yes, that's correct."

Adish continued to stare at his face as if examining a rare specimen.

"How old are you, Dave?"

"Fifty-four."

Adish's mouth fell wide open after taking a closer look at his skin. Dave started to feel uncomfortable, and Harvey noticed.

"Adish, he just arrived today. He must be overwhelmed. We'll have plenty of time to examine him over the next few weeks. He told me the Juvenatrust building burned, and they found four bodies. I guess they tried to make it look like it was us."

Adish now looked shocked and affected, and Dave saw a tear appear in the corner of his eye. In a trembling voice, he said, "Horrible! My wife Chahna must be devastated."

Adish cried a bit and Harvey put his arm around him.

"We'll talk further tomorrow, all right?"

"Thanks Harvey," Adish said, and they left the room.

Back in the corridor, Harvey gestured to a door on the right.

"Let me introduce you to Suzy Cheng, who's down the hall."

As they walked five doors down, Harvey continued talking.

"Besides Adish and Suzy, we also have Rob Hamilton here. Rob went rogue last week and I think they're holding him in some prison cell downstairs."

Harvey peered through the doorway as they arrived at Suzy's room. Dave saw an Asian-looking woman sitting at the desk working. He vaguely remembered seeing her once at Juvenatrust.

"Suzy?" Harvey said, and the woman looked up at them.

"Good evening, Harvey."

"This is Dave Wilson, a journalist from Science Magazine, and this is Suzy Cheng, one of Juvenatrust's top scientists."

He shook her hand, and she asked, "What's a journalist doing here?"

She apparently hadn't recognized him. Harvey explained the whole story. She was dumbfounded to hear the story about his theft, but showed no emotion in her face.

"Stealing from Mr. Broch!? I don't think you realize yet what a mistake you've made. You're in deep trouble! He's ruthless! Anyway, you're an interesting case for us to examine."

Dave felt embarrassed, but also a little frightened by her chilly remarks. She stared at his face, fascinated by his transformation. When Harvey told her about the four burned bodies, she barely responded. Her lack of response and empathy perplexed him, especially given Adish's emotional reaction a moment before. Later, back in the corridor, he asked, "Harvey, how come Ms. Suzy Cheng was barely affected when you explained about the burned bodies?"

Harvey replied, "Well, I'm not sure, but I believe she doesn't have any family or husband or boyfriend. She was always someone working late and on weekends at the company. So, I guess for her, the whole kidnapping didn't affect her that much. As soon as she arrived here, she started working like nothing had happened. Rob had a lot more difficulty accepting. That's why he got into trouble."

Dave looked at the door numbers.

"Ah, number twelve, that's my room."

Harvey grinned.

"How ironic. We're neighbors. I'm in number fourteen, right next to your room. We have much to discuss. Shall we have coffee or tea in my room?"

"Okay."

Dave followed him to his room, which looked exactly like his room, with only one difference. Harvey had a laptop on his desk.

"How come you have a laptop in your room?"

Harvey filled the kettle as he replied, "Oh, I asked for one, so I can work a bit in the evenings. I believe Suzy has one too and quite a few other people."

"Do you think I can get one, too?"

Harvey shrugged his shoulders.

"Well, you can always try. Do you have sugar or milk in your coffee?"

"No, black, please. Has anyone tried to get out of here yet?"

Harvey looked startled and gestured him to shut up.

"No, I don't think so. Escape is virtually impossible. Here's your coffee."

He booted up his laptop and opened a word processing program. Dave noticed that the laptop's camera had some black tape stuck on it. Harvey typed and gestured him to look at the screen. Dave read what Harvey had typed. Meanwhile, Harvey turned on the TV and turned up the volume.

"Be careful with what you say to people. The wristbands contain a microphone and they can hear what you say."

Harvey looked at him to see if he had finished reading the message, and then deleted the text and typed something else. Dave nodded to Harvey and looked at the screen again.

"Rob got into trouble last week with his laptop and these microphones, and they have put him in isolation. Also watch out with the guards if you do not obey or do something that is not allowed, they can shock with their taser. Sometimes the wristband can warn you that something is not allowed and then, if you continue, it can give you an electrical shock."

He deleted the text as soon as Dave had read it. Dave got it now and raised his thumb as soon as he had read the text. Harvey spoke to break the silence, not to arouse suspicion.

"So, have you tried the TV in your room yet? It has quite a few channels?"

"No, not yet, but I'll try it later. Mmm… nice to have some coffee. I saw some people on our floor entering the elevator in sport clothes. Do you know where they went?"

Dave gestured Harvey to move up a bit so he could type something on the laptop. Harvey shifted as he answered, "Ah, they're going to minus six, where there's a big gym and a large swimming pool. I go swimming sometimes."

Dave started typing on the laptop, and Harvey looked at the screen.

"Mary had trouble identifying the burned body and asked the police to cross-check the body with your dental records. She had become suspicious and doubted the burned body was yours. The police have found traces of gasoline in the building and they launched a criminal investigation."

Harvey smiled as he read it, and then Dave deleted everything. Harvey typed, *"Typical Mary, she always wants a real proof. Nice. Maybe the police will start looking for us."*

He deleted the text after and Dave typed, *"Before I got kidnapped, I warned my girlfriend and the police that some men were trying to kidnap me. So, surely, they will treat it as a kidnapping and start looking for me. Do you have any idea where we are?"*

Harvey deleted the text and typed. Dave started talking, not to have a too long silence.

"A swimming pool and a fitness center. I'll definitely try to go there tomorrow when my headache is gone."

He read what Harvey had written.

"Rob was working on that, and I believe he almost figured it out. Unfortunately, he got caught and locked in solitary."

Dave typed now.

"Do you have internet on your laptop? Can't you just localize our position using the internet?"

Harvey deleted the phrase and typed, speaking to break the silence.

"Yes, I imagine you must have a headache. I see the bump on your head. Let me take a look."

Dave read what Harvey had typed.

"The internet on the laptop is different in here. I believe it works like a one-way internet, you can read and look up. But if you want to log into your mail account and send something through, it seems blocked. The localization function also seems to be disabled. Initially, we tried to find our location using this function on a map website, but it did not work as usual. It is like there is a sophisticated firewall active."

Harvey deleted the text and Dave said, "Ah yes, they hit me hard on the head. It still hurts. Especially the bump is very sensitive."

Harvey typed, *"Be careful everywhere around here. In most public spaces, there are cameras. Except in the showers and toilets. In your room, the television screen has a small camera. Always be mindful of the angle of the camera. Like now, I am under the screen and the laptop screen is not facing the camera, so they cannot see what I am doing. I put the desk as close to the wall as possible, away from the camera's angle."*

Dave read the message and refilled the coffee cups while Harvey deleted the message. A moment later, Dave typed, *"Have you considered escaping?"*

Harvey deleted the message and typed, *"Most people want to get out of here. We have to talk further tomorrow, or we will attract too much attention. Just be careful. You cannot trust everyone here, but you can always check with me. I am still disappointed in you because of what you did, but now you are in the same trouble as we are and we will have to work together to find a way out of this mess."*

Dave nodded as Harvey deleted the message and closed the laptop.

"So, what do you do here to keep from getting bored?"

Harvey pointed at the stack of books next to his bed.

"I often read at night. There's a small library on minus six where you can borrow books. If they don't have a book, you can order it and usually you get it in the same week. Sometimes I read or go to the hot tub or take a Turkish bath."

Dave looked amazed now.

"You have a hot tub and a Turkish bath in here?"

Harvey nodded and pointed toward the end of the hallway.

"The sauna and steam room are in the washing area next to the showers, and the hot tub is next to the swimming pool."

"Nice! And what do you do during the day?"

"There's a large workspace and a laboratory downstairs where I work during the day with most of the people here. I'm still working on the rejuvenation drug. We're starting the first clinical trial next week, so there's a lot of work. Unfortunately, we've been missing Rob for several days and that's slowing down our progress."

"You have all the equipment for your research over here?"

He nodded.

"I'll show you tomorrow, at least if you get permission to access the laboratory. I'm pretty sure Mr. Broch wants us to examine you, and then you should come to the laboratory. It's large and better equipped than the laboratory we had in Novato."

"But how can you start a clinical trial from here? Are you allowed to go outside or do the patients come here?"

"No, we're not allowed outside and the patients remain in a hospital in California. The situation is not ideal. They only allow us to prepare everything, and other doctors outside conduct the clinical trial. We don't even know who they are."

"And all these other people, what do they do during the day?"

"Well, they're also working on projects. On my floor, there's a team working on growing new organs from stem cells. There's a team working on lie detection and brainwave manipulation. Some people are working on a helmet that lets the user focus on a particular task and greatly increases the performance of that task. At the restaurant, I spoke with people working on another floor. I believe it's the seventh floor under the ground. They seem to be working on drones and some new weapons."

Dave listened intently, and when Harvey finished talking, he said,

"This project about the focus helmet sounds like a story a colleague of mine was working on. Apparently, the military is developing a similar helmet and my colleague had heard that some helmets had been stolen. I even wonder if they aren't the same helmets my kidnappers wore when they chased me."

Harvey nodded and then replied, looking up as if to indicate someone was listening in.

"Interesting, but it's probably just a coincidence."

Harvey got up and yawned as he stretched out his arms.

"I'm dead tired. If you don't mind, we'll talk more tomorrow. I'm going to sleep."

"Of course! No problem! And again, I'm really sorry for betraying your trust and I hope one day you can forgive me. Good night."

"We'll see Dave. Good night."

He walked back to his room and looked at his watch. It was already ten-thirty. He saw William coming back from the elevator wearing a bathrobe and with wet hair.

"Hi William, did you go for a swim?"

"Hi Dave, yes, I try to swim for about an hour every night. At my age, you have to work on your fitness every day to stay fit."

"Every day? Nice! Maybe I'll try some swimming tomorrow if my headache subsides."

He was about to enter his room when, out of the corner of his eye, he noticed the double doors next to the elevator. Next to the door was a small light in the sensor.

"Oh, William. One more question. Do you know where those doors next to the elevator lead? I saw them on another floor, too, but I couldn't get them open."

"I think there's an emergency staircase that goes up and down throughout the building. I saw a guard come out once and saw a stairwell. I always wondered what would happen if there was a fire or some other emergency. We're not allowed through these doors, so I guess we're in trouble in case of a fire."

"Ok, yes, that's strange. Thanks, William. Good night."

Dave entered his room and grabbed some water from the fridge. He drank some and then walked to the washing area to brush his teeth and go to the restroom. On the way, he noticed several doors were closed now and people had gone to bed. As he entered the washing area, he saw Larry Miner at one of the sinks next to a younger, quite muscular guy.

"Hi Larry."

"Hi Dave, have you met Yakov yet? He's one of the few young people around here."

Dave looked at the younger man next to Larry. He had light blond hair and looked rather muscular and athletic. He reminded Dave of one of those Russian or Eastern European athletes in the gymnastics discipline at the Olympics. The young man extended his hand to him with a friendly smile.

"Hi, I'm Yakov Cherepanov. I'm a software programmer."

"Nice to meet you, Yakov. I'm Dave Wilson. I'm a journalist for Science Magazine."

"A journalist? What's a journalist doing in here?" Yakov said with a puzzled look on his face.

He spoke with a heavy Russian accent. Dave explained what he had done, and Yakov grinned.

"You stole from Mr. Broch!? I like you already. You have balls, almost like a Russian. This drug you took makes you younger!? How old are you then? I thought you were my age or younger?"

He grinned back at Yakov, who seemed to have a good sense of humor.

"Well, I'm fifty-four. How old are you?"

Yakov looked amazed now.

"I'm thirty-two and I thought you were younger than me. Nice drug!"

Dave brushed his teeth. Meanwhile, he thought he had heard Yakov's name before, but he couldn't remember where. When he finished brushing his teeth and Yakov was about to walk out of the washroom, he asked him, "How long have you been in here, Yakov?"

Yakov looked grim now.

"I was kidnapped and brought here about two months ago. Too long! I still can't get used to it."

Dave nodded.

"Yes, I can imagine that. You don't really get used to it, no?"

"Never. Have a good night, Dave, nice meeting you."

"You too, Yakov!" and he went to the restroom.

He noticed a camera overlooking all the sinks before going to the toilet. After that, he took a quick shower and dried off. The washroom was now deserted. He walked back to his room and noticed all the doors were closed. Suddenly, the lights in the hall dimmed and only the light in the washroom stayed on. Back in his room, he looked at the wristband. It was one minute after eleven. He could see light under some doors, but most were dark now. He closed his door.

He flipped open the blanket on the bed, undressed, and put on a pair of pajamas from the cupboard. He took another glass of water and then pressed the power button on the remote control. He checked what channels there were on the television and all the popular ones were on it. In most places he visited, there were always some local stations, and he hoped he would find them on the television to get a clue as to his whereabouts. After zapping through over a hundred stations, he concluded that there were no local stations. Looking at the number of Canadian and Mexican stations, he thought it could even be possible he was in another country and no longer in the United States. Given the desert looking landscape he had seen today, it could be he was in Mexico. But then again, it would be fairly easy to manipulate the list of channels to make him believe what they wanted him to believe. He zapped to an American news channel, hoping to find anything about his kidnapping. Unfortunately, his abduction had not made the news, and it seemed as if the world just went on as if nothing had happened.

About half an hour later, he turned off the television screen and turned off the light in his room. What a day it had been. He still had trouble believing he was in this place now. Just that morning, he had enjoyed breakfast with his beautiful Penelope in New York. He missed her and thought about her. Would she be looking for him? Were the police looking for him? Had the witnesses who had seen his kidnapping spoken to the police? He vaguely remembered seeing a man filming with his smartphone, so maybe the police would get the footage from him? Would they be able to find him in this godforsaken place? He lay in his bed mulling for a while until he finally fell into a deep sleep.

11. Examination

The next morning, he woke up at a quarter past seven. The room was still pitch dark, and he searched for the light switch. Still full of disbelief, he looked around his room. Just the idea that he would have to stay here for a long time depressed him. He felt much better physically than before, and his headache was gone. He touched his head and still felt a bump, but had the impression it had gotten a lot smaller. After meeting all those scientists yesterday, he wondered what he was supposed to do all day, and no one had told him anything. He got dressed, opened his room door, and walked toward the washroom. The corridor was still dark like last night, and only the light in the washing area was on. One of the doors to his right opened and Yakov came out.

"Morning! Good to see that you too are one of the few who wake up before the alarm."

Dave smiled at him, a little puzzled.

"Morning Yakov. Alarm?"

"An alarm awakens everyone every morning at seven-thirty sharp."

"Ah, okay. I often wake up early, I guess too much energy."

He grabbed his shaving gear from his locker while Yakov disappeared into the shower. He put the shaving foam on his face and was about to put the razor on his skin, when suddenly the wristband in his left arm vibrated and startled him. He felt lucky he was holding the razor with his right hand, otherwise he might have cut himself. He continued shaving and slowly more people came to the washing area. He met more people he had not seen before and chatted with them. At one point, Yakov started shaving at the sink next to him. Yakov chatted with him and they got along well.

"If you have too much energy, try the fitness center on minus six. They've lots of fitness equipment, treadmills, rowing machines and more. I work out every night. It clears the mind."

Dave had missed his regular workout and was glad to hear he could continue working out here.

"Yes, I certainly will tonight, especially now my headache is gone. Do you know what time breakfast is?"

Yakov continued shaving as he said, "Always between eight and nine in the morning. You can ask that kind of thing from your wristband. It helped me a lot in the beginning."

Yakov got a big smile on his face and said, "Look."

He held his wristband with his other hand and asked, "How can I order a hot dog?"

Yakov showed the message to Dave with a big grin, which read: *"Sorry, we do not offer this service."*

They both laughed and then Yakov asked, "Where can I find the sauna?"

He showed the message to Dave: *"The sauna is in the washroom next to the showers."*

"Thanks for the demonstration, Yakov. See you later," said Dave and returned to his room.

In his room, he looked back at the wristband and said, "What time is breakfast?"

The wristband now showed a message: *"Breakfast is from 8 to 9 in the morning."*

He looked at the time it was seven-forty and turned on the television screen to check again if there was any news about his abduction. He zapped between different news channels, but found nothing. A bit bored, he asked the wristband, "What floors can I go to?"

It said: *"You have access to floor -3 and floor -6."*

"Where can I get books?"

"You can borrow books in the library on floor -6," the wristband showed.

He was afraid he would get bored and thought about what Harvey told him yesterday, so he asked, "Can I get a laptop in my room with internet access?"

The wristband displayed: *"Request submitted. Awaiting response."*

He decided to kill some time and do some push-ups. He continued until he had done a hundred, then he turned and sat on the floor. He started doing some sit-ups to exercise his abdominals. To his surprise, he could do them quite easily, and he aimed for one hundred. As he approached the hundredth sit-up, he began to sense a burning feeling in his abdominals. After the hundredth sit-up, he relaxed flat on the floor.

Suddenly, he heard a voice say, "Impressive for a man of your age!"

He looked up and saw Yakov standing in the doorway with a grin on his face.

"Are you joining us for breakfast?"

He looked at his wristband. It was almost eight o'clock.

"Of course!"

He got up and walked with Yakov. On his way to the elevator, his wristband vibrated, and he looked at the message.

"Proceed to the restaurant on floor 2."

He noticed Yakov was no longer even looking at the wristband, although it also had a message on it. On their way, Pierre Lavoisier and Adish Bharara joined them. Larry Miner was already waiting in front of the elevator. As they entered the elevator, he noticed a line forming in front of it. Everyone scanned their wristbands as they entered the elevator, and it quickly filled up. After scanning, he realized he had been granted automatic access to the second floor during breakfast. He had the impression there were nearly twenty people in the elevator when Harvey was the last to enter. Most of the people he had already met, yet there were some unfamiliar faces. The elevator doors closed and started moving up to the second floor.

On the second floor, everyone got out, and at the restaurant, another line formed as people began to fill their trays with breakfast. Dave followed Yakov to one of the tables close to the large window where two people were already seated, a blond woman and a dark-haired man with a short dark beard.

"Dave, have you met Judith and Gary yet?" Yakov asked as he set his tray on the table.

He shook his head, set his tray down, and extended his hand to the middle-aged woman first.

"Hi, I'm Dave Wilson. I'm a journalist from Science Magazine and I arrived yesterday."

"Hi, I'm Judith Anderson. I'm a neuroscientist and I've been here for several weeks now after being kidnapped from my sailing boat."

He shook her hand, and she had a firm grip. He looked into her eyes and noticed her determined look. The man next to her stood up and held out his hand.

"Hi Dave, I'm Gary Pratt, I'm a specialist in aeronautics and electrical engineering and have been in here for almost six months."

As they sat down, Judith asked, "What's a journalist doing among all these scientists?"

He smiled at her and explained the whole story. They both listened with fascination and stared curiously at his face and hair as he explained what had happened to him. Then he asked, "Enough about me. What are you working on?"

Gary looked at Judith in a gesture to let her answer first.

"I'm working on several projects, but mostly on brain stimulation. You may have seen a metal cap on the back of Jeff Broch's head. That's a brain stimulator designed by me and William Ashton," she explained.

"That little cap with a wire attached to it? What does it do?"

"Well, this version has several functions, but the main one is that it allows the brain to focus on certain areas and improves brain performance. It also has a brain stimulator function, which improves the memory function of the brain. Basically, despite being sixty years old, Mr. Broch has a memory function of a twenty-year-old."

"How does that work?"

"The electrical pulse closely targets the prefrontal cortex and the temporal lobe. In young adults using their working memory, these two areas synchronize the rhythm of their activity. The tighter the synchronization, the better the working memory performs. With age, this tight synchronization slowly vanishes, which seems to be the cause of working memory decline. We synchronize those brain areas that are uncoupled or uncorrelated or less synchronized in the elderly."

"Fascinating!"

"And you Gary, what are you working on?"

"A completely different field than Judith. I work mostly on drones," he said, gesturing enthusiastically with his hands. "All kinds of different drones, ranging from Nano drones to larger drones."

"Nano drones?"

"Yes, tiny drones that can travel through someone's body dose a medicine or target specific parts of a body to heal. A little bigger, you have micro drones, which are mainly used to spy on people or assassinate people secretly and then, of course, larger drones for warfare, transportation or other functions."

"We just developed a micro drone the size of a mosquito that can inject a deadly poison into a person. The drone's so small and fast you would have a hard time seeing it."

"That sounds like scary weaponry, Gary. What does Mr. Broch need that for?"

"I'm not sure, but I believe he sells them at a very high price through dubious intermediaries. But you're absolutely right. It's scary stuff that will change the world of warfare."

They talking on as they ate their breakfast. At a quarter to nine, Judith left to brush her teeth. Dave continued talking to Gary and Yakov while they enjoyed their coffee.

At nine, everyone's wristbands vibrated at the same time. His wristband showed a message.

"Go to floor -3."

As they stood up, Dave asked Yakov and Gary, "What floor do you need to go to now?"

"I have to go to the lab on floor minus five," Yakov replied.

"And I work on floor minus seven. Where did they send you to?" Gary asked.

"I've got to go back to minus three. I guess I'm supposed to get bored all day."

They got in the elevator and headed back down.

"I'm sure they have something in mind for you, Dave. With us, it was also unclear at first. Try the library on floor minus six. At least they have plenty of books," Gary tried to comfort him.

"Well, have a nice day and see you later," Dave said as he stepped off the elevator. Judith just came out of her room and walked toward the elevator.

"Going back to your room?" she asked.

"No work for a journalist, apparently in this place."

She shook her head in disbelief.

"But there's plenty of writing to do, though. I believe Harvey's team is about to start a clinical trial and they need to write instructions for the medical staff. Let me bring it up to him."

"Thanks Judith, that's kind of you. Although he's probably still mad at me, but it's worth a try. Have a nice day!"

"You too, Dave."

He walked to the washroom and brushed his teeth. The entire floor was empty. He went back to his room and watched the news, but again, nothing about his abduction. He realized that kidnappings were rarely on the national news channels, usually on the local channels, and those were not available here. Wanting to get some books from the library, he walked to the elevator. He noticed the doubled door next to the elevator again. Curious, he saw no harm in trying to open the door. He put his hand on the door handle, but it was locked. Then he held his wristband next to the sensor, and it vibrated. The double door did not open and his wristband showed a flashing message.

"Access not authorized."

He walked to the elevator and pressed the button. A few minutes later, the doors opened, and he stepped in. He pressed the button to floor minus five and his wristband vibrated. He looked at it and it displayed another message.

"Access to floor -5 not authorized."

He realized he might have confused the floor numbers and asked the wristband, "What floor is the library on?"

The display showed: *"The library is on floor -6."*

He pushed the button to minus six and now the doors closed and the elevator went down. At floor minus six he got off and there was a door to the left in the corridor with a sign "Library". The corridor was much shorter on this floor, and other than the door to the library, there were only two other doors further down the corridor. He explored a bit and the first door on the right gave access to what looked like a bar. The door was open, and he took a peek. The lights went on as he entered, and there was no one inside. There was a bar on the left and on the right, there was a sitting area with tables and chairs and in the back were all kinds of games, including darts, a pool table, a soccer table and an air hockey table, followed by some restrooms.

Back in the corridor, he opened the other door where a sign "Fitness Room & Pool". He went inside and first passed some changing rooms, and then there was a large gym with a wide selection of different fitness equipment, treadmills, rowing machines, etc. To his right there was another corridor, and he passed more changing rooms and showers, and then he saw the swimming pool. It was big enough to do some nice laps, and he decided he would go for a swim later on. In the corner, there was also a large hot tub.

The creepy thing about the place was that he had not seen anyone yet. He walked back to the library and noticed the cameras on the ceiling in the corridor. He entered the library and even here there was no one. Next to the entrance there was a desk with two screens on top and the rest of the room was filled with many shelves full of books. He sat down at the desk and looked up some book his son had recommended to him, and he had been wanting to read for a while. It was a scientific thriller about some new revolutionary drug by a relatively unknown author, and to his surprise, the computer indicated that the book was available. He walked to the indicated bookshelf and found it there. He looked further and picked up another book. At the entrance, there was a sign telling him to scan the books and his wristband. He did so and returned to the elevator with the books. The whole place felt spooky, and he was glad to go back to his floor.

Back in his room, he made coffee, sat at the desk, and read the scientific thriller. About an hour later, he felt like moving, so he looked in the closet and took out the swimming shorts and bathrobe. He changed clothes and headed back to minus six. All the way to the pool, he saw no one, and there was no one in the pool. He dove into the water and started swimming laps. It felt great to move through the water. The lack of windows and the fact that he had lost his freedom had made him depressed, but swimming took his thoughts away and he could finally relax. He forced himself to swim faster than he normally would, and after an hour, he felt tired but satisfied. He took a shower and dried off. Back in his room, he put his light blue clothes back on and read his book until his wristband started vibrating.

"Proceed to floor 4 for a meeting with Mr. Broch."

He walked to the elevator, waited for it to arrive, and pressed the button to the fourth floor. This time the wristband did not vibrate, and apparently, he had automatically gained access to the fourth floor. He was nervous, and on the fourth floor, an armed guard waited next to the elevator. Dave greeted him.

"Good morning. Proceed through the doors straight ahead, please," the guard said.

He opened the dark wooden door, and the woman behind the reception counter looked at him.

"Good morning, Mr. Wilson. You can go right in. Mr. Juncker is already with Mr. Broch."

"Okay, thank you," he said.

He opened the thick wooden door and walked into the large office. Jeff Broch was sitting behind his desk in a dark suit with a white shirt, and Harvey was sitting in one of the chairs in front of the desk.

"Good morning, Dave. Take a seat," Jeff Broch said, gesturing with his hand to the chair next to Harvey. Jeff stared at his face as he entered and approached his desk.

"Good morning, Mr. Broch. Hello Harvey."

Harvey smiled a bit at him, but seemed tensed. He took the seat next to him and looked outside at the desert. It was cloudy today.

"Dave, I understood you have already enjoyed our swimming pool. You must have noticed by now that we treat our people well and do our best to make their stay here comfortable. I've just discussed with Harvey what we're going to do with you. He'll continue to administer the drug to you and will examine you thoroughly to see what the treatment does to your body. Ideally, we would have done a thorough examination before the start of the treatment to have a zero measurement and focus on any changes from this starting point, but we don't have that now because you sneakily started the drug treatment. Although with your medical records, Harvey should be able to analyze some changes."

Jeff pointed at the thick medical file in front of Harvey with Dave's name on it.

"How did you get my medical records?" he asked, astonished.

"They're not so difficult to get, especially with the dedicated people working for me. Everyone always believes the blanket statements that their records are safe with medical institutions, but nothing connected to the internet is safe," Jeff replied with a grin on his face.

"This week, Harvey will examine you in our laboratory and use these findings to prepare for clinical trials beginning next week. You're giving us an excellent opportunity to study the drug and its effects on people. This way, I may be able to sell the drug to some people even before we've gotten FDA approval through the clinical trials."

"But that's illegal, isn't? Who would buy an unapproved drug?"

"You're telling me something's illegal!?" Jeff replied and started laughing with a horrible, loud laugh.

"Ha… ha… ha! I can't believe what I hear from the journalist willing to steal and try a drug treatment that hasn't gone through a clinical trial yet. Now imagine a rich, aging billionaire who has come to the sad conclusion that money can't buy the one thing that is most valuable to him and that he's just as mortal as any other poor bastard. They pay a fortune for any treatment that enables them to live longer and healthier lives. Several billionaires have already asked me if they can be part of the clinical trial or get the drug sooner."

"Just out of curiosity, why don't you sell the rejuvenation drug at a reasonable price to the entire population?"

"Dave, that's very simple. I don't believe the world can handle a population that lives much longer than it does now. The world already cannot cope with the current growing population. We're depleting our planet's resources and polluting the Earth at an unprecedented speed and scale. If humans all lived much longer, this process would only accelerate further. For as long as humanity has existed, we've dreamed of immortality and eternal youth. I believe this dream will become a reality in the next twenty to thirty years. I also believe that this dream should be realized only for the few richest people in the world. The masses can only aspire to this dream, just like with the American dream. Fewer and fewer people actually realize this dream, and for everyone else, it's like opium for the people. In the coming decades, we'll see the rise of a new species, which I call the superhumans. With biological engineering and cyborg engineering, we'll create superhumans."

Jeff showed off his sophisticated bionic arm to back up his claim.

"Aren't you afraid that people will revolt if you make these drugs and technologies affordable only to the rich?"

"No, Dave. You're implying I'm proposing something new. The world is already unfair, and rich and poor already do not have equal access to medicines and technologies. The rich and the poor live separate lives in different worlds. In ancient times, when the rich got too rich, and the poor got too poor, sometimes there was a revolution. Like we had in France with the last king, Louis the Sixteenth. Ironically, with our current system of democracy and capitalism supported by new technologies, it has become much easier to control the population and make them believe in the dream that they can become rich as well and one day they'll have access to all those technologies and health improvements. In reality, most poor people in America do not have or can't afford our current healthcare, and in our democracy, politicians aided by artificial intelligence in conjunction with social media have caused people to vote against increasing access to healthcare for the poor. Last year, the twenty-six richest billionaires in the world owned as much as the poorest half of the world's population. The biggest gap between rich and poor ever and no one is starting a revolution or doing much against this. And do you know why, Dave? Because our current so called democratic capitalistic system uses internet technology and artificial intelligence to keep the masses living in a dreamworld. And even if one day they stopped believing in this dream and revolted, they're facing a government that'll try to maintain the status quo and suppress a revolt because they're addicted to the financial support of the rich. We already have the most power in the world because the politicians are so sensitive to our strong lobby. Money rules the world, Dave. Meanwhile, we're creating superhumans who will rule and dominate the world."

"Don't you think governments will regulate all these new technologies and drugs and prevent their abuse by individuals and corporations? Like now they're thinking of regulating genetic manipulation," he asked, stunned and shocked by Jeff Broch's radical views.

"Yeah, sure, Dave. They think about regulating genetic manipulation, like they think about regulating artificial intelligence. Governments don't understand these developments, and the technological revolution is happening so fast that governments can't keep up. Wealthy individuals and corporations are jumping on this technology wave and not waiting for their governments to catch up. Even scientists move ahead like the Chinese scientist you wrote about last year who made genetically manipulated babies. The rich will build their own armies of robots and drones and become even more powerful. Even if there were a revolution of the poor, they don't stand a chance against the armies and power of the rich. Governments are too careful and afraid to attack or tax these wealthy individuals and corporations, fearing they'll leave for other countries that tax or restrict them less. A classic prisoner's dilemma. So, they distract and focus the people's attention on other problems or threats. No, I'm sure, superhumans will rule the world with their enhanced brain capacity and skills. Regular humans will become irrelevant and slowly disappear, just as many animal species are now disappearing or have already disappeared."

Dave let Jeff's words sink in a bit as he realized there was a grain of truth in his vision, but that frightened him even more. He was sitting across from a ruthless man who lived his own vision. He noticed Harvey did not engage in the conversation at all. Jeff looked at Harvey now and said, "Enough chitchat for now. Harvey, I take it everything is clear to you? You can examine and observe Dave here for the next few weeks. I expect at least a weekly report. Dave, to keep you busy, I've agreed with Harvey for you to help his team write instructions for the medical staff who'll begin clinical trials next week. You're both dismissed now."

Harvey stood up with the medical files in his hands and Dave followed suit and they walked out.

"That guy gives me the creeps," Dave said as they walked to the elevator.

"Yes, sometimes it seems like he's from another planet. His brain capacity is enhanced, and he's always thinking several steps ahead. He was surprisingly talkative to you, probably his ego took over."

They took the elevator, and Harvey pressed the button to minus five.

"Ah, can I go to minus five now too?" Dave asked.

"Yes, since I have to examine you and you'll be working with my team, you get the same access to minus five that we have," Harvey answered, still quieter than usual.

"What's wrong Harvey, you look down?"

"I guess I'm a little down and miss my freedom."

"You were quiet in there. Did something happen?"

"No, nothing. Don't worry about me, I'm just not feeling well today," but as he said this, he pointed to the wristband to indicate that he could not talk freely now.

The elevator doors opened at minus five. The floor was buzzing with activity. To his right, he saw a large laboratory with many people working in a large open workspace, and to his left was another large laboratory, both with windows in the corridor. On the other side, there were several doors with no windows. Harvey walked to a desk in the laboratory on the right. Dave greeted Suzy and Adish, who were sitting at the desks nearby. Harvey put the medical file in a drawer under his desk and looked at his wristband.

"I'll give you a tour after lunch. Since it's almost noon, there's no point in doing that now."

"How was the meeting with Mr. Broch?" Adish asked, and Suzy also looked curiously at Harvey.

"We must continue as planned, preparing for the clinical trial that begins next week. I've insisted a lot on having at least one of us present at the medical facility to supervise the clinical trial, but Mr. Broch has made it very clear to me that he won't allow that."

Harvey sighed and then continued, still a bit stressed, "Dave will spend the next week assisting us in writing all the manuals for the medical staff who will be conducting the clinical trial. In addition, we need to examine him thoroughly over the next few weeks, as he'll continue his drug treatment in here."

Everyone's wristband vibrated and people stood up.

"Let's have lunch first and then talk further," Harvey said, and they walked to the elevator.

In the restaurant, he sat at the table with Harvey's team, and they talked about the clinical trial. Dave could not help but stare out through the large windows at the nearby mountains. He wondered where this strange prison was located and how he could get out of here. It seemed impossible, especially since discussing it openly was not possible with the wristbands eavesdropping on everything. He thought about how he had woken up next to Penelope the previous day and how peaceful everything had been. He missed her and stared out onto the dirt road with no cars or any building in sight. He had to find a way out to get back to her. Someone called his name several times, and then he felt a hand on his shoulder pulling him out of his deep thoughts.

"Dave? Hey, Dave? What planet are you on?"

He turned his head and looked at Yakov's square face.

"Oh, hi Yakov!"

"It looked like you left us. Daydreaming?" Yakov said with a big grin.

"Oh... uh… yes, I was deep in thoughts, I guess… wondering what the hell I'm doing here."

"Ha! Yes, that's the question we all ask ourselves. Well, don't forget to come to the fitness center tonight. That'll relax your mind a bit."

"I will, Yakov. Right after dinner."

"See you then, my friend!"

After lunch, they went back to minus five to the laboratory. Suzy and Adish went back to work, and Harvey turned to him.

"Let me first give you a tour before we start with the examination."

"Perfect."

Harvey showed him around the laboratory and explained what everyone was working on. When he arrived at the desk where William Ashton worked together with Judith Anderson, Dave saw several dark helmets all connected to a machine.

"I've seen those helmets before. The men who kidnapped me wore them," Dave said, surprised.

"About three months ago, they brought us those helmets. I think the U.S. Army developed them and Mr. Broch ordered us to improve them. They help people focus on certain tasks. The first version was for relatively simple tasks, but we improved them and now they can be used for a wide range of tasks," William said.

"Well, I can tell you those guys were very tenacious and fast. I was able to shake them off for a while, but eventually they caught me."

"Yeah, those helmets are scary. They make the brain focus on a particular task and reduce the distraction signals coming from the brain, enabling users to perform tasks which they wouldn't normally be able to accomplish."

They continued walking through the laboratory. When they arrived at Yakov's desk, he looked up with a big smile.

"So, Dave, is Harvey giving you a nice tour of the facilities? Let me show you one of the projects I'm working on right now."

He moved a camera mounted on a metal stand and pointed it at Dave.

"All right, tell me how you ended up here, or tell me something about yourself."

Dave was a bit puzzled, since he had already explained that to him, but he played along, and after five minutes of talking, Yakov pushed the camera away and did something on his computer.

"Okay, thanks. It's just for the demonstration that I have to film you talking. Come watch!"

Dave stood behind him and looked at the screen. Yakov handed him a headset. Then Yakov started speaking in a microphone and at the same time Dave saw himself on the screen talking and pronouncing the words that Yakov spoke.

"Hello, I'm Dave and I'm a famous ballet dancer. I also like to fool people, and that's how I'm going to win the next presidential election in this country."

He was amazed since he saw himself talking on the screen and it seemed like it was really him, saying all those words.

"That's amazing. How did you do that?"

"This's what they call a deep-fake algorithm. I developed this software that uses machine learning techniques, and you can create indistinguishable from real videos of anyone and have them say anything. Scary, isn't it?"

"Very scary. Jesus, Yakov! I think one of my colleagues, James Cullen, was planning to do an article on deep-fake software. He was going to interview some software developer from Saint Petersburg, but apparently, he got kidnapped before they could do the interview… You're not going to tell me it was you, are you?"

Yakov looked at him in bewilderment.

"You got to be kidding me! Yes, I had an interview scheduled with a certain James Cullen. Was he your colleague? Wow, what a small world."

"A small world, indeed. What a coincidence! So, what do they want to use this software for?"

"That, my friend, I don't know, but I imagine it would be a very nice tool for Mr. Broch and his billionaire friends to manipulate a presidential election or to create scandal or confusion in the world. I just know that from now on people can't trust what they see, and this will have a huge impact on news reporting in the decades to come."

They continued their tour and crossed the corridor to the other laboratory. Pierre Lavoisier and Margaret Jones were looking through a microscope, and behind them there were some strange jars with wires in them. Inside he saw organs, one jar with lungs, others with hearts, kidneys and livers. It looked like he had entered Frankenstein's laboratory. As he inspected the jars, Margaret Jones explained, "We've succeeded in growing organs from stem cells. We are testing them on animals, but soon we'll be testing them on humans. So far, the tests have been very successful. I think this'll become a huge industry in the future and solve the global shortage of organ donors. Another advantage is that when you grow organs from someone's own stem cells, you reduce the risk of rejection virtually to zero."

"That's impressive Margaret, I heard about this before, but I didn't know they could already do this for so many organs," he said, staring at the lungs.

"Unfortunately, Mr. Broch has decided he can make a lot of money from this business and the patents associated with it. Instead of sharing this technology, he wants to turn it into a business monopoly and make sure he gets even richer than he already is. People are willing to pay a lot of money for organs," Pierre said in his French accent.

They walked further through the lab and then returned to the corridor, where they walked toward the doors in the back. Harvey opened the first door. There was quite some noise from the ventilation system and a horrible smell in the air. The room was filled with rows of plexiglass cages up to the ceiling. Harvey pointed to one of the cages with mice in them and said, "This is the testing area. Some of these mice were from our lab in Novato before it burned down and some from other labs. Further down, we have several pigs. These pigs have transplanted organs in them, like you saw earlier in the lab, grown from their own stem cells."

"Impressive," Dave said as he looked at the pigs.

"There're so many cages here. Who takes care of all these animals?"

"They have special support staff taking care of them. Let's go to the next room, because I find the smell in here really unpleasant," Harvey said, making a face as if he smelled poop.

In the other room, there were many rows of the blue fridges he had seen earlier at Juvenatrust.

"These fridges probably look familiar to you, don't they? Although it'll be harder to steal anything from them," Harvey said with a cynical grin on his face.

He stared at the rows of boxes with the drug doses in them. He recognized the metal boxes that resembled the one he had in his basement in New York.

"Mary had told me that all the doses had been burned in Novato. Now I see such a huge supply here. How's this possible?"

"One of Mr. Broch's people who worked with our company, one Yuri Petrovski, had already prepared a plan in case they wanted to continue the operation underground. Apparently, just before the fire, they moved all drug doses from the fridges in Novato here and replaced them with doses filled with water. They were quick with their operation right after the board meeting, during which I had my huge argument with Mr. Broch. I angrily walked out of the meeting and said we would publish the article."

"But was this article the reason they started this fire and kidnapped you and some of your colleagues?"

Harvey seemed to hesitate for a moment, but then answered, "I know I told you that yesterday in my anger, but it wasn't the only reason. I think I had gone too far in this board meeting. I had threatened to make the formula for the rejuvenation drug public. I told them I have the right to do that, because I had developed it. Then I walked out of the meeting and they were furious. Back in my office, I left you a message and at that same moment, several guards entered my office. They put a black bag over my head and dragged me into some truck. They sprayed something in my face and when I woke up, I was in one of the prison cells downstairs. Now I regret it. I feel so guilty because it's my fault that Rob, Suzy and Adish ended up in here."

"Harvey, you shouldn't feel guilty about what you did. It's not your fault they're here. You didn't kidnap them. The way you reacted in that meeting is completely understandable, and in a normal company, this whole kidnapping would never have happened. You know what they say: Forget regret, or life's yours to miss."

He put his hand on Harvey's shoulder, who was clearly feeling down today.

"Thanks. I guess you're right. Well, let's continue with the tour. They filled the other fridges with drugs from other projects. I understood from Pierre Lavoisier that they're even developing a pill that can repair brain damage."

"Wow, that would be huge. How would such a pill work?"

"The problem with brain repair is that neurons don't regenerate after brain damage. Apparently, they had found a cocktail of nine molecules that can convert so-called glial cells into new neurons. Recently, they simplified this treatment and reduced the number of molecules in this cocktail to four, with better results in their test on human neurons in the lab. The pill could repair brain damage caused by stroke or Alzheimer's disease."

"Impressive. With developments like this, Broch's story of striving for immortality in the coming decades becomes a lot more realistic."

"Absolutely. Decades may be a little too fast, but this century will be revolutionary and longevity will increase significantly," Harvey said as they walked toward the last door in the corridor.

"In this room, we've all kinds of equipment to produce drugs and pills in quantities large enough for use in clinical trials or to sell small batches."

They walked through the room and talked about the various machines, then returned to the laboratory. When they arrived at his desk, Dave said with a deep sigh, "You know what I miss most? To feel some fresh air and be outside. Here underground without windows. It feels depressing."

Harvey smiled and looked at his wristband.

"Funny you should mention that just now, because in fifteen minutes it's time for our daily rooftop break."

"Rooftop break?"

"Yes, normally every day at three-thirty we all go out on the roof on the fifth floor and have one hour of break. You're not obliged to go, but most people chose to enjoy the fresh air."

"What a relief to hear that, Harvey. I'd go nuts in this place otherwise."

"Okay, let's get you up to speed with the clinical trials so you can start helping us write the instruction manuals for the first phase of the trial. This first phase will begin with two patient groups. One group of patients with advanced osteoarthritis and another with cardiovascular disease."

He continued to explain about the clinical trial until their wristbands vibrated, indicating it was time for their rooftop break. They all took the elevator and on the fifth floor Dave noticed that the design of this floor was similar to that of the second and fourth floor, with three corridors, one in front, perpendicular to the elevator doors, one to the left and one to the right of the elevator. The main difference on this floor was that the corridor on the left side was very short and there were two glass doors almost directly next to the elevator. The corridor in front of the elevator and the one on the right were both blocked by two armed guards. Everyone walked through the doors on the left, away from the guards.

Warm air blew into Dave's face as he walked through the doors onto the large terrace. The sun was shining and there was not a cloud in the sky. About two-thirds of the outdoor terrace was covered by a roof, under which were a dozen tables with chairs. There was a coffee machine in the corner and a refrigerator with water and other drinks. He followed Harvey to the coffee machine and took a cappuccino, then he walked to the uncovered area. The view was magnificent, and there were mountains all around the building. He saw only one dirt road and, for the rest, nothing. Just dry desert all around. In the sun, he felt the heat more, but with the breeze, it was bearable. He peered over the edge of the roof and saw that there was a large fence surrounding the entire building. When he turned around, he noticed the helicopter on the landing pad, which was on the roof right in front of the elevator. The building was T-shaped. The roof over the outside terrace was covered with barbed wire. In each corner was a tall pole with a camera on it, one focused on the terrace and two on the desert landscape surrounding the building. In the center of the building, right at the intersection of the building's T-shape and above the elevator, was a strange square tower. It had no windows, but several roll-down shutters on each side.

"Harvey, do you know what that tower above the elevator is for?"

"No, I have no idea it looks strange now you mention it. You should ask William Ashton. He has been around here a lot longer. Maybe he knows."

He looked around but did not see William, but next to Harvey he saw Gary Pratt with a man he had not seen before.

"Hi Gary."

"Hi Dave. Nice to enjoy the fresh air and escape from that basement for a moment. Have you met Takeo?" Gary said as he touched the Asian-looking man's shoulder with his hand.

"No, I haven't, although I believe I saw you at the restaurant today. Hi, I'm Dave Wilson," he shook the hand of Takeo, who was much smaller than him, but looked square and strong, with a very determined look in his eyes.

"Nice to meet you. My name is Takeo Matsumoto. I'm an electrical engineer specializing in drones and robots. I've been here for four months now, but I haven't seen you here before. When did you arrive?"

"Yesterday, I'm still trying to get used to this prison life."

"Well, I don't think you can get used to it. After months, all I can think about is how to get out of here. I was kidnapped four months ago in Kyoto, where I had a great career at one of the best robotics companies in Japan and now I'm stuck in this godforsaken place. What were you doing before you came here?"

"I'm a journalist at Science Magazine in New York."

"A journalist? Then what are you doing here?" Takeo asked, with a puzzled look on his face.

He explained the whole story to Takeo, who was impressed that the drug treatment had made him look so much younger in such a short period. They talked until the end of the break, when they returned to the elevator. Takeo explained he worked on minus seven and sometimes on minus eight, like Gary, but that they slept on minus four, where sixteen prisoners slept. Takeo told him he had kept track of the number of prisoners and, with Dave added, there must now be thirty-six in total. At minus five, Dave said goodbye to Takeo to join Harvey and his team.

That afternoon, he worked with Harvey, Suzy and Adish to prepare for the clinical trial. He began making an outline for the manual on the desktop computer in the laboratory. At the end of the afternoon, Harvey wanted to spend some time to prepare the examination of Dave and to discuss the continuation of the rejuvenation drug treatment. Harvey had studied Dave's medical records for a while, after which he asked him, "When did you take your last dose?"

"Last Friday. That was also the end of the second week with the injections every other day."

"Okay, so now you have to switch to bi-weekly injections for the third week."

"Yes, originally I planned to take one injection coming Tuesday and one injection on Friday."

"Fine, then we'll give you an injection on Tuesday. I also want to start with the examination and I think the best way is that we go through a list of questions Suzy has prepared for all the clinical trial participants and we also need to take some of your blood to examine. Maybe we'll start with the blood and then you can answer the questions tomorrow morning, since we have to go upstairs for dinner in less than thirty minutes."

"Sounds like a good plan."

Suzy opened a cabinet, took out a syringe, and she told him to roll up his sleeve. She inserted the syringe in his left arm and blood flowed into the tube. When the first tube was full, she replaced it with a second one. Dave wondered if they would find negative side effects from the drug. He had heard of some clinical trials where people developed problems months and sometimes years after. He hoped his case would not be like that, but still could not help but worry a little. She removed the tube when it was full and removed the syringe from his arm. She put the tubes in a nearby fridge and then everyone walked to the elevator.

After dinner, Dave hurried back to his room. He had felt like exercising all day and he was full of energy. He put on the sports clothes from his closet and rushed to the fitness center. He passed the bar and saw that some people were playing pool. The fitness center was still empty and when he had just started running on a treadmill, he heard Yakov's voice.

"And I thought I was down fast, but you seem to have beaten me to it."

"Hi Yakov! Yeah, I really felt like exercising to relax and forget a little about this horrible prison we're in."

"Yeah, I know what you mean."

Yakov climbed on the treadmill next to him. Dave was taller than Yakov, but he looked very athletic, with his broad shoulders and muscular arms and legs. Yakov turned on the television screens that were hanging in front of the treadmills and put on some music channel and turned up the volume. Yakov started running and the fitness center was now alive with the buzzing sound of the treadmills and the steps of both men mixed with the loud music from the TV. After a few minutes of running, Dave asked, "Yakov, everyone in here seems so tame and accepting of their fate. They work as if it's normal to be robbed of your freedom. I just don't get it. Didn't anyone try to escape or resist?"

Some silence fell, and he noticed Yakov was taking his time to answer, as if he was thinking carefully about which words to choose. Yakov increased the sound more with the remote control. Dave wondered why he turned the music up so loud, but when looking at him, he saw he was smiling and pointing to his wristband.

"Be careful in here. It's not that people accept their fate willingly, but they see no other choice. When I had just arrived here, I saw how Pierre Lavoisier refused to work and the cameras in the laboratory must have noticed, because after he had sat with his arms crossed for an hour, his wristband vibrated and he got a warning on his screen. Still, he refused and then his wristband began to give him electrical shocks and, about five minutes later, two guards appeared and tasered him in front of everyone. They took him to Mr. Broch. I don't know what Mr. Broch had done to him, but from then on Pierre worked consistently and didn't resist."

"Wow, Pierre! Who would have thought? He looks so calm. But how do these bracelets work?"

"They work on batteries, which limits the force of the shock, but because it delivers the shock to the inside of your wrist, it does hurt a lot. But the guards' tasers are much worse. The batteries run out, and they've already changed mine twice. I think they last for a few weeks and they seem to have some sensor in it, warning them before the battery runs out."

"Okay, good to know and do you know what happened to Rob Hamilton last week?"

"I wasn't there, but I've heard from others what happened. I have met Rob, and he is quite a character. I guess by now you know the internet we have in here differs from the normal. Apparently, the system in here is a customized version created by a company owned by one of Jeff Broch's billionaire friends who also developed the internet in China. It is shielded from the rest of the world and you only have access to what they allow you. Anything you want to send is screened or blocked. They use a similar system in China, where it's a powerful technique to control and manipulate the population. But if you think it only happens in China, dream on. Last year, they changed the laws in Russia. The new law requires internet service providers in Russia to disconnect from foreign servers and requires a national domain system that allows the country to stay online if it is ever cut off from the global internet," Yakov said, getting out of breath from talking and running at the same time. "Before this law, the Russian government already blocked certain websites and banned all software and websites related to bypassing internet filtering, but this law makes it possible to adopt an internet system like they have in China and exercise much more control and censorship."

"But what does this have to do with Rob?" Dave asked.

"Ah, sorry, I strayed a bit. Rob had noticed the internet system didn't allow any of the normal localization functions when he tried to figure out where we are located. He began hacking the system, which Broch's people discovered. They took him to Mr. Broch and I don't know exactly what happened in that meeting, but he's been in a prison cell downstairs ever since."

"And do you know if anyone has tried to escape from here?"

Yakov looked concerned and pointed to the wristband again and said, "No, I don't think anyone has ever tried. This place is like a perfect prison, and it's impossible to escape from it."

He grasped Yakov was afraid to talk freely and asked no more questions. They kept running without talking until they stopped an hour later and walked to the water fountain to drink some water.

"You run well for a fifty-four-year-old, Dave. What sports do you do?"

"In my twenties, I did a lot of sports and was good at it, but later I neglected sports for a long time. I stopped playing tennis five years ago because of my back problems, and I have done little sport since. But since I started using this rejuvenation drug, I feel constantly energized and feel like exercising all the time."

"Nice! I always loved sports, especially weightlifting. In Russia I was a national youth weightlifting champion, but I stopped competitions when I went to study at a university in America. I realized I could make more money in computer programming than in weightlifting and I returned to Russia after graduation to work for a software company."

They talked further while doing exercises with the weights and on the various fitness machines. At one point, Judith entered the fitness center. She greeted them and started working out on one of the cross trainers. Yakov occasionally told funny jokes, and they laughed a lot. At one point, even Judith, who heard one of his jokes, started laughing and struggled to continue her exercises. An hour later, Dave thought he had done enough exercises for today.

"I'm going back to my room. See you tomorrow!"

"Okay. I think I'll go swimming for a while."

He walked with him to the exit, and Dave glanced around the pool. The big pool was empty, but in the hot tub he saw Takeo Matsumoto, Larry Miner and Gary Pratt. They had music on and waved at him. Yakov had quickly changed into his swimming shorts and walked toward the three men. He waved at Dave and said, "See you tomorrow and next time bring your swimming trunks."

He smiled and waved back.

"I will. See you tomorrow!"

He returned to his room, grabbed some fresh clothes from the closet, and went for a shower in the washing room. In his bed, he thought of Penelope and how worried she must be. He missed her immensely. Although they had not been dating very long, he felt very close to her and had not felt that way with anyone in a long time. He also thought about his son and wondered if Penelope had contacted him. He had spoken to him Friday night and normally they called once a week, so in theory, it could be possible he was not even aware of his abduction yet. He hoped Penelope, or the police, had contacted his son and wondered if they were looking for him. How could they find him if even he did not know where he was? He had to find some way to let them know where he was. After a while, despite his worries, he fell into a deep sleep.

12.   Escape plan

The next morning, he woke up around six thirty and jumped out of his bed. Feeling fit, he put on his swimming shorts and bathrobe. The hallway was dark and lit only by the small emergency lights. Arriving at minus six, the elevator door opened, and the hallway was completely dark. He got off the elevator and the movement must have triggered a sensor because the lights in the hallway came on. The entire floor was deserted, and he had the pool all to himself. Swimming brought back memories of his university days, when he swam early in the morning every day. He swam for about an hour and then returned to his floor to shower and get dressed, feeling physically fulfilled.

The rest of the day, he working on the manuals, taking breaks to eat and to get some fresh air on the roof in the afternoon. In the late afternoon, James appeared in the laboratory with a laptop.

"Mr. Wilson, your request for a laptop has been granted by Mr. Broch. Mr. Juncker had indicated that the deadline for the clinical trial manuals is very tight, so Mr. Broch is allowing this laptop so you can work on the manuals in your room at night. You must return it when the work is finished."

"Thank you, James."

James left, and Dave smiled at Harvey, who winked at him.

"Thanks, Harvey."

"You're welcome."

He continued working, and after dinner, he rushed back to his room, for he had been looking forward to his workout in the fitness center all day. This time he put on his swim shorts under the sport clothes and hurried downstairs. He was the first in the fitness center and started running on the treadmill to warm up. While running, he remembered that today was the day of Juvenatrust's lawsuit against Science Publications to prevent the publication of his article. He was anxious to see the outcome. The lawyers of Science

Publications had not been so concerned, but now he saw how ruthless and fanatical Jeff Broch was, he was less certain of the outcome. After a while, Yakov entered the fitness center.

"Hi Yakov."

"I see you beat me to the punch again today," Yakov said with a smile and started running beside him.

"Did you bring your swimming shorts today?"

"Sure did."

"Good, you'll love the hot tub."

After about an hour of running, he began his workout on the fitness equipment. They talked about all sorts of things during their workout. At one point, he asked how Yakov had ended up here. He explained what had happened to him and how he was still angry that his dream to start his own company was smashed. After the workout, they walked to the pool, which was empty, but in the hot tub, he noticed the same faces as the previous day.

"Hi guys," Yakov said as he entered the warm water.

Gary and Takeo made some room for Dave and Yakov. Everyone was up to their necks in the tub, which was bubbling loudly.

"Ah, this is nice," Dave said as he entered the tub.

Yakov grabbed Dave's wrist and held his arm under the water. He looked a bit puzzled at him.

"Are you sure we can trust him, Yakov?" Larry asked in a low voice.

"Yes, I checked him out and Harvey vouches for him, too. He wants exactly the same as we do."

Dave did not know what to make of this, but before he could ask anything, Yakov explained.

"Just make sure you keep your wristband underwater at all times. Then they won't be able to hear anything we say. We're pretty sure there must be a microphone in that camera on the other site of the pool, so never raise your voice."

He nodded and looked at the camera hanging from the ceiling at the very back of the pool. Gary explained what they were up to.

"I understood from Yakov that you're also motivated to escape from this place. But because we're constantly being watched, we have to be extremely careful. Basically, we meet regularly in the hot tub to discuss how to escape from here. Dave, keep everything we discuss here secret and don't discuss anything with anyone who's not in our group. Harvey Juncker's also involved and joins us from time to time. Besides Harvey, only Rob Hamilton is also part of it, but he's in a prison cell downstairs. Sometimes we stop our meetings abruptly when someone steps into the pool or joins us in the hot tub. We also don't meet for too long or every night, and we vary the composition of the group, because we don't want to arouse suspicion."

He listened intently as Gary explained all about their group and how they worked together. He felt relieved that there were more who desperately wanted to escape. Many people seemed to have given up and seemed completely cooperative with what Mr. Broch was demanding of them. He did not understand those people, after all, your freedom was the most important thing. All he wanted was to get out of here and back to Penelope. Most people in prison were careful what they said, which made free communication and conspiracy much more difficult. So had he from the moment he knew they eavesdropped on them all the time through these wristbands.

"Good to hear there're more people who want to escape. I was beginning to believe everyone here had already given up. Do you already have a plan on how to get out of here?" Dave asked.

"We're working in parallel on a few possibilities, but before we tell you anything about our plans, we want to start by picking your fresh, unspoiled brain. Let's start by brainstorming all the possibilities. This is to prevent us from anchoring you on our plans and perhaps missing new great ideas. I guess this sounds a bit too scientific as an approach, but hey what do you expect from a group of scientists?"

They laughed, and Yakov showed a big grin and said, "Okay, before we get serious, first a joke about scientists. Newton, Pascal and Archimedes are playing hide and seek. Archimedes starts counting. Pascal hides in a bush, and Newton draws a square on the ground and steps into it. Archimedes, of course, finds Newton first, but Newton replies, 'Nope. One Newton on one square is equal to one Pascal'."

Again, they all laughed and when the laughter died out, Gary looked at Dave and said in a low voice, "Okay. Let's start the brainstorming. You should with the first ideas that come to mind about how to escape. After the first five, we'll throw in our spontaneous ideas as well. The rules are simple, no one criticizes any idea. All ideas are good."

As Gary stopped talking, the four men looked at him, and Dave tried to focus.

"Interesting method. Let's see how we can get out of here. We can dig a tunnel and leave at night. Alternatively, we can kidnap Mr. Broch and force him to let us go. Or we can try to reprogram the access codes on the wristbands and gain access to the ground floor, where we all run out the door together. Or we can try to capture a guard and take his wristband. One of us dresses up as a guard and tries to get into the control center, which manages all the wristbands' access codes. He gives all prisoners access to the ground floor and we all escape from there."

He paused as he ran out of ideas for a moment and the men looked at him until he continued in a low voice, "Or we could make parachutes and jump off the rooftop during the break and try to run for it."

Takeo smiled and said in a low voice, "Nice start, Dave. That was number five. Everyone can join in now, but keep your voice low."

"We can jump off the roof using a long cord," Yakov said.

"Or we could break into the helicopter platform during the break and get away in the helicopter," Larry said.

"Or we could send a message out in a drone and have the police come and get us out," Gary said with a smile on his face.

"We could also simulate someone having a heart attack and then they would have to take this person to the hospital from where this person could alert the police or try to escape," Dave said.

"We hack into the computer network and send out a help message," Takeo said.

"We... we... we could break the window in the restaurant and all jump out the window and run away as fast as we can and all in a different direction," Dave said.

Suddenly Larry stood up and said quite loudly, "I'm going back to my room. Good night, everybody!"

Dave looked perplexed at him getting out of the whirlpool bath and didn't understand until he noticed Suzy Cheng entering the swimming pool and starting to swim some laps. Yakov told another scientist joke, and they all laughed, after which Takeo and Gary also stepped out of the hot tub. Yakov and Dave moved away from each other to use the extra space.

"Thank God we have these sport facilities in here, otherwise I would really go nuts being locked in here."

"Yeah, you can say that Dave and I can tell you after two months here, you really have to exercise to keep going every day. My skin's getting all wrinkled. Time to get out of the bath."

They returned to their floor, and Dave said goodbye to Yakov. After showering and brushing his teeth, he went back to his room. The laptop was standing on his desk and, like Harvey, he had put the desk against the wall to make sure that the camera on the television screen could not see what he was doing. He checked out the internet a bit. The laptop had a browser on it he had never seen before and was not at all like the browsers he had used before. The camera on the laptop's screen caught his eye, and he looked around in the room for something to cover the camera with. At one point, he found some sticker stuck to the inside of the desk lamp he used to cover the laptop's camera with.

First, he searched for news about the lawsuit against Science Publications, but he could not find anything about it. Then he started searching the New York State Courts electronic filing system, but again, he found nothing. Perhaps there would be some delay before the hearing outcome became available online, so he decided to try again the next day. Then he navigated to his private online e-mail account. He logged in and, to his surprise, it worked, and he discovered his mailbox was full. He scanned through the mails and his eye fell on an e-mail from Andrew. The e-mail was from the previous day and the message read:

"Dear Dad,

I am not sure if you will get this message or not, but just a quick mail to let you know that I spoke with the police and Penelope. We are all looking for you and I will not rest until we find you. I hope you are okay and that you find a way to communicate with us. We all miss you very much.

I love you, Dad!

Andrew."

He cried while he read the email. He missed his son, Wendy, and Penelope so much. He realized how worried they must be. With his sleeve he wiped away his tears, pushed the reply button and typed:

"Dear Andrew,

I am so happy to hear from you. I am alive and in some kind of prison in a desert with mountains all around, but I have no clue where I am. I have been kidnapped by Jeff Broch, the owner of Juvenatrust. They are treating me well. Miss you all so much! Send my kisses and love to Wendy and Penelope.

I love you!

Dave."

He clicked the send button and, to his surprise, the message disappeared as if it had been sent. He checked the sent items box, but the message was not there. Strangely, the outbox and the drafts box were both empty. It was as if the message had vanished. He feared that the message probably had not been sent. He felt sad and turned off the laptop. That night, he thought a lot about Andrew and Penelope and missed them more than ever.

The next day he went swimming early again and, in the water, he thought about the meeting in the hot tub the previous day. He figured that if they could only meet in the pool in the evening and discuss things, this whole escape plan would take a long time. He thought back on all the ideas, but the more he thought about it, the harder it seemed to get out of here. At breakfast, he sat at a table with Harvey, Judith, and Adish, and when he finished, he stood up and saw Gary coming toward him.

"Hi Dave, good morning. Did you sleep well?"

He was friendlier than before and shook his hand. Suddenly he felt he put something in his hand.

"Yeah, I slept like a rose. After some exercise, I always sleep well."

He put his hand in his pocket and put the object inside.

"Maybe I'll see you again tonight. I might go for another swim after dinner."

"All right, see you later Gary."

Dave took the elevator to minus five to work in the laboratory. There he first went to the restrooms, where he took the object out of his pocket. It was a gray USB-stick. He put it back in his pocket and returned to the laboratory to work with the team on the instruction manuals for the clinical trials. The day passed quickly and, in the afternoon, they all went for a walk on the roof. It was raining, and most people stayed on the covered terrace. He walked around toward the edge and the warm rain fell on his head. He looked at the mountains and at the barren and dry landscape. Except for some small bushes, he saw no good place to hide and get out of sight. So even if they managed to get out, it would be so easy for the guards to spot them and catch them again. It all looked hopeless. He became increasingly curious about the USB-stick.

After the break, they went back to the laboratory and continued working. Around six o'clock, Harvey got up and walked to the storage room in the back. After a while, he returned with a tube in his hand.

"Dave, it's time for you biweekly injection."

Harvey searched in one of the lab's cabinets and took out a syringe packed in plastic foil. He unwrapped it and began to fill it with the liquid from the tube.

"Okay," Dave said, and rolled up his sleeve.

Harvey inserted the syringe into his arm and slowly emptied it. Suzy peered through a microscope, and when she looked up, Dave asked her,

"When do you think you'll have the results of my blood analysis?"

"I think later this week, maybe early next week," she replied in her serious tone.

"We have to run quite a few tests."

"Okay, well, I'm curious to see if everything is okay with me. I mean, I feel healthier than ever, but you never know what's going on under the hood."

"We'll have to test a lot more than your blood, and ideally we'd do some scans like an MRI scan, but we don't have the equipment here."

Harvey looked at them and said, "I think we should take our time with the examination and probably do more tests this week and next week. However, this week the focus should be on preparing for the clinical trial."

Dave rearranged his sleeve and sat back down at the computer screen to continue writing the manual. Harvey threw away the syringe, and then walked back to Dave and looked at his screen.

"Let's see how far along you are."

Harvey started typing on Dave's computer and typed,

"I am trying to slow down the examination and health assessment, because I know that as long as we have many question marks about the drug's impact on your health Mr. Broch will see the need to continue to give you the drug and keep you around here longer."

He stopped typing and deleted the typing as soon as Dave read it.

"Is this what you have in mind for the manual?" Dave asked, so as not to arouse suspicion and he typed,

"Do you think I am in danger?"

Harvey looked at the screen and then typed,

"Not immediately, but I am afraid that once we have examined everything and have no more testing to do, that Mr. Broch might decide we do not need you anymore. He already hinted at that during the last meeting. This Friday I have to report to him about our findings from our examination of your body and I want to make sure that after Friday I still have to do a lot of testing and research. The password for the USB-stick is Alcatraz."

He read the message and deleted it after. He understood very well what Harvey meant. The only reason he was still alive was because Jeff Broch wanted to know what the drug had done to his body, and if there were any negative side effects. The other scientists could work on different projects for a very long time, but Dave was of little use to Jeff Broch after the examination would be finished. Logically, he could not just let him go and would most likely have him killed.

"Yes, I think you're on the right track with the manual, but when you finish it, we all need to read it carefully to make sure everything's correct and that we don't forget anything."

"Okay, thanks Harvey," he said and put his hand on Harvey's shoulder. He continued working, but remained a bit distracted for the rest of the evening. It had become clear to him he needed to get out of this place as soon as possible.

After dinner, he went back to his room and put on his sports clothes. As he undressed, he felt the USB-stick in his pocket. He inserted it into the laptop and found several files on it, which were password protected. He opened a file named "list one" and after typing in the password "Alcatraz", he found the complete list of all the people held as prisoners, including what floor they slept and worked on, how long they had been there, their backgrounds and where and when they had been abducted.

In another file called "list two" he found a list of all the ideas from the previous day's brainstorm session, as well as all the ideas from previous sessions. Next to it were lists of things to check and a whole risk analysis. For example, next to the idea of digging a tunnel was a whole analysis. The main problem with this idea was how to keep the tunnel undiscovered. Since the wristbands were equipped with microphones and apparently included a location tracker, it would be too easy for security to notice they were digging. Another challenge was getting rid of the huge amount of sand and debris. He found a whole list of ideas on how to get rid of the sand, but it seemed like a very difficult option.

He quickly scanned through the file and opened another file, called "list three". This one contained drawing of parts of the building with many details, such as the locations of the security cameras. Another file contained a schedule of when and who would meet in the hot tub. He looked at it and saw that today on Tuesday his name was also on the list and he had to be there at fifteen minutes to eight. He looked at his wristband and saw it was already in five minutes. He took the USB-stick from the laptop and hid it in the back of the small refrigerator in his room. He rushed out of his room and took the elevator to minus six.

This time, he went straight to the pool, and when he entered, he saw Takeo and Harvey already sitting in the hot tub. Gary and Larry were swimming laps in the large pool. He greeted them and undressed in one of the nearby cabins. In his swim shorts, he walked over to the hot tub and sat next to Harvey.

"How do you feel after your injection?"

"I feel perfectly normal. Since the beginning, I've felt nothing different after any injections. In fact, I usually feel even more energetic after."

Larry and Gary also entered the hot tub and Larry, with his long gray hair and wrinkled face, said, "Harvey, maybe you can give me some of those injections, so I can look and feel young again, just like Dave here. Maybe then my hair will lose its gray color."

"Well, Larry, I've some bad news for you. After Mr. Broch heard Dave stole tubes from our stock, he implemented a new barcode system and all tubes are now marked and tracked with RFID tags. He even put a camera system in the storage room. When I take a tube out of the fridge, it is immediately registered. I now have to ask permission to take out a dose."

"You can just take out the drug and fill it back with water, right? For a good friend like me, you'd do that, right?"

Harvey laughed.

"I'd still have to explain to Mr. Broch and you know how efficient he can be in getting the truth out of you. I'm not risking that at my age."

"Just kidding Harvey. I think Dave will be the only lucky one here."

Gary looked around, and everyone was sitting in the hot tub with their hands under water.

"Okay guys, let's get started before someone comes in again. First, I'll explain the USB-stick procedure to Dave. We use the USB-sticks mainly to keep track of the progress of the various escape plans and to plan the meetings in the pool. We change the composition of the participants frequently so as not to make it too conspicuous. I keep the master file and make sure it's updated each time. Once a week, I hand out a new USB-stick on Tuesdays. So, be sure to give yours to me every Tuesday morning and I'll give it back to you in the evening or at lunch. You can add your ideas or findings, but make sure they're clearly marked. Be very careful and hide it well, since we'll be in trouble if they get their hands on it."

"Don't worry, I'll be very careful. I didn't have enough time to read through all the documents, but I will tonight," Dave said.

"No problem. All right, let's start with the progress on our GPS location plan. As you know, Takeo and I work on minus seven and Takeo occasionally on minus eight. The big difference with your floor is that we constantly have guards around and several very loyal employees of Jeff Broch. We help them develop all kinds of military drones and weapons. However, on most projects, they only let us work on part of the project and regularly check what we're doing. The drones are all equipped with GPS receivers. The drones make regular test flights, and the trajectory traveled is recorded. We've been trying to read those GPS receivers for a few weeks now, because that should give us the exact geographical coordinates of our location. Jeff Broch's people do the testing and flying of the drones, and they won't let us get near those receivers. We've tried to get our hands on those receivers, but it's difficult. Takeo and I are working on a plan to get access to the drones' GPS receivers, but we can't tell you much more about it, because it's better that you don't know. We're waiting for the right moment, so hopefully more news soon. Takeo, how far along are you with the wristband analysis?"

"I discovered we can block the signal in the wristband by covering the whole band with aluminum foil. The big challenge is that when the signal stops transmitting, security eventually notices. The key question is what their response time is. On floor minus eight, I've been experimenting with electromagnetic weapons and there's a metal cage which acts like a Faraday cage."

"What is a Faraday cage?" Dave asked.

"A Faraday cage is an enclosure that blocks electromagnetic fields. I entered this cage several times last week, and then it blocks the signal from the wristband. I measured the time it took for the guards to notice my signal was gone and come and check on me. This takes them at least twenty minutes. I told them I had to do some work on sensitive equipment in this cage and that's why the signal was gone. After that, they started reacting even slower with me, as they found me in this cage every time."

"Interesting, Takeo. So, we can basically disappear off the radar for twenty minutes. That's good to consider in several of our ideas," Larry said.

"Can't we find a way to change the authorization codes on the wristband to get access to different floors?" Dave asked.

Larry nodded and replied, "I've tried to read the signal the wristband transmits, but everything's encrypted and so far, I haven't been able to crack this code. Some very professional and talented people must have developed the whole system. I keep trying, but I have to be careful not to get caught like Rob."

"Has anyone gotten any information out of the guards or support staff?" Dave asked.

"Well, I guess we've all tried, but they're tight-lipped and so far, no useful information has come out," Harvey replied, and the other men in the hot tub nodded.

Larry now looked at Gary and asked him, "Any luck with stealing a drone from the storage room?"

Gary smiled triumphantly at him and answered, "They don't allow us in the storage room without a guard, so it's very difficult to steal anything. But today they asked me to fix a drone, and I had told them some parts were broken. I had tossed the parts in the bin in front of them and they gave me all the new parts. I repaired the whole drone and when they left, I phished the parts out of the bin. I hid them under my desk attached with tape to the back of one of the drawers. I hope to collect enough material to build a new drone that we can use for one of our plans to send out a message. Unfortunately, we must be patient and wait for an opportunity."

"Have any of you considered taking one of the guards or support staff hostage and then negotiating our way out of here?" Dave asked.

Harvey shook his head and replied, "That won't work with someone like Jeff Broch. The man is ruthless, and he would just sacrifice the guard without hesitation, and one of us will probably get killed in the process."

"I guess you're right. It's a bit of a desperate method."

Gary looked around and asked, "Does anybody have anything else for this meeting? Otherwise, I suggest we close this meeting."

Everyone shook their heads, and slowly, one by one, they left the hot tub. Dave went to the fitness center and worked out for almost two hours. Back in his room, he looked on his laptop to see if he could find out anything about the outcome of the lawsuit against

Science Publications, but again, he found nothing. He spent the rest of the evening reading the files on the USB-stick. Unfortunately, he did not get a good feeling from what he was reading. From all the comments he had read, it seemed almost impossible to escape from this place. After all this time, they had not even managed to figure out the location where they were being held captive. Only Gary and Takeo were still actively searching for the location. Rob Hamilton had been close, but had been put in solitary confinement. He felt sad and missed his friends and family more than ever.

The next day he continued working on the manual and in the evening, he did not go to the hot tub since it was not his turn to attend the meeting. He ran on the treadmill at the fitness center and could not help but think of Penelope. After running, he did his exercises on the fitness equipment and after a while Yakov joined him when the meeting in the hot tub was over. He started telling jokes again, and Dave felt better, at least for a while.

On Thursday, he finished the manuals, and Harvey's team reviewed them. In the evening, he saw Takeo and Gary at dinner, both looking excited and happy. He sensed something was up, but over dinner they only talked about the children they had seen on television, marching in the streets around the world, demanding tougher measures from their governments to halt global warming and curb the carbon dioxide emissions. It was encouraging to see all these young people fighting for their future.

After dinner, he rushed to the hot tub, and this time he was the first. Gary arrived a bit after him, followed by Yakov and Takeo. Harvey and Larry were not scheduled for that evening. He noticed Gary and Takeo were more enthusiastic than usual and he sensed they were onto something. Once they were all seated, Gary started talking.

"We finally had a breakthrough today. We were able to read out our location on one of the GPS receivers. With the geographical coordinates, we could find our location on a map on the internet. Gentlemen, we're in what they call the Sonoran Desert in Arizona."

"That's great news! The Sonoran Desert, that's close to the Mexican border, isn't it? What's the nearest town?" Dave asked enthusiastically.

"We're south of Phoenix, but the closest town is Maricopa, which is less than ten miles from here," Takeo answered.

"How did you get the coordinates?"

"Well, we've been waiting and observing the drone operations for weeks now. Today, one of the guards made a mistake. The man from the support staff, who usually does the repairs, wasn't there. He came to ask us if we could fix the drone. We kindly repaired his drone, and he observed us the whole time, but after our lunch, he was called away for about ten minutes. We immediately downloaded the drone's GPS tracking information, and that's how we found the geographical coordinates of our location. The guard took the repaired drone back and had no idea we had taken the information," Gary said. Then he looked at Dave and Yakov.

"After this meeting, I have the coordinates for each of you on a piece of paper. Dave, maybe you can give it to Harvey? And Yakov, maybe you can give it to Larry? At least that way we won't lose the information if they catch me or Takeo."

"What do you mean by catching you or Takeo?"

"Well, Gary and I have been working on a plan to get a message out for a while, but since we finally have the coordinates, we want to execute our plan in the coming days. We can't and won't say anything about it. This way, if we fail and get caught, at least you guys can continue working on other plans to get out of this place."

"Can we help you somehow?" Yakov asked.

"Thanks, but I think it's better you all stay out of it."

William Ashton showed up and started to swim laps in the large pool, and the meeting ended instantly. Yakov told a joke, and they all laughed. Takeo left the hot tub first, and then the other three men followed. They dressed in the cabins and Gary passed the pieces of paper with the coordinates to them. Dave and Yakov went for a run on the treadmills and then did their workouts as usual.

Back on minus three, Yakov walked straight to Larry's room. Dave went for a shower first, and afterwards walked to Harvey's room. The door was half open, and the light was still on. Harvey was sitting behind his laptop. Dave greeted him and sat next to him, then he took the paper with the coordinates out of his pocket and put it on the desk. Harvey looked flabbergasted and smiled at him.

"Are you having a nice, relaxing evening in your room?" Dave asked with a huge smile and started typing on the laptop to explain the whole story.

He returned to his room after and hid the coordinates behind the refrigerator. Feeling optimistic, he wondered what Takeo and Gary were planning. He searched the internet again for the lawsuit, but again he could find nothing, except that they had filed the case. Tomorrow they would normally publish his article, and he hoped it would go through because it would mean a small victory against Jeff Broch. That night, he had more hope of ever getting out here, and he quickly fell asleep.

The next morning, he went back to work with Harvey's team, and by the end of the morning, they had the instruction manuals ready. The clinical trials would start next Wednesday. All the manuals, materials and drug doses would be transported on Monday to San Francisco where the trials would take place. They had also finished examining the sample of Dave's blood. Suzy explained what she had concluded from the blood test.

"I've analyzed Dave's blood, and we'll have to repeat this every week to see if there are any changes. We'll also have to take more samples and test other body fluids, but the current sample shows that the drug has eliminated all senescent cells from his blood cells and currently the cells resemble cells of a young person."

During and after lunch, they discussed the results in further detail, and they discussed what tests they still wanted to do. Suzy also wanted to focus more on his arthritis, which was well documented in his medical records.

"Ideally, we would do a detailed MRI scan of your body to zoom in on your bones and joints to examine how the arthritis has developed compared to the scans in your medical file. The only problem is that we don't have an MRI scanner in here. So maybe we'll start by examining the other body fluids first."

"Good idea, Suzy. I'll address the MRI scan with Mr. Broch at the next meeting," Harvey said.

They all nodded. Then it was time for the rooftop break and they all went upstairs. Dave always enjoyed the fresh air, although it was very hot today on the terrace. The guards waited by the door as they walked around. He talked to Yakov, and they stared at the mountains. When Dave turned his head, he noticed Gary and Takeo in the corner. They were standing close together as if they were trying to hide something. Yakov had noticed it too, and immediately looked at the guards under the covered part of the terrace. They were not paying attention. Gary and Takeo pulled out some metal pieces from under their shirts and put them together. Yakov suddenly whispered in his ear, "It looks like they're putting together a drone. Let's distract the guards."

Dave followed him to the covered terrace, and they walked to the refrigerator with the cold drinks, a few meters away from the two guards. Yakov opened the fridge and said, "Here's your water, Dave! Oh, shit!"

He dropped a bottle in the fridge, causing a bunch of other bottles to fall out and roll across the floor. Dave helped pick them up, and both guards looked at them. Then suddenly he heard a faint buzzing sound. He immediately yelled at Yakov, "Oh Yakov, what are you doing!? You dropped all the bottles. I just want one."

The buzzing sound faded away quickly, and with all the wind on the rooftop, it seemed like the guards had noticed nothing. Gary and Takeo had walked away from each other, but were both looking at the mountains now. Dave looked in the same direction and saw a small dot quickly getting smaller, which was probably the drone flying farther away. A few seconds later, the dot had gotten so small that they lost sight of it.

Suddenly, he heard a loud noise above him. He looked up at the square tower above the elevator in the center of the building, right at the intersection of the T-shape of the building. The shutters on the tower opened, and then he heard a loud buzzing noise. Everyone on the rooftop now looked up, and they saw four drones flying out of the tower with a low buzzing sound. They flew at high speed in the same direction where the other drone had disappeared out of sight, and the buzzing noise quickly faded. Now everyone was looking in that direction, and he saw Gary staring at the guards. He looked terrified. After a few minutes, they heard a popping sound and saw dark smoke in the sky above the mountain range. Everyone had gone to the edge of the roof catch a glimpse of the spectacle. Slowly, the buzzing sound increased again, and he saw small dots on the horizon growing larger. The drones flew back at high speed, and just above their heads, they slowed down and landed again in the square tower above the elevator. Then the buzzing sound ceased, and the shutters closed again.

He saw both Gary and Takeo looking anxious. He looked at the guards, but they had no clue what had happened. Gary and Takeo were talking together in the corner. People walked away from the edge, but about ten minutes later, a dozen ten guards stormed out of the elevator onto the roof.

"There they are! Those two men over there in the corner!" a guard shouted.

Takeo ran away from Gary, but there was nowhere for him to go. Gary just stood still. The guards got to him first and yelled, "On your knees!"

He immediately got on his knees and the guards pushed him onto his stomach and tied his hands behind his back. The other guards went after Takeo and chased him into the corner of the rooftop. He looked desperate and moved nervously on the edge of the railing. Dave was afraid he would jump off the roof, which would surely kill him. A guard yelled at Takeo, "On your knees!"

He stressed out completely and tried to run past one of the guards, but another guard grabbed his taser and fired it at him. He screamed and made jerky movements, clenching his hands. His movement froze, and he was now just shaking on the floor and the guards jumped on him. They carried both of them away toward the elevator. People moved out of the way as they passed. Everyone on the roof looked shocked. Yakov was still standing next to Dave and as the elevator closed, he said, "Shit, they're in pretty serious trouble now."

"Jesus, you can say that. Did you see what that taser did to Takeo? He looked frozen in pain."

Suddenly, everyone looked at their wristband, and his band was also vibrating.

"Return to your work floor immediately!" the display showed.

Everyone walked back to the elevator, and they were all agitated. He went back to minus five, but they had difficulty to get back to work, so they hung out around the coffee machine and talked about what had happened on the roof. Everyone was worried about Takeo and Gary. After about an hour, most people had returned to work.

Harvey worked with Dave to take more samples from other body fluids from him. He had to pee in a bottle and Harvey took some samples of his saliva. He stored everything in the refrigerator to examine later. Suzy, who seemed least affected by all the events and had gone back to work almost immediately, explained to him what else they had planned for him.

"Dave, we'll examine the body fluids tomorrow. Ideally, we should also measure your heart and lung function and take some x-rays to see how your arthritis has developed since you started taking the drug."

Harvey interrupted her now and said, "I'll ask Mr. Broch for all the equipment the next time I have a meeting with him. Let's focus on these tests first Suzy, we're not in that much of a hurry. Dave, it's time for your drug injection."

Dave started unbuttoning his shirt as Harvey walked to the storage room and, five minutes later, returned with a tube. He filled a syringe and injected the drug into his arm.

"All right. We're done with week three of the injections and starting next week, we'll only inject one dose a week every Friday afternoon."

Harvey marked something on the schedule he had on his desk and continued, "Next Thursday, we can take blood again to see if there are any changes."

Suzy nodded, and they now switched topics to discuss the upcoming clinical trial. Dave listened, but felt he was the only one there not really adding much value. His thoughts wandered, and he thought back to one of the mornings when he woke up early and looked at Penelope beside him. He longed for those moments together. The vibration of the wristband shook him out of his thoughts, and it was time for dinner.

After dinner, he changed into his swim shorts and wore his sports clothes over them. He took the elevator to minus six. Yakov was already in the hot tub together with Larry. He joined them, and about five minutes later, Harvey arrived. The atmosphere was depressing, and they were all feeling down because of the day's events.

"What a mess!" Larry said when everyone was in the hot tub. "I hope they don't kill them."

"I believe they're crucial to some of Mr. Broch's projects, but you never know. Maybe in an emotional outburst of rage, he would kill them anyway," Harvey responded gloomily.

"Did we know there was a drone defense system in the tower?" Dave asked.

"No. We had our suspicions, but we couldn't be sure until today. They must have some kind of special drone radar to detect flying objects. This puts a cross through some of the ideas on our list. On top of it, we now no longer have access to floors minus seven and minus eight, where all the drones, robotics and weapon technology are developed. We need to see if we can find someone else with access to these floors we can trust. The problem is they all sleep on minus four. Of the people I know, I don't see any candidate for now," Larry said.

"Me neither. Some of those people seem to like their projects a little too much and don't seem in any rush to get out of this place," Harvey said.

Yakov nodded.

"I guess we should all focus on alternative plans. At least we know our location, so we should focus on getting a message out so people will start looking for us," Dave said.

"Yes, well, let's all think about that tonight and tomorrow. I don't see what else there is to discuss, so I propose we reconvene tomorrow," Larry said.

They all nodded and Yakov and Dave left the hot tub and headed back to the gym to go for their daily run and workout. That evening they made no jokes, and the atmosphere remained sad.

Dave went back to his room after his workout and prepared for the night. He turned on his laptop. Today his article was supposed to be published, and he looked at the website of Science Publications. When he clicked on the page of Science Magazine, his mood suddenly changed. On the website, he saw a picture of the cover of Science Magazine and the main title read:

"Rejuvenation breakthrough!"

He immediately rushed to Harvey's room next door. His door was closed, but he could still see some light from under the door. He knocked on the door and then swung it open. Harvey sat on the edge of his bed in his pajamas and looked startled at Dave storming in.

"They published the article!" he shouted at Harvey, who couldn't believe what he was hearing.

"Come see!"

Dave hurried back to his room, and Harvey followed him. Looking at the screen of his laptop, Harvey cried out while he made a fist in the air.

"Yes!"

Harvey even hugged him, so happy was he.

"Can we read it online?"

"No, I tried, but we have to buy it online and it doesn't work with the security on the internet here."

"Still, this is great news. At least my work will now be known to the world."

"Yes, exactly, and we could use some exposure at the moment. At least they won't forget about us now."

"Well, thanks for letting me know. I'll sleep much better now. Sleep well, Dave."

"You too!"

Despite the day's events, he felt upbeat and fell asleep shortly after going to bed.

13. A new plan

The atmosphere in the restaurant was dreary the next morning. Takeo and Gary had not shown up at dinner yesterday, and now at breakfast, they were absent again. It seemed to affect everyone's mood. They were afraid that Jeff Broch had them killed. Harvey had asked one of the guards what had happened to them, but they said nothing about it. He found it so unreal to sit in the restaurant and be surrounded by this desert and mountains. Even now, knowing that they were in Arizona did not change much, because they still had gotten no message out. He missed his freedom more than ever.

He continued to help Harvey's team prepare for the clinical trial, and was quite surprised that they were allowed to take their daily outdoor break on the roof that day. More guards were present than usual, though, and they were not allowed near the railing. At one point Pierre Lavoisier walked to the edge, and they immediately shouted for him to keep his distance, already keeping their hands on their tasers. Pierre was horrified. Still, it was nice to be outside in the fresh air and to enjoy the view of the mountains and the desert in front of it.

After the break, he continued working with the team in the afternoon until they all went for dinner at seven. Before he sat down, he gazed out at the mountain range. The sun was hiding behind the mountain range and the light was mysterious. He really had to get out of this place somehow. He sat down at the table with Harvey's team, and Yakov joined them.

After a while, Margaret Jones walked up to them, and in her squeaky voice, she said, "You're famous, Dave!"

He looked at Margaret in surprise and had no clue what she was talking about.

"Haven't you seen the news yet? You're all over it. You're the big news event of the moment!"

He was still confused.

"What news channel and what's it about?"

"Almost every major national television station, Dave. They're talking about your kidnapping. Go check it out!"

"All right, I will. Thanks for telling me, Margaret."

He tried to eat his food as fast as possible and noticed all the people at his table were doing the same. They were all curious. He hurried down to his room and turned on the television screen. On one of the channels, they were talking about a political debate about a new tax bill that had been submitted to Congress and he zapped to another news channel. Behind him, Harvey and Yakov entered the room. He found another channel where they showed the headline:

"Reporter from Science Magazine kidnapped in New York."

His room filled up with people. Larry entered, and behind him he saw Adish, Judith, William and Pierre. He raised the volume of the television.

"Yesterday, Science Magazine published an article about a breakthrough with a new medical drug aimed at rejuvenating the human body. A research lab in Novato, California, led by a scientist called Dr. Harvey Juncker, tested a drug on mice and succeeded in extending their lifespan by about thirty percent. The lab is owned by a company called Juvenatrust, and they tried to prevent publication of this article last week. Today the New York Police, along with Science Publications, announced that last Saturday the author of this article, Dave Wilson, was abducted in broad daylight in the middle of New York at the corner of Fifty-Seventh Street and Seventh Avenue. Witnesses saw Mr. Wilson try to run away, but several men wearing black helmets and black clothes tasered and dragged him into a black SUV, then quickly drove away."

In the background were images of the press conference given by the New York Police Department. He moved closer to the television screen and saw behind the police officer the face of Craig Pathfinder, his boss. He was glad to see him there, which meant he was on top of his kidnapping. He wouldn't even be surprised if he was the mastermind behind the timing of the press conference right after the article in Science Magazine was published. Perfect timing for maximum publicity. He focused on the crowd behind the police officer and suddenly he spotted the Andrew's face and next to him at the level his chest he saw Penelope.

He pointed to the screen and shouted, "That's my son! And that's my girlfriend!"

He felt shivers go through his body and felt deeply touched when he saw them both in the crowd. All the time, they were showing a picture of him in the corner of the screen. It was a recent photo taken by Penelope on which he looked young, much younger than his fifty-four years. He figured she had probably explained everything to Andrew, but he wondered if they had also informed the police of his theft and subsequent injections of the rejuvenation drug.

"The police explained that Dave Wilson, based on testimony from several witnesses, was apparently being chased through Central Park by these men in black helmets, and this wild chase continued until they kidnapped him at the corner of Fifty-Seventh Street and Seventh Avenue. Several bystanders witnessed the abduction."

In the background, they showed a video made with a bystander's smartphone. You could see how he got tasered and dragged quickly and violently into the SUV. They showed a few testimonies of witnesses, and he recognized the old lady who had been violently pushed to the ground. The reporter further explained: "The New York police are investigating the abduction of Dave Wilson and any links to the publication of the article. They are also investigating whether there is a connection to the recent fire at the Juvenatrust laboratory in Novato, California. About two weeks ago, the laboratory burned down and four scientists were killed. Initially, the Novato police had announced the names of the victims, which were four scientists at the laboratory, including the facility's director, Dr. Harvey Juncker. Recently, the police called this disclosure erroneous and launched a criminal investigation. The Novato police, along with the FBI, are still investigating the deaths and identities of the four bodies found. Today a large, violent tornado rips through Oklahoma, leaving a path of destruction."

He turned down the volume on the television and rubbed a tear from his eye. The sight of his son together with Penelope had made him realize even more how much he missed them. The people in the room were talking excitedly about the news. Harvey put a hand on his shoulder and said, "At least the article is out in the open now. That'll feed the curiosity of many people. Let's hope they all start looking for us."

"Yes, let's hope so. It seems they're still investigating your so-called death. That the FBI is involved looks promising."

"Yes, indeed, it does."

Yakov slapped his hand on Dave's shoulder and said with a smile, "Dave, that's good news for you, but also for us. The more they look for you, the better chance we have of getting out of here."

He smiled back.

"Let's hope so. Well, I guess we go for a run and a workout?"

"Brilliant plan. See you downstairs."

Everyone left his room, and he changed clothes and went downstairs to the fitness center. He ran on the treadmill and did his workout on the machines. The news had given them hope, and Yakov was also in a better mood and told quite a few jokes. At one point, Yakov stopped his exercise and walked toward the pool.

"Let's go next door. It's time to relax in the hot tub."

Dave had completely forgotten about the meeting. He finished his exercise and stood up.

"Good idea."

Harvey and Larry were already in the hot tub. Yakov and Dave sat down next to them. Larry started talking as soon as everyone's hands were under the water.

"Good news that the press is doing a story about your kidnapping, Dave. It looks like they've linked it to the fake death of Harvey. I'm taking over Gary's role to update and redistribute the USB-sticks. We're sticking to the original schedule. Does anyone have any new ideas?"

He thought for a moment and asked, "Has anyone tried opening the double doors next to the elevator?"

Everyone shook their heads and Larry replied, "The problem is that access is through the sensor next to it, which is similar to the sensor of the elevator. To hack that, we either have to access the general security system that registers all access codes for all wristbands or we have to change the sensor locally. There's a camera monitoring the double doors and the hallway, so they see everything. Change the sensors would take some time, and I tried fiddling with one of the sensors once, but within five minutes a guard came through the double doors and threatened me with his taser. We thought about covering the cameras, but that wouldn't give us much time either because that also triggers an alarm. We'll have to find an easier way out."

Yakov nodded and said, "I believe Gary and Takeo were on the right track. Now that we have the coordinates of our location, it would be safest for us if we find a way to inform the outside world of our whereabouts. Then the police might come to investigate and get us out of here. The drone was a nice idea, but apparently security is too tight, so we'll have to find another way to get a message out."

Everyone agreed, and Harvey thought out loud, "So, we need to understand what people or things are moving out of this facility and how can get a message out there?"

"Maybe with the support staff or guards?" Yakov said.

"Too risky. They could find the message and most likely inform Jeff Broch," Harvey replied.

"What else moves out of this facility?" Larry asked.

Dave suddenly brightened up and said enthusiastically, "Harvey, the clinical trial starts next week. The manuals and drug doses leave here on Monday."

Harvey started smiling and nodded.

"You're absolutely right. That's a great idea. Maybe we could stick a USB-stick with a message in one of the metal boxes where we keep the drug doses."

"It has to be out of sight, otherwise the guards might see it," Dave said.

"Yes, I'll see tomorrow what the best spot is."

"I'll write a message and put it on a USB-stick," Dave said.

"It sounds like a good idea, but be careful, both of you. If they find the USB-stick, you're in big trouble," Larry cautioned them, but Yakov laughed cynically and said, "No risk, no glory!"

They all laughed, but Dave realized full well that they might end up like Takeo and Gary, and the thought alone gave him the chills.

The next day, Harvey and Dave examined the refrigerators in the storage room and the metal boxes to figure out the best place to hide the USB-stick. Harvey had been instructed to send out just enough doses for one week of clinical trial, because Jeff Broch was afraid people would steal the drugs. Each week, one refrigerator would leave with the drug doses in it. The first refrigerator would leave on Monday, and Harvey had to prepare it for transport. The refrigerator would return at the end of the week with all the empty metal boxes. Jeff Broch was so paranoid that he wanted to recycle the boxes himself to prevent that some outside recycling company from being able to analyze the drops of drugs left in the tubes and somehow figure out the formula.

The challenge was to find the most appropriate place to hide the USB-stick. If they hid it too well, the doctors and nurses conducting the clinical trial might never find it, and it might return with all the metal boxes and empty doses and then there was a good chance that the support staff or guards handling the return and recycling of all the empty drug doses would find it. If it was too visible, the guards might spot it before it even reached the outside world. They shifted one of the refrigerators out of line and pushed it together in front of the storage room, where the guards would pick it up on Monday. He could see Harvey was struggling to handle the heavy fridge, and a month ago he would have had the same difficulty with his weak back, but now he felt strong and it was no problem for him. Harvey had to count and check the drug doses. Dave helped him and as they pulled out all the boxes one by one, they had plenty of time to figure out the best place to hide the USB-stick.

Half an hour later, suddenly both their wristbands vibrated. It showed a message:

"Proceed to floor 4 for a meeting with Mr. Broch."

He looked frightened at Harvey.

"A meeting now? Any idea what it would be about?"

Harvey also looked anxious.

"No, I've no idea, but I think we'd better go straight to the fourth floor since Mr. Broch doesn't like to wait."

They walked silently together toward the elevator, and he feared they might be on to them and their plan. Were they on to them? There were cameras hanging in the hallway and in the storage room, but since Harvey had to prepare the shipment of drug doses for the clinical trial, it seemed logical that he would ask someone to help him with that. Harvey looked concerned, and when they arrived on the fourth floor, a guard was waiting for them. The guard just stared at them and pointed to the double doors in front of the elevator. They walked through the door and reported to the front desk.

"We had to come upstairs for a meeting with Mr. Broch."

The woman at the desk did not smile and seemed busy. She glanced up from her computer screen and said, "Mr. Wilson and Mr. Juncker, you can go right in. Mr. Broch is expecting you."

He followed Harvey through the thick wooden door next to the reception desk. Inside, their eyes had to adjust to the blinding light of the sun shining through the large windows. Jeff Broch sat behind his desk and stood up as they entered.

"Gentlemen, welcome! You both must have been happy yesterday that they published your stupid article after all. I hope you don't delude yourselves, as it won't change much, anyway. In a few weeks, everybody will have forgotten about it and everything will go back to business as usual."

Jeff approached the two men and shook Dave's hand and kept holding it. He was afraid Jeff might suspect something about their plan and ask about it while using the lie detector in his bionic arm.

"What's more annoying, however, are those two people who tried to send a drone to a police station. Now I had to punish them and they won't be able to work for a while, so I'm missing two talented scientists on my team. Were you aware of their plans, Dave?"

He felt extremely uncomfortable as Jeff's grip around his hand tightened. Jeff stared into his eyes as he waited for his answer.

"Uh, well no, not really."

Suddenly, he felt a tremendous pain in his hand as the grip of Jeff's hand became even tighter around his hand. He felt the incredible force from his bionic arm squeezing the bones of his hand.

"You know you better not lie to me, Dave. Don't be stupid! Did you know about their plans?"

The pain became unbearable and Dave had tears in his eyes. He had the impression his hand was going to break at any moment.

"They had told me they were planning something, but not what or when."

Jeff stared into his eyes and waited for a moment, then he said, "That's a good boy!"

Jeff loosened his grip and then released his hand. Dave looked at his sore hand. It was all red and you could see the marks of Jeff's fingers on it. Jeff now turned his attention to Harvey and shook his hand.

"Harvey, old chap, did you also know about these plans?"

Harvey looked extremely stressed and nervous. He was sweating and the warm bright sunlight from outside made it worse.

"I... I... had also heard they were planning something, but I didn't know what or when, either."

Jeff did not tighten his hand with Harvey, but he kept holding it.

"Okay, I believe you, Harvey. How's the preparation for the clinical trial going?"

He calmed down a bit and replied, "We prepared a package with all the instructions, and today we prepared the first batch of drug doses for transport. I'll make sure everything is ready to be picked up for transport tomorrow morning. Tuesday, they can unpack and prepare everything, so the clinical trial can start on Wednesday."

"Sounds good, Harvey. How's the examination of Dave going?"

Jeff Broch continued to hold his hand the entire time and Harvey remained nervous and shaking with fear.

"We did a blood test last week and studied his medical records. The blood test showed the drug eliminated all senescent cells from Dave's blood cells and resemble cells of a young person."

"So, can we conclude the drug worked properly?"

"Well, we need more time for that. We're currently examining other body fluids and we'll repeat the blood tests on a weekly basis. It'll take time to see if side effects develop. The interesting thing about Dave's case is that he has a medical history of arthritis. We want to study how this disease has progressed and what the medication has done to it. I also want to do a general health test to check his heart and lung function. We also need to scan his body to see if there are any negative side effects, such as the development of cancer. The problem is that we don't have the right equipment for all these tests. We lack, for instance, a machine to measure heart and lung function, an MRI scanner and an X-ray system."

"Make a list for me with all the equipment you need and I'll see what I can arrange for you, but I want results within a week."

"Within a week? That's only possible if I get all that equipment today, but even then, this is too ambitious."

"Harvey, just make it work! I'm expecting a potential client to visit by the end of next week. I need a conclusive test report for him."

Harvey was still very nervous and stressed, and his head bowed down somewhat desperately.

"I'll do my best, Mr. Broch."

"Mail me the list immediately and I'll take care of the equipment."

"I will, Mr. Broch."

Jeff released Harvey's hand and Harvey rubbed his hand, relieved.

"Dave, I want you to help Harvey write the test report. I want a full report on the drug and its benefits and risks, if any. Make it nice with pictures of you before and after the treatment and describe what changes you experienced. I'll ask my staff to send you some pictures from your cell phone."

"Okay, Mr. Broch."

"You can go now."

Jeff walked back to his desk. They left his office, and Dave felt relieved. At least he had not found out about their new plan to send out a message. In addition, they had learned that Takeo and Gary were still alive. Back in the lab on minus five, Harvey made a list of all the equipment he needed and sent it to Mr. Broch.

"I doubt he can get me all those machines in a week. It seems impossible to me."

"He seemed quite convinced, Harvey. We'll see. I guess I'm more amazed he has a customer visiting as early as next week."

"That doesn't surprise me at all. This drug is most people's dream. It's like a fountain of youth. Especially for rich people who are so used to buying what they want and realize that despite their money, they are mortal like the poor. Their money already gives them some extra years compared to the poor, but they compare themselves to other rich people and living longer is the ultimate treasure. I remember this Health Inequality Project that showed that in the U.S. the richest one percent of men live fifteen years longer than the poorest one percent. Fifteen years! For women, the difference was ten years. The rich don't care about this difference between poor and rich. Their goal is their own immortality, and that's priceless. With this drug, they can live up to thirty percent longer compared to their rich friends who would not take the drug. That's about twenty-five years longer. So, you can imagine people wanting to get their hands on this rejuvenation drug before their rich friends get to it."

"I guess you're right. Look at me, I'm the living example of how far people will go to extend their lifespan. Although for me, the main drive was to get rid of my constant back problems."

"Yeah, I know, and betraying someone's trust didn't stop you, either. Okay, let's continue with the clinical trial preparation."

Dave was dismayed that Harvey was still pissed at him. Their contact had improved, but apparently, he still reproached him for the theft. He began typing on the computer and asked Harvey if he had a small USB-stick to hide in the metal boxes containing the tubes. Harvey looked in a closet and found one in a metal color that would perfectly match the color of the metal boxes. He handed it to him and Dave began typing a message to put on the USB-stick. He sat in the corner of the lab, half hidden behind Harvey's desk and out of view of the cameras. Adish and Suzy were working at a microscope farther away, so he could write a message with nobody able to see what he was doing. He wrote:

"WE NEED YOUR HELP! Please pass this message on to the nearest police station as soon as possible!

Make sure they inform the New York Police Department, the Novato Police Department and the FBI.

We are thirty-six people (see attached list) held captive by Jeff Broch in a heavily guarded facility in the middle of the desert, south of Phoenix and east of Maricopa, Arizona. Our coordinates are latitude: 33.152310 and longitude: -112.213495.

They keep us in this building on several floors under the ground level, from floor minus three to minus nine. The building has ten floors under the ground and five floors above ground. Mr. Broch is located on floor four. The guards are all armed and dangerous, and the facility is heavily protected.

PLEASE HELP US! LIBERATE US!"

Dave's first reflex was to write his name below the text, but he realized that could be suicidal. Better to keep it vague, in case the message was intercepted by Broch's people. He had Harvey read it. When he approved it, he saved it to the USB-stick and erased the temporary memory on the desktop so as not to leave a trace. He tucked it away in his pocket.

After lunch, he quickly passed to his room on minus three and added the list with all the people's names to the message. Then he removed the USB-stick from the laptop and put it in his pocket. Back in the lab, he went for coffee with Yakov, then continued with Harvey to prepare the shipment of the drug doses. The refrigerator was still in the middle of the corridor and they began scanning all the drug doses that would leave the facility for the clinical trial. The new inventory system kept track of all the tubes, and Harvey had to enter the list for the clinical trial into the system for approval. Meanwhile, they gestured to each other and chose a metal box to put the message on. He bent halfway into the fridge and took the USB-stick out of his pocket, but held it carefully in his closed hand to make sure it would not be visible on any of the security cameras. He showed Harvey where he would tape it into the box. Harvey moved Dave's hand to take it to the best spot. The only problem was that the metal USB-stick now blended in so much with the metal background that Dave feared it would not be visible. He went back to the laboratory and wrote with a marker on one side,

"HELP US!"

and on the other side he wrote,

"GIVE TO POLICE!"

He walked back to the storage room and showed Harvey, who nodded in agreement. They stuck the USB-stick in the right place with transparent tape and the visible side now showed,

"HELP US!"

He was convinced this was the right spot, and maybe they had a chance it would be found. His worst nightmare was that it would not be found by the nurses but by Jeff Broch's security people. They placed the tubes in the metal box and the USB-stick was no longer visible from the outside. Once the nurses would take the tubes out, they could see it. They put the metal box in the back of the fridge. Harvey checked the computer again and all the tubes in the fridge were now marked in the system for the clinical trial. He closed the refrigerator, and they wrapped it in bubble wrap. Harvey taped a paper on the outside, listing the contents. He put stickers on all sides indicating which side was up and that the contents were fragile. He looked satisfied when they finished and they went for coffee.

That evening in the hot tub, Harvey explained to the others what they had done and that tomorrow the fridge would be transported to San Francisco. Everybody was all excited, but the meeting was cut short quickly when Suzy appeared in the pool. Dave went off with Yakov to do some running and fitness.

Later that night, as Dave lay in his bed, he thought about what they had done. All kinds of scenarios haunted his mind. On the one hand, he was afraid. Afraid of being caught. On the other hand, he felt all excited, because for the first time they might have a good chance of getting the message out and hopefully they would be freed. Just the thought of getting out and being reunited with Penelope and his son made him feel better.

The next morning, after breakfast, he went down to the laboratory with Harvey. As they came off the elevator, they saw two guards coming out of the storage room. One of them looked at them agitated and shouted, "Mr. Juncker, please come over here at once!"

Harvey walked quickly toward the guard and Dave watched from the door of the lab, worried that the guard might have found the USB-stick. Then he heard the guard say, "Mr. Juncker, please tell me exactly which refrigerator I have to take with me. I can't risk taking the wrong stuff and getting Mr. Broch's torn over me."

Harvey looked a bit baffled, since it looked so obvious to him, but the guard was stressed.

"It's this packed fridge over here. I'll also give you an envelope with all the documentation in it to be delivered with it."

The two guards placed the packed fridge on the trolley they had brought, and they dragged the trolley with the fridge toward the elevator. Harvey walked ahead to go to his desk. He had a large envelope ready with all the documents in print and a copy on a USB-stick. He handed the large envelope to one of the guards.

"That's all, Mr. Juncker? Nothing else we have to take with us?"

"Nope. That's all, gentlemen."

"Okay. Thanks, Mr. Juncker."

The two guards put the trolley in the elevator and left.

"Everything all right?" he asked Harvey when he returned to the laboratory.

"Yes, they have everything they need."

Dave was feeling excited. So far, everything had gone according to plan. He hoped someone would find the USB-stick and alert the police. He spent the rest of the afternoon working with Harvey on the test report on his drug treatment. James stopped by and gave him a USB-stick with the pictures from Dave's cell phone.

Dave got tears in his eyes when he looked at the pictures and saw a picture of him next to Andrew. The photo had been taken the weekend he had gone to visit Andrew and Wendy, and they had announced she was pregnant. That was more than a week before he began the drug treatment, and the photo showed what he looked like before treatment. He dreaded missing the birth of his grandchild, and the thought made him sad.

That evening in the hot tub, Dave and Harvey explained to Larry and Yakov that the fridge with the USB-stick had gone on transport. They were all glad that after Gary and Takeo's failed attempt, they now had another chance, even if it only had a small chance of success. At one point, Harvey looked serious and said, "Something was bothering me today. Mr. Broch interrogated Dave and me about Gary and Takeo's escape attempt. With his lie detector it's impossible to lie, and we told him that we knew about their plan, but we didn't know what their plan was or when they would do anything. I'm afraid he might find out about our hot tub group, and that would jeopardize all our plans. Has anyone else also been questioned by him?"

Harvey looked at Yakov and Larry, and they nodded. Larry replied first, "It's good that you brought it up. Just after breakfast this morning, Yakov and I were summoned to his office to report on the progress of that artificial intelligence program we're working on for a facial recognition application for use in war zones. He questioned us both using his bionic arm, but since we didn't know any details, it seemed all right."

"That's not good. He'll eventually figure out that only the four of us were aware, and then it would be easy to see the link with our encounters in the whirlpool. Thank God Gary and Takeo hadn't told us too much about their plans. There's a risk he starts focusing on our group and interrogates us further about new plans. We're all aware of our current plan, unfortunately, and everything might be for nothing. We must be extremely careful, at least for the coming weeks, because he must not find out about our plan too soon, or he may still stop it. Let's stop our meetings, at least for two or three days. Let's schedule the next meeting on Friday evening and skip all the rest, all right?"

They all agreed and ended the meeting. Larry went swimming, and Yakov and Dave went for their usual workout. Harvey stayed in the hot tub for a while longer. Dave went to bed early that night, with mixed feelings, full of hope but also fear of being caught and because of all the things that could go wrong. With the police looking for him and the fact that he was not a scientist with unique knowledge, Mr. Broch might decide to have him killed and disposed of.

Tuesday morning, he was working in the lab with Harvey's team when James came in with a guard pushing a heavy trolley.

"We have equipment that Mr. Broch ordered for you. I'll have to leave it in front of the lab, but please empty it before lunch so we can pick up the trolley at lunch."

Harvey looked at James and then at the trolley of boxes.

"Is there more to come?" Harvey asked him.

"This is all there is," he replied. "I'll be back at lunchtime to pick up the trolley."

"Thanks, James."

After they left, Harvey looked at Suzy and Adish.

"Obviously no MRI or X-ray scanner, that already seemed impossible on such short notice. Well, let's unpack the rest to see what equipment he managed to get for us."

Dave helped them unpack, and they began planning the tests they wanted to do. In the afternoon, they installed some equipment in the fitness center next to one of the exercise bikes. Dave changed into his sports clothes and had to perform a test to see how his heart and lung function were doing under intense exercise. He gave his maximum on the exercise bike while Suzy checked the results on the monitors. He performed extremely well on the tests, and everything confirmed that his fitness had improved and was comparable to a twenty-year-old. They were all impressed.

The next day, they took several samples from his skin, bone marrow and of some of his organs. He was not so happy about the examination because they stuck needles into him several times, but they had assured him it was all harmless. Just as Adish was about to stick another needle into him, Harvey noticed Dave was not amused.

"Are you okay?"

"I guess so, although I feel like a lab rat."

"I understand, but Mr. Broch didn't give us much choice. He wants conclusive answers and within a week."

"I understand, but it's still not pleasant."

They continued to take their samples for the rest of the day, and that day Dave enjoyed the rooftop break away from the needles more than usual. Yakov cheered him up with his jokes. At dinner, he was happy to hear from Harvey that they had all the samples they needed. After dinner, they went to minus three and he was about to enter his room when Adish came running to Harvey. As he tried to catch his breath, he said, "Have you seen the news? They're talking about us."

Harvey rushed into his room and turned on the television screen. Dave followed him along with Adish.

The news host was talking about another topic, but the titles on the bottom of the screen read:

"Bodies found in fire in rejuvenation lab not of missing scientists."

Later, the presenter spoke about the fire.

"The police announced today that the bodies found in a recent fire at a research center in Novato do not belong to the four missing scientists. One of the missing scientists is Dr. Harvey Juncker, a renowned specialist in the field of aging. The police have devoted additional resources to the investigation into the scientists' disappearance. The police, along with the FBI, are also investigating a connection between the kidnapping of journalist Dave Wilson in New York a few weeks ago and the missing scientists in Novato."

The presenter moved on to another topic, and Harvey turned down the volume on the television screen.

"Well, I'm glad to hear I'm not dead," he said jokingly.

"This is fantastic news, Harvey! It looks like they're finally connecting my kidnapping to your disappearance. The more they investigate, the better chance we have of ever getting out of here."

"I hope so, Dave. Hope is all I have for the moment."

They talked some more, and then Dave went for his usual workout in the fitness center. Later, in his bed, he thought of Penelope. He missed her a lot. He felt more optimistic now. It was good to hear that the police were still searching, and he thought about the USB-stick, wondering if they had found it yet. He still feared that one of Broch's men would find it, or that it would not be found at all. He would know soon enough.

The next day, he worked with Harvey on the report, while Suzy and Adish examined all the samples that they had taken the day before. Harvey had indicated to Mr. Broch that one week was too tight because he did not have enough people and could not perform all tests as he did not have an MRI scanner or an X-ray machine. That morning, a tall blond man with an arm in a cast suddenly entered the laboratory. Everyone looked perplexed, and Harvey, Suzy and Adish all stood up enthusiastically.

"Rob! You're still alive," Harvey said and hugged the tall man.

"Yes, out of the blue, they told me I had to go back to my original room and that I'd have to work with you guys."

Adish and Suzy both came to greet Rob.

"Let me introduce you to Dave Wilson. Dave, this is Rob Hamilton, one of our team members."

"Nice to meet you, Rob."

"Likewise, Dave."

"They kidnapped Dave after he stole the rejuvenation drug from our laboratory in Novato and used it on himself."

"Really? How interesting!"

Rob stared at Dave's face in fascination. Dave looked at Rob's cast and asked, "What happened to your hand?"

"Mr. Broch wasn't happy with my behavior and broke my hand. I have to keep it in a cast for another five weeks. They locked me in one of the prison cells downstairs and I had already given up hope until this morning when they told me they needed me in the laboratory."

"Good to have you back," Harvey said, and began to explain that they were working on a test report about Dave on top of the ongoing work and research. After catching up, Rob helped Suzy and Adish examine all the samples.

They all worked hard that day, and the next day they continued in the morning. They had not met in the hot tub since that Monday, and Dave was looking forward to their scheduled meeting that evening. Nothing had happened since they had smuggled the USB-stick on the drug shipment, and they had not talked about it. Before dinner, they took another blood sample from him, and after that, Harvey injected the weekly drug dose into Dave's arm. He had certainly had his share of needles that week, and after dinner, he was happy to relax a bit in the fitness center. The meeting in the hot tub was not until nine o'clock, so Dave and Yakov had plenty of time to do their daily run and workout before that.

After their workout, they went next door. Larry, Harvey, and Rob were already in the hot tub. Rob had a plastic sleeve around his right hand to keep the cast dry, but had submerged his left hand with the wrist band attached. When Yakov and Dave were also with their hands under water, Harvey started the meeting.

"Larry and I updated Rob on what happened during his absence. I have no news yet regarding the message we sent out with the drugs for the clinical trial, which I think is good news. If Broch's men had discovered it, we probably would have heard it by now. Still nothing to cheer about, because they could still find out, or maybe the stick wasn't found and will come back with the empty boxes. Coming Wednesday, we should receive back the fridge with the empty doses, and then we can check if the USB-stick has been removed. Monday, we will send out a new shipment, and I think it would be a good idea to include another message in the shipment."

"Excellent idea, Harvey. We need to keep doing this as long as possible," Dave said. "I was also thinking of an alternative means of escape. It looks like Mr. Broch will not provide us with the MRI and X-ray equipment to examine me. Harvey, perhaps you could insist with Mr. Broch to send me to a nearby hospital for the MRI and the X-rays. If he accepts, I can try to escape, or at least leave a message for people to contact the police."

"Good idea, Dave. I doubt he'll accept it, but let's try."

"I'm glad to hear you've all been creative during my absence. I can tell you that hacking into the computer system like I tried is far too risky. They have a way of being alerted quickly, and they found out right away that it was me trying to break into their system. I believe any attempt to do something with the computer system is too risky. The security is just too good."

Rob explained in detail what he had done before they put him in the jail cell. They agreed they needed to find alternative ways to escape, and that they all needed to think about that. They decided not to get back together until Wednesday, and they left one by one.

Over the next few days, he continued to work with Harvey's team on the test report, and the days passed slowly. He despaired more and more, worrying that he would be stuck in this place so long that he would miss the birth of his first grandchild. Day after day passed without any news from the outside world, nor any sign that their attempt to get the message out had worked.

On Sunday, he helped Harvey prepare a new shipment of drug doses for the clinical trial. He put the same message on a USB-stick, and they stuck it in one of the metal boxes in the fridge. They filled the metal box with tubes and put it back in the fridge. After this, they packed the fridge to prepare it for transport.

Monday morning, the guards came to pick it up, and everything seemed to go according to plan. They had transported the second message outside. All they could do now was hope it would make it somehow to the police. They had also finished the test report on Dave's medical evaluation, and Harvey mailed it to Mr. Broch.

Later in the afternoon, Dave and Harvey both received a message on their wristbands that Mr. Broch wanted to see them right away. They were both nervous when they went to Mr. Broch's office. He expected he wanted to talk to them about the test report, but he was not sure. In his mind, he also thought about the possibility that they had discovered the USB-sticks or that Mr. Broch had become suspicious and would interrogate them. As they entered the office, they saw Mr. Broch standing at the window and he was holding something in his hand that looked like a gun.

"Gentlemen, good afternoon! Just in time for the test of one of our new drones."

Harvey and Dave looked at each other, not sure what to make of this.

"Good afternoon, Mr. Broch," they both replied.

Mr. Broch turned his head toward them and gestured with his arm.

"Come look over here by the window!"

They walked to the window and looked out. In front of the building, they saw two guards get out of a large black SUV. They dragged someone out of the car, but the person was not moving and was completely stiff. Dave quickly realized it was a dummy that looked like a man. The guards set the dummy upright, then drove off, leaving it in the middle of the desert.

"Now look and pay attention," Mr. Broch said, all excited as he moved the strange pistol in his arm and pointed it at the dummy. They saw a green light appear on its head, apparently coming from the pistol.

All of a sudden, they heard a high-pitched sound, similar to what they had heard the day the drones flew out of the tower on the roof of the building. They saw nothing move, but a few seconds later, they saw the dummy's head explode into pieces.

"Nice, huh!"

Dave was confused because he heard a drone but had seen nothing flying.

"How's that possible, Mr. Broch?"

"One of the new creations from the guys downstairs. A mini drone that flies at high speed toward the marked target and explodes as soon as it hits the target. Works well, but they just need to reduce the noise on the thing and then it will be perfect."

Harvey looked horrified, for he hated violence and weapons. Dave, curious by nature as he was, however, wanted to know more.

"Impressive! What's the range of the drone?"

"The current range is about a mile, but they're still trying to increase that. Well, you can tell your friends in here they better not try to escape, or we'll send one of those things after them," Mr. Broch said and laughed viciously.

Dave felt less comfortable now and wondered if Jeff was on to them. Did he know about their meetings in the hot tub? Mr. Broch walked back to his desk and put the gun down.

"Have a seat! I want to discuss the test report with you."

They both sat down in front of the desk and Mr. Broch stared at Dave's face with his piercing eyes, then said, "The pictures are well chosen, and the zoomed-in pictures showing the differences in wrinkles and hair are excellent. If I understand correctly, Harvey, the conclusion is that the drug has done exactly what we expected, with no side effects. I guess I could start selling it to some selected number of people already?"

Harvey looked at Mr. Broch and felt uneasy. He was afraid that if admitted too soon that the drug worked perfectly, Mr. Broch might decide he no longer needed Dave.

"Well, I'd say it's too early to start selling. The time Dave has been taking the drug is too short to draw definite conclusions. Maybe side effects show up later or we missed some side effects because we couldn't examine him with an MRI and an X-ray. I also haven't been able to examine his arthritis, which would be necessary before we can draw definitive conclusions. And finally, but also important, Dave's only one test case and we need to have the results of the clinical trials to make sure he wasn't just an exception."

Mr. Broch looked annoyed by his comments.

"Harvey, I understand, and I need the FDA approval to sell it more widely, but I already have some people who are interested and they are eager enough to use it already without FDA approval. I also understand you want to examine Dave with an MRI and do some X-rays. I've asked my people to get me the equipment, but they told me there're long lead times and it may be quite a while before we receive them. I asked them to look for used equipment or a faster solution."

"Perhaps you could send Dave to a nearby hospital for an examination?"

Mr. Broch looked at Harvey now, and a grin appeared on his face.

"To a hospital? His face has been all over the news and everyone is looking for him, so I don't think I want to risk that. But if those tests are so important, Harvey, we can just cut him open to examine the tissues and his arthritis."

Dave could not believe what he was hearing, and felt fear and adrenaline coursing through his body. He looked in despair at Harvey, who also looked shocked and stuttered as he responded to Mr. Broch.

"Th… th… that's way too risky. Dave could suffer permanent damage or worse… and besides, we'd need a surgeon, which I'm not, and an operating room."

Mr. Broch grinned.

"One of my staff members used to be a surgeon before he was convicted of malpractice. He can conduct the examination. As for the damage to him, I'd say it's a low price to pay for the advancement of science."

"I strongly object to this. You can't do this!"

Mr. Broch remained calm and now looked at Harvey condescendingly.

"It's not your decision, Harvey, but I'm waiting for my first client to see if it's necessary. He should be here this Friday, and if he prefers the examination, then I'll instruct my surgeon to perform it. My client may also want to meet you, Dave, and ask you some questions. I want him to buy the drug, so you'd better answer him convincingly and if you do or say anything I don't like, I'll make your life miserable! Is that clear?"

"Yes, Mr. Broch!" Dave replied anxiously.

"Enough for now. I'll ask my marketing people to complete the report so I can share it with my client on Friday. You're dismissed!"

Mr. Broch began typing on the computer on his desk and stopped looking at them. They left his office both in shock. In the elevator, Dave had taken in what Mr. Broch had said, and now feared for his life.

"Do you really think he would let a failed surgeon operate on me?"

"If this client of his thinks it necessary, I fear he'd just do that. He is ruthless. I actually believe he doesn't feel emotions the same way as we do."

He felt all his hope sinking and became desperate. He had to get out of here.

That night he had trouble sleeping, and Mr. Broch's relentless words kept running through his mind. He hoped the USB sticks would reach the police soon and be freed. But what if the USB sticks did not reach the police or what if the police arrived here too late and this mediocre surgeon had already maimed him for life? He feared for his life and felt desperate. After hours of turning and turning, he finally fell asleep.

The next morning, he still felt down. They had finished the report, and he had not been given any new assignment. He felt like he was of no use to anyone. Harvey noticed and involved him in their research, and assigned him some tasks to keep him busy. Still, he could not concentrate and kept thinking about what had been said the previous. He felt in great danger and considered more drastic options. Like jumping off the roof with a rope to escape. They had returned the security to normal, and it was easier to get to the edge of the terrace. Still, it seemed like a desperate plan. They could easily spot him and with the desert all around, he might not get away undetected and even if he did, he would probably die of thirst in the desert. Or Mr. Broch would send one of those deadly drones after him. He ran many options through his mind, such as killing Mr. Broch at their next meeting. He wondered if he would have the courage to do that. He had never killed anyone before. Even if he succeeded, the guards might kill him afterwards. The more he thought about it, the more he felt was in a hopeless situation. Yakov cheered him up a bit in the evening with his jokes, but he kept that feeling of hopelessness and despair at the back of his head.

On Wednesday, the guards brought back the refrigerator from the week before and put it in the storage room. As soon as the guards left, Harvey and Dave went to check it out. They pulled out all the metal boxes out and began taking out the doses to check whether the USB-stick had been removed from the box or not. After examining a few boxes, they found a box with a piece of the clear tape still attached to it, right where they had stuck the stick to the metal box. Their plan had worked and someone had removed the USB-stick. He looked at Harvey, and they both nodded in satisfaction. They cleaned up and arranged all the material, then continued working in the laboratory. The rest of the day passed slowly as he felt excited and looked forward to the meeting in the evening to share the good news with the rest.

During dinner, he struggled to concentrate and strike up a conversation with the other. He looked outside and saw the sun disappearing behind the mountains and thought of Penelope again and of her soft skin and sweet smile. He stared outside like that for quite some time until Yakov brought him out of his thoughts.

"Dave, Dave? He-ho on which planet are you? Time for our workout."

He nodded and got up. After their workout, they went to the hot tub. Only Harvey was already there, but a few minutes later, Larry and Rob showed up.

"Okay, I have good news and bad news," Harvey said when everyone had their wristbands under water.

"I prefer the good news," Yakov said with a smile on his face.

"All right! The fridge came back from the clinical trial today and the USB-stick was no longer in it. Someone removed it, so now let's hope it gets to the right people. On Monday, we hid another USB-stick in the second shipment for the clinical trial. I guess all we can do now is wait and put USB-sticks in each shipment every week."

"Well, if the first stick had reached the police, we should have heard something by now," Larry said, who seemed to be in a somber mood.

"Not necessarily," Harvey said. "Maybe they didn't find it until the end of the trial, which was yesterday. No, I think we have to be patient. At least it didn't come back on the shipment, and Broch's men didn't find it, or we would have heard something by now."

"And what's the bad news?" Rob asked.

"Last Monday, Dave and I met with Mr. Broch and he doesn't want Dave to have an MRI scan outside this facility. Worse, Mr. Broch said we can also examine Dave without a scan by cutting him open and examining him directly. I told him we don't have a surgeon for that, but apparently, he has one in the facility, although it sounds like a mediocre one. Apparently, this surgeon lost his license to practice due to a malpractice conviction. I told him he risks disabling or killing Dave, but he didn't seem to care."

"Does he really need that extra examination?" Yakov asked.

"I don't think it makes a big difference, but he told us he has a potential client visiting him this Friday. If this client wants more certainty, Jeff might order the examination to rule out some risks of the drug treatment."

"I think I met this so-called surgeon. He put the cast on my hand. He's quite sadistic. They had no equipment to make an X-ray of my broken hand, so this doctor looked at my hand and touched all the bones to check which one was broken. I cried out in pain, but he kept touching my bones several times and smiled sadistically at me, while some guards held me tightly. Horrible guy!" Rob said, and they all looked shocked.

"The more reason to come up with a plan. What are we going to do if Mr. Broch decides to let this guy operate on Dave? We can at least organize a strike or an uprising. We could all stop working, and by all, I mean all prisoners. If we all join in, it could work," Harvey said.

"I'd prefer a revolt to a strike. We must all protect Dave and prevent the guards from taking him," Yakov said.

They continued discussing what they could do, and together they drew up a plan. They decided to wait until Friday, since the potential client might not find it necessary to undergo all the extra tests. After the meeting, he felt touched that they all supported him and were willing to risk everything to protect him. Still, he remained concerned.

14.   Three strikes

On Friday he woke up rested, but anxious about what that day would bring. That wealthy client of Mr. Broch would be visiting today. As he sat in the restaurant eating breakfast, he felt his worries returning. He gazed out into the desert as he thought about the meeting with this client and realized he should try to convince him of the drug's success and imply that no additional testing would be necessary.

After breakfast, he continued to help the team with their research, but he had never been more distracted than he was that day. Harvey noticed he was more nervous than usual and tried to comfort him. His anger seemed to have turned into compassion. During lunch, he stared out the window the whole time. Yakov tried to cheer him up, but it did not help much, and he remained worried. They walked back to the laboratory and went to the coffee machine. He had just taken his coffee when his wristband vibrated. Harvey and Adish looked at him when Dave checked the message and looked worried.

"I have to go see Mr. Broch, probably to meet this client. Wish me luck."

He rushed to the elevator and went to the fourth floor. There, a guard was waiting, gesturing for him to walk through the dark double door. At the reception, the woman greeted him.

"Good afternoon, Mr. Wilson. Mr. Broch and his guest are expecting you. You can go right in."

With sweat in his hands, Dave opened the heavy wooden door and entered the office. Inside, Mr. Broch sat at his desk and an Asian-looking man sat next to him. They were looking at some photos of Dave on the computer screen. They looked at Dave when he had entered. Mr. Broch stood up and wore a dark suit with a white shirt.

"Hello Dave. Come on in! I'd like to introduce you to Mr. Xu Huacheng, one of my business partners."

The Asian-looking man smiled at him, but in his eyes, he had a ruthless look. The man wore a dark suit with a silk burgundy dress shirt. His hair was black with no gray, but his face was rugged and filled with what looked like a mix of wrinkles and scars from heavy childhood acne. Mr. Huacheng was a lot shorter than Dave and when he stood up and walked toward Dave, he moved like an old man with a hunched back. He extended his hand to Dave.

"Nice to meet you, Mr. Wilson."

"Pleased to meet you too, Mr. Huacheng."

Xu Huacheng stared up at Dave's face and hair.

"Amazing! What a smooth and healthy skin and what a difference from the pictures. I understood you started the drug treatment about five weeks ago?"

"Yes, that's correct."

"I read the full report Mr. Broch had given me, but I still wanted to see for myself. What was the biggest improvement in your daily life since you started taking the drug?"

He thought for a moment and tried to remember how he felt before, then answered, "I'd say the biggest improvement for me is the fact that I no longer have pain in my back and limbs. I used to wake up with constant pain in my back, and getting through the day was a struggle. I had given up exercising long ago. After I took the drug, I gradually began to feel better and started exercising daily. I can now sport for hours and have no pain at all. I wake up every morning feeling energized."

Xu Huacheng listened intently and nodded, apparently pleased with his answer.

"I understood from the report that you were diagnosed with arthritis before?"

"Yes, that's correct."

"Interesting. I also have severe arthritis and recognize what you described as daily agony. I've been living that scenario for too long. That's also why I told Mr. Broch that I'm very interested in the drug and would prefer not to wait for final FDA approval, which may take years," Mr. Huacheng said, as Dave looked at his hunched back. Mr. Huacheng moved slowly to avoid any painful movements. A behavior Dave recognized all too well. "I saw in your file the arthritis diagnosis and the X-rays. The only thing I was missing is the medical proof that your arthritis is really gone."

"Well, I know it's gone, since all the pain is gone," Dave said nervously.

"I understand, but you have no medical proof of it."

"Uh… well… no."

Jeff Broch grinned and moved closer.

"Xu, that shouldn't be a problem. We'll get you this analysis within a week. I have an excellent surgeon who can verify that the arthritis is gone."

"Perfect, Jeff. We can close our deal right after you sent me the results, assuming they confirm that his arthritis is gone."

Dave felt his hopes evaporate, and it felt as if someone had pulled the floor out from under him. He felt dizzy and sweaty.

"Are you all right, Mr. Wilson? You look pale. Sit down and have some water," Mr. Huacheng said kindly and handed him a glass of water.

He sat down and took a sip from the glass.

"Thank you."

"Do you have any other questions for Dave?"

Mr. Huacheng shook his head.

"No, thank you for coming over here, Mr. Wilson!"

Jeff Broch looked at Dave.

"Thanks for stopping by Dave. You can go now."

He nodded and left the room, feeling worse than before. As he passed the reception, the woman at the counter noticed his pale face.

"Are you feeling all right, Mr. Wilson? You look pale. You want an aspirin?"

"No thanks, but I need to go to the restroom. Where can I find one?"

The woman pointed him to a little further on.

"Just over there, Mr. Wilson."

"Thank you, Miss."

He hurried inside to one of the toilets. Just in time, he bent over the toilet bowl and threw up in it. After throwing up, he felt a little better. He had heard that stress and anxiety can make people nauseous and make them vomit, but this was the first time it had happened to him. He drank some water from the tap and looked at himself in the mirror. It looked like he would not escape this mediocre surgeon's examination. Feeling a little better, he went back to the lab at minus five. Harvey immediately saw from his face that the meeting had not gone well.

"How did it go, Dave?"

He shook his head and stared at the floor. Rob Hamilton stopped looking into a microscope and came closer to listen.

"Not so good, Harvey. This Mr. Xu Huacheng wants to see proof that the arthritis is effectively gone, so Mr. Broch said it wasn't a problem and that his surgeon will take care of it."

"Oh, shit!" Rob said when he heard that and walked over to Dave and put his hand on his shoulder to comfort him.

"Don't worry. We won't let that bastard cut you open!"

"Thanks, Rob, but I wonder if we can stop all this."

"If he dares to touch you, we'll show him!"

Harvey began typing on his computer, and they looked at the screen, which read:

"Let's discuss this tonight, gentlemen. The walls here have ears and eyes."

Later, their wrists bands vibrated, and it was time for their rooftop break. The light breeze on the terrace did him good, and he felt a little better. Actually, Rob's reaction had made him rebellious and ready to fight and resist this surgery. He was not going to give them what they wanted easily.

Just before going to dinner, Harvey reminded him it was time for his weekly injection. Harvey retrieved another tube from the storage room and filled the syringe. Dave rolled up his sleeve and Harvey injected the drug. Another week that passed in the blink of an eye, he thought to himself. Initially, he had thought staying locked up in this prison and missing the birth of his grandchild was the worst thing, but now he feared it could get worse for him.

That evening in the hot tub, the five men discussed their plans to prevent Mr. Broch from having this mediocre surgeon cut into Dave's body. They needed all the prisoners to participate in their plan. After the meeting, they spent some time that evening informing all the prisoners on floor minus three. This took quite some time because they had to be careful that the wristbands would not overhear them. They had to whisper into ears or inform people by typing on a laptop and showing it. It shocked everyone to learn that Mr. Broch wanted to perform the risky surgery on Dave. The only challenge left was to inform the people on minus four who were working on the weapons and drones. Since Gary and Takeo had disappeared, they had no regular contact with that floor. Yakov said he knew a way to address this problem, but that would only be possible tomorrow morning because he had to approach someone about it at breakfast.

In bed, he reflected on his day and felt supported by all the prisoners. Still, he worried about the days ahead. That night he slept with the Stanley knife he had gotten from Yakov under his pillow. All the stress of that day had tired him and he fell into a deep sleep.

A little later, he woke up and could no longer feel his right foot. He looked around, and it was completely dark. He tried to sit up straight in bed, but could not get any grip using his right leg. His bed felt wet and warm. He rolled onto the side and tried to sit on the edge of the bed, but the moment he tried to stand on his right leg, he fell. He fell to the floor with a big smack and his face hurt from the fall. The door opened, and the light came on. He saw a man standing in the doorway in green clothes, and wearing a green mask like a surgeon. He looked upset when he saw Dave lying on the floor.

"I told you not to get out of bed, Mr. Wilson. I still need to open up your spine to see if all the arthritis is gone there, too."

The surgeon held a sharp, bloody knife in his hand and had blood on his green clothes. Dave panicked. Suddenly, he was startled and looked down at his leg. Or at least where it used to be. On his right leg, only the upper part was still there. Around his knee was a bloody bandage and his foot and lower leg were completely gone. The bed was all red with blood and he saw the cut bloody foot half under the covers. He screamed, and the sweat broke out of him. He moved and spun around, and then suddenly woke up. He sat upright in bed. His room was dark, and he immediately touched his right leg. He could feel his lower leg and foot. Thank God it was just a nightmare, he thought. He looked at the door, but it was closed. He slowly calmed down and fell asleep again.

The next morning at breakfast, he sat at the table with Harvey, Rob, and Yakov. It was a beautiful day and the early morning sun played with the dry arid landscape outside. He tried to act normal, but he was still anxious and thinking about his nightmare. Yakov was in a good mood, though, and he managed to get everyone laughing at his jokes. Perhaps it was because of the stress that was discharging, but he laughed along, and at one point, they laughed so hard that his stomach ached. When they finished breakfast and walked to the elevator, Yakov whispered in his ear that he had given a letter to a certain Helmut Meier, an expert in explosives who slept on the fourth floor. He believed they could trust him and the letter explained their plan, and asked Helmut's help to inform all the people on his floor and convince them to join them. Dave felt a little better after all the support from everyone.

Not much happened that morning, but after lunch, Harvey was suddenly summoned to Mr. Broch's office. Dave wondered why Harvey had to meet with Mr. Broch again. Was he on to them? Had they found the USB-stick, or did it have something to do with the examination of his arthritis? He could barely focus on his work while Harvey was upstairs. Time seemed to pass more slowly than usual, and he tried to pass the time by chatting with Yakov at the coffee machine. Then, about an hour later, Harvey appeared in the lab and Dave rushed over to him.

"How was it, Harvey?"

"Tense. Mr. Broch wants to do a thorough examination focused on your arthritis. I explained to him that to do that we need an MRI or some X-rays. He reiterated he won't have the equipment available within a week, so he told me to explore the alternative way. I asked him what he was thinking of and he suggested a surgery where we look inside with cameras and examine the arthritis. I explained to him that this could be risky and that we don't have a proper operating room with equipment for that. Mr. Broch cared little. He also summoned his surgeon. He's a dark-looking Eastern European man, named Ivan Văduva. He has a gold tooth in front of his mouth, and as Rob said, he looks like a sadist. This Ivan told Mr. Broch he was eager to perform the surgery and would prepare a room for it on floor minus ten. He'd see what tools he could find and if he was missing something, he'd let Mr. Broch know. Mr. Broch asked me to check what procedure the surgeon would need to perform to examine the arthritis properly in your body. I told him I needed to check your medical records and look on the internet to see how best to perform this procedure. He gave me one day to prepare it all."

Dave had taken a seat while all the people in the lab stood around them, listening to Harvey.

"Shit, that doesn't sound good!" Dave said as he held his head with both hands.

Yakov patted him on the shoulder and said, "Well, that gives us a day to prepare everything."

Everyone nodded and agreed. He still felt bad, thinking that so much could go wrong in their plan. His worries did not disappear, even though everyone seemed to support him. He felt the Stanley knife in his pocket as he sat on the chair. He saw the shape of the knife in Yakov's and Rob's pockets. At least they all seemed very serious about carrying out their plan. The buzzing of the wristbands interrupted the conversation. It was time for the rooftop break. Feeling like some fresh air, he got up and headed for the elevator with the others.

Upstairs, the sky was clear and blue and it was hot, but thanks to some wind, the heat remained bearable. He took a bottle of water from the fridge and walked to the edge of the roof. Yakov and Harvey joined him, and later Larry and Rob also joined the group.

Harvey looked at them and said with a smile, "I'm looking forward to some swimming tonight."

They all understood what he meant and nodded.

"Yes, with this heat, everyone feels like swimming," Larry said.

He was glad they could meet tonight, since there was so much to discuss and plan now.

Judith Anderson joined them and asked him, "How're you holding up, Dave?"

"I've never been this stressed and restless in my life, which is new to me."

Judith suddenly stopped looking at him, and stared far away behind him and then stuttered,

"Wh... wha... what the hell is that?"

She pointed her finger toward the horizon. They all looked in that direction and at the very end of the dirt road, they saw a cloud of dust. Slowly, the dust cloud got closer and they could see some dark vehicles approaching. Later, they saw the vague shape of four vehicles rapidly approaching.

"This is the first time I have seen vehicles on this road," William Ashton said in amazement. All prisoners were now standing close to the edge of the roof, looking at the dirt road.

"It looks like a police car in front of those other vehicles," Judith said enthusiastically. Dave suddenly felt hope again. Apparently, the attempt with the USB-stick had worked. They had found it, and now they were coming here to free them. As the vehicles approached, it was now clear that the car in front was a police car. The other cars were driving in the cloud of dust and were dark and less clear.

A moment later, Yakov said, "Look behind the police car. Those are two black armored vehicles, followed by another police car."

Rob nodded and said, "I've seen those armored vehicles before. They are from the police SWAT teams and are heavily armed. It looks like they're planning a major police raid!"

"That we live to see this day. What a wonderful moment!" Harvey said in amazement.

As the four vehicles rapidly approached, they could clearly see the four cars now. The black armored vehicles each had a heavy machine gun on the roof. Dave looked at the guards. One was looking over the edge and talking into his headset, but he could not hear what he was saying. The other guard stood in front of the door to the hallway with the elevator.

He turned his head back and looked over the edge of the roof. The cars had approached the big fence around the building. They all looked down now as the first police vehicles braked in front of the small guard post at the main gate. They saw two armed police officers getting out of the first car. One of the officers took a paper document out of his pocket and showed it to a guard at the guard post.

"I think I heard the police officer talking about a search warrant," he said.

They saw the guard disappear into the guard post and the other two officers waited beside their car. After five minutes, they saw four armed guards coming out of the main building, carrying heavy machine guns.

"Jesus, they carry M4 Carbine assault rifles. Usually, only the army uses those in heavy combat. This doesn't look good," Helmut Meier said.

They all observed the scene at the entrance gate. The police officers shouted and prepared their weapons.

"Put your weapons on the ground!"

A few seconds later, they heard the heavy sound of the assault rifles.

"Thud… thud… thud… thud… thud…"

The two police officers fell to the ground as bullets from the assault rifles riddled them. The back doors of the police car in front of the row of cars opened and two officers got out and hid behind the doors with their rifles in their hands. At the same time, the doors of the black armored vehicles opened and a dozen or so heavily armed SWAT team members emerged from the two vehicles. A hatch opened in the roof of each armored vehicle, and two more SWAT team members began operating the heavy machine guns on the roof of the vehicles. Another four police officers came out of the last police car and hid behind the doors of the car and started shooting at the guards. The SWAT team members ran toward the guard post behind the large bulletproof shields they were carrying. There was shooting back and forth. Dave saw one guard after another fall to the ground, dead. About five other guards came out of the building with their heavy assault rifles. Bullets were flying everywhere. One of the members of the SWAT team fell to the ground dead after a bullet hit him in the head. Suddenly, the sound of the guns was drowned out by the much heavier and louder sound of the heavy machine gun on top of the first armored vehicle. Now the guards in front of the building fell dead on the ground, and some of them tried to run back to the main building and were shot in the back.

The firing stopped when all the guards were dead and no new ones came out of the building. The heavy machine gun stopped firing, and the officers advanced toward the main entrance. The sudden loud noise above them startled everyone on the roof. All the prisoners looked up at the square tower behind them above the elevator, in the center of the building, right at the intersection of the building's T-shape. The shutters of the tower had all opened, and they heard the loud buzzing sound they had heard earlier. Although the sound was louder than before. Yakov immediately called out to the police officers at the building, "They are sending drones after you! Watch out!"

Dave saw a bright green light on each face of the SWAT team members, and he saw the same lights on the police officers' heads. Small drones began flying out of the tower at high speed with a low buzzing sound. They were barely visible and flew rapidly toward the police officers and SWAT team members. The officers now looked up at the approaching buzzing sound.

"Drones!" one of them shouted as he pointed up into the sky.

One of the first drones exploded when it hit the head of a police officer. Half his head was gone, and he fell like a bag of potatoes to the ground. The SWAT team member on top of the armored vehicle aimed his heavy machine gun at the sky where an entire swarm of drones was now approaching. Within seconds, Dave saw multiple explosions in the faces of the SWAT team members next to the armored vehicles and the police officers next to the police car at the end of the line. Their heads exploded like ripe melons and all the men dropped dead to the ground. It was a horrible and bloody sight. The machine gun stopped firing when the SWAT agent operating it was hit by a drone. His headless body dropped lifelessly onto the roof of the armored vehicle.

"Jesus, what a massacre," Harvey said in a low voice.

In less than a few minutes, the drones killed all the police officers and SWAT team members. They were no match for the drone army. They were all shocked and horrified.

"Look! There're still people alive inside the armored vehicles!" Adish shouted.

The two armored vehicles got moving, and one of them had to drive over the corpses next to the dirt road to make its turn. The two vehicles turned and drove away fast from the building, back toward the mountain range. They caused a huge cloud of dust as they sped away.

Another loud buzzing noise startled the prisoners on the roof. They all looked up and saw two larger drones flying over their heads in the direction of the two armored vehicles, which were now speeding away from the building. The two drones each headed straight for the two armored vehicles. Two loud explosions followed and two large fireballs were visible as the drones exploded on top of the two armored vehicles. On the roof, they felt shock waves caused by the explosions. The remnants of the two vehicles were on fire, sending large black clouds into the sky in the middle of the arid desert. Everything became silent now. Dave looked at the others in horror. They all looked deeply shocked. Their hopes of finally being freed from this modern prison had been shattered overnight. The police officers and the SWAT team were no match for Jeff Broch's modern drone army.

The silence got interrupted as the wristbands of all the prisoners vibrated. Their break was over, and they all had to return to their work. Most were still in shock, and some discussed what had happened.

"Did you see how that cop's head got blown away? What brute force!" Someone told his neighbor.

Dave was less surprised since he had already seen the deadly effectiveness of the drones during the demonstration in Jeff Broch's office. He was shocked to see how ruthlessly Jeff Broch deployed his weapons without hesitation. The attack had blown away his hopes for freedom, and he began to worry again about his upcoming encounter with Ivan Văduva, the surgeon. He went back to the laboratory on minus five with Harvey and the others, but for the rest of the afternoon, he struggled to concentrate.

At dinner he was sitting with Harvey, Rob and Yakov at the table, when Yakov suddenly looked at the elevators and said, "Well, what do you know? Look who just got off the elevator!"

They all looked at the elevator and were all perplexed.

"Gary and Takeo! They're back," Harvey said.

Takeo was limping, but had a big smile on his face when he saw his friends at the table. They both walked straight to their table and everyone stood up and greeted and hugged the two men. After picking up their trays of food, Gary and Takeo joined them at their table.

Larry also joined the table and asked them, "So, what happened to you guys since your drone experiment on the roof?"

"Well, they took us violently to the prison cells on floor minus nine and they used their tasers on us several times. They questioned us for a long time to find out who might have helped us plan our drone escape. They even took us to Jeff Broch for questioning, but since we planned the attack, just the two of us, he could not detect any lies. Takeo had a big mouth against Jeff Broch and the guards had kicked him so hard he's still limping and his ribs are still sore," Gary said. "We spent days in these cells, and they separated me from Takeo. I didn't even know where he was or if he was still alive until this afternoon, when the guards suddenly showed up and took us down to minus seven. They told us to help the guards evacuate the entire stockpile of drones and weapons on floors minus seven and eight. No one told us why, but we were happy to be out of our prison cells after all this time. To our surprise, a little after seven, they told us we could have dinner in the restaurant, so here we are."

Takeo had been silent all this time, but now he asked, "What the hell happened today? It must be something serious, because Jeff Broch would never evacuate this facility if it wasn't absolutely necessary."

Harvey explained what had happened, and Gary and Takeo listened and were astonished to hear that so many officers had died that afternoon. It profoundly shocked them that Jeff Broch had used the weapons they had developed for him. At the end of the dinner, they all walked toward the elevator and Harvey said, "Why don't you come for a swim tonight? I think you could use some exercise after all this time in the prison cell?"

Takeo shook his head and answered, "We'd love to, but they told us that after dinner we have to continue helping them to evacuate all stock and materials. I hope they don't make us work too late tonight."

Dave went back to his room and put on his sports clothes. He could use some distraction after the shocking events of that day. At the fitness center, he and Yakov did their usual workout until they saw Harvey and Larry going to the pool. They changed into their swimming shorts and joined them in the hot tub. Rob arrived five minutes later and as soon as he put his wristband under the water, Harvey started the meeting.

"Gary and Takeo have been released to help Broch's men evacuate, and it's clear that Jeff Broch is preparing to leave this facility completely. I'm surprised that he didn't order us to evacuate our laboratory. It's not clear if all the prisoners will be evacuated, or if he will leave us here. I also don't know if this means that Dave won't have to undergo this risky surgery. I'm guessing from previous discussions with Jeff Broch that he can make hundreds of millions of dollars selling this drug to Xu Huacheng, so I don't think he'll let Dave go. We should be prepared to defend him and resist if they try to take him for surgery. He should be safe until tomorrow, since Jeff Broch asked me to come tomorrow with the required procedure for the examination. I have no intention of giving him anything useful tomorrow and I'm waiting for him to ask for it, so let's see what happens tomorrow."

They continued to discuss their plan, and Dave was glad for all their support, although he continued to feel anxious about the whole thing. That night, he had trouble sleeping again and longed for Penelope. He missed her and the thought of her made him relax a bit and after a while, he finally fell asleep.

The next day, he felt anxious as he went for breakfast, and every time he saw a guard, he feared they would come to him and take him away. After breakfast, he was having coffee with Yakov in the laboratory on minus five. When Dave saw two guards enter the lab, he suddenly felt weakness in his legs and fear coursed through his body. They walked not to him, but to Harvey's desk and spoke to him. He saw a look of disbelief on Harvey's face, and then the guards walked away. Harvey looked at him, but also at the others, when he stood up and made an announcement.

"The guards have just ordered me to prepare the evacuation of all stock of medication, prototypes, machines and equipment. Everyone has to help, and we must begin immediately!"

He instructed everyone what to do and at the end he walked up to Dave and said, "Dave, Rob and Adish, help me put the fridges with all the drug doses in the corridor."

"Okay, Harvey. What a relief to hear we're evacuating. I was afraid of something else," Dave said.

"Yes, I thought the same thing when those guards showed up, but we have to remain vigilant, Dave."

The four walked toward the storage room at the back of the corridor and began preparing all the refrigerators for transport. They move the fridges into the corridor and set them ready right in front of the elevator. The guards periodically came by and took the refrigerators into the elevator. They worked all morning and afternoon until the storage room was completely empty. Guards walked in and out all day, and the place had never been livelier. At three thirty, his wristband vibrated to announce the daily rooftop break, and they all took the elevator to the fifth floor. It was a beautiful day and a warm breeze blew in his face as he walked up the terrace. He noticed that the helicopter on the roof was gone and made a comment about it to Yakov. They took some water and walked to the edge of the roof. The road had been cleared and where there had been bodies and exploded armored vehicles yesterday, there was nothing today.

"Amazing! They cleaned everything up as if nothing happened," Yakov said.

"Incredible. Ah look, I think they put the armored vehicles under those brown camouflage covers inside the fence," Dave said as he pointed down.

"They are efficient," Yakov said and turned his head when he heard a noise behind him.

On the horizon, they saw a helicopter approaching the building with its heavy chopping sound. It flew very low and fast until it reduced its speed and landed with a lot of noise on the helicopter pad next to the terrace. The helicopter did not turn off its engine, but left its rotor spinning. Everyone watched the helicopter and suddenly they saw the elevator doors open and two guards came out, followed by Jeff Broch. He wore a black suit and was carrying two briefcases. He looked for a moment to his left at the terrace where all the prisoners were looking at him. Dave looked too and suddenly their gazes met, and he saw a ruthless look in Jeff's eyes that scared the hell out of him. Jeff turned his head away and hurried to the helicopter. Five minutes later, the helicopter's rotor made a louder chopping sound, and they took off. The helicopter flew away from the building, staying low above the ground again, and the chopping sound slowly decreased as it disappeared from sight.

"Ladies and gentlemen! Jeff Broch has left the building!" Yakov announced loudly.

People laughed and cheered, but Dave thought it was a little nervous laughter. They all wondered what would happen to them, now that the facility was being evacuated. Would Jeff Broch just let them go, or would he evacuate all? Dave was even more worried about what would happen to him and if this Ivan would still show up. Harvey still had not sent out any information about the procedure to Jeff Broch, but that meant little, because this Ivan might have his own ideas about this examination. He laughed along with everyone, but didn't feel comfortable at all.

Back at the laboratory, they continued packing the last of the refrigerators, and Harvey noticed his anxiety.

"Let's go get coffee," Harvey said, and put his arm on Dave's shoulder.

They chatted a bit at the coffee machine, and Yakov joined them, trying to cheer him up with his jokes. It helped a little, and after that, Dave continued working with Harvey. By the time their wristbands started vibrating to announce dinner time, they had moved almost all stock, equipment and machinery out. Only some furniture and computers remained on the floor and some heavier mixing machines in the back. They all went to the restaurant. They pushed two tables together, and he ate with the group from the hot tub and Helmut Meier joined them as well. He felt relatively safe with all these friends around him, and he relaxed a bit. The slowly setting sun outside also calmed him a bit.

Yakov told another joke and when everyone was laughing, Takeo suddenly stopped laughing and stared at the window. He pointed his finger at the horizon and said, "Look... look... at the horizon... further down the dirt road!"

The sun had just gone set behind the mountain range and the desert was in a gray shade, making it much harder to see anything. They all peered at the horizon, following the dirt road, and at the very back, they saw a small dust cloud moving. The small dust cloud seemed to be coming toward them and slowly grew larger.

"Maybe the police are coming back already?" Larry asked.

"Or maybe some vehicles for the evacuation," Harvey said.

They stood up and moved closer to the window to get a better look. It was hard to see the vehicles, and as they got closer, they saw why. The vehicles were of a brown color, almost like the desert surrounding them. It was the dust cloud that gave them away. The first vehicle was most visible as the rest drove, hidden in the dust cloud behind it. It looked like an armored truck with something large on the roof.

"Look at that truck over there. It has a big radar dish on the roof!" Takeo said.

Helmut Meier moved closer to the window and stared at the large armored truck with his mouth open.

"Wow, if that's what I think it is, it looks like they're finally bringing the right weapons to the battlefield."

"What do you mean, Helmut?" Dave asked him.

"Well, I heard about this new system the US Air Force has developed against drone attacks. In the war in Syria and Iraq, the rebels had used drones and even destroyed several US Army vehicles with them. A few years ago, they used a Patriot missile, which cost about three million dollars, to take out a drone, which probably cost two hundred dollars, and the military realized they needed a cheaper and more efficient way to take out drones. The US Air Force announced a new system called THOR, which stands for Tactical High-power microwave Operational Responder, designed to take out swarms of drones. I had seen a prototype similar to the radar dish you see on the roof of that truck," Helmut said, while everybody listened.

Suddenly, they heard the buzzing sound they had heard the day before, although it was less loud since they were now inside. They all moved closer to the window and looked up. They saw several larger drones flying away from the roof toward the convoy of army vehicles. The drones kept coming, and more and more drones flew in the convoy's direction. They saw the swarm of drones rapidly approaching the convoy.

"They're almost at the first truck," Larry said excitedly. "I sure hope this THOR system works, because yesterday was a massacre."

"I hope so too," Helmut replied and looked at the approaching convoy of vehicles farther down the dirt road.

They were all watching the first armored truck now, and as the large radar dish turned toward the drones, Yakov called out, "It's moving!"

Soon after, they saw the first drone fall to the ground like a dead bird falling from the sky. When it hit the ground, it exploded, revealing a large fireball. All the other drones fell toward the ground, and the barren desert in front of them lit up with several explosions as the drones hit the ground. The large windows of the restaurant shook from the shock waves. Everyone cheered and jumped for joy.

"Yes! Yes! They're destroying the drones!"

The convoy kept advancing, and they saw another seven armored vehicles behind the big truck with the radar dish on top. All the trucks had a heavy gun on the roof. At some point, the first large truck stopped on the road at quite a distance from the building with the radar dish aimed at the rooftop, even though the stream of drones had stopped. It seemed they had taken out all the drones with this THOR system. The seven armored vehicles passed the big truck and advanced toward the front gate. They saw some guards in the guard post firing at the vehicles with their heavy rifles, and more guards came out of the building and ran toward the gate.

"Look, the first armored vehicle has some kind of rocket launcher on the roof!" Helmut Meier said excitedly.

Suddenly, they saw flames coming from the heavy launcher, together with a loud bang.

"KABOESH..."

In a blink, the entire guard post exploded in a large cloud of flame and when the smoke cleared, there was nothing left. The building shook, and cracks appeared in the windows of the restaurant. Inside, everyone cheered again with excitement. "Hooray! Hooray!"

The second armored vehicle used the heavy automatic rifle on its roof and with a loud sound, it fired at the guards coming out of the main building.

"Thud... thud... thud... thud."

One by one, the guards fell to the ground, dead or wounded. A loud voice behind them suddenly interrupted the spectacle.

"Attention! Dave Wilson, step forward immediately!"

Everybody turned, and Dave suddenly felt his hopes sink again. In front of them were nine guards standing and a dark-looking man in the middle. The man in the middle smiled broadly at Dave, revealing the gold tooth in the front of his mouth. Rob was right. The man had a sadistic look on his face. Dave felt a surge of fear as he realized they were coming for him.

"There! That's Dave Wilson! Come here, Dave!" Ivan Văduva said as he pointed at him.

He looked at Ivan and felt the adrenaline rushing to his head. Anxiously, he now looked around at his friends and saw that they were sticking to their plan. They all motioned slowly forward and around the guards, forming a semi-circle around them. They were now holding the Stanley knives, which most had been carrying for some time. The guards and Ivan watched the semicircle of people slowly moving closer. Ivan got nervous and shouted, "Stay where you are! All of you! Don't move an inch!"

Still, the crowd kept moving and was closing in on the guards and Ivan. One of the guards looked at his wristband and pressed it. Suddenly Dave felt an electrical shock on his wrist and so did all the others and some of them dropped their knifes to the floor. Ivan yelled at the guards while pointing at Dave.

"Get him! Take him away!"

Six of the guards quickly advanced on Dave and grabbed him by the arms. Yakov, who was the first to pick up his knife from the ground, saw it happen and jumped on a guard and slit his throat with the Stanley knife. The guard dropped to the floor, bleeding profusely. The other guards fired their tasers at Yakov and at some of the people next to them. Yakov dropped to the floor and his body trembled with the electric shock. Some of the prisoners backed off except Larry, who headed with his knife to the guard holding Dave and cut him in the arm and immediately stabbed the guard another time, this time in his chest. The guard let go and dropped to his knees. Another guard tasered Larry, and he fell to the floor. At the same time, the guards moved quickly and now began tasering the people around Dave, and more people fell to the floor trembling. Dave used all his strength to shake off the two remaining guards and pushed them away, but then he was tasered by another guard. He felt pain everywhere and fell to the floor, shaking. Four guards grabbed him again. The other guards continued tasering more people, and some people backed away. The four guards twisted his arms behind his back and they quickly carried him away from the crowd while the other guards continued tasering people who got too close.

Ivan ran after the four guards, dragging Dave to the elevator. Suddenly, an enraged Rob ran past the guards and jumped on Ivan. With his speed and weight, he pushed Ivan to the floor with a big smack and Dave had never seen Rob so angry. He started stabbing Ivan with his box cutter. Blood flowed from Ivan's body in the places where the enraged Rob had cut him. Ivan struggled to push Rob off him, who kept stabbing him and pushing Ivan down with his arm in a cast and after resisting for a while, Ivan stopped moving and his head fell to the side. One of the guards tasered Rob, and he fell next to Ivan to the floor, making epileptic movements with his body. The guard checked on Ivan, and since appeared dead, he left him on the floor.

"Let's move out!"

The seven remaining guards quickly retreated toward the elevator, dragging Dave with them. One of the guards had already called the elevator, and the doors opened. The prisoners stormed after them, and he saw Takeo and Gary jump on the guard closest to the crowd. They knocked him down, and another guard tasered Gary, but Larry and Helmut attacked the guard who was tasering. At the same time, the other five guards pulled Dave into the elevator and quickly closed the doors, leaving the other guards behind.

He tried to resist and get out of the guards' grip, but they held his arms tightly behind his back and his struggle was futile. He gave in and listened to the heavy breathing of the five guards around him, all trying to catch their breath. He looked at the electronic panel in the elevator and saw the elevator had already reached the fifth floor. The doors opened and two guards were waiting in front of the elevator. They carried heavy rifles instead of tasers. The guards pushed him out of the elevator and led him to the doors leading to the helipad. Dave felt he was in big trouble. Apparently, Jeff Broch had decided he needed to be evacuated as well so he could sell his drugs to this billionaire for a lot of money. The guards opened the doors for Dave and dragged him in front of the helicopter pad.

Surprisingly, the helicopter was not on the platform. He felt the warm evening breeze on his face as the guards waited with him on the edge of the platform. He heard a guard talking into a phone.

"We're waiting with Goldilocks on the helicopter platform. How far are you? All right, see you shortly."

Dave looked around and it had gotten darker outside. He heard some gun shots below. When he looked behind him, he saw the square tower with all the shutters open, but there was no movement and no more drones. In the distance, he heard a low chopping sound that slowly grew louder. He stared back across the helicopter pad toward the desert. In the twilight, he could not see much. He tried to listen to determine where the chopping sound was coming from, and then he spotted a dark shape with some flashing lights. He stared at the lights and after a while he distinguished the shape of a helicopter. He felt desperate and his arms hurt from the firm grip of the guards. He had come so close to being freed, and now everything seemed to be falling apart for him. He was going to be taken away. He struggled and pushed the guards one more time to get out of their grip, but the more he struggled, the stronger the guards held him. It was no use.

Four other guards were right in front of him, and he tried to look between their heads to catch a glimpse of the approaching helicopter. One of the guards hit him in the face with his fist. The blow dazed him. He ceased his struggle and waited for the helicopter to arrive. The roaring chop sound grew louder and louder. The helicopter approached the platform now. Suddenly, he heard a whooshing sound and saw a beam of light flash toward the helicopter, followed by a huge explosion. Dave felt a big bang on his head and everything went dark.

15. Epilogue

A blurred shadow was standing above him, and he could not see who it was. He heard some faint sounds around him, but his eyes could not focus and he only saw some blurred light, and then the light went out again.

A while later, he heard some low voices murmuring in the background, but he could not understand what they were saying. He heard a slow beeping sound in the background. He felt numb and tired, but tried to open his eyes. The bright light coming into his eyes blinded him, and he closed his eyes a bit to let them slowly get used to the light. When he opened his eyes a little more, he heard a female voice he did not recognize.

"He seems to be waking up. I'll page the doctor."

Later, he saw a friendly nurse looking at him as she bended over him to check him out.

"Can you hear me, Mr. Wilson?"

He tried to nod, but his head felt heavy. Beside her, a dark-haired man in a white doctor's coat appeared. The man looked at him and shone a small light in his eyes, which made him blink.

"That looks good," the doctor said, and held his pulse to check his heart rate.

"Can you hear me well, Mr. Wilson?"

"Y... y... yes," he muttered wearily.

"How many fingers do you see in front of you?" the doctor said now while he showed him three fingers.

"Th... th... three."

Slowly Dave woke up more and regained his senses. His body felt sore, and it felt like a big truck had run over him. The doctor put his wrist back down and looked at him.

"Hello Mr. Wilson, I'm Dr. Reeves. Do you remember what happened to you?"

He tried to remember what had happened, but then he felt his headache get worse. He waited a moment, took a deep breath, and then he slowly remembered how all his friends in the restaurant tried to defend him and attacked the guards.

"The… the… there was a fight in the restaurant…but where am I?"

"You're in the hospital in Phoenix, Arizona. What else do you remember?"

Slowly, he remembered more things.

"They dragged me into the elevator and took me to the fifth floor and the last thing I remember is a helicopter arriving on the roof."

The doctor nodded.

"Very well, Mr. Wilson. I'm glad your memory is coming back so quickly."

Dave looked at him, still a bit puzzled.

"What day is it today?"

"Today is Tuesday. They brought you in on Sunday night. The soldiers had found you under the dead bodies of four guards. You were extremely lucky, because the guard's bodies were full of shrapnel. It seems their bodies shielded you from the explosion, because you only have a slight concussion, some bruises and some minor cuts on your legs and arms. You've been unconscious the whole time. Just last night we thought you would wake up, but then you passed out again. How are you feeling?"

"I feel tired and have a headache. My body feels sore and heavy," he answered, trying to look around the room. He saw the nurse next to the doctor, but for the rest, there was no one else. Through the window, he saw the blue sky.

"You took a huge blow from the explosion, but the guards in front of you must have absorbed most of the shock. We found no lasting damage and you should recover quickly. Actually, if you feel up to it, we have some visitors waiting for you outside. They've been at your sickbed since Monday. Shall I let them in?"

Dave nodded, curious to see who had been waiting for him. The nurse gave him some water and helped adjust his electronic bed so he could sit up straighter. His body ached as he changed positions. He looked at the cuts and bruises on his arms and noticed the catheter sticking out of his arm, which was used to infuse an intravenous drip. The nurse shifted the pillow behind him until he was in a more comfortable position.

"I'll let your visitors in now and come back later to check on you, Mr. Wilson," the doctor said as he left the room.

He heard the door close, and the nurse shifted some chairs. When the door opened again, he looked at the doorway. Dave felt a moment of pure happiness when he saw the pretty face of Penelope, followed by his tall son Andrew, along with a pregnant Wendy. They slowly entered the room and walked toward him.

"Dave, my love! I've been so worried about you," Penelope said. She looked at him with tears in the corners of her eyes and gently kissed his lips. Dave now felt tears in his own eyes as a wave of emotions swept over him, a mix of happiness, relief, and love.

"Dad! Good to see you're back in the land of the living."

Andrew stood next to him on the other side of the bed with tears in his eyes and gave him a kiss, then Wendy slowly stepped forward to kiss him.

"Hi Dave. We're so happy to see you're alive and survived that explosion."

Wendy was now looking at his face with watery eyes.

"I couldn't believe the pictures, but seeing you now, it's even more amazing. You really look so much younger."

He smiled at her and said, "Well, at the moment, I feel like a truck ran over me."

They smiled at him, and Andrew said,

"You were very lucky, Dad. I talked to an army officer involved in the liberation operation who explained what had happened. Apparently, they fired a missile at the arriving helicopter because it had ignored all the army's warnings. The blast destroyed the helicopter and much of the roof. They found you under a pile of rubble and under some dead guards in front of what was remaining of the elevator. At first, they thought you were dead, because you were unconscious. Late Sunday night, they called me to tell me they had found you and brought you to this hospital. I called Penelope after that to let her know they found you back alive and that you were in the hospital in Phoenix, Arizona. On Monday, we all arrived here and have been waiting ever since."

Penelope was holding his hand and when Andrew finished talking, she added, "Immediately after your abduction, I looked for Andrew's phone number in your apartment to contact him. I explained everything about the drug treatment, the burglaries, the Harvey's disappearance and everything else. Together, we spoke regularly with the police during the search and investigation. Your colleagues, Craig and Henry, also helped tremendously in the search and getting the right press coverage. Andrew and Craig got in touch with Mary Lewis, and that's how we convinced the police that Harvey's disappearance was related to your kidnapping. I have since gotten to know Andrew and Wendy very well and you can be proud of them."

"And what an amazing girlfriend you have, Dad. Penelope was trying so fanatically to find you, through her contacts and with her brother's help we were to speed up the whole investigation and get the FBI involved," Andrew said with a broad smile as he continued. "With the help of the FBI, they could broaden the whole investigation. Still, time seemed to pass so slow during the investigation. We were so worried about you. The real breakthrough came when the police got a visit from a nurse involved in the clinical trials who had found a USB-stick with your location on it and now you're finally back with us."

He looked at Penelope and then at Andrew and Wendy, and with tears in his eyes, he said, "I'm so glad to see you all. I've been through a lot of hard times and the thought of you has kept me going."

At that moment, they all put their hands on his, and Dave felt truly happy.

"We couldn't believe what had happened to you," Wendy began to explain. "Penelope explained you had been kidnapped, so we flew to New York immediately. She told us about the drug treatment you had taken and showed us some recent photos. We couldn't believe our eyes. I still can't believe it. You look so much younger."

Andrew stared at his face as Wendy continued talking and when she finished, he jokingly said, "Amazing, Dad! This is so much better than hair transplants. Your skin looks so smooth and young. Other than the bruises and cuts, you look great. You could pass as my younger brother now. I understood from Penelope that your back problems are gone, too.”

“Yes, that’s right. I felt great physically, at least until that helicopter exploded in front of me,” he said with a smile, thinking back to the fight in the restaurant. “What happened to all the other prisoners?”

“Well, Dad, they were all rescued. The Army officer I spoke to yesterday explained to me all the details of the raid. Apparently, on the first attempt, the police SWAT team had lost all their troops in the unexpected attack from the drone army. Immediately, the army got involved, and it took quite some time to prepare for the second raid and come up with a strategy to attack the drone army. When they stormed the building the second time, many guards resisted and were killed. They rammed the front door and entered the building. Some guards surrendered and on the second floor, they found all the other prisoners trapped in the restaurant.”

The door opened and suddenly Harvey and Mary entered, followed by Yakov.

“We heard you regained consciousness. Welcome back to the free world, Dave,” Harvey said with a big smile as he gently touched Dave’s hand.

“Good to see you, Dave. That was close. We thought we wouldn’t see you again,” Yakov said and tapped him on the shoulder.

“Hi Mary,” Dave said as she came over to kiss him.

“Good to see you all got out in one piece! And the others?” he asked.

“Everybody got out unharmed. Larry will organize a reunion to get together in a few weeks,” Yakov replied enthusiastically.

“And Jeff Broch?”

“Well, they’re still looking for him. The other shareholders of Juvenatrust also seemed to have disappeared, and they’ve issued international search warrants for all of them, so I think it’ll be a matter of time before they catch them,” Harvey said.

They talked for a while longer about all the events, and he felt so happy to be free again.

The next day, he sat with Penelope in a cab on the way to the Phoenix Sky Harbor International airport. They sat close together, and he kept his arm around her while she stroked his chest with her hand. He looked up at the sunny sky and thought about everything that had happened.

He wondered if they would ever catch Jeff Broch. People like that tend to get away with things and have every means to disappear. He thought about the rejuvenation drug and wondered if it would become available to the public or if it would become a luxury drug for the rich, dividing the world into people with money who could live a long time and poor people with a much shorter life. Or would the government force pharmaceutical companies to make these drugs available to everyone? Everyone has the right to a long and healthy life, regardless of your wealth. It was certainly a beautiful and hopeful thought, but in most countries, this was already not the case. Only time will tell what the future holds. One thing is certain, though, interesting times are coming.

BY THE SAME AUTHOR

The Dome is a riveting thriller about a young man's quest to find his biological parents in a world ravaged by the catastrophic consequences of climate change. The first book in the Dome series.

ISBN: 9789464007343 (paperback)
ISBN: 9789464007350 (hardback)
ASIN: B08NFCFSQC (eBook)

The Breach is a thrilling story about a young man's immersion in the world of refugees suffering from the catastrophic consequences of climate change. The second book in the Dome series.

ISBN 9789464007367 (paperback)
ISBN 9789464007374 (hardback)
ASIN: B09L64DTN3 (eBook)

Nemesis is a fast-paced thriller about revenge, love and hope in a world where shocking events are taking place. The third and final book in the Dome series.

ISBN 9789464007381 (paperback)
ISBN 9789464007398 (hardback)
ASIN: B0BKLQ5JBJ (eBook)